LIVING THE GIMMICK

BEN PELLER

Ⓦ A Time Warner Company

ISBN 0-7595-5004-2

First edition: October 2000

Visit our Web site at www.iPublish.com

To all the professional wrestlers I have
ever watched or worked with, for making a
small piece of my heart a place where
dreams will always be possible.

And to my father, for giving me the spark.

*What shocks the virtuous philosopher
delights the chameleon poet.*

—John Keats

1

LADIES AND GENTLEMEN . . .

I yank the final lace of my left boot tight, preparing to commit fraud in front of ten million witnesses. Most of them will be watching through closed-circuit television, but eighty thousand of them are just outside, seated on folding chairs lining the field of Giants Stadium or in the bleachers above. Their cheers ease dully through the dressing room's concrete walls, all four of which are painted a blank white. Only a full-length mirror provides a pocket of variety; it stands in the middle of the far wall, intimidating and unapologetic.

The crowd lets out another series of cheers. They have been growing more and more animated all afternoon, and now with evening, their moment of truth is almost here. Within minutes they will be watching two characters engage in a fantastic battle for a world championship belt that glitters high above an everyday life of mortgages and kids and bills and asshole bosses. I am one of those characters. The challenger. Mister Michael Harding, young lion seeking to fulfill a childhood dream. They are going to watch me attempt to defeat the World Wrestling Organization Heavyweight Champion in the main event of tonight's annual professional wrestling extravaganza known as SlamFest.

There is a knock and the door opens before I can respond. "Michael," comes a voice I recognize as belonging to "Hippo" Haleburg, an executive for the WWO. "They're gonna take it home in about five. Then you're on."

I stand and pull up my yellow knee pads. In the mirror, a reflection confronts me. Long thick brown hair curling at the ends. Arms and chest and legs all shaved, and expanded from years of steroid use and weights. Bronzed, of course. A tan so blatant it looks like the skin has been permanently stained, forced to relinquish any hold on natural color.

Michael Harding, I mouth the words to myself. The movement of my lips is strange. My tongue clicks against my teeth like an intruder. Sweat has already collected on the wide scars lining my forehead.

"Whattaya say, Michael?" Hippo Haleburg prompts. "Ready to give 'em what they came here for?"

"What did they come here for, Hippo?" I ask, even though I know what his reply will be.

"Shit, if you don't know that, we're in trouble." He claps his hands. "Come on, kid, let's give 'em a good show."

This is the answer. They have come to lose them-

selves in the brutality of choreographed violence. They have come to see a world that is contained within the very chaos it exhibits. They have come to see if I can become a champion and achieve what I have long believed to be my dream. They have come for a good show.

But there is no guarantee they'll get one. Because there is a key variable that will make this bout like no other I have ever wrestled. Tonight, for the first time in my life, I will be stepping into a ring with absolutely no knowledge of how the upcoming match will end.

Participation in the world of professional wrestling is desired only by a unique few. I was one of them. Throughout my career I met countless *fall-ins*, a term for those who found themselves in the business by default. They were former gym teachers, frustrated body builders, and football players who were forced into premature retirement because of ineffectiveness or injuries. One former amateur wrestling champion told me he considered professional wresting a basic career change. That's like saying a switch from pauper to millionaire is a basic status change. They are two different worlds, pure and simple.

The groundwork for my wish to become a professional wrestler was laid at a Cub Scout Father-Son softball game during the summer of my tenth birthday. I'd gone there with another boy, Max Egan, and his father. Max and I were in the same fourth grade class. He was a moody kid who loved attention. He constantly picked fights with others, then backed down the moment his opponent landed anything other than a glancing blow. Often there were two or three other kids following him around, latching on to the safety of his aggression.

Max and I didn't know each other that well, but his mother, a den mother with thin precise features, had insisted I tag along. "You two can be like brothers for a day!" she exclaimed brightly.

When I got up to bat at the picnic, nobody called out any words of encouragement. Half the kids there probably didn't even know my name because I rarely spoke at meetings. But still I felt that everyone was watching me, wondering which of the grown-up men was my father. The pitcher was studying me. Why didn't he just pitch the ball?

Two men standing along the first base line were whispering to each other. One of them laughed. My ears burned. Was he laughing at the fact I was here as Max's "brother-for-a-day"? I cursed the fucking Cub Scouts for organizing this idiot event. The pitcher finally wound up and then the ball was looping through the air at me.

I swung, wanting to get a hit, any kind of hit, just so I could get away from being so exposed at the plate. The jolt sent a satisfied vibration up my arms. I watched the ball fly away, half-expecting it to come rushing back and hit me in the face. Only when someone shouted "Run!" did I drop the bat and take off in the direction of first base.

I made it to third, sliding in and triggering a mini-storm of dust. I leapt up and looked around, flushed with excitement and exertion from running. Mr. Egan was in the dugout, drinking a beer and talking to another kid's father. Someone went up and motioned toward me, and Mr. Egan turned his whiskered face in my direction and hollered: "Good job, kid!" Even though the compliment came out in a bored and slightly slurred tone, it still felt good. My back became suddenly hot, invaded by something other than sweat. I turned to see Max standing in the outfield, his eyes narrowed and fixed on me.

After the softball game, groups of fathers and their kids congregated with a shared economy. All of them were following a code involving high fives and enthusiastic tones that looked and sounded so easy, but remained a mystery to me. I retreated from their booming voices to the shade underneath an oak tree. There I sat, trying to eat a hot dog while constantly pressing my finger into the bun and then to my flesh. This was my habit for as long as I could remember, the need to touch something in order to confirm its actual existence. The thing I most often touched was my own body; scratching my arms, poking my legs, anything to make contact. To make sure I was still here.

A painful itch came alive on my arm. I looked and saw a large mosquito there. Its fang, no wider than a pin, sucking out blood.

I slammed an open palm against this easy target. When I took my hand away, I saw its dead body lying tangled in a small smear of blood. My own blood. For an instant I felt victorious. I had conquered something that had made me itch. I was real.

But then the fresh bite erupted. It felt like a million tiny bugs were inside its swelled red cap, tickling just under my skin. With this came guilt. The mosquito still lay mangled against my skin. I picked up its body between two fingernails. Then I pressed the evidence into the grass, digging my fingers under the dirt. Instead of being silenced, the itch now throbbed harder. I scratched the wound furiously, causing more blood to run. I took another bite of my hot dog and chewed miserably. The bun was stained with blood from my fingers. More evidence of the bug I'd killed so effortlessly, like everything in the world could be killed. I touched my arm hesitantly, then took a breath.

Still alive. For now.

"Hey, Mikey!"

The words were like a high pitched shotgun blast. I knew they'd come from Max even before I opened my eyes and saw him approaching with a group of four boys behind him. My fingers tore at the hot dog bun. "Why are you here, Mikey?" Max spat. "You don't have a father!"

"Yes, I . . . ." I dropped the shredded bun and scratched my hand. "I did."

"Then what happened to him?" Max asked, his voice tauntingly curious.

My throat seized up. I jumped up and turned to walk away. "Chicken!" Max shouted excitedly. "Chicken!" My feet whirled around and ran toward a blur. When I regained focus, my hands were slamming into Max's shoulders. He fell to the ground.

One of his friends stepped over and shoved me and shouted: "Bastard!" The word was unknown to me, but the shove was familiar enough. So I shoved him back. Hands collided with my back. I stumbled and turned to face whomever had pushed me. A different pair of hands hit me from behind.

The kids closed in, each of them chanting "Bastard. Bastard. Bastard." This word saturated the surrounding air with hostility, a chorus of hammers striking steel drums. I stumbled through a hole in the ring of boys and ran. I kept running until the sound of their laughter disappeared completely, taken over by the sounds of younger kids playing on a swing set at the park's edge. I ran all the way home, even though I wasn't due back for hours. My eyes never left the pavement, where a blurred shadow remained a constant step ahead. I tried to catch up, pushing myself harder and harder until I stumbled and sprained my ankle. I jogged the rest of the way home with my eyes closed.

Mom wasn't home, so I let myself in with my key, which hung on a thin leather rope around my neck. The inside of my throat was dry, still on fire from the combination of running and tears. I went into the kitchen for a glass of water, avoiding my favorite big brown mug. Punishment for letting Max and the other kids push me around, for my lack of faith in my own body's existence.

I hurried into the living room, wincing on my ankle, and pulled a large dictionary down from its home on the top shelf of a rickety bookcase. The word was simple enough to sound out . . . bass-turd, bass-turd . . . and I tracked it down right away: Bastard 1. an illegitimate child. 2. anything inferior, spurious, or not standard.

I slammed the book shut, but the word lay embedded in my stomach. The mosquito bite on my arm screamed and I clawed at it. If I just stood there I would vomit, so I limped over to the television and snapped it on. Then my hands went to my thighs. Tapping over and over. I commanded my hands to stop, but they wouldn't. I cursed myself with a soft sob and focused on the unfolding light of the television screen. Two gigantic men were throwing each other around a ring. My hands became still. These two monsters were exchanging blows that looked crippling, but they kept getting up after every fall. The blows must have hurt; their faces registered intense pain. But they kept fighting. It was like they were invincible.

Do men that big really exist?

Two more titans in spikes flew into the ring. Three of them began to pound on one. The image made me think back to the park where Max and his gang had jumped me, and tears of outrage welled up. But then something amazing happened; the one man actually fought back with a flurry of blows so overwhelming that he knocked the other three men out of the ring. I watched, awestruck, as he stood triumphant in the middle of the ring and flexed mightily.

When Mom arrived home a little while later she found me leaping around the room, my sprained ankle forgotten, throwing blows at invisible opponents in imitation of those dancing warriors on the screen.

During the next week I went into the boys' washroom every afternoon to examine the scab slowly growing over the mosquito bite. The third afternoon, Max and two other kids marched in while I was at the mirror.

"Oh, look," Max hooted, "Mikey's posing. Think you're tough, huh, Mikey? Think you can whip me?"

I knew if I tried to fight Max the other two would jump in. Besides that, I didn't *want* to fight. I wanted to be left alone. My face hovered motionless in the mirror as they got closer. Instead of fear, a hot anger was erupting inside. I imagined my blood was lava, coursing below a skin that felt weirdly foreign. I'd done nothing to deserve this treatment; for one of the first times in my life I felt *right*. I was a good guy being unfairly attacked, and remembering how that wrestler on television had fought back, I fastened my face into an aggressive sneer. Max's grab for my shoulder was cut off when I spun around and knocked his hand away. "You want some of me, little man?" I roared in a voice that, although unfamiliar, was immediately comfortable. It seemed an inevitable discovery. The tiled floor under my feet became solid. "I'll take on all three of you! But you remember one thing!" The words flowed so naturally, made all the more intense by my opponents' stunned looks. "I will show you no mercy! I will beat you . . . One. Two. Three." With the last word I shifted my weight toward Max, who retreated quickly.

I was surprised to find my arms rising. They locked outstretched at my sides and I stood in imitation of a pro wrestler poised to leap off a turnbuckle. Although this stance left me wide open to attack, my body remained frozen. My heart was beating so loudly I was sure it was audible throughout the bathroom, but if they could hear it they gave no sign. All three just kept staring at me, their jaws hanging open in vacant surprise. They may as well have been looking at an alien.

"You're weird," Max finally pronounced, then turned and walked out of the bathroom. Their leader gone, the other two kids looked at each other and found matching confusion. They left.

Max was right. I was weird. I was also victorious, without even having to throw a blow. A feeling of freedom fanned out inside of me like a warm blanket gliding cleanly onto a bed. This was something I could use. I turned and faced the mirror. The scab on my arm was still visible and ugly. I picked at it and watched the blood run.

Max and his crew didn't ever bother me again and the bite eventually healed, but left behind a scar as small and unique as a snowflake.

———————————

I turned fourteen in 1984. That was the year I attended my first World Wrestling Organization show at the Rosemont Horizon. The main event featured "The American Dream" Sonny Logan defending his WWO Heavyweight Championship against "Cowboy" Jesse Buke. Logan stood 6'7" and boasted twenty-three-inch biceps (which he referred to as cannons). In between successfully defending his title for the past three years, he'd been steadily spouting an all-American rhetoric with such grace and charisma that he became a fixture on late-night talk shows. Logan won that night, of course, then flexed as a sea of flash bulbs exploded. Before the house lights came on, I scurried underneath the bleachers and slipped backstage. After hiding behind a mountain of sound equipment for a half an hour listening to voices and footsteps pass by, I stepped out and launched myself blindly up a flight of stairs. In the bare light of the stairwell a hulklike form was descending. As the figure approached, I recognized it as belonging to Sonny Logan himself. His face stretched into a smile and he extended his hand. "How's it goin', brother?" he asked.

"Hi, Dream," I whispered, taking his extended hand. His grip was relaxed, but his eyes reached forcefully into mine. His skin was stained with a permanent tan, and strands of blond hair cascaded from the sides of a prominent forehead. It was the first time I ever shook hands with one of the men whose image I had taken from the wrestling ring and used to fill the vacant place in all the pictures of my mother and me. Then his touch was gone and I was watching the World Gym insignia on the back of his leather jacket descend down the next flight of stairs.

I followed quietly, stopping at the door that led out to the cavernous cargo area. I peered outside and saw technicians and workers rolling up cables and loading pieces of the ring into a truck. Sonny Logan was standing by a limousine, talking to "Cowboy" Jesse Buke. They shook hands and then Sonny Logan got into the limousine while Jesse climbed into another car. Witnessing this brief exchange only fueled my excitement. I was privy to a special secret; something meaningful had just been laid out before me.

It is an illusion. They will do this night after night and all will work out as it should.

A few minutes later I floated out of the arena into a night sewn together by sticky heat. I felt a peculiar absence of fear. Everything was all right. A hero had touched my hand and acknowledged my individual existence; suddenly, I could be anything or anyone I wanted to be.

Two extraordinary things happened that next week. I didn't feel the need to touch that hand to confirm its existence, and I began lifting weights.

My desire to be a professional wrestler was with me all the time, as powerful and well-defined as other kids' dreams of becoming a magician or an astronaut. Although pro wrestling was as esoteric as those professions, it lacked their respectability. This made it even more appealing. Although not technically an *illegitimate* child, the world had branded me different and inferior because of circumstances I couldn't control. I savored the idea of being at odds with that world.

My physical stature made taking on giants like Sonny Logan a long shot; when I started high school, I was only 5'5" and 115 pounds. It was impossible to look to my father as evidence of future growth; he had died of prostate cancer when I was six. My only memories of him were of a gaunt, hollow-eyed figure struggling to sit up in his hospital bed in order to give me a hug. I had been too scared to hug him, afraid that if I so much as touched him, his bones would burst through his skinny sheet of flesh.

"Was my dad big?" I asked Mom a few weeks after I started lifting weights. She halted her work on the back

door's loose handle. The kitchen was silent as she studied the screwdriver in her hand.

"Yes, I suppose," she said. Her eyes left the screwdriver and found me, sitting at the table and rolling an
orange from one hand to another. "He had a desk job,
you know. At the Board of Exchange—"

"But he had a big build, right?"

She nodded slowly. "Yes. He had a big build." Her
voice came slowly and her eyes were far away. She
might have been studying an old picture in her mind.
There were none that I knew of in the apartment. "Why
do you ask?" she asked.

"I want to get big," I said. "I want to be a pro
wrestler."

She raised her eyebrows and smiled. "A pro wrestler,
huh?" She nodded and went back to the door handle.
"All right, kiddo. Just don't get too big."

I didn't tell her that in order to get into the ring, I
would *need* to get too big. For me, part of the attraction of
being a pro wrestler was the requirement of being larger
than the average human being, larger than life itself.

Hours and hours of reps, the same movements
either pulling or pushing, but the weights kept increasing. I fell in love with lifting huge amounts of weight.
After a workout I would multiply the number of reps by
the number of pounds I used for each exercise, then
dutifully record the total in my "Muscle Journal." A
vague goal of a million pounds had formed in my mind.
This goal made it possible for me to endure those first
few months of pain, when my arms would hurt so much
from the previous day's workout that I found it hard to
raise a pen in class.

But I soon saw that as far as muscles were concerned, pain signaled growth. Every hour spent in the gym brought Michael Harding one step closer to climbing into a wrestling ring.

I reached one million pounds by my sixteenth birthday. After noting this in my Muscle Journal, I threw the book away. By that time, there was enough physical proof of my body's growth to inspire me.

During these years, I saw my efforts to bulk up as evidence of determination, drive, and growth. My family had their own adjectives to describe my goal, "crazy" being the most popular. My mother settled for "murky."

Murky or not, by the end of my junior year I had grown seven inches and built myself up to 192 pounds. At a Christmas dinner with my mother's sister, my relatives said that I was looking "too big."

"No such thing." I waved their worries away with a sweep of my arm before taking a large bite of the chicken leg I held. We had come out to the suburbs of Chicago, where my Aunt Shirley lived in a compact two-story house, complete with a portable pool in back and a spacious basement recreation room.

The house was located on a street lined with other houses differing only in minor details such as the type of wood paneling on the front door and what kind of bushes lined the driveway. A few brave souls risked neighborhood censure and threw up bird feeders in their front yards. My Aunt Shirley found them "tacky and offensive." "Birds can make very offensive noises," she had explained on more than one occasion.

Now she sat regarding me with an air of self-righteous suspicion as I gnawed at the chicken leg. Her black hair was set in flammable curls. "I don't think those people make much money, dear," she said to me as I reached for another helping of mashed potatoes.

"Sonny Logan makes two, maybe three million a year," I said. In fact, I had no idea. "At least," I added.

"But that's before taxes," my cousin Jim pointed out from across the table. "After taxes, he's probably only doing a million. These days, a million isn't all that much." Jim, a year older than me, had a medium-build, medium-complexion, and a medium-personality. He had already been accepted for early admission to Harvard, where he planned to major in economics. He had been seeing the same girl for three years, and the two already had plans to get engaged soon after high school graduation. He allowed himself a beer and a half at parties (the other half of the beer he allowed his girlfriend to consume) and had never been drunk in his life. He smoked one cigar a month and thought people who sold "pot and all that other crap" should be given life in prison. He based his objection not on the standard conservative argument that drugs were deadly, but that the illicit drug trade messed up the pharmaceutical industries. Not that he wasn't a rebel. His one "trip astray," as he put it, came when he had just turned seven and had hatched a plot to disfigure every bicentennial quarter he came across. He figured the proof sets his parents had given him for his seventh birthday would be worth a fortune if he destroyed all the others. He once confided that he and his Boy Scout knife had scarred over fifty bicentennial quarters before he finally came to grips with the unlikelihood of knocking the millions of other quarters out of circulation. He also conveniently overlooked the fact that his was not the only proof set in existence.

"Plus," Jim now said to me from across the table, "that stuff's all fake."

"Oh yeah?" My voice jumped. "How would you know? Ever been in the ring?" To hear Jim dismiss a carefully orchestrated illusion like pro wrestling as "fake" rankled me. It was like calling a classic car "old." Years as a pro wrestler would hone this defensiveness to a fine edge. What Jim didn't know was that I had already written several scripts for matches, which I per- formed with a pillow laced with extra stuffing. My bed served as the ring for my one-sided battles. These matches never failed to draw pounding on the ceiling from the apartment just below my bedroom. In my imagination, I had learned to transform the angry beats into the roar of the crowd.

But someone like Jim didn't want to understand the subtle magic that made pro wrestling much more than a "fake" sport, and my own inability to explain frus- trated me as well. I kept up my attack. "Have you?" I demanded again, with the mounting anger I believed a pro wrestler would display in that situation.

"Honestly, Bonnie." My aunt threw the words at my mother while casting anxious glances at me. "Can't you talk to him?"

Mom just shrugged and attempted the nonchalant grin she relied upon whenever this subject came up. "Harry, what do you think?" Shirley turned to her hus- band, who took the matter seriously enough to give it a few seconds of silent thought, a spoonful of peas poised before his thin lips.

"College," he determined. Then he plunged the peas into his mouth and chewed with careful motions. He was a small-framed man, and his actions were always tainted with a hesitation so precise that it must have taken years to perfect. "Go to college." Harry finally swallowed. "Then find a good job and marry a nice girl."

"Why?" I asked.

"Because . . ." He became flustered at the question. "What do you mean 'why?'"

"Why does it only have to be a 'good' job? I think being a pro wrestler would be a dream job," I told him, then felt embarrassed at revealing this much to someone who probably wouldn't get it anyway. "And I think nice girls are boring," I added.

Harry stabbed another group of peas with his fork and said nothing for the rest of the meal.

On the ride home that night, Mom spent the first ten minutes in the smoldering silence that always came before a big talk. I waited, gripping my left forearm like a vise for ten second intervals. Houses shot past my dim reflection in the passenger window. "Shirley's worried about you," Mom announced. I responded with a weary sigh. "Michael—" she began.

"I don't want to go back to Shirley's again," I said, turning to face her. The car rumbled over a rough portion of the road before smoothing out.

"Michael." She sighed again. "They're concerned about you. I am, too." As I opened my mouth in protest, she added quickly: "In a way. I mean, it's great that you have such a clear goal. But why . . ."

"I don't know," I said quietly. My forearm was ready

to explode from the pressure, but my hand didn't release.

"Is it . . . anything to do with your father?" she asked cautiously.

"No," I snapped, embarrassed that she felt she had to be so tentative. "It's got nothing to do with him. It's about having pride in myself." I went on quickly, gesturing now with both hands free. "And taking advantage of being an American and going after my dream." This regurgitation of one of Sonny Logan's trademark rants was enough to convince myself that I was making sense. I kept talking, afraid to stop. "That's what life is for, for hunting down your dreams. Would you feel better if I wanted to be an accountant like good little Jimmy?" I asked.

"Michael, stop it," she said, voice rising. "I don't want you to make a mistake. Besides," she added, "you are getting too big."

My arms were curled at my sides, and I flexed both biceps in armored defiance. "Too big is never big enough—"

"Damn it, Michael! Don't give me these goddamn pro wrestler speeches! They're a bunch of overgrown ignorant kids! Is that what you want to be? Some ridiculous cartoon?"

"What did you want to be when you were growing up?" I demanded. Several seconds of silence. I watched the road markers being eaten up by our car.

Then came her quiet response: "A mother."

"Sorry if I've disappointed you," I said. Her silence found a way through my sarcasm. I snapped on the radio.

"Dusk or dawn?" she asked in an uncertain mono-tone.

"Dusk," I offered. Without moving our heads, we found each other, both forgiving, in the corner of our respective ranges of vision.

—————————

When I was around eight, two years before pro wrestling entered my consciousness, I got my mother a painting for her birthday. It was of a small building shaped like a boat and colored a pristine aqua-blue. A small chipped sign reading "Bed and Breakfast" dangled just above the small doorway. The building's hull was perched just above a cliff strewn with bushes and a stairway of different sized rocks leading to a smooth ocean below. Half of a burning sun hovered expectantly above the sheet of water. A red haze emanated from it, as though it was in the throes of a slow explosion. Its redness overtook the entire picture, giving the sun the intensity of a fiery diamond cutting through the sea of glass. The cliff's landscape offered no clue as to what coast this scene portrayed. As soon as I hung it up in the living room, my mother and I had engaged in a good-natured argument over whether it was "dusk or dawn."

"What's it called?" she had asked.

Broken Dock.

"Oh, that's a big help," she had replied. And we had both laughed.

This became our anchor of sorts; and we clung to it as our arguments grew more heated throughout my teenaged years. This was a mystery we agreed to both be puzzled by.

I never told her that I sometimes had the strange feeling, after studying the picture for a long period of time, that it was neither dusk nor dawn. That instead the sun was approaching the earth (I read somewhere that in a billion years this would really happen) and was setting the entire planet on fire. I imagined that painting was of earth's last refuge, the one place the sun hadn't yet consumed. The ship had tried to crawl onto land in order to get away from the ocean's boiling water. It was the end of the planet, of life as we know it, and of a predictable orbit that had been in place for billions of years.

I revealed this to no one, storing it away in my mind like some rare collectible weapon that was too dangerous to keep in plain sight but too valuable to throw away.

Still, it troubled me enough to inspire me to create my own artwork. I wanted to tap into the strange mystery that *Broken Dock* proposed. During high school, art was the only subject that even came close to igniting the same kind of enthusiasm in me that professional wrestling did. I stored all my sketches in a small cardboard box I kept on the window sill. Its fold-up top was covered with heart stickers from several Valentine's Days ago. My sketches were done in pencil, all of simple colorless objects shaped not by their own essence, but from the surrounding features. A vase would be outlined against a mirror floating in the background, illuminated by its own reflection. I sometimes imagined that the sunlight shining through the window down onto the box would awaken color from the sketches within. But every time I emptied the box to make room for new sketches, I saw the sun hadn't made a damn bit of difference.

My grandfather on my father's side, Jerald Harding, had played an integral part in the Chicago real estate boom back in the 1920s, and then again after the Second World War. He now lived in the penthouse apartment of a building located two blocks inland from the "Gold Coast" of Lake Shore Drive. In addition to helping design the structure, he had overseen its construction, greasing necessary political wheels and extracting various permits from key city government offices. The end result was that it was located on a strategic corner and had possessed one of the best views of Lake Michigan until 1956, when larger buildings had sprouted up closer to the lake. Angels and clouds festooned its brick facade.

Every Saturday after working out, I would take the bus over to see him. He let me drink beer so I could "get a bit of a glow on" for the nighttime festivities of hanging out with my friends. My grandfather was the kind of man who was able to pontificate about his youth without becoming maudlin, and share life lessons without sounding pedantic. He believed in a certain old school of responsibility that he claimed was distressingly absent in the modern world. But, true to his self-restraint, he never belabored this point or any other. "Keepin' your mouth shut is the best way to keep your options open," he would murmur contentedly as we sat on his porch in silent contemplation of the buildings around us.

We spent a good portion of our afternoons together playing gin rummy with a deck of cards he claimed once belonged to Al Capone. I had beaten my grandfather steadily in these games up until the time I was sixteen. Then he began trouncing me every game, and it took a few weeks before I realized he had simply been letting me win all along. I was flattered that he now believed I was worthy of beating.

One afternoon a few months before my eighteenth birthday, we were taking a break from playing cards and simply sitting on his deck staring at the water. Slivers of Lake Michigan squeezed between buildings like light through a row of giant metallic fingers. He wrapped a large hand around a moist beer bottle. "You're really serious about this pro wrestling?" he asked. In spite of the pack-a-day cigarette habit he maintained for sixty of his eighty-three years, his voice had managed to retain a smooth layer just above its gravelly strength. His scalp still boasted a fair amount of hair, although its color had faded.

I began to nod. "Yes," I said for further emphasis.

"How's your ma feel about it?"

"She thinks it's a phase."

His eyes were growing more and more curious, and I was finally able to stop nodding. "Maybe it is," my grandfather chuckled. "Hell, I still look at smoking as one of my phases." He leisurely exhaled a cloud of smoke, which was soon broken apart by winds whipping in from the lake. "Life is all about phases.

Everything you see here . . . all these buildings . . . they
were a phase. In 1928 I designed and built a row of
apartment houses on Belmont. We made sure each of
them was tailor made to the buyer's requests." He
drained the remaining beer from the bottle. "Now
they're knockin' 'em down for rows of identical ones.
Tract houses. Fuck me if I know why someone would
wanta raise a family in one of those."

He sighed. "If I give you something, will you promise
to keep it?" he asked.

"Sure," I replied.

He excused himself and rolled his wheelchair inside.
A few minutes later he emerged with two fresh bottles
of beer in each hand and an old mitt resting on his lap.
"Thanks," I said, accepting one of the bottles from him.
He kept studying the mitt as though he half-expected it
to suddenly leap off his legs.

Finally he spoke: "I used this mitt while I was growing up, playing in the pick-up games down on the south
side. This was back in 1919, 1920 . . . the days when
scouts still hung out in neighborhoods. I was a pretty
good player. A scout even offered me a contract once."

He lit a fresh cigarette with his old one and exhaled
again before continuing. "Couldn't take him up on it, of
course. My father was dead, and I had brothers and sisters to support," he said, looking up at me. "You don't
have any brothers and sisters. And your mother doesn't
need supporting." He extended the glove to me. I took it.
The leather was hardened with age, but I managed to
work it down over my fingers.

"Thanks," I said quietly. He nodded. The glove's
insignia was faded, but when I brought it to my nose I

could still pick up a stubborn trace of rich leather
scent.

An hour later, after he trounced me in several
rounds of gin rummy, I got up to leave. He went with me
as far as the door, where we stared at each other for a
time that seemed longer than the few seconds it probably was. "Are you sure . . . you want me to keep this?"
I asked, indicating the glove I was holding tightly in my
right hand.

"Yes," he nodded firmly. "Please."

———————

The basement of my high school was always hot and
sticky, even in wintertime. I spent a lot of time there,
lifting weights in "the cage," a weight-lifting area surrounded by chain-link fence. It was located in the center of the basement, and inside were bench presses,
squat racks, dumbbells that went up to seventy
pounds, and slabs of metal weighing as much as a hundred pounds each. The football coach, Chuck
Grabowski, a former pro football player who looked as
though he still ate bottle caps for breakfast, supervised
the cage from behind a copy of *The Sporting News*.
Whenever someone would release a particularly powerful grunt, he would look up with a hint of approval
flickering through his perpetual scowl.

A track surrounded the entire perimeter of the basement, and it was used primarily by the girls' track team
and the cheerleading squad. Oftentimes the girls would
watch us through the small holes of the cage, reacting
with questioning glances to the same grunts that would

elicit Grabowski's approval. We greeted their stares of mingled attraction and distaste with the casual indifference we thought would make us look even more unapproachable. For a while I dated one of the cheerleaders who could always be seen doing laps. Had Uncle Harry known of Charlotte Fischer, he would have most certainly approved. She embodied his notion of "a nice girl." Her honey-blond hair always looked recently washed, and her face maintained an air of innocence even after our marathon make-out sessions. Although I really liked her, I found myself haunted by a hatred for her laugh— a high-pitched nasal shriek that made her sound like a witch. Even in the moments I felt truly drawn to her, her horrible laugh would sound in my head like a taunting chorus.

"I want to have your children," she said quietly to me on the night of our senior prom. We were twenty-five stories up in the bedroom of a hotel suite. She was standing against the window, her body draped with a white lace nightgown. She looked like a ghost against the dark sky, visible through the glass. "You being a wrestler would make it hard to raise a family," she continued.

"Family?" I cried. "I just turned eighteen, for chrissakes!"

"My parents got married when they were eighteen. Two years later, they had me."

I nodded helplessly.

"How old were your parents when they had you?" she asked.

"I don't know."

"Well . . . did they meet in high school or—"

"I don't know," I barked, fingernails digging into both my thighs. I pressed them down further, sighing with the sharp licks of pain. Pain that reassured me I was alive.

"I'm sorry," I mumbled, "but I don't know."

"I Remember You" by Skid Row filtered obscurely through the closed door, the words as mournful as the stalemate that hung in the air. "Come here," I said and patted the bed. She did, and we lay there, hands clutching at each other's backs, until long after the song ended.

Later that night, we made love with a passion we had never been able to capture before. As we lie there afterward, she closed her hand lightly around mine. "It's okay," she whispered.

When I called her the next weekend, she told me, very gently, that she had a date that night. I almost thanked her. As we promised to remain friends, sadness and relief collided in my gut.

"That sucks, man," Marty said to me later that week, as we lay on the high jump mat stationed about thirty yards from the cage. "She was hot, too."

"Phone breakups are pretty bad," Bryan added. The three of us had been best friends since grade school. Almost every day after working out, we would have matches on the mat, its surface as bouncy as a trampoline. Marty and Bryan were rabid pro wrestling fans, and they viewed my dream of becoming a pro wrestler with a mixture of support and disbelief.

"Me and her are still friends, at least." I shrugged. "That's important."

"Hard to be friends with a chick," Bryan said, nodding his head. He would make a hell of a psychiatrist one day. His neat, thoughtful face was made to ponder. Marty was the opposite, with angry freckles and a face that always managed to shape itself into an expression of defiance.

"How the hell would you know?" Marty teased him, then said to me: "At least you popped her, right?"

"Well, yeah."

"On prom night?"

"Yeah."

"You musta failed the test," Marty chuckled.

"Eat me," I barked, face flushing. "It was . . . special."

They both hooted. "Oh, I'll bet. If it was so special, how come she broke up with you?" Marty demanded.

"Because she wanted to get married and I'm not gonna be able to do that if I'm on the road all the time wrestling."

"Jesus," Bryan whistled, "are you *really* serious about this pro wrestling stuff?"

"Hell, yeah."

"Sure," Marty chided, scratching his chest. "I'll bet you a hundred bucks you're at University of Illinois next fall, just like the rest of us."

"Fine. Let's bet," I started to extend my hand then saw his already waiting.

"Come on," he said, fingers fluttering. "Let's do it."

I pulled back, my cheeks hot enough to explode. "If I know you, you won't have the money to pay me," I said in a lame quivering voice.

That night, I wrestled with my overstuffed pillow a half hour longer than usual, repeatedly slamming it on my mattress, stopping only to acknowledge the pounding accolades from the apartment below.

A week before graduation, the school newspaper printed all the names of the graduating seniors and where they intended to go after high school. Out of six hundred people, five hundred and sixty-four were going on to college. Thirty more were listed as: "full time workers." And there were six whose future after high school was dismissed as "unknown." I was one of them.

This pissed me off because on the questionnaire they'd given us the week before I had clearly printed "Shane Stratford's Wrestling Academy." While others had sent for packets of information from various universities, I had written a letter to Buck Dipter, the editor for *Pro Wrestling Monthly,* asking for a list of any pro wrestling schools he might know of. The magazine's 250,000 circulation apparently kept Buck busy, because he failed to respond. Finally, I stumbled across an article in another magazine listing a half dozen schools. I sent off a batch of inquiries, and Shane Stratford had been the only one to respond. His information packet had consisted of several photocopied articles citing his school's "superior manner of teaching" and "great adherence to the sport's dignity." But what interested me most was that he was the West Coast representative for the World Wrestling Organization. Included was an application that asked questions that ranged from the benign (Who was my favorite wrestler?) to the more sinister (Did I bleed easily?). A week after I submitted my application, he called me at home and invited me to come out for a tryout. "Can't guarantee that I'll take you on," he had warned. "You sound like someone who's serious about this. But if you aren't, I don't want you wasting my time." Assuring him that I was damn serious, I promised that I'd be out there sometime before the end of summer.

But my school newspaper didn't consider this a pursuit worth acknowledging, and neither did my speech communications teacher and classmates. The teacher had assigned a speech on "My Dream Job." Several people had talked about becoming musicians or actors. The teacher praised these vocations as "artistically challenging," while professions such as architecture or financial consulting were "grounded and secure." When I announced my choice, he paused for several seconds, his lips chewing air. "Strange," he finally proclaimed. I seethed in my chair, throwing up a coiled silence in response to the outburst of laughter.

That afternoon when I got home, my mom was waving an envelope from Oakton Community College. She had pestered me so much that I had finally mailed off an application just to satisfy her. Now they'd sent a letter of acceptance. Reading the letter over my shoulder, my mom let out a delighted cry.

"I'm not going," I declared. Her face darkened immediately.

"I'm going to go to California," I continued, "to Shane Stratford's Wrestling Academy."

"No, Michael. You're not."

"What th—"

"You can go to Oakton for a few years and get a handle on a basic education," she galloped on, her words sounding very precise and planned, perhaps practiced in bed at night, "and get an associate's degree—"

"I don't want to go to Oakton," I interrupted.

"And *then*, if you still want to try out this pro wrestling thing, we'll see about you going—"

"*We'll see?*" I echoed incredulously.

The phone let out a shrill ring. Mom rose and answered it in a weary tone. The thing I hated most about these conversations was how much they always seemed to exhaust her.

Mom began answering "yes" in a suspicious voice. I looked up to see her staring blankly at the refrigerator door. She bit her lip, set the receiver down on the counter, and looked at me. "Jerald's dead," she said quietly.

I blinked hard, body growing numb. Death. It was so real I could feel it inside me at that moment. Waiting. I gripped my biceps, rubbed my arms over and over. Only when I felt dizzy did I realize I had been holding my breath. My lungs gasped, sucking in air frantically. I began coughing and pounding my chest. "Michael, are you okay?" Mom asked urgently. "Do you want some water?"

"No thanks." I coughed again and turned away, tapping my own chest. The sound was reassuring. Steady and reliable; an artificial heartbeat that I could control.

I went to my room, closing the door quietly behind me. The baseball glove peeked down from the bookshelf, where it lay nestled securely between two sketches. I lay on the mattress, tapping my chest. If I stopped I would die.

———————

My grandfather's estate had been considerable, but taxes cut it down to a modest amount. He left most of it to my mom, much to the chagrin of his flesh and blood daughter, Annie. Annie had left home at eighteen and by the time she turned twenty was married to the heir of a hotel chain and living in Boston. She dove into the society life of parties and dinners with ease, divorcing and marrying six more times in the next twenty-two years. Throughout this whirlwind of matrimonial activity, she had found the time to call her father exactly twice. "She's a heartbreaker," he once told me wistfully. "I wish she was more like your mother."

So it was no real surprise that Annie wasn't mentioned in his will. What shocked everyone, including me, was that he had left specific instructions that $7,000 go to me "immediately, for upkeep of the glove." That was the exact reading of the sentence. I didn't share the story he had told me with anyone. I thought it was something he would've liked to have kept between us.

His will stated that his final wish was to have his ashes thrown into the legendary Chicago winds from the top of the Sears Tower. He'd often made reference to this during our afternoons together. "I never want to touch the ground," he had said. After many tense phone calls, Annie had agreed to come out to participate in this last bit of cleanup regarding her father on the second of July, en route to a Fourth of July party at a North Shore mansion owned by some governor's son.

This was the first time I had met her. She was a

slight woman with hardened features that bore the evidence of years spent constantly willing the world into a form that would suit them. Her hair was dyed red, and her nose had obviously been sculpted to remove any trace of her family's Russian Jewish ancestry. She spoke with an affected Boston Brahmin accent that warped even casual observations into stubborn declarations.

On the morning we met in the lobby of the Sears Tower, she was restrained in her greetings. The man standing a few feet behind her, her seventh husband, reached over and introduced himself as "Jed Smythe with a y and an e." His face hovered above a neck overcome with fat. He looked like he weighed at least 275 pounds, and I wondered if I was capable of body-slamming him.

As soon as we were all in the elevator, Annie's eyes locked on me. About halfway up she spoke: "My father left you seven thousand dollars. Is that correct?"

"Yes."

"What are you planning to do with it?" Her chin pointed at me accusingly.

"I don't think that's any of your—" Mom began.

"I'm going to use it to go to professional wrestling school," I said. "Anything that's left over I'll put in the bank."

There was a sharp *ding*. The elevator doors opened and I stepped outside. The observation deck was lashed by wind screaming off Lake Michigan. "I don't think that's very funny," Annie's voice came at me from behind.

"I'm not kidding," I said, raising my voice in order to make myself heard.

"Let's all remember why we're here," my mom interjected, holding up the ash-filled urn as though it were a peace offering.

I hurried to the railing. Chicago sprawled out before me, a collection of patchy roofs and dark streets. There were millions of tiny cracks running through the concrete that supported the city, and each winter these cracks grew and new cracks sprouted when more salt was spilled to melt away the frost. In the summer this same ground was dipped in a soupy heat and cooked by a ferocious sun. My grandfather's death wouldn't stop this city's cycle, and I now confronted the sober fact that mine wouldn't either. My feet rocked back and forth in a hectic rhythm. I located my grandfather's old building. The movement of my feet grew more rapid, and I gripped the fence as though it were a cage.

Annie flew up beside me. "What kind of a joke are you trying to make, anyhow?" Annie asked.

"It's not a joke," I said. Looking out at the city fanning out into a blurry green horizon, my feet kept rocking with wild restlessness. The one thing I had that was mine and mine alone was a goal of being like the men who had elicited so many of my cheers and emotions. If I didn't leave this city to follow that goal, I had a sick assurance that one day I'd find a roof with no fence, nothing to stop my body from throwing itself off.

"It's not a joke!" I said louder. Her arms were crossed, and her face a mask of blank disgust. "It's something I need to do."

"It's perfectly ludicrous," she spat back.

"You don't know me," I told her. My words were even and full. "You didn't even know your own father!"

Her lips parted in shock. "Aren't you going to say something?" she commanded my mother.

"Yes." Mom looked at me. After a few seconds, she turned back to Annie. "Shut up, Annie."

Annie shook her head. "I think you're both absolutely ridiculous."

"I think you're a pompous bitch," I said.

Jed angrily protested that I couldn't talk to his wife that way. I glared at him. He suddenly didn't look so big. *I can slam your fat ass, no problem.* His next few words were lost in the wind, and then he lapsed into silence. Air rushed against goose bumps on the back of my neck as I hurried over to Mom, grabbed a handful of ashes, and flung it over the side of the building. I looked over at her. "Mom . . . I've gotta go," I said. She nodded. "Thanks," I said, then was gone.

After making it out to the sidewalk, I stopped and looked up, imagining that a gust of wind had captured at least a few of my grandfather's ashes and for endless summers would keep them in a perpetual dance above the city he spent his life building. Then I turned and started moving again. There was a lot to do.

————————

That night I went to a party at an apartment on Belmont Avenue. It seemed like half of my graduating class was there. Like always, people asked in joking tones when I was planning on leaving for pro wrestling school. This time I had a concrete answer: "Tomorrow morning." The Amtrak ticket was on the top shelf of my closet along with the cashier's check for $7,000. Two duffel bags were packed; one had only clothes, while the other contained pro wrestling magazines, workout books, my faithful wrestling pillow, and my grandfather's glove.

There was a keg at the apartment. A stereo in the corner was at full volume, blaring rock songs by Motley Crue, Van Halen, Warrant . . . all their lyrics about being young and crazy screamed over drunken conversations about our futures. As midnight approached, the party began breaking out of self-contained chaos into genuine bedlam. People were vomiting through open windows, making out wherever they fell, and singing different songs with a shared intensity that made them sound as one.

Sometime around two in the morning, Bryan, Marty, and I staggered out of the building. A warm breeze blew through the street, bringing the leaves that were in full summer bloom to life. A maple tree stood in front of us, its branches waving gently to the tune of the night wind. To my blurred vision, its movements were not unlike signals of a conscious farewell. I was between Bryan and Marty, with one arm draped around each of them. "Hey," I slurred, letting my face swing toward one and then the other, "I love you guys."

"Love you too, man," Bryan said. Our hug was broken by Marty's frenzied voice.

"Check this out!" he was shouting. We turned and saw a firecracker in his hand, its wick blazing. He chucked the flames into the air a second before it exploded. The blast unleashed an echo down the street. Marty came up and locked his arms around my shoulders. His beer-tinged breath poured over me. "Let's steal a car!" he whispered with aimless urgency.

"No way, bro." I started laughing. He broke away.

"Aww . . . ," he sneered. "You gotta go home and get your beauty sleep or somethin'?"

"No," I fumbled, unsure of something. "Well, yeah. I gotta catch that train tomorrow morning." Bryan and Marty and I had been together for as long as I could remember . . . six, seven years old . . . and now I was leaving. Next year they would both be at University of Illinois and for the first time in what seemed like forever we wouldn't be together. I didn't want to piss away this moment in a drunken blur; it was too damn important.

I stood there silently as attempts to express this whirled in my head. By the time I determined there was no real way to say it all, they were already staggering off in the general direction of the downtown Loop. I turned and headed in the other direction. As I passed underneath the shelter of a tree, I stopped at the sound of footsteps. When I turned, I discovered that I had only heard the echo of my own. Somewhere in the distance came the hollow blast of three rapid firecrackers followed by desperate cackling.

The alarm clock's steady beep sent consciousness rushing at me head-on. My eyelids snapped open in horror. I pushed myself out of bed and yanked the plug out of the wall, silencing the thing. I wrapped the wire around the clock and stuffed it in the duffel bag alongside my grandfather's mitt.

My mom was sitting up in the rocking chair by

the living room. "Here," she said quietly, and extended a wrapped plastic bag. I peered inside and saw a brand new toothbrush and a tube of toothpaste.

"Thanks," I said.

"I already called the cab," she said.

"Thanks," I repeated with honest surprise.

"Kind of a late night last night, huh?" she asked, flirting with a smile.

"I had to say goodbye to some people," I said. I didn't feel as hungover as I should've been. In the years to come I would learn all about the wonders of adrenaline.

"Mom, I'm afraid," I blurted. This admission took me by surprise. Her lips surrendered into a full smile. She rocked slowly in response.

"I don't always understand you," she said slowly, "but I guess most parents don't always understand their children." I walked over and fell into her warmth. "I think this is sort of the way it's supposed to work," she whispered in my ear. "I hope so, anyway," she added. My eyes wandered up the wall behind us, finally landing on *Broken Dock*.

"Dusk or dawn?" I asked quietly.

"Dawn."

We remained in each other's arms until a horn came from outside. "Go," she said.

Union Station's high ceilings reflecting off an immaculate floor inspired enough awe in me to keep any sort of hangover safely at bay. But once on the train, with the buildings of Chicago drifting by the window, I leapt to my feet and careened toward the bathroom. Vomit burned my throat and stained the cool gray of the toilet bowl. I knelt there, unable to move until knocking at the door forced me to stand and look at myself in the mirror.

I had already chosen a wrestling persona for myself. I was to be a "good guy," a la Sonny Logan. Good guys didn't get drunk the night before they left home and then throw up in train restrooms the next morning. At least that's what I believed then.

"I was not drunk last night. I am not drunk now, not running from anything," I said this out loud to the mirror, and the unshaven guy with a thin strand of puke clinging to his chin morphed into a man on his way to greatness. A date with destiny.

As the train traveled west with the morning sun, taking me away from everything I had ever known, I concentrated on my new image.

It would be the first of many.

2

WELCOME TO THE FAMILY

After Hippo Haleburg leaves, I apply a final layer of baby oil to insure that my skin will glisten beneath the spotlights. Smearing the oil over my chest and arms makes me feel like a classic car being waxed down before a show. My skin tingles with the application of moisture; it knows this ritual means a match is coming up. I dry my slippery hands with a towel and head out-side.

The hallway is packed with wrestlers, many of whom are already starting to party. Hammer and Nale, two beefy bald men who call themselves "The Handymen," are celebrating their winning the tag-team belts earlier in the day by downing champagne out of beer bongs. "What a waste of good champagne," I say to them as I pass, just to be saying something. "You can't taste it that way."

"Hell, that's the point." Hammer belches. "Champagne tastes like shit."

Nale finishes what's in the bong and backs away. After swallowing, coughing, and gasping, he grins at me. "We'll save ya a bottle." He winks. Champagne dribbles down his chin.

I wave and move on, returning to the uncomfortable company of my own thoughts. The towel is still clutched in my hand.

"Look out, Mike!"

Rob Robertson, a former pro wrestler now turned company executive, rushes up. His face, wrinkled with age yet still cherubic, seems out of place sprouting from his three-piece suit. He looks like a kid playing dress-up. As we all do.

He pulls me over to where a group of wrestlers are gathered. "They're brawling all the way back here!" he cries.

For a moment I'm confused before I remember that the current bout is a strap-match between two former tag-team partners, Wild Joe Irvin and Stud Hoss Mauler. The added stipulation of the strap means the two come armed with straps that they use to lace across their backs.

"Everyone stay behind that white line!" Rob points to a strip of tape running from one side of the hall to the other. I step back behind it, watching a cameraman hustle for position. He aims at the curtain separating backstage from the outside world. A few other wrestlers mingle around me, talking quietly and laughing. There's Tug Tyler, a four-hundred-pound behemoth with a weakness for cats. He owns fourteen of them. Daytrader Duke, a slim clean-shaven guy with a rich kid gimmick who in reality is the lowest paid guy in the company because he just joined. Tony Martino, a Columbian drug lord gimmick. He's got the five o'clock shadow and the rough barrio accent. You'd never guess he was born and raised in Minnesota.

Their voices drift around and through me but their words are hard to focus on. "Seen that cute little rat in the third row. She was giving me the eye—"

"Fuckin' bonus for this show better be good or I swear I'm quittin'. If I don't go over six figures this year, I'm gone."

"This dude came up to me at the banquet last night. Thought I was his fuckin' long lost cousin from Cuba! I almost fell down laughing."

"What's up, Champ?" Tug says to me. This gives me a jolt.

"I'm not the champ," I reply, trying to smile.

"Not yet," he laughs. "Come on, what's the big secret? You gotta be goin' over—"

Thankfully, Irvin and Mauler burst through the curtain, drawing everyone's attention. They both have straps and are belting the shit out of each other. Large welts blossom on their backs and arms. Mauler's head and shoulders are covered with a reddish substance too thin to be blood. He boots Irvin in the stomach, throws him face first into the wall, then unleashes a flurry of blows against Irvin's back. A series of thin explosions echo around the backstage area as the strap slaps against skin already chapped with welts. "All right!" Rob whispers. "Go!"

Tug, Dave, and Tony launch over and separate the

two. As they pull Mauler away, the cameraman subtly approaches and allows them to back into him, which makes him jerk the camera up toward the sky and wave it as though it were an out of control machine gun.

The walkie-talkie in Rob's hand crackles. "You're clear!" a voice buzzes.

"Cut it!" Rob yells. "We're clear!"

Immediately Mauler is released and the three wrestlers are sharing a giggle. "Yo!" Tony hoots. "We're the peacekeepers!"

Mauler and Irvin shake hands. "You took some good blows, pardner," Mauler drawls.

"Damn, I thought this shit was fake!" Irvin jokes. He winces as he tentatively feels around on his back, which is a map of angry welts. Everyone murmurs respectful comments about going all out. You always give it something extra for a live event like SlamFest. "Fuck it," Irvin barks. "You can't fake strap shots." He retreats to a table by the wall, where he leans on his hands with his inflamed back to us. Every few seconds he wipes at his face.

"He's hurtin'," Mauler comments quietly.

"What's all over your face, Hoss?" Tony asks.

"Tobacco juice." Mauler shakes his head. "Shit, I thought the only place where you could get tobacco juice dumped on you was Texas!"

He looks at me. "When you go out there, watch out for the assholes in the fourth row, right side of the aisle."

"Thanks," I tell him. His eyes are darting around in search of something. I toss him the towel I brought from my dressing room.

Wild Joe Irvin turns and faces us, still using the table for support. "Boys, is this really what we wanna do when we grow up?" he asks.

"What else is there?" Mauler hollers.

I stand, struck silent by both questions.

On July 6th, three days after I left Chicago, I arrived in San Bernardino, California. San Bernardino is the hub of what is known as the Inland Empire. This area consists of several towns scattered about fifty miles east of downtown Los Angeles. An ocean of desert surrounds them, and temperatures routinely climb above 100 degrees in the summer. The train station was in an advanced state of decay. Huge chunks of the walls were missing. The other buildings on the block were in no better condition. Older American cars chugged between the potholes littering the street.

I found a pay phone just outside the train station. Nearby, a figure in rags sat on the corner curb coughing violently. Across the street, the temperature flashed in broken yellow numbers on a display nestled above the entrance of a bank: 103. Only half of the 3 lit up, as though the electricity powering the sign was dying along with its surroundings.

"Shane Stratford's Wrestling Academy," a deep voice boomed from the receiver.

"Shane, it's me, Michael." I exhaled. "I'm here."

"Michael?" he said. Then he immediately exclaimed, "Michael!" as though it were the answer to a riddle. "You're where?"

"Downtown," I said. "Outside the train station. I wanna come over there."

"Right *now*?" he asked. "Sure you don't want to rest up or—"

"No," I said. More intense even than my fatigue was my need to see what I had traveled all this way to find. Scratch marks crisscrossed my forearms, evidence of anxiety-ridden hours spent on the train. If some proof of this journey's validity wasn't provided soon, the identity I had nursed throughout the trip (that of a Young Man Going After His Dream) would implode.

The shape in rags spewed forth a series of deep moist coughs. "I'd like to come over now, if I could," I told Shane.

Shane told me which buses to take and I boarded the first with renewed vigor, happy to be leaving the crumbling train station behind. But each time I transferred to a new bus the city outside my window grew more depressed. The promotional packet Shane had sent me bore an address, but when I got off the bus and found myself standing before an auto repair shop, I sighed inwardly, assuming there had been some mistake. Then I saw the group of bandana-wearing kids loitering on the corner. They glared at me, and the duffel bags in my hands immediately became a hundred pounds heavier. I hurried around to the side of the building and saw a brick addition. Above the door was a white sign whose red letters proclaimed this to be SHANE STRATFORD'S WRESTLING ACADEMY.

The door, its paint peeled long ago, was answered by a bearded 6'4" Coke machine with human features. I recognized Shane Stratford from his picture in the pamphlet, but I wasn't prepared for the sheer size of the man. He was as wide as the doorway, with no discernable neck and an inflated belly that nevertheless suggested strength earned by some exercise other than eating. His scalp was covered with a mass of long tangled hair that disappeared below his shoulders.

He looked me up and down and nodded, his mouth stretching into a grin that revealed a set of perfect teeth. "You must be Michael," he said.

I extended my hand. "Good to meet you, Mr. Stratford."

He let out a strange matronly giggle. "*Mr.* Stratford!" he exclaimed. "Been a while since I been called that."

We shook hands and I told him my situation. I had just arrived in town, had no place to stay, no car, and no immediate plans other than to learn what it took to be a pro wrestler. He listened patiently, then shrugged. "Well, how about a tour of the place?"

"How about a lesson?" I countered. His eyes narrowed.

"You on the level?" he asked.

"You bet," I nodded.

Slowly he removed from his pocket a folded piece of paper. I recognized the handwriting on it as my own; it was the completed application. "You say here that Chuck 'The Stud' Beastie is your favorite wrestler." He tapped the sheet with a thick scarred finger. "Why is that?" he asked.

Chuck "The Stud" Beastie, the current WWO International Champion, was a man about my height whose tight musculature and long frizzy black hair suggested that an electric current whipped through his body at all times. He spoke in a guttural rasp that I was able to imitate to a degree which had always amazed Bryan and Marty. But the voice wasn't the only thing that made him "The Stud," there was also his beautiful valet, Mimi. She was a woman with gentle features; her honey-blond hair and small face gave off a radiance that appeared as mild as Beastie's demeanor seemed savage.

While "The American Dream" Sonny Logan was my idol, Chuck Beastie occupied a different place in my mind. When I was eleven I had written him a couple of times, inviting him to upcoming Father-Son events. Once I hit thirteen I realized how silly those letters had been and by that time had quit the Boy Scouts anyway. But since then I still allowed myself to indulge in the occasional fantasy that there was some deep significance behind my ability to imitate Chuck Beastie's voice, not to mention the fact that we had the same color hair. Ridiculous, sure. But all these years later this hopeful ember still refused to go out.

I was too embarrassed to tell anyone about this, particularly Shane Stratford, who was still studying me with curious eyes and my application in hand. "Chuck Beastie incorporates visual flair and style with a gut-level intensity," I heard myself explaining. "The same juxtaposition can also be found in his combining high-flying maneuvers with a bare-knuckle brawling approach." The answer sounded as prepared as any essay answer I had completed on a high school test.

Shane nodded and broke into a smile. "Good answer." He folded the application and tucked it back in the pocket of his floppy pants. From another pocket he pulled out an unlabeled brown bottle. "Well, all right!" he exclaimed, uncapping the bottle and taking a long whiff. "Let's get goin' with this SlezamFest!" he howled.

I wondered briefly if I had imagined his bizarre pronunciation of that last word. Later I would learn it was an example of "carni," a language every pro wrestler learned sooner or later. I changed into spandex pants and he lent me a pair of wrestling boots. "They'll make ya two inches taller." He winked. Then for the first time in my life I was climbing into a wrestling ring. Even though I could see that I was in a small, stuffy low-ceilinged gym, my adrenaline was whisking me into a battleground as grand as Madison Square Garden or even the Rosemont Horizon itself. Posters of wrestlers lined one wall of the gym, with the other three joined by a strip of mirrored glass six feet high. I caught a glimpse of myself in that glass and a strange fear burrowed into my stomach. I regarded my reflection as one would that of an imposter.

"First thing." Shane's voice brought me back to the ring. "Falls. If you gotta know one thing in this crezazy business, it's how to take a fall."

He then hurled himself backward and ended up sprawled face up on the mat. The resounding thud was eaten up by the stuffy air. He leaped to his feet and ordered me to try it. Pro wrestlers fell countless times during a match, how much could it hurt? I threw myself backward and found out: one hell of a lot. A cloud of pain poured across my neck as the back of my head recoiled off the mat, which boasted a surface much harder than the high jump mats my friends and I had wrestled on a lifetime ago.

Shane laughed. "Not bad for the first time," he said. He helped me up and explained that the key was to always keep my neck tucked so as to avoid giving myself "a permanent hezeadache." I also learned to always arch my back, thus allowing my shoulders to absorb the full brunt of the blow.

"'Course, you'll get head and backaches anyway." He chuckled as I rose dizzily to my feet after yet another fall. "But that's what pezainkillers are for."

I forced a laugh, my head and back throbbing.

But soon I was kicking my feet up into the air and managing to slam my shoulders into the mat, all while keeping my neck tucked against my chest, thus sparing the back of my head any actual contact with the mat. "Good!" Shane exclaimed after one particular fall, and the exhilaration his compliment caused vanquished my headache. Soon he was launching off the ropes and plowing into me, and by the end of the hour, I could absorb his three-hundred-pound blow and fall correctly. When he announced the hour was over, I rolled out of the ring and settled unsteadily onto a folding chair. Shane hopped out of the ring and ambled up to me. "How ya fezeelin'?" he asked.

"Tremendous." I lied. "Could do this all day long."

"That's what I like to hear," he hooted, sitting down next to me. "How this works is, I usually give people three free lessons. If at any time they wanna quezit, no problem. But if they wanna continue, I collect for those lessons."

"Fifty bucks per, right?" I asked, leaning down to retrieve my jeans, which lay folded by the chair.

"Yeah. But like I said, wait until the third—"

I had already plucked a fifty dollar bill from the back pocket and was holding it out to him. "I'm not gonna quit," I said. "Take it."

He took it.

"Mind if I ask you something?" I said.

"Sure." He shrugged.

"Are you mispronouncing these wezords on purpose, or is it just me?"

"Next couple lessons." He chuckled with gentle dismissal. He pulled out the brown bottle once again and inhaled deeply. "Nail polish remover," he explained, "better than Valium. Want a hit?"

I took a tentative sniff.

"Nah," he corrected, "You gotta smell it like you would a woman!"

I snorted violently and tilted my head as the liquid's sharp sterility penetrated my nostrils. Head spinning, I sat back in the chair with a jagged smile. Shane nodded and tucked the bottle back into his pocket. "You said you had no place to stay, right?" he asked.

"Just got into town." I shrugged. "You're my first stop."

"Tell you what," he said, "every Tuesday, Thursday, and Sunday, I have an advanced class here. Now since this is your first day, you're not ready for that. But the class ends at ten-thirty, and if you wanna head out and grab something to eat or whatever, you can come back around then and sleep here tonight."

I thanked him, left my bags there, and took a few buses back toward downtown. I ate at a Del Taco and found the main library, where I sat until six o'clock with a book of Giorgio De Chirico's collected sketches in my hands. I didn't look at a single picture, choosing instead to stare out the window at the palm trees that sprouted like exotic weeds beyond the rooftops of buildings. They were the first I had ever really seen, and I kept studying them even after the sun had set and their leaves were shadowy prisoners of their own shape.

By the time I returned to the academy it was 10:45. I walked through the door and saw Shane shrugging on an overcoat. "Right on time." He smiled, then gestured at the chair in the small office. "That's probably the most comfortable place," he said.

"How'd it go tonight?" I asked.

"Went all right." His head bobbed contemplatively. "Brutal. Bloody. A little shooting."

"Shooting?" I asked.

"Next couple lessons." He winked, heading for the door. "Sweet drezeams."

"Hey, Shane!" I called, "Tuesday, Thursday, or Sunday?"

"Huh?"

"Is it Tuesday, Thursday, or Sunday?" I asked again.

"Tuesday." He frowned. "Remember for tomorrow," he added, "watch the back of the head when you fall." Then he turned and went out the door, leaving me to the stillness of the gym's shadows. The wrestling posters hovered like ghosts against the walls. Outside, the only sound was an occasional squeal of car tires.

I circled the ring three times before leaping to the apron and climbing through the ropes. "Ladies and gentlemen," I announced to the surrounding silence, "The Heavyweight Champion of the World!"

I threw myself back onto the mat, making sure to

keep my chin tucked. After repeating this maneuver a couple of dozen times, I finally lay down in the middle of the mat, using my curled up jacket for a pillow. With sleep's approach my breaths deepened, and I abruptly registered the pungent smell of blood. My eyes snapped open and focused on a dark stain about two feet away. My left wrist tapped the mat in a haphazard series of soft, dull thuds. After a few minutes of straining to recall if the mark had been there earlier that afternoon or not, exhaustion overcame excitement. My arm came to rest and I crashed into unconsciousness.

In my dream, a body that I recognized as my own was in a ring. My hair hung to the small of my back. With the omniscient perspective unique to dreams, I became one with every person in the screaming audience. As both participant and observer, I was aware that this was a "mask vs. hair" match. If I won, I would be allowed to strip off my opponent's mask. If he was victorious, he would be able to shave off all my hair. I leapt off a turnbuckle and landed on the masked figure. The referee's hand slapped the mat three times, whereupon I had the sensation of rising. One of my arms raised in victory while I tore at the mask—

Then an explosion ripped the ring apart, and I turned toward the audience only to see their bodies flying in all directions. A severed head, flames rising from its hair, whipped toward me. I woke as it collided with my face and saw not a head, but one of Shane Stratford's legs. The bridge of my nose throbbed angrily.

"Never let your guard down while you're in a ring," Shane said with a stern smile as he rolled off of me.

We began to practice falls. "Good," he said and nod-

ded after only five minutes. "Looks like you're getting
the hang of them." I beamed in response. He then suggested we try chops. I quickly discovered that a chop is
one of the most *legitimately* painful moves in professional wrestling. The only way to create that sharp
report that sounds like the crack of a whip is to legitimately slap the shit out of someone's chest with the
palm of your hand.

For thirty minutes we stood in the middle of the ring
and took turns striking the other's bare chest with an
open palm. At first we used polite restraint, but as soon
as the pain kicked in, we were slashing at each other's
flesh with horrible force. Drops of blood began seeping
through our raw skin. I didn't care. I knew that if I suggested we stop first, then I would've failed some kind of
test. After fifteen minutes, my nerve endings were no
longer responding. Soon splotches of blood decorated
our hands, making us into two children indulging in the
goriest kind of finger painting imaginable. As we kept it
up, I told myself that every chop would bring me closer
to a title belt, that this was a test to get into heaven, that
if I surrendered now I would die. I was feeling light-
headed as hell from all the pain, of course, and that
helped.

"All right," he bellowed, after my last chop burst yet
another pocket of blood on his left pec. "Good enough,"
he panted, allowing himself to wince at last. We both
lowered our hands and simultaneously howled in pain.
He insisted on cutting the lesson short that day and
only charged me twenty-five dollars. I went apartment
hunting and found a place about three blocks from the
academy right next to the freeway for $450 a month.

When the ashen landlady inquired guardedly as to my occupation, I told her that I was a student.

"Oh!" she said, her lips relinquishing their taut frown. "At the junior college?"

"Yeah," I agreed numbly, wincing as my chest throbbed as though it were being struck with a thousand pins. I was in too much pain to even eat that night. All I could rouse myself to do was sit in a small chair by the window, listen to the cars shoot past on the freeway, and wonder what kind of a person paid twenty-five dollars to have their chest turned into raw hamburger.

The next day, after covering lock-ups and head-locks, Shane suggested we spar a little. After locking up, he promptly hurled me out of the ring. I fell sloppily through the ropes and tumbled onto the floor. Before I could climb to a solid footing, he grabbed me and threw me headfirst at one of the steel bars that hold up the four corners of the ring. My forehead slammed against the bar. Stars burst into my vision. Drops of blood trickled down into my eyes.

I was fuming. *I'll be damned if this fucker's gonna split my forehead open and get fifty bucks for it.* Wiping the blood away, I climbed back into the ring. Shane was watching me carefully. He lunged for me, but I cut him off by booting him hard in the gut. He exhaled sharply, and I grabbed his arm and threw him into the ropes. As he launched back at me, I came at him with a flying clothesline that snapped his head back with a furious jolt. He plummeted back onto the mat and lay there staring up at the ceiling. I ran the ropes once and paid him back for the leg-drop he had given me the previous morning by giving him one that would have made Sonny Logan proud.

I rolled off, preparing to run if necessary. But when I turned, I saw that he was still prone, an ecstatic smile now on his face. "Pin me!" he shouted gleefully. "Pin me!" Dutifully, I covered him and slapped the mat three times. He sat up and extended his hand.

"That's shooting," he said. "Welcome to the fezamily." I took his hand.

He went on to explain that he always tested newcomers to make sure they weren't reporters or people just looking to uncover the workings of the business. With the recent popularity of professional wrestling had come a rash of controversy about just how much of the action in the ring was staged.

"Now," he announced proudly, as I tended to my wound with a couple of butterfly bandages, "you're gonna learn how this business really works."

As if to cement the deal, he passed me the nail polish remover. I took a hit, and my forehead felt a little better. So I took another one.

3
GREATEST SPORT IN THE WORLD

"So what's gonna happen out there? You're goin' over, right?" Tug whispers to me. We're standing by the wall, watching technicians scamper about. The miniature ring that I will ride down the aisle is being readied.

"You're just gonna have to watch and find out," I say. My own voice sounds so far away, as though it were coming from the end of a long tunnel.

"I hope you win it, man," Tug blurts out in a strangely petulant tone. I study his face, searching for jealousy. But his face seems more frustrated than anything.

He shrugs and covers himself, "I mean you like posing with kids and all that shit, right?"

"Don't you?"

He shrugs again. "It can get tiring. Like those auto-graph sessions."

I nod. The meet-and-greets before the shows. Some take place in convention centers near the arena, others in record stores or malls. Fans line up, linking up to form a chaotic snake of humanity, and wait for the chance to meet wrestlers and get signed pictures. It's not uncom-mon to sign a thousand autographs at these things. Afterward, we have to plunge our hands into a bucket of ice to numb the cramping. The cold stings at first but after twenty minutes you can't feel a thing. It's either that or get a shot of Xylocaine to kill the area's nerves completely. Just as long as you can work the match that night.

Tug is talking about the night he begged off after his hand seized up on him. "My right hand was shot. I couldn't even grip the goddamn pen any more," he says, "so I just shook everyone's hand with my left. I've got the right one stuck in a bucket of ice, right there at the table. So I hear some guys bitching about how a big tough pro wrestler is too much of a wimp to sign autographs. They're getting closer in line and saying how I'm proba-bly faking it. Usual bullshit. So when they come up to shake my hand, I grab one of their hands and pull it into the ice and hold it there. He starts shouting and I tell him, "You think I'd be keeping my hand in there if I wasn't in pain, asshole?""

He laughs a lot harder than I do. "Fuck," he deter-mines, "be a champion for those people? Who needs it?"

"You've been a champ before," I remind him. "International champ."

"Fuck it. The only good thing about winning a strap is

it means you're finally gettin' a push. The fans don't know who to cheer for. They just want a champ."

"You really believe that?"

He picks at the red tape still wrapped around his wrists. "I dunno," he says. "I guess people kinda think it's time for some new blood. Someone who really wants it, you know?"

I nod. Like most pro wrestlers, Tug was a fan as a kid. Once you've been a pro wrestler, it's hard to see wrestling through the eyes of a fan. Because to be a fan is to be a mark. Wrestlers, a collection of characters towering above life, inhabit a world that is uniquely theirs. Anyone outside that world is a mark.

But there have been moments while watching a match on the backstage monitor or through the curtain that tickle something lost inside me. A feeling, a conviction, a promise that everything was always going to be all right so long as I remained in pursuit of my dream.

The kind of promise that does not age well.

——————

The next couple of weeks brought daily bursts of knowledge at a pace so hectic that I sometimes felt like a sponge in a river, surrounded by more water than I could ever hope to absorb. The first thing Shane filled me in on was the language he had been using when he said things like "bezody slam." This variation on pig latin involved inserting an "eez" directly after the first consonant of a word. Wrestlers use this technique when talking to one another in the ring or in the presence of "marks" (fans). By distorting the words in such a fash-

ion and saying them quickly, it makes relevant com-
munication sound like gibberish to untrained ears. The
language is known as carni, and got the name from its
use among carnival workers dating back to the eighteenth century. Shane claimed he had been speaking it
for so long that he now used it out of "unconscious hez-
abit."

Our lessons often extended to almost two hours,
with equal amounts of time given to the physical and
the psychological side of the business. I learned that
pros didn't *wrestle* each other. Rather, they *worked with*
one another. "When you're in the ring, you've got eight
thousand things to be thinking about," Shane said to
me one day. "There's the crowd, how long the match
has gone . . . the last thing you need to be doing is trying to hurt the person you're working with. You need
him alive so you can wrestle him the night after that
and the night after that." In wrestling, there was no
winning or losing. If you were victorious in a match, you
went over. If you were pinned, you merely *did a job*. A
draw was referred to as a *broadway*, because it enabled
both wrestlers to move up in fans' estimations.

I learned how matches are structured. Shane told
me that pros who toured with the WWO often worked
with the same person every night, and some of them
would memorize a match move for move, performing as
actors would a stage play night after night. "I remember
one time," Shane told me, "Marty 'Madman' Mikiwolski
and I had our match down so pat that the boys backstage would time us. Every night, the match would go
exactly thirteen minutes and twenty-four seconds. We
had it all nailed . . . every grimace, every gesture, every

curse to the crowd." However, Shane pointed out, frenzied travel schedules often made this kind of structure
impossible. "So you need to know how to improvise,"
Shane said. "Gotta be able to call spots while you're in
that ring."

A spot referred to a series of moves. Oftentimes
spots would be planned out beforehand in the dressing
room. Then in the ring one guy could say "drop-kick
spot" and both would know that the spot consisted of a
specific series of moves finished off with a drop-kick.
Then there was pacing, with matches usually alternat-
ing between high-spots and rest-spots. High-spots were
several moves following one another in rapid succes-
sion, while a rest-spot would involve one wrestler holding his opponent in a headlock while both caught their
breath. One wrestler, often the heel, set the pace, or
called the match.

Toward the end of the second week I asked Shane
something that had been on my mind since I had spent
the night in the gym. "What did you mean that first
night," I said, "when you said there had been some
shooting?"

Shane smiled. "Shooting is the term used for when
wrestlers really go at it."

"You mean sometimes wrestlers just start brawling
with each other?"

"It happens." Shane shrugged. "Someone gets pissed
off, starts throwing blows that really connect. The other
guy takes offense, and next thing you know you've got
a shezoot match."

He made a clear distinction between shooting and
merely working stiff. "Working stiff means you're throw-

ing blows that connect. And they hurt. But you're doing it because there's a sold-out crowd or it's a pay-per-view or whatever." He took a long snort from his ever-present bottle of nail polish and sighed. "Shooting is the real shit," he said dreamily. "Two animals tryin' to kill each other."

During these weeks of lessons, I slowly grew more comfortable with seeing myself in the ring. Looking at the posters on the wall, I was able to envision my own picture up there. My face and body tensed and ready to pounce, flexing mightily just above a name distinguished only by its own intangibility in my mind's eye.

My past life fell away as easily as a spent skin. Soon the streets of San Bernardino consumed my thoughts and memories, effortlessly replacing the streets of Chicago I had walked for eighteen years. I called my mom once from a pay phone to let her know I had arrived safely, but couldn't give her any home phone number. Who needed a phone? The only constant connection I maintained with my past life in Chicago came through my old wrestling pillow, which I would faithfully elbow-drop in farewell every time I left my apartment.

Slowly the days evolved into a pattern. Every morning except Sunday I went to the academy and learned yet another aspect of professional wrestling. Then I had lunch alone at a nearby cafe, sitting on a stool at the counter alongside manual workers from the tire factory just down the street. Even though the same waitress, her cheeks recessed and littered with pockmarks, was always behind the counter and I always greeted her with a hesitant wave and ordered the same thing (a French dip with French fries and a chocolate milkshake), she insisted upon the ritual of pointedly asking what I was "plannin' on today" while holding a pen to her order pad and giving no indication of ever having seen me before. She might as well have been asking me about my complete day's itinerary, which was almost as unvarying as my meals. After lunch I headed over to a gym and worked out with weights. Then it was to the library, where I would pick up a few art books.

Back in my room I would spend afternoons admiring the world through my window. The freeway was just below, and beyond it a mini-mall. The parking lot was a constant whir of activity. Fights, fender benders, ambulances speeding in and out—the glass pane filtered all these scenes, keeping them at bay like a television screen does the reality of the ten o'clock news. After the ink of night spread through the sky, I followed the headlights soaring along the freeway below. The art books I held at those times brought me some contentment, even though I had no desire to open them. I had left all my drawing supplies behind in Chicago and that was just as well. I had enough to think about, because in spite of their structure, my days were lived in a vortex of raw emotions brought on by my new circumstances. I had never come home to an empty room before, and found myself greeting imaginary fans on the street and inviting them home. I would buy a pack of cigarettes, smoke one, and then throw out the rest of the pack. I tried the same with chewing tobacco. All I ever bought at the grocery store were cans of soup and bottles of water. I worried what the checkout girls would think of me. That I was alone, a loser, had no friends? But I wasn't lonely. I had the fans in my apartment, and every night I spoke out loud to them, discussing whatever latest intricacy of pro wrestling I learned from Shane Stratford that day. I conducted interviews with myself while walking down the street, discussing my humble beginnings in the hot desert town of San Bernardino, ending each with "only two things grew there: the tumbleweeds, and me."

I was still scratching my own skin, but being in the ring helped lull the urge into a temporary silence. I felt comfortable in a ring. Four roped off boundaries.

One day Shane made reference to the comeback Sonny Logan worked into every one of his matches. "He's in the ring, gettin' the shezit kicked out of him, but he's reachin' out toward the crowd," Shane explained, "grasping power from all his little Dreamers, and all of 'em cheer and feed right into his gimmick."

"What's a gimmick?" I asked him.

Shane gestured around at the poster-lined walls. "They are," he said. "They're all gimmicks."

I scanned the posters needlessly. I knew them all by heart. Ivan Tostoff, "The Russian Tiger." Tod "The Bod" Malibu. Johnny "The Devil" Satanic. Dozens of men like these snarled down from their posts on Shane Stratford's Wall of Fame.

"A gimmick is," Shane explained, "a wrestler's character. It makes the marks boo or cheer. An all-American, a cocky boy-toy, a renegade cop, a rock star, a matador . . . anything that gives 'em an identity the crowd can relate to."

"An identity." I moved my head up and down. "So Sonny Logan's gimmick would be like an all-American?"

"Not quite deep enough." Shane picked at the salt-and-peppered stubble on his chin. "Logan's gimmick is that he's the American Dream. But at the same time he makes his fans believe that his very existence is completely due to them. They're convinced that they give him the strength to do what he does in that ring."

"You don't think they are?" I asked quickly, remembering the narrow stairway and the warm grip of Sonny Logan's hand. That night his grasp pulled me up into this world of "body slezams" and gimmicks.

"Who knows?" Shane shrugged. "It doesn't matter, as long as they're convinced. When does an illusion stop being an illusion?"

A few seconds passed before I realized the question wasn't rhetorical. I raised my shoulders and dropped them.

"When someone becomes convinced of its existence enough to respond to it as their perceived rezality." Shane smiled and clapped once. Twice. Three times. "Lesson's over for the day."

That night back in my apartment I sat staring at the art books which lay stacked against the wall. A tower made up of different sized bricks. It was impossible to summon any kind of hope that if I held one of those books in my hands, I might actually open it. I sat on the edge of my bed, held still by a mute terror.

Am I real? Is any of this world real?

A hope sprung up. I reached down and picked up a

Carl's Jr. napkin and a pen. Slowly I traced a square. Then another square within the first. And then a third. My hand vibrating, tapping the pen against paper, now against my wrist. Black dots nicked my flesh. I flung the pen and napkin to the floor. Then I paced, hitting my tensed stomach until the pain was real enough.

After two and a half weeks and $750 worth of lessons, Shane announced to me that I was ready for the advanced class.

The advanced class consisted of maybe two dozen people who had either undergone training at Shane's or somewhere else. Some of them were actively pursuing wrestling as a career, while others were passionate hobbyists.

My knees were shaking the first night Shane introduced me to the group, but when he announced that he and I had chopped each other for a full thirty minutes there were impressed exhalations, and I was granted immediate respect. It turned out that no one else there had gone over ten.

Every session basically consisted of people getting into the ring with one another and staging impromptu matches while a third man played the role of a referee. These sessions went for two hours and Shane charged us twenty dollars each for "ring maintenance." As I worked with various people in the advanced class, I learned how to adapt to different styles of wrestling. Hubert, a man six inches shorter than me with a massive beer belly and arms as thick as hams, liked to work slow and stiff. Juan, a 160-pounder who had grown up watching the fast-paced Mexican style of wrestling known as *lucha libre*, enjoyed incorporating various flips and high-flying maneuvers.

Shane spent every class observing and critiquing the matches. It was important to wrestle before a discerning audience, he constantly reminded us. "Many people don't think of professional wrestling as a sport because a sport is defined as a competition between opposing teams or single participants." Here he would pause. "Well, consider this: You and whoever else is in that ring with you are on one team. The crowd is the opposing team. You're competing against their skepticism and powers of observation in order to make them believe and appreciate what you're doing inside that squezared circle. Your job is to make a match *appear* as violent as possible while at the same time imposing a conscious order on the very chaos you're creating and using to entertain. You want to pop the crowd, make 'em say 'wow.' Break down their barriers of disbelief and they'll keep coming back. That's the competition that qualifies pro wrestling as a sport." At this point he would stop, take a deep inhalation of nail polish remover, and conclude, "And I happen to think it's the greatest sport in the world."

Everyone always applauded that speech.

During my first week I gravitated toward another student in the class, named B.J. Thomas. Although the B.J. stood for Bobby Joe, his nickname in the class, much to his chagrin, was "blowjob." He was a couple years older than me, as were almost all the people I wrestled with. (Due to this fact, I automatically increased my age by almost three years, telling people I was six months shy of turning twenty-one.)

B.J. was exactly my height and had the same sub-dued facial features I did. His body boasted an overall thickness mine didn't have, and this along with his curly hair and black skin were the only things that really differed in our appearances. B.J. also happened to be as dead serious as I was about pursuing pro wrestling as an actual vocation, and this bonded us immediately.

B.J. explained that since his father had worked sixty hours a week as a limousine driver to support a family of six ("Growing up with three sisters, imagine that," B.J. would say, rolling his eyes), the only real father-son time came on Saturday nights, watching All-Star So Cal Wrestling.

B.J. had been indirectly guided to a career in pro-fessional wrestling by a wrestler known as "The Billion Dollar Baby" Ricky Witherspoon. He had been in the WWO for about a year, and his gimmick was that he was the son of an oil tycoon and believed he could buy anybody off with his immense wealth.

"So, I'm two years out of high school," B.J. explained. "I'm living at home. I've got this nothing job at a drug store while I'm taking general education courses at a junior college. And one night about six months ago Dad comes home and shows me a hundred dollar bill. He had driven Ricky Witherspoon from the airport to his hotel, and Witherspoon had laid that bill on him and told him to keep the change. I had always loved wrestling, and I knew I could take those dudes on. So I decided right then and there, doc . . . I wanted to be the one being driven instead of the driver." He had called Shane Stratford a week later.

B.J. had a unique rule he followed whenever in the ring: He would never deliver a head-butt. It was a staple in pro wrestling that any African-American or Samoan wrestler would possess a devastating head-butt. This angle reeked of the racist notion that their heads had to be harder to protect their weak minds. "Used to drive Dad crazy." B.J. would shake his head. "That was the one promise I made him. Well, second promise. First, I told him I was gonna make a million dollars as a wrestler, and second that I was gonna become a world champion without once throwing a head-butt."

"Come on," Shane Stratford said after one session, testing him, "if the WWO offered you a contract on the condition you go out as 'Hard Hat Mac' or something, you'd sign quickern' a whezore swallows."

"No, I wouldn't," B.J. replied simply, and Shane raised his eyebrows as though he believed B.J. was sincere. I knew I did.

By my third week in the advanced class, I was a regular visitor to the apartment B.J. shared with his girlfriend, Terri. They had been sweethearts since junior high and were planning on buying a house within the district of West Covina Junior High so that their child could go to the same school where they had first met each other in sixth grade gym class. They already had this child named. "T.J.," Terri revealed proudly.

"He'll love it," B.J. hooted.

"*She'll* love it," Terri teased.

They would often refer to details of their future

together as if they were vacation plans. Whenever I was around them I found myself gripped by a hopeful longing, which soon blossomed into fear that made me a blur of repeated movement.

"Why do you do that?" B.J. asked one afternoon. We were at the gym, resting between sets of bench-presses.

"Do what?"

"Touch yourself." He tapped all the way up and back down his arm. "You don't notice it?"

I leaned on the end of the barbell, its steel cold and reassuring. "It's a habit, I guess." I shrugged.

"That's it?"

I shrugged again, thoughts popping in my skull like hyper-kinetic popcorn. *Isthisbodyreal? If its skin was cut woulditbleed? Do I exist?* "I guess." My voice stumbled over these silent questions. "I don't know."

B.J. gave a careful nod. "Let's keep this show goin'," he said. After a few confused moments, he laid down on the bench press, and I realized he had meant the lifting. I exhaled.

Picking me up at my apartment one afternoon, B.J. noticed some art books from the library. They were scattered on the floor below the window. "Crazy stuff, doc," he said in a careful, noncommittal tone as he flipped through one. I didn't tell him that in the last four seconds he had seen more of their contents than I had.

Sometimes B.J. and I hung out with another guy in the class named Aries Watori. Aries was twenty-three, and his father owned a couple of used car lots and a few higher-end apartment buildings in downtown Los Angeles. He was around 5'10", with a stocky barrel-chested upper body balanced on two skinny legs. "A castle held up by twigs," Grabowski would've mumbled from behind his newspaper, had Aries ever stepped into the cage. Aries claimed to get off on pain and often rammed his own head into the turnbuckle several times, particularly if people were watching him. He often took insane chances, such as diving on tables and somersaulting off the turnbuckle onto the mat for no apparent reason. He once told me that his hero was Jim Morrison, because he had "hated his father."

"My father treats my mom like shit," Aries informed me one night. We were headed to the wrestling academy in a BMW from one of his father's lots. "He's a fuckin' joke," he spat. I nodded mutely. "They're both a fuckin' joke," he added, taking a corner at forty-five miles per hour. Aries always drove as recklessly as he wrestled.

———————

One Saturday afternoon the three of us were at Del Taco, where we usually went after class to stuff ourselves with forty-nine cent tacos. Aries had performed a particularly risky maneuver in class earlier that day, diving off the top of a turnbuckle onto a table positioned on the floor fifteen feet below. He had broken the table in half to great applause from the dozen or so wrestlers present, as well as Shane Stratford. "You're nuts, man," I told him as we sat down at a patio outside with a half-dozen tacos each. "You could've been killed," I said, my tone halfway between admiration and disapproval.

Aries smiled and nodded. "I know," he acknowledged, "but it got a reaction, didn't it?"

"Jesus," B.J. belched, "you risked your life to get a
reaction from fifteen people during a practice session?"

"Damn right I did," Aries' voice lowered. "I remember
when I was like eight or nine years old my dad took me
to one of these IMAX theatres. They were showing this
film about speed. Drag racing, planes breaking the
sound barrier, that kind of stuff. Well, there was this
one story about this guy. He was a teenager speeding
along the road and gets pulled over by this small town
cop. The guy's all excited, and he asks the cop how fast
he was going. 'Over a hundred miles an hour,' the cop
replies. 'Did you hear that, Mary?' The guy turns to his
girlfriend. 'A hundred miles an hour!' The guy loved
speed, pure and simple. Then the screen shows, 'So and
so won the 1965 Indy 500. Won the 1966 Indy 500.
Died leading the 1967 Indy 500.'"

We sat silent for a few seconds, munching thought-
fully. "That was when I realized," Aries declared,
"there's no shame in dying if you're doing what you
love."

"Sounds pretty admirable," I admitted.

"Sounds like a bunch of sentimental horseshit," B.J.
scoffed.

"What was the guy's name, Aries?" I asked.

"I forget," Aries said. "But it was a great fucking
movie."

I raised my large Mountain Dew. "To living and
dying doing what you love," I announced.

"To living and dying doing what you love," Aries
echoed with appropriate zeal. B.J. raised his cup in

dubious silence but gave in to a grin as the three of us touched paper cups. Then we drank, happily swallowing the conviction that whatever we loved was not only pure, but destined to be; that mixture which enables people to believe in truly fantastic toasts.

4

MUSCLE MAN

The champion's dressing room door remains closed. The murmur of the crowd reverberates through the high-ceilinged backstage area. Through a series of mellow cries and whoops, the fans are issuing a collective exhalation before the main event. They need their strength to unleash the enthusiasm required for the night's climax. Rarely does a match succeed or fail solely on the efforts of either the wrestlers or the crowd. Each feeds off the other, and when the energy is right, they produce a union as wondrous as sex.

Thousands of hands find a common rhythm and are soon clapping as one. The bleachers above our backstage area vibrate from perfectly timed stomps. "Marks are gettin' ready," Tug says, his cheeks filling with a hot flush.

The pounding now fills the air; my breaths are rapid and shallow, matching their rhythm. I need to get out to that ocean of people.

The technicians back away from the miniature ring. Three ropes of red, white, and blue surround the four-by-six platform.

Rob Robertson lowers his walkie-talkie. "Three minutes to intro of Michael Harding!"

My legs tremble as I climb into the shrunken ring. I recall my first trip down an aisle and am surprised that this memory is tinged with sadness. Although too nervous to enjoy the experience, that first time possessed a perfection spread over all of its panicky blurs. A diamond made even more precious by glaring flaws.

Standing in this mini-ring, I suddenly feel like a museum piece. I could be a mummy, cordoned off by this patriotic colored three-rope barrier. The crowd's unanimous claps and stomps have become the beats of a death march. How many more ring entrances will I be able to make before the thrill is completely gone, when the possibility of becoming WWO Champion will be more of an inconvenience than a goal?

"Ladies and gentlemen . . . and wrestling fans!" The announcer's voice tunnels under the crowd's rhythm and surfaces: "This is the main event!" Instantly the beat is scattered into thousands of separate cheers and howls that rise in a tidal wave of noise. It frightens me.

This is the biggest match of my career, and for the first time a fear of what I will either have to destroy or be destroyed by makes me dread heading down that aisle.

———————

My first match in front of a paying crowd came soon after I started my advanced training at the academy. A promotion based in Los Angeles was putting together a show at the YMCA down near San Diego. Shane knew the people in charge and got the three of us on the show. I was slated to wrestle B.J. It would be his first paying gig as well. His gimmick was a psycho dentist.

For five nights I sat up well past midnight, trying to conjure up a gimmick of my own. The cars shot by outside my window while I ran my nails over my chest and arms. I had an uncertain hope that if the skin broke just once, an identity would be released with my blood. But my flesh held firm.

Lying in bed was torture. Sleep had become an orgy of shadows; I was convinced that one night my lack of identity would enable them to absorb me and I would never awaken. *Why can't I think of a fucking gimmick? What's the big deal? It's just a gimmick.*

Just a gimmick.

The nights passed and I remained gimmickless. Back when I had been sketching in Chicago, I had found subjects for drawings effortlessly. The shape of a vase could spark a dozen possible sketches, each one its own story. But now when I consulted my surroundings for any clues as to a gimmick, *one* gimmick, there was no assistance to be found. I stared at the cracks, which spread like aimless spider webs in the ceiling, but they remained cracks in a wall and nothing more. I conducted interviews with myself, playing the roles of both announcer and wrestler. But the announcer simply referred to the subject as Michael. *Michael?* I rubbed my temples. *What kind of a fucking gimmick is Michael?*

When I turned to Shane for help, he just smiled. "It's your gimmick," he said firmly. "You've gotta pick one you feel comfortable with." There was no way I was going to tell him I wasn't even comfortable in my own skin.

The day of the show B.J., Aries, and I all drove down in the new Mercedes Aries' father had given him for his twenty-third birthday. "I'm nervous, guys," I admitted on the way, trying to make my voice casual. "What the hell should I call myself?"

As the car streaked toward San Diego County, we tossed some possible ideas around. It quickly turned into a game:

"Mike the Mangler?" *Too football.* "Mikey the Moocher?" *Too bluesy.* "Malicious Mike?" *Rhymes with delicious.* "Marble Mike?" *Sounds like an ice cream flavor.* "Michael Myers?" *Too Hollywood.* "Mike Starr?" *Too porno sounding.* "Mr. X?" *Not porno sounding enough.* "Mikey, he likes it?" Aries suggested.

"Fuck you." I gave a chuckling Aries the finger. My eyes snapped away to the open window. The foliage streaking by on either side of the highway made me think of Chicago. Home. The maple tree outside that final party. In the same way that maple's leaves had waved goodbye, these leaves now appeared to be waving in greeting. The petals fluttered by in a blur as though they were the hands of well-wishers lining a drag strip. I tried to picture whatever connected the leaves to the plants out here traveling underground and linking up with the roots of the Chicago tree through a vast network of intertwined vegetation. I extended my arm in a closed fist salute. A warmth licked my body, for this arm indisputably possessed the thickness required of a professional wrestler. I kissed the rounded head of its right bicep. B.J. laughed from the backseat.

"Tonight's the night, boys," I boomed. "Muscular Mike Maple makes his pro wrestling debut."

They hooted, slapping me on the back as I flexed my neck in the rearview mirror. Fucking immortal, having found a gimmick at last.

We arrived two hours before show time and found the promoter pacing in the narrow backstage hallway while guzzling ferociously from a bottle of beer. He was a pale guy with hair peeking out of the top of his weathered Harley-Davidson T-shirt. Moderately sized arms and legs extended out of a massive upper body, making him look like a Popsicle with four sticks. He shook our hands with a limp grip (the standard pro wrestler greeting, indicating you didn't work stiff) while introducing himself as Steven Winters. It turned out he was a pro wrestler himself who claimed to be Sonny Barger's cousin and went by the name of Jack "Rude Boy" Daniels. I introduced myself as "Mike Maple."

The ring had already been set up, and a couple rows of folding chairs surrounded its perimeter. The bleachers were pulled down expectantly. Steven informed us there had been twenty advance sales of tickets but he had high hopes that the gate would exceed two hundred people.

A half hour before the card was set to start, I changed into multicolored spandex and a Gold's Gym tank top I had fortuitously brought along. It added another level to my muscle persona. I was posing in a mirror above the sinks when B.J. tracked me down. "Hey, Muscular," he said, "let's go over that power slam spot again."

"I should press slam you," I decided.

"Say what?"

"You know." I turned to face him. "Press you over my head."

"You're nuts." He laughed. "Hell, we haven't even practiced that."

"Hey guys!" Aries bounded over and clapped each of us on a shoulder. He was clad in a long black robe glittering with sequins that his father had paid $700 for in honor of Aries' first match. "I'm gonna be a champion tonight!" he announced. "One of the guys no-showed, and Steven says my pirate gimmick'll work perfectly. So I'm gonna be one half of the team that wins the tag-team championship."

"Hell," Steven crowed as he ambled over, a beer in hand. "That robe is probably worth more than I paid for the two tag-team title belts." Aries looked down and gave a sharp shrug as Steven chuckled tipsily. "Hey, Muscular Mike, you're gonna be the face in your match with B.J., right?" he asked.

Since B.J.'s gimmick was that of a psychotic dentist called "Dr. Eddie Extraction," I told Steven that it looked like I would definitely be the one shaking hands and kissing babies.

"Then you're going over," Steven said. "I'm workin' as a heel and winning the title tonight, so we need some face victories to round everything off."

Steven was functioning, as most independent promoters do, as both the promoter and the booker. In pro wrestling, the booker decides not only who's going to wrestle who, but also determines the winners, the angles or story lines, feuds, and the general direction of the promotion. Given this, it's not surprising to find that when a wrestler is serving as a promotion's booker, he's generally also serving as that promotion's champion.

"What's your finishing maneuver?" Steven asked me.

"Press slam," I answered before B.J. could speak. I pantomimed the maneuver by plunging both my hands up into the air. My palms collided with the low ceiling.

"You can do that?" Steven asked.

"Hell yeah." I grinned and hit a double biceps pose. "I'm Muscular Mike Maple."

"Damn." Steven belched laughter. "You really live the gimmick, huh?"

"Every second of the fucking day."

Steven went weaving off, still chuckling and drinking. Aries was studying his robe in the mirror with defensive eyes. "I may just toss this thing into the fuckin' crowd tonight," he grumbled.

B.J. shook his head. "All right, Mr. Maple. You better not drop me," he warned, "or I'm gonna kick your fuckin' gluteus maximus from here back to L.A."

Twenty minutes later I was flexing my way down to the ring before a listless crowd of around seventy-five people. The half empty bleachers mocked me as I hoisted myself into the ring and immediately began posing in hopes of stirring the apathetic silence. Muscular

Mike Maple was announced and met with scattered lackadaisical cheers. Then B.J. made his entrance dressed in a dentist's smock smeared with red paint and a handheld drill. The crowd booed him thoroughly and he ate it up, responding with equal vigor in the form of threatening gestures and fiendish cackling.

Then he was in the ring. "A pro wrestling match is like any other work of art," Shane had often advised us. "Make the opening three spots and the closing three spots the best. That's all anyone'll remember anyway."

B.J. and I glared at each other for several motionless seconds. A shout of "Boring!" rang out from somewhere in the stands. The crucial opening window of the match and my career was slipping away. A drop of sweat crawled down my forehead and found its way into my left eye.

I was melting into just another shadow shaped by an unstoppable sun.

My eyes closed, and when they opened their vision was clear and Muscular Mike Maple was nailing Eddie Extraction with a devastating clothesline that sent the evil dentist down to the canvas. My first movements in a ring were swept up in a whirling compound of the opening bell's clangs and the audience's cheers.

The rest of the match was sloppy, with our spots stiff and rushed as a result of sheer nervousness. In spite of the mistimed pacing, the crowd popped for several of our moves. After every big move such as a power slam or suplex, I ripped off a few poses. To alleviate my nervousness, I focused on individual faces in the crowd. Down in front was a pigtailed little girl whose pudgy face was dominated by a pair of wide distraught eyes.

At the end of one row slouched a man, sitting by himself and clad in a trench coat and a top hat. Drops of sweat traveled the wrinkled map of skin clinging to his shrunken face. He had his legs spread and both were bouncing up and down with a restless rhythm. In the bleachers, three guys in high school letter jackets hooted with exaggerated sarcasm, trying too hard to show their three weary-eyed dates that they were here simply as a lark. One of the girls' blond hair reminded me briefly of the girl I had gone to prom with, although I wouldn't be able to actually remember Charlotte's name until I got backstage.

B.J. and I had only gotten through about half of our planned match when the referee, a bearded Samoan with a massive girth, tapped me on the shoulder and muttered, "Nine minutes by. Better take it home, guys."

"Say what?" I murmured back, slamming an elbow against the surface of B.J.'s neck. It seemed like we had been in the ring for only three minutes at the most.

"Take it home," the referee implored. "End the freakin' match."

"All right, baby," I said quietly to B.J. as I backed him into the ropes. "We're takin' it home. Press slam time."

"You'd better pull this off—" he hissed as I threw him across the ring. I had practiced the maneuver a few times in advanced class, but not with any real consideration of ever using it. However, that was before I became Muscular Mike Maple.

B.J. bounced off the opposite ropes and flew back at me. I jammed one hand on the fleshy part of his leg just above his kneecap while my other went to his chest. He gave a little leap, and in the next second I had him successfully pressed above my head. In that moment I glimpsed a reflection of the ring in the dark window of an office located on the far wall. The distance shrunk our image, but it was still unmistakably that of a pro wrestler in a ring pressing an opponent above his head. Then I stepped forward and released B.J., letting the vision slip from my sight as I turned to watch him plummet to the canvas. I bolted against the ropes and came down on his prone form with a splash. Then I rolled him over for the pin, and three seconds later had won my first professional match.

The referee raised one of my arms and I raised the other. Like wings I had just used for the very first time.

Back in the locker room, B.J. and I shared an exultant embrace. "We did good, huh?" he asked.

"We did good," I agreed.

Steven came up and clapped both of us on the back. "Great stuff, you two," he said, "but for future reference, remember the first three matches of a card are preliminaries. They shouldn't be anything too fancy. No false finishes, brawling outside the ring, or any of that shit."

"Oops," B.J. said. We had brawled outside the ring for a good ninety seconds.

"It's cool." Steve shrugged. "But you should still know this kinda stuff. If you're ever in the first three matches, don't shoot the show's load too early. Save the chairs and other shit for the main eventers." He paused and grinned. "But I wouldn't sweat it. You guys won't be in the prelim spot for long."

Basking in this immediate praise, B.J. and I watched the other matches with pleasant interest. The other wrestlers were wide-shouldered blocks of flesh; rolls of fat ballooned over their spandex tights. Their gimmicks were fairly standard; most were simply playing themselves in variations of a rowdy biker character. Aries teamed with a guy who dressed up as a Navy Seal and billed himself as "Sergeant Rox." Aries and Rox won the tag-team titles, according to plan. Immediately after triumphantly bursting through the curtain, Aries scanned backstage for the robe he had neglected to throw to the audience. After spotting it draped over a folding chair, he looked again at the title belt in his hands with a relieved smile.

Twenty minutes after the card ended, Steven finally paid off the wrestlers. He was pretty blitzed by that time; he had been stumbling noticeably during his main event title win. "You guys work pretty good." His beer-soaked breath wafted over us as he handed each of us a well-worn twenty dollar bill. "This was your first time out, huh?"

B.J. and Aries just nodded and shrugged. "First but not the last," I stated, giving a most muscular pose.

Steve laughed and hiccuped. "Well, there was this manager who used to work in the South. He's in the big leagues now. He said you're still a mark until your hundredth match."

"Damn," Aries remarked.

"How many matches have you had?" I asked.

Steven belched. "This was my eighty-fifth tonight,"
he groaned. "Fifteen more to go."

————————————

The next week was spent lifting weights with a ferocity
I hadn't known since the first year I picked up a dumb-
bell. I squeezed out forced reps, driving my muscles to
growth through exhaustion. Also, with religious adherence to the advice in pro body building magazines, I
increased my level of food intake. Whenever my friends
and I went out to Del Taco after class, I now inhaled
twelve tacos instead of six.

But all this added exertion and force-feeding did was
give me achy joints and serious indigestion while at the
same time increasing my weight by seven pounds, most
of which settled around my mid-section. I was now 211
pounds and had reached a plateau of some kind. It was
becoming more and more obvious to me that B.J. possessed a muscular denseness that I lacked. His muscles
came in levels; mine were large but one-dimensional.
Instead of feeling validated when I flexed, I was now
becoming alarmed. Muscular Mike's muscularity
couldn't touch that of wrestlers in the WWO or even a
few local southern Californian wrestlers. Without muscles, Muscular Mike Maple couldn't exist.

And without a gimmick, I would be back to being
Michael Harding.

When I mentioned to B.J. that I needed to get a lot
bigger very fast, he was pleased. "I was wondering when
you were gonna come around," he beamed. "You're at
the point where your body's taken you as far as it's

gonna. There's only one way you can get bigger from here on in, and it isn't by eating tacos, my man."

"Roids?" I asked.

He nodded. "Fuckin' A," he affirmed.

B.J. proudly displayed pictures of himself just a year ago. He had been taking steroids on and off for the past year and in that time had gained twenty pounds. In spite of the bullshit declaration by the American Medical Association, he assured me roids worked. They were easy enough to obtain. "Just across the border in Tijuana, doc." He smiled. "Go over, buy 'em, get drunk, and walk back through the border just like another college schmuck down there for the weekend. Only difference is we got roids stuffed in our crotches."

On the Saturday following Muscular Mike Maple's fourth match, B.J. and I drove down, parked in the United States, and walked into another country through a revolving door constructed of metallic slats. With each complete rotation the top rung would swipe a metal lever that rose briefly before falling back into a collision of metal-on-metal. Each toll signified the passage of another person.

Our first stop was an island of three buildings perched on a small corner between dusty roads. One store used the sidewalk in front to display leather jackets and vases in the shape of cartoon characters. The building nestled between this store and a glitzy jewelry shop was the *farmacia* B.J. dealt with. Our entrance caused the lone clerk behind the counter to look up with a start. His thin cheeks quickly stretched into a smile. "*Anabolica!*" he cried.

"*Anabolica!*" B.J. responded with a thumbs-up. By

the time we reached the counter, the clerk had dug a box out from underneath the counter and placed it on the glass. B.J. and I rifled through the various jars and tubes with the considerate motions of soldiers scrutinizing a collection of semi-automatic weapons. The names were all familiar: Dianabol, Anadrol, Testosterone Cypionate. My junior year project had tackled the question of whether or not the risks involved in taking steroids outweighed the benefits. The twelve-page report had been fueled by many hours spent in the public library, reading countless articles that detailed possible side effects such as premature balding, high blood pressure, aggression, heart disease, kidney malfunction, impotency, and possible death. My conclusion had been that athletes who took these potentially dangerous drugs were risking their lives, and it was up to them to make that decision.

Now, two years later, Muscular Mike Maple is making that decision.

We wound up buying so much that the clerk threw in a few extra bottles for free. He smiled and nodded while watching B.J. and I shove tiny blue bottles of D-bol and vials of testosterone into our pants. "You two . . . ," he began, and then his eyes expanded as though they had just fallen upon the sight of an unexplainable natural wonder. "Be gigantic!" he proclaimed with the excited fervor of a Sunday morning preacher. Or, perhaps not so ironically, a professional wrestler.

After tucking our bounty safely inside our pants and socks, we made our way to one of the many bars lining Avenida Revolucion. The drinking age in Tijuana was only eighteen, making it a popular destination for students from San Diego State and other nearby colleges. Kids my age flooded the streets in a quest to drink away this late Saturday afternoon. They threaded through a bevy of vendors hawking wares such as jewelry, cigars, and small hot dogs of suspicious nature.

B.J. and I sat at a window table on the top floor of a club, well above the madness. Our completed mission set us apart from the frat pledges getting bombed on tequila shooters.

"You know . . . ," I commented as we finished our third round of Dos Equis, "steroids are bad for the liver. We probably shouldn't be drinking." I said this resignedly, almost as an afterthought.

"Just this once won't hurt us." B.J. waved my weak attempt at caution into the cool darkness, where it was seized and trampled by the howling frat guys at the bar. As B.J. launched into a description of the cycle of steroids he was planning, I let my eyes wander out to the lined street below. I wondered how many of the kids clad in "SDSU" T-shirts were freshmen. I tried to picture Marty and Bryan, both wearing "U of I" T-shirts, downing beers or shots at some University of Illinois watering hole. I hadn't talked to either of them since leaving Chicago. I looked away from the churning bodies below and caught my reflection hovering in the window against a sky colored by the setting sun.

Or is it rising?

I squeezed the thought from my head by flexing my arm, Muscular Mike Maple's arm, then turned and waved to the waiter. *"Dos cervezas!"* I called.

B.J. whooped. "Everybody in the business takes 'em, doc," he said, carelessly patting his crotch. "And everybody parties hard, too. And ain't nobody dropped dead yet."

In my junior project I determined that one of the reasons there were no documented deaths linked to steroids had to do with the newness of the abuse. But there was no point in bringing that up now. Muscular Mike Maple hadn't written that paper, and it was his survival that was at stake.

And so it was Muscular Mike Maple who unzipped my pants and reached inside. After extracting one of the small bottles (each contained one hundred Dianabols), he shook out two dusty blue tablets and washed them down with beer.

I took a breath and waited. There was no remorse. No elation. No strike of lightning. A wry disappointment snuck into my thoughts. The world should have ended. The bar should have become a sea of fire, with every one of us consumed by an angry sun.

But the light outside the window continued to fall and the frat pledges at the bar were still howling with drunken delight. I was still alive and could already feel my muscles growing. Having survived an initial attack against its natural processes, my body throbbed with invincibility. I was going to be bigger than nature ever intended. I raised my beer bottle, snug and cool in my palm. All as reassuring as a beer commercial. What good was fate if you didn't tempt it? "Die young," I said. "Die huge."

"Fuck that." B.J. laughed, touching his beer bottle with mine. "Live forever."

————————

"This is Muscular Mike Maple. I'm probably at the gym or in the ring, so leave your name and number and I'll get back to you whenever I can. Stay pumped." I had finally gotten a phone and an answering machine so as not to miss any calls from promoters. I had grudgingly given my mom the number, telling her to call only in emergencies. I kept telling myself that I was too busy to call Bryan or Marty, and maybe I was. In the weeks after our Tijuana visit, B.J. and I were working out with the discipline of monks and the fury of savages.

Steroids definitely worked. I was walking proof. My strength increased, and my muscles swelled within the first few days. Much of this growth came from water retention, but it made me appear bigger when I looked in a mirror and that was what I was after.

Three weeks into my cycle, I wouldn't leave my apartment without posing in the full-length mirror leaning against the wall next to the closet door. Before I entered the ring at the academy I had to flex into each of the three mirrors on the different walls. If I rode in a car I would gaze into the rearview mirror and flex my neck in time to whatever song was pounding out of the radio. The only times mirrors betrayed me were when I focused on my eyes. A rabid uneasiness would invade my body, making me feel so small and insignificant that I would immediately have to flex with all my might in order to feel whole again.

Aries' stubborn disregard for his own body finally caught up with him during his third defense of the tag-team title. During the match, he was hurled over the top rope and launched himself into the air with a velocity that made it impossible for him to control his landing. As a result, he came down awkwardly and broke his ankle. "I wanted to make it look good," he said later, seemingly unconcerned that he would be out of wrestling for at least two months.

People are often shocked when they discover that pro wrestlers actually endure injuries. "But I thought that stuff was fake," they say. The truth is that not only do all pro wrestlers suffer injuries throughout their careers, but the lack of an off-season makes it impossible for most of these injuries to ever fully heal. Consequently, a lot of wrestlers are always working in pain. It is a point of honor not to stop a match because of an injury. There was the story of one guy who had wrestled in the first match on a pay-per-view extravaganza. The match went on for thirteen minutes and ended in a scripted victory for him. He collapsed in the ring at the end, weeping what everyone backstage felt were rather extravagant tears of joy. It was only after he made it back to the dressing room that everyone found out he had suffered a compound fracture in his elbow during the first minute of the match. Also contrary to public belief, not all injuries are the result of screw-ups. One wrestler in a promotion up in Canada was shoved off the top of a steel cage and fell fifteen feet onto an announcer's table, cracking three ribs and dislocating his shoulder in the process. There hadn't been any mistake. He had simply told his opponent before the match, "Shove me off the top of the cage and let's see what happens." The rush that comes from putting your body in jeopardy is as addictive as any drug. In the same way time is rendered meaningless by being in the ring, so too is the possibility of death reduced to simply another move, another angle, or as Aries sneeringly referred to it one afternoon a couple days after his accident: "the ultimate job."

Around mid-September, the World Wrestling Organization arranged television tapings in San Diego and Long Beach. Shane's main function as the WWO's West Coast representative seemed to be scrounging up enough jobbers to throw into the ring to be slaughtered by the organization's superstars.

Shane explained the concept of jobbers: "People wanna see superstars wrestle each other. But how does a federation create a superstar? By showing them pezummel young rookies like yourselves. You're there to make these guys look like superstars; it's your job. How do you do that? Ya let 'em kick you around the ring and pin you in three minutes. Then the audience sees this on TV and goes to the live shows at arenas to see the superstars go at it with each other. All part of the beziz. Believe me." He inhaled a shot of nail polish remover, then solemnly nodded. "Most of those guys were once jobbers too."

Two weeks before the WWO was set to come to town, Shane pulled B.J. and me into his office during an advanced class. My nose was bleeding slightly as a result of one of B.J.'s stiff elbows. The spot above his left eyebrow was growing puffy from my retaliatory jab. "You guys are looking good." Shane nodded at us. B.J. and I exchanged grins.

"As you know, the WWO is coming to town. They

need jobbers." Shane opened a drawer and removed a gallon jug with a label identifying it as *high grade* nail polish remover. "I'll recommend you two if you want. But my advice is don't do it."

"How much does it pay?" B.J. asked.

"A hundred and fifty. I take twenty of it for my . . ." His voice wandered off in search of a proper word.

"Kickback," I offered.

"Managing fee," he countered with a smile as he opened the jug.

"Why don't you want us to do it?" B.J. asked.

"As you know, I worked for the WWO. And I saw these jobbers come and go." He slid one end of a rubber tube into the jug and carefully placed the other end into the small brown bottle he constantly carried with him. "And I'll tell ya . . . these WWO executives see you come in as a jobber just one time, and that's how they're gonna always remember you. 'Once a jobber, always a jobber,' we used to sezay," he said, licking his lips as he tilted the jug. I watched in bewildered fascination as fluid snaked down the tube. It was like watching a deranged episode of *MacGyver*.

"What about what you said before," B.J. said, "about how most of the superstars used to be—"

Shane cut B.J. off with a snort. "That was to give those boobs something to shoot for," he said as he squeezed the tube and let the remainder of the fluid glide back into the jug. "They're not as serious as they like to think they are," he added, stashing the rubber tube back into the drawer along with the jug. "They're sure as hell nowhere near the level of you two," he concluded.

I felt a quick glow of pride snake down my throat and warm my stomach. He capped the refilled bottle, gave it a good shake, then uncapped it and took a tentative sniff. He followed this with a deeper one, then reclined back in his chair as he scrutinized B.J. and me. The jagged rhythm of bodies falling in the ring broke through the office's thin walls, all four of which were adorned with pictures of professional wrestlers. "You guys are on the jezuice, right?" His voice was leading, almost as though it was required that we be in order for him to continue.

"Yeah," B.J. said immediately.

"All right." Shane nodded. "I think I can get you guys some jobs with the Southern Wrestling Association. They promote in the Mid-South area. Gotta warn you, though, it's a tough region."

My palms tingled. Hell yeah, it was common knowledge in the business that Mid-South was one of the toughest territories around. But that reputation also lent the area its distinction as a hotbed of pro wrestling. The SWA alone had produced legend after legend. "The WWO's been raidin' the area of talent," Shane was saying. "And a promotion like the SWA would be a nice step up for you guys."

"That'd be great, Shane," I said. "We're ready."

"We'll see," he said with an impartial smile.

"What kinda . . . managing fee should we give you?" B.J. asked.

Shane broke into a halting laugh. "Shit, kid. You're gonna be gettin' your brains beat out for forty bucks a nezight. I get you two into the SWA, you're on your own."

His eyes roamed the growling, groaning, taunting visages that lined the walls of his office. He leaned down and snorted from the bottle and smiled back up at the two of us. "But I'll tell you what," he said in the first soft voice I'd ever heard him use. "Either of you guys become a world champion, you tell everyone where you were trained. Deal?"

"Deal," B.J. and I agreed simultaneously.

———————————

A couple weeks later I dislocated my shoulder during a match at the San Bernardino arena. After the match I slammed the thing back into place against a concrete wall to the applause of my fellow wrestlers. Although my body cried out in pain, I managed to grit my teeth and stretched my lips into the requisite sneer that Muscular Mike Maple used to show that pain didn't affect him. Later, Steven (aka "Jack Daniels") came up to me and asked if I was hurting. "Nah," I managed to growl. "I'll be all right."

He nodded knowingly and extended a small plastic bottle. "Try some of these." He shook the container, the loose pills inside making it sound like a maraca.

"What are they?"

"Soma."

"Soma. Sounds like some good bud."

He laughed. "Just muscle relaxants, man. They sell 'em over the counter in Mexico. Hold out your hand."

He spilled two pills into my palm. White pills with 250 etched into their surface. I popped them with a shrug, forcing them down my dry throat with no liquid.

A half hour later my shoulder was still on fire. After the show ended, the owner of the arena (who was pleased that the gate was close to three hundred) let us drink free beer from the tap at the snack bar. Several beers helped reduce the flames to a steady throb. I found Steven. "Jack, those pills suck," I told him. "I still hurt."

He poured three more into my hand. I downed these with a swallow of beer.

After another couple rounds of beer a group of us headed to Denny's for a post-show snack. On the way I hit Steven up for a few more. The pain was still there. "Give it some time, man. These things are good."

"I swear, I must have a high tolerance," I reassured a hesitant Steven. "I still feel the damn thing." So he gave me two more pills.

At Denny's I realized I had fucked up; Soma don't really kick in until there is something else in the stomach for your body to absorb. After wolfing down a few bites of one of my French dips (having ordered two), I was suddenly suspended between my chair in San Bernardino, California, and a pleasant cloud that was floating in a world I had never visited before. "Hey, check out Muscular Mike!" I heard a voice come from one of those dimensions.

"You are fucked up, man," B.J. commented with a melting smile.

"I'm fine," I slurred. Drool was leaking down my chin, and when I tried to pick up a napkin my fingers stubbornly refused to close. Getting up from the table, I stumbled at first; clouds had taken the place of a floor.

I was wading toward the exit when I heard a young

voice calling from behind: "Muscular Mike!" At first I worried that I had split into two beings and left part of myself back at the table, but when I turned, there was a boy who appeared to be about eight years old standing there, holding a napkin and pen. "I saw you tonight," he said shyly. The words came out like nervous high-pitched static. "You were great."

He looked behind him, and I followed his gaze to a man and woman perched by the cash register. They nodded at the kid and made urging motions with their hands. When I looked back down, I saw he had thrust the napkin and pen out and was gazing up expectantly.

"Thanks . . . ," I slurred. My tongue felt like a freshly caught fish flapping uncontrollably. "Little dude," I drawled with great effort. Then I gripped the pen with stiff fingers and planted the napkin against the wall. "What's your name?" I asked.

"Devin," came the shy reply.

My hand jerked across the napkin: "To Devin . . . Best, Muscular Mike Maple." After I finished, I took a look at the napkin and saw that "Muscular" was the only collection of jumbled symbols that resembled an actual word. I handed the napkin and pen back to Devin, then looked away from the confusion devouring his eager expression as he stared at the incoherent name. "Sorry . . . Devin. My hands are, um . . . ," I stuttered while Mike Maple scrambled for a reasonable answer. ". . . kind of messed up from the match."

"Sure," he nodded quickly. "I understand."

I grinned and extended my hand for him to shake. But my concept of distance was distorted; my fist slammed into his chest. He stumbled backward, staring at me with startled and frightened eyes. I began to apologize but then saw his parents inching forward or maybe charging forward, so I just waved and ran through the restaurant doors into the parking lot. "Shit," I inhaled, acutely aware of my heart's panicky beat. "Shit, shit, shit!"

"Hey!" Steven called out from his car. "Mister High-tolerance!" He laughed. I nodded wearily. The last thing I tried to think of before I blacked out was a joke, so that I could laugh along.

I awoke in my apartment, terrified and disoriented. I had just had the dream of being in the ring. This time, the finishing maneuver had been a press slam. But before the mask came off everything exploded in a display of multicolored lights.

My eyes swept the dark room. No one else there with me. But outside the night was being tickled by a web of rotating red and blue and yellow lights. The same ones I saw in my dream.

My heart was still railing with an angry irregularity. I stood, determined to ignore the lights outside. They signaled some kind of chaotic event, something completely out of my control. I closed my eyes and jogged in place, trying to forget about my heart, forget about the fact that the signing of my first autograph, an event that would never come again in my lifetime, would never be anything more than a jumbled blur of shapes with distorted voices. Finally I gave up and wandered over to the window. About a half mile down the freeway, a sea of squad cars surrounded a jack-knifed semi that lay sprawled in the road like a fallen dinosaur.

In the sober moments of the next afternoon, I was able to repress my dread by putting the situation into a thoroughly proper perspective. I had been hurting and had taken a few too many muscle relaxants, pure and simple. The cause was nothing more sinister than inexperience. With this lesson learned, I felt certain I was capable of handling Soma any time there was some pain to kill. To prove this to myself I ended up trading Steve one hundred Dianabol for two hundred Soma. Over the next two weeks a few moderate doses of Soma caused no embarrassing intoxications, and I easily fell into a pattern of four Soma a day, two before I worked out and two before bed. The pre-workout intake masked any lingering aches from matches and enabled me to work out with greater intensity, and the two doses before bed granted me a blissfully dark and dreamless sleep.

One morning my phone shattered through another Soma-induced coma at an entirely ungodly hour. Raising my eyelids haltingly, I glimpsed the clock display reading 7:04. No one would call this early unless it was really important, I thought, springing for the phone with the anticipation of hearing Shane's proclamation that we were heading south.

What I heard instead was my mother calling to check up and make sure I wasn't dead. Why hadn't I called in so long? What was I doing? *How* was I doing? Had I heard about the flood that had closed down half of State Street in the Loop? She asked all this in a carefully veiled tone that made the questions seem like a maze designed to lead to an ultimate query that would no doubt be along the lines of, "When was I going to come to my senses and give up this pro wrestling?"

Before she unleashed this final question, I tore my tongue away from the roof of my mouth and provided some short answers: Fine, I was fine. No, I hadn't heard about the flood. I didn't have a TV—

Didn't have a TV? Her voice sprang at me. What about the newspapers? How would I be able to keep up with what was going on in the world?

I replied that I didn't read newspapers and that I really didn't care what was going on in the world.

"How are you, darling? Really?" she asked, her tone leaning toward a suspicious tenderness.

"I . . . signed my first autograph the other night," I mumbled. "I've had twenty matches so far. And I'm getting bigger—"

"Bigger?" She sounded alarmed. "What do you need to get *bigger* for? You're too big already!"

"I've gotta go, Mom." I groaned. "I've gotta go . . . work out."

"Don't work out too hard!" she implored urgently. "Damn it, Mike, are you sure you're doing the right thing?"

"Muscular Mike," I said.

"What?"

"Muscular Mike. That's my name now."

"Muscular Mike," she spat out the words as though it was the name of a newly discovered lethal disease. "I see."

A few cautiously spoken exchanges broke the line's crackling silence. It was ten below wind-chill factor in

Chicago. No, I didn't really miss the snow. How's the apartment? Still the same, oh good. Mine is small. Yes, very small but I don't mind. They put the Christmas tree up in the Loop already, where'd the year go? "When do you think you're coming out?" she inquired.

My fingers gripped the phone for support. "I'm not," I said steadily.

"Why not? It's Christmas, we're—"

"I don't want to go to Shirley's place," I said. "I don't want to see them. I—"

"Don't you want to see me?" she asked.

"I have to do some things out here," I said quietly. "I have three matches Christmas week." I lied in a wavering voice.

"All right," she said, her tone suddenly subdued.

My next few attempts at small talk disappeared into the silent void on her end of the line. "So, I'll talk to you later, okay?" I suggested finally.

She didn't respond, although a tightly labored breathing indicated she was still there. The silence stretched on. "All right," she said quietly. "Merry Christmas. I love you."

A deep regret gripped me, and I flexed my arm angrily. "Love you, too. Bye." I hung up the phone. The muscles in my legs expanded as I urged them to life. I hopped out of bed, then flexed into the mirror and didn't stop until I could clearly see the figure of Muscular Mike Maple, who decided to screen his calls from then on.

———————

Contrary to popular opinion, there are season changes in California. I discovered this on the Christmas day, my first away from home, that I spent walking the dry empty streets of San Bernardino. My landlady thought I was visiting in-state relatives. B.J., Aries, and all my wrestling pals thought I was going back to Chicago. My mother thought I was insane and off doing God knows what. Only the latter was perhaps true. I shuffled from one deserted street corner to another in the chilled afternoon light. The air was surprisingly cool, forcing my hands into the pockets of my jacket. The day's wary sunlight suggested a reluctance on nature's part to invest any energy in these quickly interrupted daylight hours.

Taking step after step after step, I walked on in a daze and didn't stop until I became aware of the air's change. Rusty urban dampness had been replaced by a warm blanket of chocolate and smoke. I looked around and saw a residential area of flat one-story homes. Many of them had a swarm of old worn cars in front. The houses' front windows were shut tight. Most of them were encircled by narrow strips of Christmas lights, ornamentation that seemed cheerless without the snow I was used to. The main color behind the lights was the fuzzy blue of a television.

I looked back the way I came, trying to spot a land-mark that would provide some kind of clue as to the route I had just drifted down. But nothing was familiar. I was lost. Lost on my first Christmas away from home.

By the time February came I was halfway to shedding my status as a mark. Fifty matches down. The second weekend of March, B.J. and I worked a match at an old-time rock-and-roll club in the San Fernando Valley. Merv Evans, the promoter, had erected a ring on the stage and taken out several ads in weekly Los Angeles newspapers as well as in *The Pennysaver*. He was known throughout the business as both a savvy businessman and a deceiving little snake. In pro wrestling, as in most fields of entertainment, the two descriptions often seem to go hand in hand.

Merv was about forty with brittle black hair that looked as though it had last been shampooed with bacon grease. His eyeballs didn't seem to be able to move all the way up, so when facing you he always seemed to be focused on your crotch. If he said something he wanted to sound earnest, he tilted his head back and you'd be greeted by two long hairs poking out of each nostril. His body appeared elongated to an unnatural degree, as though he had spent years as a child hanging from a bar in order to stretch himself to additional heights.

Like a starving ferret, I thought, shaking his thin hand.

"Good to see you two guys. I've heard fabulous things about you two," he said.

"From who?" I asked with genuine interest.

"Oh. Here, there, ya know. People in the biz . . . ," he said, and waved his hands and apparently felt the gesture was significant enough to take the place of actual names because he ceased talking for a few seconds while studying me and B.J. intently.

"You're the heel, am I right?" he said suddenly to me. I shook my head.

"Right, of course." He turned to B.J. "The pay is fifty each, but you can make a hundred if you want."

"No shit." B.J. exhaled. "How?"

"Juice, kid." Merv's head reclined slightly as he kept an eye on B.J. "Juice."

Juice meant blood. Thanks to a mention of our feud in a national wrestling magazine, B.J. and I were in the semi-main-event slot. Semi-main eventers usually juiced. B.J.'s eyes registered a momentary alarm before easing into a thoughtful mode. "Fifty bucks more, huh?" he asked.

"And the crowd'll love it." Merv smiled, his nostrils aimed assuredly at B.J.

A veteran named Hal Duncan, known to wrestling fans as Al "The Landlord" Hoover, was also on the card that night. With his shaved head, handle-bar mustache, and thick frame, he fit perfectly into the physical stereotype of the evil landlord found in old-time melodramas, all the way down to his practiced evil laugh and tongue-rolling rrrrrrrrs. He was the one who showed B.J. how to juice.

"Just keep that baby tucked there," Hal said, placing a small razor blade against B.J.'s index finger and wrapping a bit of tape around it. "Then, after Mike throws you against a ring post, hit the ground facedown and do what you gotta do."

B.J. peered at the hidden razor blade. "And it won't . . . pop out or anything?" he asked nervously.

"Just be careful. Don't pick at the damn thing," Hal snapped as B.J. fingered the tape.

"Where should he cut?" I asked. Hal thrust his face at me like a charging bull. Scar tissue crossed the top of his forehead in a puffy maze, as though miniature creatures had been burrowing underneath the skin for years.

"Take a wild guess," he remarked. I nodded mutely and he laughed. "Scars are good," he added, rolling the "r" heavily. "They're a symbol of dues paid."

Two minutes before the match, Hal came up to where B.J. and I were standing behind the curtain and handed B.J. a pill. "Take this," he said, "it'll help."

"What is it?" B.J. asked. "Speed, Valium . . . ?"

"Aspirin." Hal winked. "It'll thin out your blood so you won't have to cut too deep to bleed." After a slight hesitation, B.J. popped the pill.

There were about four hundred people in the crowd, and most of them were young drunk rockers who had ventured to the show out of idle curiosity. They were the kind of audience who regard the whole show with a sloshed skepticism, coiled for one slightly pulled punch that will give them an excuse to release an onslaught of jeers: "Bullshit!" "You fucked up!" "Do another take!" and other validations that they are in on the joke. They were the kind of crowd Shane had told us would be our toughest opponent.

Because we knew they would heckle us at the slightest excuse, B.J. and I worked a very stiff match. After a couple minutes, my forehead was throbbing from B.J.'s repeated punches. It's a rule that you never give stiff punches to the neck or throat or side of the face. "If you're gonna go stiff," the saying goes, "go stiff on the hardest part of the body."

We had that crowd popping, especially when B.J. busted open my nose with a drop-kick. "Sorry," he whispered as he picked me up for a suplex.

Then juice time arrived. We went outside the ring, where security guards were shoving back a few rowdy fans trying to scramble onto the stage. I hurled B.J. into the ring's post and watched him go down. A delighted roar erupted from the audience in response to a security guard shoving a fan off the stage.

Figuring I had given B.J. enough time to do what he had to do, I walked over and picked him up. "Oh, shit," he was whispering. "Oh shit!" I glanced at his face and instinctively released him. He had made a common rookie's mistake—cut too deeply. A gash split the skin across his eyebrow and almost reached his temple. The blood streamed down his cheeks and dripped off his chin like rivulets of lava from an erupting volcano.

The crowd saw this and went insane. I felt like vomiting and passing out. "Do something," B.J. pleaded. I did the only thing I felt I could; I picked him up and body-slammed him on the concrete floor.

The cheers soared passionately, and the knots in my stomach eased. As I pushed B.J. back into the ring, I heard a chant go up: "Ma-ple! Ma-ple!" It was the first time a crowd had ever chanted my name. I turned and flexed to their adoration. They responded with throaty cheers. A stray flashbulb went off.

People don't take pictures of nothing. My heart thumped in triumph.

I climbed to the top turnbuckle and leapt to the mat with my hands clasped like an axe handle. My fists collided lightly with the top of B.J.'s head and he went down. I covered him. "You wanna keep goin' or take it home?" I whispered.

"Take it home," he croaked back.

I quickly stood and he gave me a crotch-shot, which involves throwing your arm up between your opponent's legs without actually contacting anything. I keeled over and the crowd cried out in angry retaliation to this cheap shot. B.J. crawled to his "dentist's bag" sitting in a corner of the ring. The finish called for him to go over via disqualification. So out came the "dentist drill," its gigantic bit obviously meant for boring holes in wood, not teeth. He hit me in the stomach with the tool's handle and the referee called for the bell. "Hit me again," I whispered, "in the head."

"Huh?" he asked, wiping blood from his eyes.

"Make me bleed, man," I urged through gritted teeth.

He whacked my forehead with the drill. The blow launched streaks of pain through my head into my shoulders and down my arms, but failed to puncture the skin. He gouged the drill bit into my flesh. The crowd's violent enthusiasm was now a force of nature gone a little crazy; being one of its targets made me exhilarated and uncomfortable. "What are you guys doing?" the ref hissed. The drill nibbled through my skin and then I was in ecstasy, feeling blood flowing down my forehead. My blood.

"Now hit me!" I demanded. B.J.'s blow split open the cut and blood ran down over my pupils. "Thank you." I exhaled.

"Get me outta here, doc," he said.

I kicked him in the stomach and tossed his compliant body out of the ring. As he staggered back toward the curtain, I turned to confront the crowd. Blood shielded my eyes, sparing me the need to focus on any of them. As I fired off poses, their frenzied chants of "Ma-ple!" blended with the blood to make me an entire being. One who could bleed and be cheered. I wanted to kill them all as they worshiped me. I felt like a god, and I did not want it to end. Ever.

"Are you feelin' all right?" I asked B.J. later, back in one of the dressing rooms. He was sitting on the edge of a table holding a formerly white T-shirt that was now deep crimson. Like Achilles, only the part of the T-shirt that B.J. held was untouched by blood.

"Yeah," B.J. replied, dabbing at the gash. "Hal looked it over. Said I cut a little too deep."

"No shit," I said in a deadpan tone, igniting his laughter. I examined the cut. It was deep, but didn't appear as wide as it had before.

"Did we have that crowd goin' nuts or what?" A slow grin took over his face. Combined with the dried blood, the smile made him look like a contented vampire.

"Bet your ass we did." I nodded. The frenzied storm that had gripped me in the ring had passed, leaving behind a mellow uneasy glow. "Thanks for cutting me."

He nodded, his lips parting uncertainly. A chorus of shouts erupted from the hallway. "Let's go check that out." B.J. slid off the table. We hurried into the hall and spotted a throng of our fellow wrestlers. They were surrounding Merv who, it seemed, had been trying to duck out before the show was over. Merv was hurriedly explaining that he was a busy man and that he couldn't be expected to remember everything.

"One thing you can always be counted on to remember is taking the gate money with you!" a rotund man in a farmer's outfit cried out.

"And you always seem to forget about paying wrestlers for the matches they've worked!" growled Hal, rapping his fleshy knuckles against the concrete wall with intimidating ease.

"But I can't pay anyone!" Merv whined, his head arched fully back. "I haven't even been paid yet."

"*Cabron!*" a dark-skinned wrestler wearing an Indian headdress cried out. "Search his pockets!"

Triumphantly, Merv pulled out his front pockets. Both were empty. He did the same to his rear pockets. "Try his socks!" a wrestler draped in the outfit of a mental patient called out.

With dramatic indignation Merv removed his shoes and socks, unleashing a foul odor into the air but revealing no money.

"Fuck all that," Hal said, advancing menacingly, "I'm checkin' his jock."

"Okay, okay," Merv screeched. He explained that although he had stashed an envelope with a fairly large amount of money in his crotch (due to the muggers roaming L.A.), he *needed* that money in order to put a security deposit on the next place. But if we could give him all our addresses he'd be more than happy to send us—

"Hey, motherfucker!" I growled, pushing my way through the other wrestlers. "If you don't pay us, we're

gonna carry you out there and feed you to that pack of
animals we just wrestled for!"

We all paused a moment. Outside, the main event
was in full swing. A chant of "Make him bleed" was
being sent up by the crowd.

Merv's hands began shaking rapidly. He slowly
reached into his pants and removed a mildly soggy
envelope. "These fuckin' bills better be dry!" Hal
warned. Merv began counting out cash.

He handed B.J. five twenties and then quickly
placed a fifty in my hand, snatching his hand away as
though I were a mongoose. But I caught him and said:
"This is fifty." I pointed to the red gash on my forehead.
"You owe me a hundred!" I snarled at his nostril hairs.

"You juiced on your own. I didn't ask you to!" he
whined huffily. "Everyone knows you don't double-juice
except for in the main event. Everybody knows that!
What are you, a mark?"

I slammed him up against the wall. This money was
needed to validate my blood—to make what had happened out there real. "I bled to pay dues," I snarled.
"Now give me what I earned, goddammit."

Merv pushed another fifty in my direction. I grabbed
the bill and released his jacket. "You'll never amount to
anything in this business," he seethed.

"Trim your nostril hairs, asshole," I said. Laughter
and hoots followed Merv as he fled out the back door.

After the show ended and the riotous crowd had
finally dispersed, Hal and I exchanged numbers and
talked a little bit in the parking lot. "You handled yourself pretty well," he said.

"Thanks," I responded, taking the compliment with

proper gruffness. "Guess I can kinda count on Merv not calling me up for work any time soon."

"I wouldn't sweat it if I were you." Hal laughed. "Merv doesn't put on that many shows. Damn near every wrestler in the business knows what a weasel he is. Whenever a promoter tries to skip out without paying the boys, it's called 'pulling a Merv.'"

"'Pulling a Merv,'" I laughed. "I like that."

B.J. dropped me off at my apartment that night. "You sure you're all right?" I asked him, my right leg dangling out the passenger door.

"Yeah, I'll be okay."

I got out of the car. "Hey, Mike." His words contained a careful steadiness. I turned back. "Why'd you bleed tonight?" he asked.

"I bled for you." I lied uneasily. Focusing on his eyes that shone against the bleak light of the car's interior bulb. I noticed with a strange relief that his irises displayed a distinctly richer shade of green than my own.

"No, you didn't," he said quietly.

Heat swam across my face. "No. I didn't."

"What for then, man?" B.J. asked, his tone deep and curious, "I know why I bled—to get an extra fifty dollars to take Terri out for a nice dinner. But I know you don't need fifty bucks that bad."

I sat, paralyzed except for my tense biceps. The wound on my head was still offering reassuring throbs. The cut was real, Muscular Mike Maple was real, I was real. But that mosquito I had so easily killed years ago had been real, too. I wanted to tell B.J. about this, but kept swallowing the words and preventing their escape. Sweat rolled down the inside of my Gold's Gym sweatshirt.

B.J. rescued me by placing a hand on my shoulder and saying, "Whatever it is, doc . . . it's cool. Do your thing, all right?"

"Yeah." I nodded automatically and placed my hand over his. We held this for a few seconds before we both pulled back and threw out farewells laced with overzealous vulgarity.

After hopping out of the car, I watched his taillights disappear around a corner inhabited by a three-story apartment building that had once served as a lamp factory. The night was hot with only an occasional timid breeze for relief. A rush of air prodded my wound. I had bled. My body was real enough. But what was inside this body? I exhaled this silent question into the dry heat, then turned and headed into my building to finish off the night with a few more Soma, a beer, and another art book I wouldn't open.

5

ROAD TRIPPING

Opening chords of my entrance music skate across the crowd's cheers. Their voices rise to meet this fresh noise. I grip the ropes on either side of me and lose myself in the movement of the red curtain. It is rippling lightly with breeze, a crimson sea.

We call these curtains wide red lines. This term has a vague Midwestern origin; an old saying spoke of a thin red line between the sane and the mad. The backstage area is our land of sanity, where we plan and structure matches. The arena is where a bunch of crazed marks watch this structure blossom into simulated war. All that separates these two realities is a felt curtain, the wide red line.

I slowly realize the ring isn't moving.

I turn to see Rob Robertson kicking at the ring's

wheels, which sit motionless on the metal track that leads outside to the stadium. "Come on, you sonofabitch!" Rob howls, switching his assault to the ring's corner post.

"Everyone push!" Hippo Haleburg shouts. Several wrestlers jog over and press their weight against the cart. It begins to creep along.

"Fuck it, I'll walk," I say, parting the ropes to step out.

"No!" Hippo commands, "The champ's gonna be walking. You gotta ride."

The ring inches toward the curtain. Outside, the crowd's cheers have begun to dip. Timing is now crucial. If I don't appear soon, they'll find it hard to gather a second wind.

Moments slip by as the ring grinds along inch by inch. "What the fuck is going on in there?" a voice screams from Rob Robertson's walkie-talkie.

"The cart's malfunctioning!" Rob shouts back.

"Get that piece of shit moving!"

"We're workin' on it!" Rob groans.

"Momentum!" Hippo grunts. "Enough momentum'll kick it in gear." I wipe my forehead and find it cool and dry. Even in the World Wrestling Organization, the number one wrestling promotion in the world, things go wrong. Carts can malfunction, injuries can occur, wrestlers can ignore storylines and hijack their matches. Anything can happen.

The cart is jarred by a force that sends me tumbling against the ropes. I grab them for support and look back at Hippo Haleburg, who backs up a few steps and slams his bulk into the cart again. The cart begins moving, but as the curtain parts I'm still looking back at

Hippo, who is kneeling on the ground panting and clutching his chest. "Go!" he pants, gesturing with his other arm at a spot above my left shoulder. His next words are too weak to break through the crowd's thunderous onslaught as I pass through the curtain. My last sight before the curtain closes is of Tug and Rob Robertson kneeling over him.

The wide red line has been passed. I'm in motion.

Awakened the next morning by the telephone's shrill ring, I yawned groggily and peered at the clock: 7:10. The answering machine clicked on and spewed out Muscular Mike's greeting followed by a beep.

"Hey, Mike. Get your ass outta bed," commanded the voice from my machine. "It's Hal. You know, from—"

I plucked up the phone. "Yeah, Hal," I slurred through the Soma-induced grogginess. "What's up?" I asked.

"We got a tour set up. It's five days, four shows. Gonna run through Arizona, New Mexico, and Colorado. Fifty bucks a night and hotel's paid for. You interested?"

"Is Merv a weasel?" I said, shaking my head to dislodge the strands of sleep still lingering there.

Hal laughed and went on to explain that I was being called as a last minute replacement. One half of a tag team had been in a bar last night and had blacked out. He had woken up in jail and called Hal just twenty minutes ago asking for bail money. The charge was assaulting an officer of the peace, and the bail was

$100,000. Hal had gotten very upset, not at the fact that this guy was facing a possibility of twenty years in jail (he was a nasty drunk and generally rotten person, Hal explained) but that the guy's irresponsible behavior had jeopardized the tour. Hal had promised the promoter a certain number of wrestlers. Based on Mike Maple's handling of Merv last night, Hal had immediately thought of me.

By this time, adrenaline had whisked me up to an acute state of consciousness in such a short time that I felt dizzy. "I'm in," I said simply.

"Great!" he replied. "I'll pick you up in half an hour."

"*Half an hour?*"

"Forty minutes, tops." He went on, "We're wrestling on an army base in Somerton, Arizona, at seven o'clock tonight." I nodded dumbly at the receiver. "Oh, one more thing," he announced hurriedly, "the tag team uses a rock-and-roll gimmick, so think up another name besides Muscular Mike Mailer."

"Maple," I corrected.

"Whatever," he laughed. "Drop it and think up a rocker name. I'll see you in thirty."

I hung up and got out of bed. The floor chilled my bare feet as I padded over to the mirror. There was a small reddish mark over my right eye, but no giant scar. I turned away from my reflection, vaguely ashamed.

Twenty-eight minutes later, I was waiting outside, drinking a beer. *Drinking a beer at 7:38 in the morning is something a rocker would do.* I had left the apartment without flexing in the mirror or elbow-dropping my pillow from home. In addition to those two rituals, also left behind was Muscular Mike Maple, who was doomed to roam southern California as the ghost of a character that had enjoyed a lifetime of sixty-eight matches.

The early morning's tight briskness matched how I felt inside; Muscular Mike Maple's sudden absence was causing neither sadness nor relief. All I could get a grip on was the same numbness that I experienced in Tijuana after Mike Maple had enabled me to pop my first steroids. Steroids were a given in my life now. Perhaps my lack of remorse at Muscular Mike Maple's passing indicated that he was a gimmick I no longer needed. As simple as outgrowing a bicycle or winter coat. An excited cry fought its way up my throat but I swallowed it back with a question.

Who will take his place?

A rocker. Hal had said a rocker so that's what I would become. I exhaled and saw my breath frost up in the chill of the morning desert air. This reminded me of many winter mornings spent waiting for the school bus in Chicago. This memory tumbled into another and yet another until I was back at the party on the night before I left home. Motley Crüe's "Kickstart My Heart" erupted in my ears, as though a juke box stagnating in some stale corner of my mind had just been kicked to life. "Chicago!" I flung the name at the arid chill and frowned at how strange it made my mouth feel.

Five minutes later a minivan consumed with thin rivers of rust roared up to the curb. I tossed the empty beer can onto a patch of parched brown grass. "How's it goin', Mike?" Hal's grinning face called out to me from the open driver's window.

"The name's Mick," I drawled back, "Motley Mick Starr."

By one that afternoon we had crossed over the Arizona border into a sea of sand populated by small islands of cacti, all of which led to mountains rising far off on either side with the imposing grandiosity of undiscovered countries. By this time I had downed ten beers from the cooler nestled at Hal's feet ("road cocktails," he called them), relieved myself twice in an empty Gatorade bottle, and hadn't once felt a need to flex my neck in the rearview mirror.

In addition to Hal and me, there were two others in the van. My future tag-team partner, "Jammin' Jimmy Nitro," was riding shotgun. His build was beefy without a predilection toward either muscle or fat; it seemed to be a naturally dense shield that had accumulated through his fifteen years in the business. Curly hair traveled down his head like an unruly plant, stopping just before his upper back. He had to keep it relatively short, he told me, because his day job was as a psychology and physical education teacher at a Los Angeles junior college. He had given up the idea of wrestling full-time, but still found it "physically and mentally stimulating," even on a part-time basis.

Our other tour companion was Summer, a girl about my age with smoldering eyes that matched the color of her sandy-brown hair. Her body was taut, and a sharply defined tricep could be seen lurking beneath the sleeve of a T-shirt that announced *These Aren't My Eyes, Pervert* in bold red letters that ran across her substantial chest. A playful lilt in her voice lent everything she said a mildly sarcastic tone, but she had a kind nature. It was she who had given me her empty Gatorade bottle after Hal had sadistically cackled that he wouldn't stop for anyone to relieve themselves until lunch.

A half an hour into Arizona, we stopped for lunch at a truck stop that also sold supplies such as doughnuts, ephedrine, and porno magazines for travelers that were embarking on what a sign had warned us was a 170-mile stretch with no services.

This stop on the edge of potential starvation is where Jimmy explained the dynamics of tag-team wrestling to me. He obviously enjoyed imparting information, rising to frenzied conclusions, and emphasizing his sarcastic phrases with shrill glee. "Most tag-team matches start with the faces . . . we'll call them A and B . . . having a hot-spot," he explained. "This means they perform several moves demonstrating their *brilliant teamwork*. Thus, the heels . . . we'll refer to them for our purposes as X and Y, will be the victim of double drop-kicks, double clotheslines, *double anything*. After this initial burst, the pace slows down, and the heels get the advantage. Then they perform the requisite cheating, such as taunting A into the ring, then double-teaming B while the referee is distracted and struggling to get A out of the ring."

At one point he mentioned a "false tag" and I actually raised my hand. He paused and looked at me alertly. "What's a false tag?" I asked.

"A false tag involves one of the faces . . . let's choose A . . . struggling valiantly to get close enough to his corner in order to tag B. X is holding him back but A is making progress. The crowd is chanting, clap-

ping, urging A on. Then just as he's almost at the corner, Y comes trundling into the ring and is corre-
spondingly pushed back by the referee. Now is the
moment when A finally pushes X off and leaps to his
corner to make the tag—!" He held his barbecued
chicken sandwich in one hand and smacked it triumphantly with the other.

"But wait!" he shouted. Through the streaking waitresses, I caught a glimpse of the truckers sitting at the
counter. Some of them were watching us curiously.
"The referee didn't *see* the tag, of course, because he
was struggling with Y. Therefore, the tag is no good. The
crowd boos mightily at the injustice of it all. They are
forced to stew until the *hot tag*, which is when A finally
manages to tag B in sight of the referee and B storms
in and beats on both X and Y at the same time." He bit
into his sandwich and munched with a complacent
rhythm. "*Cleaning house,* as they say." He smiled with
lips exaggerated by the barbecue sauce clinging to
their edges.

I nodded and bit gently into my double cheese-
burger. A row of shelving wound around the perimeter
of the restaurant; toy trains, old action figures, Hot
Wheels cars, and other trinkets gave the place a
museum-like air. The rumble of activity in the diner was
like a symphony improvised by an orchestra who has
played together for years. Knowing that I was immediately going back on the road made me appreciate the
diner's intricacies even more. It was like prom night,
when Charlotte and I achieved a connection fueled by a
shared knowledge that our relationship had to end.
Now the same thing was happening, but instead of

another person, I was having a fling with a potpourri of bacon grease and chatter.

———————

We reached the army base around six o'clock. The first person who greeted us was Mark, the promoter. Two nervous eyes whose motion never stopped tweaked my curiosity, but the rest of his face was haphazard: a crooked nose jutting out from a thin mass of premature wrinkles supported by a weak jaw and a patchy field of hesitant whiskers. He was the victim of a vicious stutter, a hacking cough that caused his body to shake with alarming force, and a constant drool. His lips were chapped, no doubt rubbed raw from the rag with which he was constantly wiping his mouth.

In the van that afternoon, Mark's name had come up. "Kind of a funny name for a promoter to have." I commented, given that fans were usually termed marks.

"Not for this one," Hal said mysteriously.

Jim broke into chuckles. "He's a little . . . unorthodox," he began. Then Hal shushed him.

"Let him find out on his own." Hal smiled. "He's gotta find out on his own."

But so far all I could tell was that he was one of the most agitated human beings I had ever seen and that he drooled.

After disengaging my hand from Mark's sticky fingers, I headed back to the dressing room for another beer. I saw the back of a longhaired woman standing in the doorway. She said something I didn't catch, but whatever it was prompted a warm wave of laughter. *This must be Shawna,* I smiled.

Shawna's name had been mentioned in the van as well. She was going to be working with Summer on the tour. "Very cool chick," Hal said.

"Great worker," Summer remarked, snapping her gum.

"Knows how to work a crowd," Jimmy Nitro said admiringly.

The first thing I noticed was the pleasantly tight fit of Shawna's jeans as they formed a second skin on her lower body. Her shape gave them an allure that managed to be provocative but not obvious. Thick red hair cascaded down her black shirt. Her clothes didn't flatter her; she flattered them.

I judged her height to be an inch or two shorter than my own. As I was busy taking her in, she glanced at her shoulder as though a whisper of breath touched her there, then seemed to sense my presence and turned around to face me with a curious expression.

Smooth tan skin stretched taut over a delicate facial structure. It was a capable face; I thought, one that could manage a barroom brawl or a child on a swing set with the same ease. Though not overly muscled, her sinewy body seemed to suggest great strength. Her lips curled upward. "You planning to come in any time soon or just stand out there and look silly?" she asked in a teasing voice that kneaded every bit of gravelly temptation out of the words. Her remark prompted a round of chuckles from all present in the dressing room. Even though I was blushing, her demeanor seemed playful enough to invite my participation.

"I don't know." I shrugged exaggeratedly. "The view's pretty good out here."

"Really?" she asked, still smiling. "I'm glad to hear that. My boyfriend'll be really glad to hear that too."

She walked into the locker room to a chorus of *ooooooohs.* I followed, and as soon as I was inside stopped very quickly. She was standing beside a behemoth seated on a stool. He had a piece of fur draped over his loins. His massive body was covered with hair. He was bald, and a vein throbbed in his scalp as he glared at me.

"You hittin' on my girlfriend?" he roared, and leapt to his feet with surprising agility.

A second later he was standing before me. He was at least 6'5". "Bet you wanna fuck her, huh?" he growled, and I noticed all his visible teeth were either chipped or crooked.

"No," I replied too loudly. My heart was beating in my ears.

"Then why'd you make that comment about the view, huh?"

What would a cocky rocker say? "I appreciate great works of art," I blurted.

The man slammed a fist into his other hand, holding me there with a killer's gaze. If I tried to run he would catch me and tear me apart. My eyes began to creep over to Hal, when suddenly the giant broke down into scattered giggles. "Sorry, Shawna," he said to the woman, "he got me with that one."

Everyone in the room started to laugh. The monster clutched my limp hand with a gentle grip, introducing himself as Taz and assuring me he wasn't Shawna's

boyfriend. I had been ribbed. My heart was still pounding as I glanced over at Shawna, who smiled, cocked
her finger, and simulated shooting me. I gripped my
chest and smiled back, feeling special and singled out.

Two of the wrestlers on the show were old pros. They
had been in the WWO for some years, and now wrestled
only part-time in main events of independent shows such
as this one. The heel was named "Allah Abdullah Khan."
His real name was Errol Whittaker, and he had been an
amateur wrestling champion in England back in the
1970s. He had started with the WWO in 1980; his first
gimmick being that of a haughty English lord. This had
failed to go over. When the Iran hostage crisis occurred
in 1983, the WWO had, as he put it, "given him an over-
haul." He grew a moustache, shaved his head, and began
barking out pro-Iran proclamations in a halting Middle
Eastern accent. This new gimmick was a whopping success. In the first month, Allah had been attacked twice
with bats, three times with knives, and shot at once by
an ex-army general who had served in World War Two.
Errol confessed to us that he wasn't entirely at ease
wrestling on an army camp as Allah. "Bloody
Americans," he scowled, "so damned emotional."

The face was a man who had enjoyed a brief stint as
the national champion in the WWO, where he had been
known as Richie "Golden Boy" Rutger. His brown hair
had been repeatedly bleached to a brittle white. He used
makeup to cover the scars in his forehead and kept a
perpetual wad of chewing tobacco tucked in his gums.
Richie traveled these small tours with a Polaroid camera and posed with fans for five dollars a picture. I had
seen him wrestle many times at the Rosemont Horizon,

and he had even been on the card the night I met Sonny Logan.

During the intermission, I went out with Richie and took pictures of him posing with fans for five bucks a pop. Two blue jean clad girls approached me. Although neither of them appeared to be over sixteen, their faces were thick with makeup. "Can we get a picture with you?" the slightly taller one asked me, fluttering her mascara-crusted eyelids. The shyness in her voice surprised me and led me to offer them a picture for free. But Richie insisted that he needed the five dollars for film. It was with more than a little surprise that I watched the two girls cough up five singles. I posed with my arm around each of their slender hips, then autographed the picture: *Motley Mick Starr.* Immediately after I handed them the picture, they both turned very bashful. They thanked me and quickly retreated into the crowd.

When we got backstage Richie slipped me a five dollar bill. "Here you go, brotha. Just wanted to make sure you didn't give yourself away for free." He smiled and placed a hand on my shoulder with awkward abruptness. "You *always* charge them. The more you charge, the more they'll think you're worth."

In spite of his hand laying gently on my shoulder, his voice sounded more resigned than fatherly. His eyes were focused not on me but on a section of the white wall that was slathered with streaks of red paint. I nodded mutely as he spat a wad of tobacco juice onto the ground. Then the hand on my shoulder was gone. I eased away, the bill clutched in my hand, leaving Richie still staring at the wall.

During Shawna's match with Summer, I stood just behind the curtain watching her. She maintained the advantage for most of the match. Her moves came fast and with a crispness that engaged the crowd and got her over with them almost immediately. Every gesture she gave them elicited cheers.

"She's great," I said to Hal, who stepped up beside me.

"Yeah," he confirmed, "she's a hell of a worker all right."

"Where is she from?"

"Arizona, as far as I know." He shrugged. "Somewhere around Phoenix. Trained back east at the Power Camp. Rogers says she came in one day and started taking bumps like she'd been doin' it for years."

"Maybe she had," I suggested, recalling the many wrestling "matches" I had conducted on my bed as a teenager.

"Yeah, maybe. He said it was like she was born to be a pro wrestler," he mused. "By the way," he added, "you might wanta forget it."

"Forget what?"

"Whatever move you're thinkin' about putting on her." Hal chuckled. "She doesn't fool around with wrestlers."

"Why not?" I asked.

"She's smart," he suggested, and we both laughed. I looked back out at the ring just in time to see Shawna perform a flying cross body from the top rope. She remained in the air for what seemed like many seconds, mocking gravity, before landing on Summer. *Born to be a pro wrestler.* The referee counted to three. The crowd unleashed a hurricane of cheers, and I joined them.

When my match came, instead of posing a la Mike Maple, I whipped my head around and let my long hair fly while flashing the universal two-finger-and-thumb-raised sign for heavy metal. The crowd ate it up, and I was pleased at how easy it had been for me to shed one skin and adopt another. But a simple nervousness kept surfacing; there was something else different about me, something with no relation to my new persona. While the crowd's cheers crashed on my ears like a slow predictable tide, Shawna's laughter ruled my mind. I replayed our interaction in my head and, while covering one of our opponents for a three-count, came to the conclusion she was someone full of surprises. The referee raised my hand in victory.

She is a person who will shelter me from myself.

My original conclusion would certainly prove correct, which would in turn doom any hope of my being sheltered from anything.

———————

After the show we retired to a Motel 6 about two miles away, located thirty yards from the entrance to the interstate. Mark had insisted on paying us at the hotel, and Hal had assured me that it wasn't all a ploy to slip out on us. "Mark wouldn't leave without paying," Hal said. "He enjoys it too much," he added, then smiled and refused to explain any more.

With the exception of Richie and Allah, who had been paid in advance, all the wrestlers had to go into Mark's room to get paid. Shawna and Summer went in together and came out quickly. Then Hal entered. A few minutes went by. There came some shouting from inside the room. Then a crash like a lamp had been thrown to the floor. I started for the door but Jimmy placed a restraining hand on my shoulder. When I asked him what the hell was going on, he just smiled and shrugged. "You'll find out soon enough," he said.

When Hal emerged five minutes later, an envelope was in his hand and a bemused grin adorned his face. "You're up, Mick," He said and clapped me on the back.

I stepped hesitantly through the open door. Mark, clad only in a pair of green skivvies, was placing the lamp back on the dresser. "Hi, Mark," I announced.

"Oh!" He turned to face me with wide frightened eyes that mirrored my own nervousness. "Close the door," he said, gesturing restlessly with his hands. "You came for the money, right?" he said with the swiftness a host offers a guest a drink. I nodded.

"Well, I don't have it!" he snapped. I frowned. He sank to his knees. "I'm sorry," he said. I took a few steps toward him, scanning the room for his briefcase.

"What do you mean you don't have it?" I asked in bewilderment.

"I don't have it!" he huffed again. Then his voice dropped to a husky whisper, "You're not going to hurt me, are you?"

I looked down at him. A small pool of sweat was collecting in the bald spot at the center of his scalp. Then my eyes fell to his skivvies. They were stretched with an erection.

He enjoys it too much, Hal had said. I felt a little ill. Did this freak want me to actually hurt him? Or just threaten to do so? I scanned his body for any possible

wounds that Hal might've inflicted. There didn't appear
to be any. He whimpered, groveling at my feet, and I
snapped into my role.

"I'm gonna kick your bitchy little ass, punk!" I
roared. He sobbed.

"No, sir!" he cried. "Please! Don't!"

Now what? "I'm gonna shove my foot up your ass
and make you bleed!" I roared again. He clutched my
calf. I caught sight of myself in the mirror and the
minor tremor of excitement I felt made me look away
quickly. A frantic whisper came from below. "What?" I
addressed Mark's scalp. He didn't respond. I cursed
softly, then bellowed: "What did you say ya little punk?"

"The lamp," he urged sharply.

I grabbed the lamp, noting that the lightbulb had
been conveniently removed. "I'm gonna slam this over
your fuckin' head if you don't give me what I came for!"
I shouted, then immediately hurled it across the room.
Mark gasped as the lamp slammed into the wall, then
sighed comfortably when it sunk to the ground unbroken.

"Okay, okay," he nodded eagerly. He scampered to
the bed and pulled a fifty dollar bill from between the
mattresses. "Here." He thrust the bill out with the same
disdainful air that Merv had given me with the extra
fifty dollars. I took the bill, pocketed it, then stalked
wordlessly to the door. When I looked back, Mark was
already picking up the lamp and carrying it back to the
small table. I wondered if he'd even bother to plug it in.

Much later that night, Jimmy, Shawna, and I were
the remains of a drunken party in the room Jimmy and
I were sharing. Jimmy was pontificating for what

must've been the tenth time on the dark psychological deviancies that drove Mark to his bizarre method of paying people who wrestled for him. I cut him off with a belch. "Guy's a freakazoid," I said. "He likes to be threatened by big muscular guys."

"Not *really* threatened," Jimmy corrected. "He likes the illusion of the threat itself. It enables him to indulge his desire to be dominated while still permitting him to enjoy it in the absence of any real threat."

"So, basically, you guys are serving as his dominatrixes as well as wrestling for him." Shawna chuckled. "He oughta pay you extra."

Jimmy spent a few more minutes delving into the psychological implications of role-playing, be it conducted in "the process of what we knew as everyday life" or "through fantasies forbidden by societal norms." Finally, having made a closing point of some kind, he staggered over to his bed and passed out. Shawna and I stared at one another across the crumpled beer cans overrunning the table. We began going over our personal histories in a revealing, somewhat desperate manner—two people drunk and getting to know each other for the first time. I learned that she had been raised by a foster family after her real parents abandoned her. The foster family consisted of an alcoholic mother and a father who gambled. She had an older brother, whom she loved very much. He protected her from bullies at school (eager to make fun of the fact that she had no "real parents"). "'I'm her real brother,' Billy would tell them," she said proudly. "Then he'd say, 'And if you don't stop teasing my real sister, I'll kick your real ass.'"

Billy had died the summer after his high school graduation while diving off a bridge above a reservoir. The water level had been low and he had cracked his head open against a rock jutting up from the bottom.

"I'm sorry," I said after she told me the story in a quiet monotone.

"He was a daredevil." She brushed her hair out of her eyes and smiled. "Had a lot of energy. We used to have pro wrestling matches in our backyard."

"So that's where you learned to take bumps," I said.

"More or less," she answered.

"Is that what made you want to become a wrestler?"

"You mean is that when I realized I wanted to be one?"

"I'm not talking about a realization necessarily," I explained. "I'm talking about *why*. Like are you trying to keep those years intact through being a pro wrestler?"

"That's a strange question," she said. "Are you drunk or something?"

"Yeah. But I ask strange questions when I'm sober, too."

"You do ask some strange questions," she repeated, laughing. "You know that?" she asked.

"Yeah," I said. Then I reached across the table and took her hand. This spurred her on to further hilarity.

"Uh-oh," she eased her hand away. "Time for me to go."

"Why?" I asked, giving what I hoped was a non-threatening smile. "Things are just getting interesting."

"I'm not big on following rules, but I do have one I never break," she said. "I never get involved with pro wrestlers."

"Never?" I repeated with teasing disbelief.

"Never," she stated. "They have too many issues. And the ones who are grown up are already married."

"Marriage probably wouldn't stop most of them."

"It stops me."

"You think I don't want to grow up?" I demanded.

"I know you just met me tonight and already want to sleep with me," she said. "I know you're a pro wrestler," she added, as if this cemented my immaturity.

"So what?" I cried. "*You're* a pro wrestler too."

"So maybe you're right," she said, her voice slipping into a tired slur. "Maybe I am trying to keep something in my past intact. Jesus, you should come out with a psychiatrist gimmick. Can see it now . . . 'Doctor Freud.'"

Jimmy's snoring was cut off as he stirred on the bed and mumbled something unintelligible. Then he snorted and started up again like a dying motor coaxed back to life.

"Well, there you go," I announced with confused triumph. "And I don't want to sleep with you," I continued sulkily.

"Oh no?"

"We could just go to bed and hold each other."

"Oh God," she moaned, rising to her feet. "Good night, Mick."

I took her hand and traced the gentle ridges of her hand leading up into her forearm dotted with small white hairs.

"What the hell are you looking at?" she snapped, yanking her hand from my grasp.

"I'm memorizing you." I smiled at the frown just

above her gently sloping shoulders. "I'm an artist," I
said. The statement took us both by surprise. The last
time I had attempted to draw had been that night
after Shane gave me a lesson in gimmicks. Since then
I had pushed the possibility of drawing far from my
mind, telling myself that I was too busy wrestling and
striving to gain more muscle for Muscular Mike
Maple.

Shawna was taking a few steps back, arms wrapped
around herself. "An artist, huh?" she stated suspiciously. "What do you draw?"

"Nothing," I admitted.

"Oh," she said. "Well, I'd be a lousy subject."

"I don't think so," I said.

"Sweet dreams, Mick," she replied as she opened the
door.

"I didn't mean it like that—" I began, but the door
had already shut behind her.

———————

Next morning the first thing I did was reach over and
grab a partially open beer on the nightstand between
my bed and Jimmy's. I shook the can. About half full. I
held my breath and took a sip and promptly spewed
beer all over the carpet. Jimmy had been using the
thing as an ashtray.

I found an unopened beer on the table and opened
it. I could hear Jimmy butchering a song in the shower.
Outside the window, the sun was up and stoking the
flat sandy terrain into glowing fullness. Cars blazing by
on the interstate provided me with a sound familiar to

my mornings of the past four months. I finished off the can of beer and opened another. *Starting a buzz at . . . I looked at the clock . . . 8:00 in the morning is typical behavior for a rocker.*

Jimmy agreed, and by the time we were checking out at 9:30, he had downed four beers and I had downed six. We bought a case for the road from a small convenience store across the road and were loading it into Hal's van when Shawna emerged from the hotel office, clad in short jeans and a T-shirt.

"Got some road refreshments, I see," she called with a grin.

"Care to join us in one?" I asked, following the separation of her thigh muscles as her legs carried her toward me.

"Up here, Mick," she said, "my legs can't hear a thing you're saying." But she was smiling as she stopped in front of me.

"You coming with us?" I asked. She shook her head and waved her hand in the direction of a Pontiac Firebird. "Nice wheels," I whistled.

"It's a two-seater," she said. "My gear and stuff takes up the passenger seat," she added quickly.

"Probably just as well." I shrugged. "I don't trust myself around you."

"I don't know whether to be insulted or flattered."

"Be both."

"I meant what I said last night," she said, her head lowering just a bit. "I don't get involved with pro wrestlers."

"You're involved with yourself," I said, "aren't you?"

She plucked a beer out of the case. "See you at the

next stop, Michael." She threw the words over her shoulder, turning away with a smile.

"Who's Michael?" I called. She didn't turn around.

———————

The fourth day of the tour was our day off. Mark had booked us rooms in a small town in southern Colorado. We were supposed to rest up for the final show of the tour in Rochester the next night. With nothing better to do, Jimmy and I spent twenty minutes aimlessly patrolling the streets in Hal's van. The houses were mostly typical single-story homes that appear pedestrian in the daytime and subdued at night.

However, as we cruised around, we couldn't help but notice we kept passing groups of women walking around. I pointed out the apparent absence of men to Jimmy. "Doesn't this strike you as odd?" I asked him.

"Maybe it's a town of women who have made a conscious decision to ignore standard sexual roles in Western civilization," Jimmy suggested.

"You mean like a town populated by a lot of lesbians?"

"You got it," he said, flashing a grin.

We were coming up on a pair of women both clad in bikini bottoms and belly shirts. "Jesus, Jimmy!" I exclaimed. "Pull over!"

He guided the van to the side of the road, warning me as he did so, "Don't be surprised if they're frightened and/or a bit hostile."

"Excuse me, ladies!" I called. They approached the van wearing inquisitive smiles that made them appear neither frightened nor hostile. "My friend and I were just driving around and I've gotta say . . . there's one hell of a lot of single women out on the streets," I explained. "Are men not allowed in this town or something?"

They laughed when I said that. "A lot of the guys went away for the weekend," the blonde explained through lips devoid of lipstick. "Some hot rod thing down by Phoenix." She eyed me with what seemed like habitual nonchalance. "What're you two doin' here?" she asked. "Besides lookin' for girls to molest."

"We're professional wrestlers," I said again. "On tour," I added. I brought my arm up and flexed as though it were a union card. They both raised their eyebrows lazily.

"We're having a party tonight!" Jimmy called out, leaning around me.

"A party?" the darker-haired one inquired.

"Yep." I nodded. I gave them the address of our hotel and our room number. "Tell your friends," I said. "They'll be other wrestlers there too. Until then . . ." I kissed the blonde's hand. She said her name was Diane. Her friend was Stevie. Jimmy and I gave them our names.

"Mick?" She seemed puzzled. "That your real name?"

"Yep," I said.

"See you tonight, Diane and Stevie."

We pulled away from the curb and whooped as we headed to a Safeway to get refreshments for the party.

With the exception of Shawna, who had already gone on to the next town, and Mark, who was probably somewhere cowering before a frothing truck driver, every wrestler on the tour spent that afternoon drinking heavily. Even Richie and Allah joined us, and after a few cocktails they began telling stories of the old WWO days. According to them, some of the wrestlers had been so blitzed before matches they wouldn't even remember them the next day. Allah mentioned a wrestler named Rob Robertson, who he claimed was "an old buggerer." "The inside joke was 'When you wrestle Robertson, always wear three pairs of tights, 'cause he'll manage to pull at least two of 'em down during the match,'" he said, popping open another beer. Allah told us that Robertson retired from wrestling a few years ago and was working as a road agent, traveling with the WWO and supervising shows at arenas across the country. He also specialized in putting the moves on the ring-boys who set up and dismantled the ring. Another wrestler, a guy with a preacher gimmick, had been busted by the DEA for cocaine trafficking. He had been transporting cocaine around the country while on tour, unloading kilos in whatever cities he was wrestling in. Richie laughed as he talked about the sexual habits of "Beautiful Steve Stallyon," who was known for his body builder physique. Stallyon would pick up overweight women, bring them up to his room, begin to get amorous, then abruptly turn on them, insulting them and shouting that he would rather beat off than fuck a woman so fat. "People used to take bets on how quick ol' Stevie could have a woman running out of his room in tears." Richie smirked. "I can't recall it ever taking longer than five minutes."

To hear these two put it, the WWO roster was a collection of drug users, perverts, alcoholics, and malcontents with assorted inferiority complexes. "How about

Sonny Logan?" I pounced, eager to get away from so much moral ambiguity.

"Sonny Logan." Richie grunted and took a long swallow of beer. "Total cokehead."

"Cokehead?" I echoed, a little stunned. "Isn't he . . . supposed to be . . ."

Richie gave me a withering look. "His gimmick," he stated flatly, "his gimmick is that he's a big teddy bear always ranting at kids to take their vitamins and say their prayers and blah, blah, blah. All I know is I worked a series of matches with the dude about a year ago, just before I left WWO, and the asshole was so coked up he damn near killed me."

I was stunned. In the back of my mind I had held Sonny Logan out as an example. Of course, I pretty much assumed he took steroids, but everyone took steroids. In an interview in a Chicago newspaper a few years ago, he had been quoted as saying he didn't drink, smoke, or use drugs. "But sometimes I cheat and have a few chocolate chip cookies," he had added. Even though I was partying, it had been my intention to settle down once I made it to the WWO. I had always envisioned myself there, wild oats properly sowed, laying claim to a position as a role model for young kids. Taking over the throne of Sonny Logan.

Now Richie was telling me that to be like Sonny Logan I would have to snort at least a gram of coke a day.

"That's what he was doin' while I worked there." Richie nodded. "He'd always say 'I'm a big man. And big men need big lines.'" Richie unleashed a harsh laugh as I tried to smile. After another drink I was able to see more humor in the situation. A couple more and it was pretty fucking hilarious. American Dream, shit. Who wouldn't want to party every day and make a lot of money and be worshiped?

By the time Diane and Stevie arrived, I was laughing my ass off. They brought along some friends, who squealed when they recognized Richie and Allah from their WWO days. A girl with plastic bracelets covering her forearms couldn't get over the fact that the two wrestlers were partying together. "Aren't you guys supposed to hate each other or something?" she asked.

Another woman, her black hair streaked with blond highlights, elbowed bracelet-girl in the side. "Duh, Cheryl. They're acting. It's fake," she said. I waited for either Richie or Allah to shoot back a response that calling pro wrestling fake was selling it short. Instead they just laughed.

"Actually," I heard myself slur, "they really do hate each other. They're just trying to patch up their differences." This inspired further laughter. I smiled and drank. I hadn't mean for it to be that funny.

Two hours later, the party was veering out of control. Richie had disappeared with the one called Cheryl (he would later tell me with a wry grin that the reason she draped her forearms in bracelets was because of a hirsuteness that she claimed ran in her family). Allah and Hal were having a makeshift match, throwing punches at each other in the midst of women downing beers and shouting out choruses to Pat Benatar songs. Jimmy was making out with a woman in the corner. Taz was peppering the wall with head-butts, forging a large crack in the plaster to the delight of three squealing women who surrounded him.

I ended up in the next bedroom with Diane and Stevie. Both women were amazingly patient, but my thoughts were lost in a swirling montage of Sonny Logan snorting coke, Allah reciting Shakespeare, and Richie taking pictures of it all so that he can auction them off to the highest bidder. Rather than feeling privileged to be in bed with two women, I found myself gasping for breath. After twenty fruitless minutes, they finally accused me of not finding them sexy. I assured them that wasn't the case. "Just too much to drink," I maintained as they left with forlorn looks. Then I was visited by an image of Shawna, and soon found myself with an erection. So I masturbated, finally gaining a release and a temporary relief from the hopelessness that Richie and Allah's report inspired.

But afterward I laid in bed, remembering Stevie and Diane's fallen faces and feeling very much like Steve Stallyon.

The first time I heard the words *kay fabe* I thought it was Spanish for shut up. But it turned out to be the way wrestlers alert each other that there are outsiders present. When kay fabe is in effect, heels and faces aren't supposed to mingle. But this rule is enforced with varying degrees. As I had seen with Richie and Allah in the hotel room, where women were concerned kay fabe was less important than getting laid.

The night after the party, we were changing for a show in the back supply area of the local community center. It consisted of a few rusty garden tools hanging from the wall and several bags of manure stacked in a wheelbarrow. Suddenly Richie's voice barked from around the corner: "Kay fabe!"

Taz, who had been going over a spot with Hal, dropped Hal's arm and walked off. Around the corner came Richie alongside a stubby-legged police officer. The flesh on the officer's face was glazed like the skin of a turkey hanging in a market, and a viscid liquid, which looked like some kind of soup, clung to the hairs of his moustache. Richie announced that this gentleman would be providing security for the show.

Once the show started, it became apparent that we might need some security before the night was over. The audience consisted of every farmer, mechanic, and blue-collar worker within a twenty-mile radius. It was Saturday night in the middle of nowhere and we were the circus that had just rolled into town. They were determined to get their money's worth and were loudly insistent of this fact from the opening match. Our security officer sat ringside and watched with bemusement as the audience made up of his neighbors (and probably some second or third cousins), assaulted the ring with cups, half-eaten hot dogs, and crumpled up programs.

One bearded man, whose well-stained T-shirt sagged over his pear-shaped body, was especially active. He called Shawna and Summer lesbo dykes and threatened to "climb in there and give ya a fuck that'll make ya blind." In reply, Shawna shouted from the ring that it would be no use to go blind *after* she fucked him. This shut him up for about thirty seconds while he groped unsuccessfully for a retort.

When we came out for our tag-team match, he roundly proclaimed us a bunch of pretty boy queers. He then screamed that he would fuck *us* up the ass like the pansies we were. Other people in the audience hooted enthusiastically, urging the lunatic to jump in the ring and back up his words. The security officer was busy taking the whole spectacle in with a look that matched the curiosity of the very people he was supposed to be controlling. "Jesus, Sammy," I whispered to one of the guys on the other team as I picked him up for a body slam, "let's get the hell *outta* here."

I power-slammed him and pinned him. The ring was immediately besieged by flying debris. A beer can narrowly missed my head as we charged down the aisle back to the dressing room. Pear-man followed us all the way screaming: "*Goddamn sissies! Buncha fake bullshit! Bet I could kick all your faggot asses!*"

The possible causes of this man's vehemence were manifold, Jimmy informed me once we reached the safe haven of backstage. He ticked them off . . . *Terrible home life, job he hated, latent homosexuality* . . . while Pear-man continued to bellow at us from just outside the curtain. The anger in his voice made his words into weapons that could slice the curtain's flimsy material that, I realized with evolving trepidation, was all that separated us from his wrath and the crowd's lust for violence. Until this moment, the ideas of the wide red line had always been an amusing concept, part of one of Shane Stratford's many lectures. Now it seemed all too real and far too narrow.

Mark came up to us. "Tell me that crowd isn't as bad as it sounds," he said wearily.

"They're worse," I said, "especially the guy who looks like a pear."

"We're talking serious repressed aggression," Jimmy added.

"Fuck," Mark scowled.

Richie and Allah had wrestled in front of hostile crowds before. But the days of dealing with violent fans were behind them. They had families now, Allah pointed out before the match. They were getting too old for this frightful nonsense.

"Speak for yourself, baldy," Richie chided him.

When the two were first announced, the crowd gave them grudging respect as former WWO stars. Mark, wearing a turban, went out as Allah's "interpreter from the Middle East." The crowd spat at Mark, with Pear-man leading the crowd in a chant of "Dune Coon." Ninety seconds into the match, Pear-man was accusing Richie and Allah of being "washed-up old queens" and others were hurling objects at the ring. Most of the crowd was drunk by this time, and their projectiles had grown more lethal. When a chair flew over Mark's crouched head into the ring, Richie immediately small-packaged Allah for the pin and rolled out of the ring.

From where Shawna, Jimmy, and the rest of us were all watching behind the curtain, the crowd seemed to be surging toward the backstage area, led by Pear-man, whose voice was now growing hoarse: "Fuckin' pussies! I'll kick your asses! I'll break your heads! Hey, you little weasel, bet you'd love that, wouldn't ya? You want me to beat your little ass, don'tcha?"

We all watched, horrified, as Mark broke away from

Allah and Richie (who by now were jogging back together), and turned to face the man. "I couldn't resist," Mark explained later. "I didn't think he'd really *do* anything."

Mark's motionlessness caused Pear-man to halt abruptly. Pear-man studied Mark for a quick second with eyes as removed as an actor scanning an imaginary page for his next line. Then Pear-man blinked and screamed: "I'm gonna tear you apart, you Middle East faggot!"

"Oh brother," Shawna whispered in my ear, and this combined with the general excitement of the situation made my neck catch fire.

Pear-man lunged, grabbing Mark by the shirt. He smacked Mark's face and the turban hit the floor, revealing Mark's patchy blond hair. By that time, Richie and Allah were by Mark's side. They grabbed Pear-man, with Richie seizing his arms in a full nelson while Allah hoisted his legs. He was howling and trying futilely to kick his way out as Richie and Allah carried him back toward the curtain. The crowd watched in inebriated awe. We stepped back as Richie and Allah barreled through the curtain, deposited Pear-man on the floor and started stomping on him. A bewildered buzz exploded from just outside the curtain. A thousand drunken voices seemed to be debating if this too were all part of the act.

Then Shawna unleashed a wide kick into Pear-man's groin, and his howl left little doubt that we were up to no good. "Stay back, just stay back, I'll find out what's going on!" came the voice of our security officer. I peeked out the curtain. He was marching sternly up the aisle.

I closed the curtain and hissed, "That cop's coming! We better get the hell outta here!"

Everyone scattered, leaving Pear-man huddled and moaning in a pool of vomit which had escaped his bloated body. I quickly grabbed my boots, my bag, and my white fringe leather jacket that I wore to the ring. The cop stumbled through the curtains and shouted, "What the hell—"

Then he saw Pear-man moaning on the floor. "You're all under arrest!" he shouted.

"Fuck you!" Mark snapped before turning and running for the back exit. "I know your names!" the cop was screaming as we all scrambled after Mark. "I know your names!"

The crowd had begun to filter in. After looking around confusedly, they finally saw us tearing down the hallway and linked all of us with the sight of their leader lying on the floor wallowing in a pool of his own vomit.

Some of them started shouting: "Come back and fight like men, you assholes!"

"Eat me!" Shawna shouted back over her shoulder. We were the last two to reach the door, which I held open for her. "Why thank you, kind sir," her words escaped in a burst of breathless laughter. I took a last glance at several beefy guys in T-shirts storming down the hall before I whisked out and slammed the door.

Hal already had the van started and was gunning the motor while in neutral. His spinning tires bit into the ground and sent a storm of dust and pebbles into the air. The lack of moonlight made it difficult for our eyes to penetrate the mounting cloud. "We're outta here!" Hal's voice came through the haze. "Meet us at the Motel 6 on Route 25. Just over the New Mexico border!" Then he popped the clutch and the van shot out of the lot, creating a momentary opening that quickly became clotted with swarming dust. Shawna and I squinted our way through the filthy vapor and found her car. There came the slam of the back door of the community center. "Oh shit!" I spat out the dust that had flown into my mouth. Shawna got into the car and unlocked the door. Through the cloudy shield, I was able to make out three human shapes. One had something clutched in his hand. It could've been a gun, it could've been a flashlight. I didn't want to find out. I slipped into the car. "Gun this motherfucker, Shawna!" I shouted.

"I love this business, I swear to God!" she exclaimed. She started the car up and tore out of the parking lot. Once we reached the interstate, she ran the car up to ninety, hit the cruise control, and flashed a relieved smile. "Too bad I can't stand most of the fans," she said.

"Do you think a lot of them are that dangerous?" I asked. She laughed.

"There was supposedly some survey conducted at various wrestling cards around the country," she said. "Out of all the fans, two percent of them truly believe that pro wrestling is on the up and up." She clutched the wheel a little tighter. "That two percent keeps me up at night."

"What about the other ninety-eight percent?"

"They're like anyone, I guess," she said reluctantly. "Looking for an escape from the grind of life. Pro wrestling gives it to 'em. It's a fucking male soap opera, is what it really is."

To hear my dream laid out in such bare terms took
me aback. I turned to my window, vaguely seeking
some external source of reassurance like the kind I had
gotten on the drive down to my first match in San
Diego. But my vision was stopped by the darkness
speeding past the window.

"You could disappear out here and no one would
ever know." Shawna's voice interrupted my thoughts.
"Be abducted by aliens," she continued, "anything."

"Should I be worried right about now, Shawna?" I
joked.

"If you could just drive down a road like this forever,
would you?" she asked wistfully, intent upon the transparent barrier of the windshield.

"I thought I was the one that was supposed to ask
strange questions."

"That's not a strange question."

"I don't know."

"Answer it."

"I just did," I replied. "I don't know. We'd have to
stop. To eat, to workout . . ."

"To wrestle."

"Yeah," I agreed with a shrug, "that too."

She abruptly whipped the steering wheel to the right,
throwing me against her as we lurched onto the sand.
After about twenty yards into the desert, she stopped
and extinguished the lights and motor. The sole illumination now came from stars poking through the blanket
of perfect blackness above. Shawna got out of the car.

"What's up?" I called nervously.

"Come out here!" she shouted. "Look at them!"

I followed her, staring up at the sky. My focus

became lost in the boundless sea of tiny orbs blinking far above me. I pictured myself on a concert stage, staring out at an infinite throng of fans holding up flames. "Just think of how many more galaxies there are like this one." Shawna's voice found me, but in the darkness her form was featureless. I thought of the people I drew in sketches and felt an urge to touch her. "They go on and on," her shadowy outline spoke again, "forever."

"I once heard that some of the stars we see could already be dead," I ventured, "but are still visible to us because the speed of light can take years and years to reach earth." I didn't continue with what I had always wondered about—that when I died, would distance provide me with an extended life to aliens observing from other worlds? *Who would they be watching?* I became aware of my heart pounding, an engine powering a starless sky. I fell back against the car for support, at least the steel felt real enough.

Once we began to drive again, the feeling of motion possessed my body as I flirted with sleep.

"Is it what you thought it would be, Michael?" A voice came from somewhere ahead of me. I struggled for an answer. Two months ago, I had been changing before a show when the promoter came back and informed us that he was canceling the thing because only ten people had shown up. I had been overcome with a strange relief, followed by nagging guilt. I was supposed to love pro wrestling. It was my dream, so why the hell had I been so relieved about not having to actually go out and do it on that particular day?

Muscular Mike had been able to swiftly chop that trepidation down to a manageable size by blaming a simple case of nerves, an "off" afternoon, or a number of other reasons both incidental and harmless. But in the twilight between conscious and unconscious reasoning, I wasn't so sure. Quickly, I struggled for another answer. And I found it.

"Gettin' paid to party," I mumbled sleepily to the darkness my closed eyes blessed me with.

"Whatever you say, Mick," a voice responded. The motion accelerated and I became lost in the dream again. The masked man was pinned. This time I managed to rip off the mask.

I jolted awake. Shawna looked over at me. "We're here." She smiled. I yawned and looked out the window. Hal's van was parked beneath a Motel 6 sign winking steadily at the surrounding night.

Mark was already gone, but Hal had gotten the night's pay for me and Shawna. The ring, apparently, had been one that Mark was ready to get rid of. Even though leaving the ring probably cost him five hundred dollars, "it was worth it," Mark had said.

From the room, I placed a call to West Covina. It was one in the morning, which meant it was only midnight in California. B.J. answered on the second ring. "Hello?"

"B.J." I said. "You'll never guess what—"

"Mike!" he cried, "Where are you?"

"New Mexico border, man. We had to leave Colorado or we were gonna be thrown in—"

"No, like where exactly? What interstate?" His voice leapt into a higher pitch of excitement with each word.

"Interstate 25," I offered.

"I'm leavin' right now, doc," he declared. "I'm picking you up."

"What?" I stammered.

"I talked to Shane today," he announced. "We've gotta be in Louisville by Monday night for a tryout with the Southern Wrestling Association."

––––––––––––

Eleven hours later I was sitting in an Albuquerque bar near the corner of Broadway and Indian School. That was the intersection B.J. had picked out on his road atlas as the meeting point, and Hal and company had dropped me off there at nine o'clock. I was on my fourth beer, heading outside periodically to search for B.J.'s Toyota.

Giant boards lining the windows barred the entrance of any exterior light. The bar was darkly illuminated by neon words. There was also a sign that was actually a miniature screen. Across it scrolled different extravagantly drawn locations. Snow-capped mountains, a festive Mardi Gras–type street, the magnificent skyline of a city at night . . . all of these scenes were strung together by the name of a beer which occupied several strategic spots in each setting. As I watched this electronic world revolve, I wondered where my current situation would fit into it. The tour was over. Motley Mick Starr was history.

I reached into my pocket and touched the neatly folded piece of paper Shawna had given me that morning before I left the hotel. It had her address in Phoenix and her phone number. "Call me," she had said and smiled, running her hand through my hair. I took out the paper and looked at the curves of her writing. I traced them with my finger, keeping my body in motion against a sudden fear that I was very, very insignificant in this world. *I'm like Jack Kerouac,* I reassured myself. Even though I had never read any of his books, I knew the title of one: *On the Road.*

A roided up Jack Kerouac, I reconfirmed. This reminded me it was time for my shot, so I went into the bathroom and injected 400 mg of testosterone while standing up in a stall.

A few minutes later I finished my beer and stepped carefully outside. As the sunlight hit me, I had the sensation of emerging from the barriers of an old photograph. For a moment I was afraid that the abrupt brightness would reduce me to ashes. But there was B.J. across the way leaning against his car, and when I raised my forearm in a salute, the flesh on my arm tingled against the sun's rays but didn't disintegrate.

6

SOUTHERN WILDMAN

A pair of spotlights ambush the mini-ring, cloaking me in a sheet of illumination so hot it sets my skin on fire. The path to the ring is clear.

Ring entrances are sometimes better than the actual matches themselves. These moments without rules, like that magical image in the opening kickoff of a football game when the ball touches its zenith. Anything is possible. The upcoming contest is a story about to be told, a life yet to be lived.

Wary security guards man either side of the aisle. I squint at the crowd, but the lights make it impossible to discern anything more than a dark mass of howling humanity. Arms slash through air. Fists pump in time to my theme music, which is a loose instrumental interpretation of "Eye of the Tiger." No words, just a powerful beat and an electric guitar slashing out the anthem of an underdog. Fans love it, the single has reached number nine on the charts.

The song is exactly three minutes and thirty seconds long, and I've been able to time my ring entrances so that I'm always inside the ring and perched on one of the turnbuckles by the time the triumphant crescendo comes. But at SlamFest the song ends while the cart is barely halfway to the ring. The song starts over and nobody seems to notice. Eighty thousand people continue to cheer and howl. A few aimless screams break apart from the pack of noise, but they are soon swallowed by the crowd's concentrated aggression.

———————

Louisville, Kentucky's sports arena earned its affectionate nickname, Rough Arena, during an event that had taken place just a year ago. A pro wrestling card, of course. There had been a title change involving Billy "The Prince" Rampart. Rampart was immensely popular in the South. In Memphis, his hometown, he was second only to "The King" Elvis Presley in popularity. When the fans in Kentucky had seen The Prince cheated out of his belt by the dastardly "Adam Prescott the III" (who was really Rampart's nineteen-year-old son), they had rioted and torn half the seats out. Prescott had been forced to flee the building still clad in his gear with the belt clutched in his hand. He had almost run three people over in the parking lot while trying to escape a half-dozen teenagers who were beating on his car. The next week on an interview segment,

Rampart had said that the Louisville arena was "a rough arena to lose in. That's why I'll never do it again." Naturally he hadn't lost there since, and the nickname caught on.

B.J. and I heard this story from Rampart himself. We had arrived at Rough Arena a few hours before the show was set to begin and were in Rampart's private "dressin' quarters." He wasn't exceptionally tall, standing a few inches below six feet, and sported the beginnings of a pot belly. His shoulders drooped into solid but unremarkable arms. Although his body's overall shape was that of an untoasted marshmallow, this only made his face more striking. It was a beautiful face, with features that managed to look both defined and reckless. A blubbery roll bulged at his neck, and one wondered if some autonomic function of his body somehow prevented any fat from traveling beyond this point. Only a few nasty scars on his forehead marred his "princely" facial features. He later confessed to me that he went to a doctor every twelve months to get his forehead sanded down.

As The Prince proudly filled us in on the history of the Rough Arena, I couldn't help staring at the drawing leaning against the mirror. It depicted a tremendously muscled man with sharp abdominals adorned in an outfit that suggested royalty. He was wearing a crown and standing on a rock, looking off at what was surely a horizon as infinite as his conquests.

"That's kind of a self-portrait," he said, his voice lapsing into a rusty shyness. "Drew it myself," he added needlessly.

I struggled to find a link between the self-portrait

and the man who drew it. As far as I could tell, only the face seemed fairly accurate.

"Heard some good things about you two," he said, pulling out a small silver tin. "Dip?" he suggested, as though offering a glass of wine.

"Sure," I said, not wanting to be ungracious. B.J. accepted as well.

"Yep." Rampart fished out an astonishing wad of chew. "Heard some things. But I gotta see it in the flesh." His last four words were obscured by the tobacco inserted between his cheek and gum. B.J. and I awkwardly followed suit. "So what're your gimmicks?" he asked.

B.J. described his psycho dentist. Rampart nodded eagerly. "I like what I'm hearin'," he announced. When B.J. showed him the ketchup-stained outfit, Rampart whooped. "Love it!" he exclaimed, then spat a wad of tobacco juice onto the floor. "How 'bout you, Mike?" he asked me.

"I was . . . a rocker," I said hesitantly. He immediately shook his head.

"No can do," he said. "Already got one of those."

"How about . . . the Wandering Weapon?" I asked. He frowned.

"The Wandering Weapon?" he repeated with distaste.

"Yeah," I forged ahead, "the Wandering Weapon . . . Michael Harding."

He scratched his head. "Can you be crazy?" he asked. "You know, like act a little loony? One oar in the water? Drool, talk to yourself—"

"He does that anyway," B.J. interjected.

I shoved him. "Hell yeah I can," I said.

"The Wandering *Wildman*," Rampart proudly christened me. "We'll have it be that you just escaped from a mental institution or somethin'. I know a nurse at Memphis General. We can probably even get you a straitjacket."

"The Wandering Wildman . . . Michael—"

"No, for Chrissakes. Don't use your real name. Don't use any name. It'll spoil the gimmick. 'Sides . . ." He spat meditatively onto the ground. "You don't want someathese fans knowin' your real name."

"Don't you use your real name?" B.J. inquired. Rampart smiled proudly.

"'Course I do, son. But I'm the Prince." He spat onto the ground with the same authority of a judge pounding his gavel and turned to face the picture. "People love me," he observed matter-of-factly.

That night, "The Wandering Wildman" made his SWA debut against "Flatliner Nelson." Flatliner's backstage nickname was Flatulence. I found out why in that match. Luckily, his farts' unsettling stench was quickly absorbed by the beer, fried chicken, and cigarette smoke emanating from the eight thousand people surrounding us.

The match itself went well. I hissed and barked at the crowd as though I were undergoing some kind of transformation into a wild animal. At various times I would space out and stare into nothing. The longer the match went on, the more legitimately crazy I felt. Soon I was standing on the second turnbuckle in the corner, howling at the crowd like a lost werewolf. The main thing expected of wrestlers in the South is to draw heat from the crowd. Drawing heat simply means making the crowd react to you. I knew that when the crowd began howling back at me, I had done my job. B.J. was also successful in his match. He menaced the crowd with his drill and had pieces of chicken and empty cups hurled at him in retaliation.

After the card, Rampart offered us jobs. "Here's how it works," he explained. "Y'all will start at fifty bucks a night. Responsible for your own lodgings. Wrestle six nights a week. Ya'll got Sundays off. It ain't exactly glamorous, but you can work your way up and you get a hellalotta exposure. We got a deal?"

"Hell, we'd do it for free," I announced. B.J. elbowed me sharply. Rampart peered at me from his stool.

Then he uttered something that would gradually evolve into the truth over the coming year: "Damn, Wildman. You really're nuts, ain't you?"

———————

Being on the road six nights a week made it difficult to locate a place to live. Most of the boys lived in Memphis, the aptly named "littlest big city" in America. Endless rows of flat two-story buildings squatted along the streets like weary troops. The only structure of note was the Hernando DeSoto Memorial Bridge, which spanned across the Mississippi River and joined Memphis with West Memphis. The well-known Beale Street offered a jumble of smoky blues clubs and darkened corners where one could obtain anything from black beauties to DMT.

B.J. and I quickly learned that wrestlers in the

South didn't bother with Soma. They preferred to pop a few Valium or Quaaludes, then wash them down with Jack Daniel's. "Valium is nice," B.J. said one night after downing two Valium and six beers.

"Valium is very, very nice," I agreed, displaying the usual wit I had after downing two Valium and a half pint of vodka. We were in B.J.'s car, which was parked at a rest area. There was no way we were going to blow half of our night's earnings on a roadside motel, so we slept in B.J.'s car when we were on the road. I averaged about three hours of sleep a night; B.J.'s passenger seat didn't tilt all the way back, plus he snored like a horny wildcat. After a month of this, I bought my own car (an investment I only half-jokingly referred to as "getting my own apartment"). My apartment was a 1985 Chevy Cavalier. I had bought the car in Memphis from a dealer who had given me a special price because I knew "The Prince" Billy Rampart. The exterior, no doubt white when it was new five years ago, had been infiltrated by a cancer of dirt that seemed to have spread even to the windshield. No matter how much I scrubbed, its glass still appeared muddy. This peculiar brand of filth seemed to infect all of Memphis; every street, every building, even the billboards advertising The Prince's weekly call-in radio show were glazed with a layer of grime.

Although dirty, the Cavalier ran well, got decent gas mileage, and most important, had a comfortable driver's seat that tilted all the way back. During the first four months we wrestled for the Southern Wrestling Association, B.J. and I lived in our cars. We showered at gyms, did our laundry at Laundromats, and became intimate with every rest area between Tennessee, Indiana, and Kentucky.

There was an unexpected upside to all this activity, and to adopting a gimmick like the Wandering Wildman. Because Wildman was so energetic in the ring and his traveling schedule so fierce, I was in a state of perpetual exhaustion that made it hard for me to worry whether or not I was real. Wildman's very active existence sapped any doubts as to my own. The way people looked at me as I slammed my head against the turnbuckle was satisfactory proof that I was no shadow. Sometimes when drifting off to sleep in the car, I would focus on a large section of the ceiling's cloth covering that had already been torn away. Secure in Wildman, I had no need to pick at the roof's wound.

Because of this security, I sought to further immerse myself in Wildman's gimmick. One Saturday afternoon I went to a barber and got the sides of my head shaved. I dyed the remaining patch orange and spiked it up into a fearsome Mohawk.

"Now you really look like a wildman!" Rampart said gleefully when he saw me.

"Yeah." B.J. laughed. "You'd have to be out of your fuckin' mind to get your hair cut like that." I took a playful swing at him.

"I am out of my fuckin' mind!" I roared.

From that night on, the fans reacted to me with greater intensity. I was loathed and cheered by an equal number of our fan pool; the former group was made up mostly of older people who called me "a no-good punk" while the latter consisted of teenagers who flashed signs at me with such slogans as *Anarchy Rules* and

Youth Gone Wild scrawled on them. I was working mostly with "Hayweeds" Duncan, an old-time country boy who stood about 6'3" and whose advancement into his mid-forties had pulled most of the bulk that once occupied his chest down to his mid-section. His beard was perpetually soaked with juice from an ever-present mouthful of chewing tobacco (I began making him take the wad out before matches). Whether relaxing backstage or dueling it out in the ring, his face remained flushed with a convivial red that furthered his look as a hillbilly Santa Claus. I enjoyed him. He had been wrestling in the SWA for twenty years, but still enjoyed working stiff and "going ballistic, as you younguns would say." As my lunatic character became more and more defined, I began to brawl more with Duncan outside of the ring. Oftentimes I had Duncan order the people in the first row to surrender their seats so he could then hurl me into the vacated row of chairs. This never failed to pop the crowd. Of course, hand in hand with this growing abandon for my safety came the injuries. During my first six months in the SWA, I broke my pinky and forefinger, sprained my right wrist and both ankles, dislocated my shoulder again, and accumulated countless bruises and cuts. One time I bladed myself and cut a little too deep and had to go to Memphis General for twelve stitches. The nurse who sewed me up recognized me and said, "My son watches wrestling all the time. You're the crazy one, aren't you?" True to form, I responded with a growl and several barks. She seemed shaken. "Wow," she whispered. "You really are crazy, huh?" Her remark made me glow inside.

"Just think, Wildman," Duncan said to me in the locker room the next day, "some day you can tell your psychiatrist about how you once drove three hundred miles a day to abuse your body for fifty bucks a night with no social security, no pension, and no benefits." It was official. Even I was beginning to happily doubt my own sanity.

———————

That Christmas I felt ready to go home and see my mom. Before I did, though, I sent her a photo of myself that had appeared in a recent wrestling magazine. In doing this, I hoped to prepare her properly for my altered appearance. When I pulled up in my car, she was standing on the front steps with a big smile despite the sub-zero temperature. As soon as I emerged, her lips plunged into a frown. By the time I reached the top step, she was shaking her head. The shopping bag that contained her Christmas gift suddenly seemed heavy enough to pull my hand through the porch.

"Hi, Mom," I began, "did you, um . . . get the pictures I sent you?"

"A wig." She hurled the word at me. "I thought it was a wig. It looked fake."

"Fake?" I stammered.

"Fake!" she repeated, as though the word were a key piece of evidence in a trial. "Fake! Fake! Fake! Like everything else in that . . ." Her voice trailed off in search of a proper description for her son's chosen profession. "Thing," she finally declared.

"Pro wrestling's not fake," I snapped reflexively. "It's known as a *work*."

"What are you doing to yourself?" she asked, once we got inside. I growled in response. It seemed easier than actually trying to explain it to her. "You're getting way too big," she complained.

The picture of the sun approaching the small building was hanging in the same spot. I howled at it.

"And what is with these sounds you're making?" she demanded.

"They're part of my gimmick." I shrugged.

"This is what you've turned yourself into?" she shrieked. "A gimmick?"

I looked back at the picture to seek a refuge from her eyes. "Dawn or dusk?" I said.

"What?" she asked in annoyance.

"Dawn or dusk?" I repeated, more audibly this time.

She glanced up at the picture, her face overcome with a frustrated incomprehension. "I don't know," she said finally, all anger absent from her voice. "I don't know."

I caught up with Bryan and Marty on the day after Christmas. Both of them found great amusement in my new hairstyle. I filled them in on the life of a pro wrestler, and they told me about life in the apartment they had rented down at University of Illinois for their sophomore year. "What are the parties like?" I asked.

"Just people hangin' out," Marty said. "Twenty-five-year-old seniors goin' after eighteen-year-old freshmen girls. What about pro wrestler parties?"

"Mostly a bunch of big guys taking pills, drinking, and passing out," I said. When described like this, my life didn't sound so thrilling. But Marty was intrigued. He questioned me as to the type of pills and the quantities in which we consumed them. Bryan shook his head as I ran down the list.

After I finished, Marty whooped and showed me a copy of *Fear and Loathing in Las Vegas*, which he kept tucked in his back pocket. He liked to have a copy always on hand so that he could reread passages at any time, and he informed me proudly that he had read the book from cover to cover at least twenty times. "They take all kindsa pills in here," he said, tapping the cover lightly, as though he didn't want to disturb the world inside.

When he went to the bathroom, Bryan informed me in a subdued tone that Marty had been reading a lot lately. "Some real crazy shit," he whispered, casting a suspicious glance at the bathroom door. "He's hangin' out with kind of a weird crowd. I told him I didn't want some of them in the apartment. I haven't really seen that much of him."

When Marty came back from the bathroom he sunk to the floor cross-legged and began studying me intently. "What?" I finally snapped. Marty just nodded.

"Wandering Wildman," he chanted. "'He who makes a beast of himself gets rid of the pain of being a man.'"

"Shit," I chuckled. "Who the hell said that?"

Triumphantly, he whipped out his copy of Hunter S. Thompson's book and opened it to the first page. It was the opening quote by someone identified as Dr. Johnson. "Cool," I said lightly. Bryan gave a derisive laugh.

I looked from Bryan to Marty, trying to remember us

all working out together. Both had obviously stopped; Marty looked to be harboring the prolonged effects of the "freshman fifteen." Bryan, on the other hand, was shrinking. An Izod shirt he had filled out our senior year of high school now hung loosely over his attenuated body like a collapsed tent. After another half hour of strained conversation I left, promising to call them as soon as I got a permanent residence.

That night I sat in my old room, staring listlessly at an old wrestling tape playing on the VCR. The room had an unfamiliar scent that irritated me, but it took several minutes before I finally determined what it was: cleanliness. After months of living in cars and changing in locker rooms crammed with other sweaty bodies, I no longer identified with a room that didn't smell.

A number ran through my head. Although I had memorized it long ago, I hadn't yet called. Before I could ponder it too much, I snatched up the phone and dialed. She picked up on the third ring.

"Hello?"

"Shawna?" I ventured. "That's you, right?"

"Well, well . . . ," she said in a tone that triggered a vision of her knowing smile. "What is it you go by these days . . . Wildman?"

"Yeah," I said. Then howled quietly. Her laughter spilled through the receiver, and I laughed as well; my first genuine laughter since being back home. "Is it too late to be calling?" I asked.

"No," she said. "It's an all right time."

I tried to think of something to say to the silence lurking on the other end of the line. An unpleasant image of Meredith Perkins galloped out of my memories.

She had been a curly-haired beauty in my eighth grade class, and I had once called her on the same cream colored phone I was using now. I had been so nervous I had used index cards to ask her to see a movie with me. She had turned me down.

"I got your card," Shawna was saying, pulling me back to the present. "I would've sent one back but it didn't have a return address. Figured you must be living in your car."

"How'd you know?"

"That's what most people do their first couple months in the SWA. That's what—" She lapsed into a coughing spell. After she recovered she continued, "That's what most people do."

"Sounds like you've been there," I said.

"It's a long story."

"I've got all night."

"Some other time."

"Shawna—" I began, taking a nervous breath and inhaling the smell of the receiver. It was laced with pine cleaner. "I wish I was there with you," I announced abruptly.

"I think you wish you were anywhere but there."

"Maybe," I agreed. "You're probably *involved* with someone anyway."

"Just myself," she replied, "like you said."

"I'm surprised you remember that," I smiled.

"How come?"

"I guess I didn't think you were really listening to me." I shrugged. "I'm under the suspicion that most people I know never really listen to me."

"I listened," she insisted. "I'll listen anytime. Okay?"

"Okay."

"Thanks for calling, Michael," she said. "Merry Christmas."

"Merry Christmas," I echoed. As I replaced the receiver in its cradle, my eyes landed on an old drawing pen that lay next to the phone. Its tip pointed accusingly at me. I inhaled, recalling Shawna's throaty voice, and this urged all my senses to life as they began to unify in a memory so complete that the sterile stink of my room was driven away, replaced by beer and the light trace of perfume she had been wearing that first night we had talked. Patches of her body began appearing in teasing phases: her sinewy neck, alert breasts, and those gray eyes whose irises thickened like an increasingly dense sky as they closed in on their respective pupils.

I picked up the pen along with a small pad of paper. I held the pen against the sheet, but the paper's intimidating whiteness broke through my hazy picture of Shawna. I sighed and looked up at the wrestlers flickering across the television; its screen cast out a bluish glow that blanketed both me and the wall I was leaning against. When I awoke the next morning, my palm had an indentation from the pen that I had evidently been clutching all night.

When I left that morning for Memphis, I took my entire drawing kit with me. My mom's Christmas present, a book titled *10 Ways to Prioritize Your Life*, I left standing on the mantel.

––––––––––

After a few more months, B.J. and I finally received a raise to seventy-five dollars a night.

"Joy," B.J. drawled later that night, as we nursed beers in the back booth of a small honky-tonk just off Interstate 65. We had wrestled in the southern tip of Indiana that night, and were due to work in Tennessee the next day.

"It's something," I said, shrugging. With careful motions, I moved my fake moustache and took a long sip of beer. The promotion was very strict about keeping up kay fabe, and since B.J. was a face and I was a heel, we weren't even supposed to be seen out in public together. Even an activity as simple as grabbing a beer together required a certain degree of espionage; in addition to the fake moustache, I was also wearing a blond wig and glasses.

"Are you really happy with that raise?" B.J. asked.

"Sure. Last time I checked, seventy-five was more than fifty."

"But look at Rampart. Living in a million dollar mansion while every other wrestler scrapes by."

"He's the prince," I said.

"He's an arrogant sonofabitch."

B.J. and Rampart had already clashed once. Rampart had insisted that B.J. throw at least two head-butts a match. "It can be your secret weapon," Rampart had implored.

"It's no secret that everyone in pro wrestling assumes black people have hard heads," B.J. had said mildly, and refused to do it. Although Rampart had accepted this, he hadn't been giving B.J. much of a push. While I was wrestling semi-main events, B.J. was still working mostly preliminaries.

"We should unionize," B.J. was saying now. At the bar, a group of three drunken men were firing coins at the floor.

"Dance you fuckers, dance!" one of them shouted. I could only assume he was talking to the roaches I had seen skittering across the tobacco-stained hardwood.

"Unionize?" I frowned. "If we threatened to do that, you know how many people would be waiting to take our place for . . . hell, twenty bucks a night?"

"Damn, doc," B.J. broke into an amazed smile, "I almost think you were serious that first night."

"What first night?"

"The night you told Rampart you'd wrestle for free."

"I suppose I would have," I swallowed more beer, "for a while anyway."

"Why?"

I ground the bottom of my beer bottle into the thin surface of dust on the table. Then I picked it up and lowered it into the ring of moisture it had just created. B.J. was watching me so intensely I checked to make sure my wig hadn't slipped off. It hadn't. I retreated into safe territory, that of Wildman.

"I'm crazy," I said, "I guess." Then I gave a soft howl.

———————

The raise in pay made it possible for me and B.J. to finally settle into apartments in Tower 99, a well-kept, three-story apartment building on the north side of town. Many of the other wrestlers lived there, and after wrestling in Nashville on Saturday nights, we would drive back to the Tower and have parties that often lasted until the next morning. They were always well attended by the wrestling groupies we called "arena rats."

"Just remember to make sure these rats are over eighteen," Rampart would remind us, "No high-school girls!" A year and a half ago a scandal had been narrowly avoided when the sixteen-year-old daughter of a Tennessee senator had attempted to elope with one half of a popular tag team. The girl had been shuttled off to a private school in Florida, and the wrestler was now working in Mexico. "Check IDs at the door," became Rampart's motto.

Aided by copious quantities of Valium, alcohol, and high grade marijuana, parties at Tower 99 most often dissolved into random coupling in different rooms, shadowy corners, or if the intoxication level of those involved was high enough, a couch right out in the open.

At first, I participated in a few of these encounters. But the next day I always felt guilty, half-suspecting that the cops were on the way to my apartment to arrest me for some nameless wrongdoing. Many of these "rats" were either reckless young girls in their late teens or the tired-cheeked women who had been left by husbands (usually after years of abuse) and now worked as waitresses in sawdust-filled honky-tonk bars. I liked the older women better, and always insisted on talking to them before sex because their stories contained a tragedy which made their presence in this world so painfully acute. Still, they never failed to depress me. When I confessed this to William Epstein (aka "Foreman Rip Tractor," a construction worker gimmick), a tall New Yorker with a shaved head and legs the diameter of ripe watermelons, he pinpointed my problem immediately. "You're supposed to fuck rats," he admonished me, "not talk to them."

Even though I eventually pleaded impotence at these parties, I still found myself drawn to the general decadence. I became content to simply sit and observe through dulled vision the blurry semblance of naked bodies writhing together. Snatches of laughter and sometimes young girls' sobs would sway into my ears in an unfocused rhythm. I would pop another Valium to numb my senses further, but would remain at the party until the sun rose. Only with this indication that a world outside still existed could I manage to get up and stagger off to sleep.

One Sunday morning I floated back to my apartment in worse shape than usual. I collapsed onto my bed and watched my brain raise out of my head and float toward the cottage cheese patterned ceiling, which was transforming into a whirlpool of tiny man-eating fish. As this image blurred, I sucked in a breath and held it in hopes that this would help accelerate my heart's lagging pace. It didn't seem to be working, and I let the breath out and inhaled again and reached for the phone.

"Hello?" Shawna's voice was groggy.

"Shawna?" I slurred. "Hi. It's . . ." I inhaled sharply as my heart gave a kick.

"I think I'm dying," I said after two more complete breaths.

"Why?" she asked. "What's wrong?"

"Valium and alcohol . . . that's . . . not a good combo is it?"

"I hear it's great if you want to die or go into a coma and have a machine breathe for you," she said. Then her tone cracked a little, "Shit, I'm making fun of you. I shouldn't do that. How much did you take?"

"I don't really know." I flexed my tongue, not as an obsessive action but simply to make sure I could still exert a measure of control over it.

"I wanta draw," I said slowly, trying to capture the thoughts melting against my skull.

"Draw?" she challenged immediately. "Like pictures?"

"Yeah," I said. Then I told her in a slow thick voice about the picture I had bought my mom. I told her about how I thought it was neither dusk or dawn, but instead the end of the world. "I've never told anyone that," I announced in conclusion, "before now."

"What do you usually draw?" she asked.

"Abstract things," I said. The word "abstract" struck me as funny, and I began giggling.

"I want you to draw something for me," she spoke intently. "Are you listening?"

"I'm listening," I replied.

"You know that bridge . . . the Hernando DeSoto . . . it spans the Mississippi River and leads west into Arkansas?"

"Yep."

"When you cross that bridge, there's a stretch of highway a mile later that straightens out and stays that way for almost ten miles. There's nothing but rice fields around it. This time of year they flood the fields and it

looks like something you would see in China. The first
time I saw that scene I couldn't believe it was right here
in America." Her voice's growing ardor made my heart
beat a little faster. "At the right time of day, the sun sets
and reflects off all the water, and you can just get lost.
You can get lost and pretend you're on the other side of
the planet. Are you listening?"

"Yes," I responded immediately.

"I want you to drive out there and get that feeling
down on paper. Draw it for me." She paused. "Will you
do that?" she asked.

"Yes."

"You better not die on me," she warned. "I want to
see that picture."

"You will," I assured her. We hung up. My heart was
beating comfortably by then. I had a mission, one that
was obviously important to Shawna, and this gave me
the confidence to close my eyes and know that I would
wake up.

A week later, I followed Shawna's directions and drove
over the bridge. Five minutes later I spotted the fields
rising up on both sides of the flat stretch of highway
that extended all the way to a tiny indecipherable point
at the edge of my eyes' range. I pulled over. The water
on either side of me absorbed the glare, throwing off
tiny fires of light that sparkled across the surface like a
carpet of diamonds. I stationed myself on the car hood
with my right hand holding a pen motionless against
the top sheet of a sketch pad. With my other hand I

slowly removed my sunglasses and closed my eyes. Twisted orbs of light danced between my pupils and the dark vacuum that protected them, and my hand began to move.

While I drew, my eyelids trembled, fighting an instinct to open and stare into the sun. They did slip for a moment, and my hand froze in the avalanche of light. Only once back in darkness was I able to resume drawing, feeding off a vision that lingered and altered itself like a dream remembered in consciousness.

When it felt done, I blinked several times before focusing on a cool suffusion of red across the horizon. The sky now served as a beacon, a means for the sun to demonstrate it was still burning deep within a temporary grave, and would rise again. Without looking at what I had just drawn, I folded up my pad, got into my car, and drove back to Tower 99 where a few Valium and my own impermanent death awaited.

"I can't believe you're still taking Valium," Shawna scolded me when she called five days later.

"I'm more careful now," I assured her. I had successfully convinced myself that my near overdose had been a result of irresponsible drug taking. Having monitored my intake more carefully over the past couple of days with no life-threatening incidents, I was able to banish the unpleasant experience to a corner of my mind that was kept under lock and key. "What about the picture?" I asked.

"I like it," she said simply. The picture had arrived yesterday, she told me, via ExpressAir.

"You like it?" I asked. "That's it?"

"It seems a little . . . ," she paused.

"Don't be shy," I said. "Say what you mean."

"Exactly."

"Huh?" I said.

"That's what you've got to do more of in your art," she concluded. "You're hedging."

"Hedging what?" I asked, confused.

"You tell me."

I let my eyes wash over the neat rows of thin white tiles that made up the kitchen floor. An ant was navigating across the ocean of neat squares with a speed that suggested some essential errand. I had read somewhere that ants were one of the strongest creatures on earth. I threw a shoe at it and missed.

"Yourself," Shawna's answer finally came through the receiver.

"I'm gonna start feuding with Rampart," I said blithely. "He told me today. I'm supposed to attack him at the next television taping."

"Oh boy," she said, "are you in for it."

"For what?"

"People down there love him," she said, "and remember what I said one time about two percent of the United States population believing pro wrestling is real?"

"Yeah."

"They all live in Tennessee."

———————

During a card at the Mid-South Coliseum on June 15th, "The Prince" Larry Rampart was ambushed by members of the "Street Warriors." As they double-teamed him in

the ring, the "Wandering Wildman" appeared in the aisle
with a twisted grin. The crowd became frantic. Rampart
and the Wildman had spent the past three months
engaging in a series of brutal matches, and his appearance seemed to spell the end of Rampart. Wildman
walked down the aisle, climbed into the ring and then,
for reasons of his own, pummeled the surprised Street
Warriors and threw them both out of the ring. He then
helped Rampart to his feet. A skeptical Rampart finally
shook the Wildman's hand, and a new fan favorite
sprang to life in the Southern Wrestling Association."
—from *Pro Wrestling Monthly*, 8/2/89 issue.

The above article was printed as an epitaph to my
feud with Billy "The Prince" Rampart. The "reasons of
my own" the article referred to was that after three
months of feuding with Rampart, I feared for my life.

The feud started well. According to plan, the
Saturday after I talked to Shawna I attacked The Prince
from behind while he was giving an in-ring interview. I
then "pummeled him from pillar to post" as they say. He
bladed himself, and as he lay bleeding in the middle of
the ring, I pranced around in his robe while the fans
hurled garbage at me.

Rampart and I began having matches all over the
circuit. The reaction was immediate and harsh. Up
until that point I had been what's known as a "hace," a
heel who is entertaining enough to be cheered by some
as a face. But my attack on Rampart immediately cata-
pulted me to the unenviable position as the most hated
wrestler in the SWA. Whenever I was introduced, fans

spit and flung a storm of half-eaten hot dogs, cups filled with tobacco juice, and other assorted bits of garbage at me. I began to carry an umbrella so I could shield myself from the assault of putrid refuse that was hurled at me during that long walk down the aisle. They unleashed an audible attack as well, their curses and insults and threats of violence peaking with a vehemence that was alarming in its confident self-righteous tone.

Pro wrestling offers a wonderfully simple distraction from the messy complexities of human nature. People are given the power to cast aside the horror of ambiguity when they enter a pro wrestling arena. Any doubt or fear in their lives can be squashed by their love for their heroes and hate for their villains. I often noted the curious fact that for the most part, the people who cursed me most violently weren't truck-driving "simple folk," as one wrestler referred to them. The people who hated me most were the middle-aged businessmen, housewives, and those most desperate for a break from the tyranny of their lives. Wrestling provided them with a fantasy world where they could love and hate and scream and yell with no repercussions.

At first, the sheer volume of hate mail I received gave me a temporary jolt. Mixed with the many grammatically challenged tirades was the occasional death threat. These especially worried me, until other wrestlers showed me some of the death threats *they'd* received. One wrestler, Jesse James Tolliver, had laminated some of his favorite hate letters and used them as place mats. The one he was most proud of read:

Dear Mr. Tolliver:

   Billy *"The Prince" Rampart's gonna whip your
ass good, boy. You need it, too, you fatassed pansy
dickwad. You're a jerk. You think you're so sexy but
you're really A FATASSED FREAK! You can't wrestle, and the only way you'll beat The Prince is to
cheat like the dog you are! I hope The Prince makes
you lick his boots, and I'll be there to cheer when
that fine day comes.*

Sincerely,
Jane Hoover

"It was a fourth grade class assignment," Tolliver
explained as I smiled down at the letter, a spoonful of
chili poised before my mouth. "All the kids had to write
letters. I got about four others from that class," he said
proudly. "The way I look at it, to make a *child* tell you
how much they hate you . . . that takes some doing."
   Tolliver, of course, had no children of his own.

———————

The night of Saturday, June 25th, found me crouched
underneath a ring in Rough Arena, where the temperature hovered around eighty degrees. The latest angle in
my feud with Rampart involved me interfering during a
cage match. Cage matches, called that because the ring
is surrounded by fifteen-foot-high strips of chain-link
fence, are billed as "the ultimate confrontation" because
there is no escape and no possibility of interference.

But I, as head SWA heel, was going to set a precedent by hacking my way into the ring with a machete. I had stationed myself underneath the ring a half hour before show time, and spent the next three hours listening to the terse explosions of bodies hitting the canvas above me. After an hour, my entire body was drenched in sweat. The darkness beneath the ring took on a more sinister feel. I was in one of the sweltering caverns of hell, while above me, God dispensed claps of thunder to the riotous approval of ten thousand sweating worshipers. I recalled crawling underneath the bleachers at the Rosemont Horizon, making my way among candy wrappers and empty cups as rats scurried just out of my sight, all to sneak backstage and meet Sonny Logan. That night, I had imagined the crowd the same way: a group of people cheering mightily as gods battled in the ring. Now, five years later, I was ready to attack one of these gods in his own kingdom. This incident would be featured in *Pro Wrestling Monthly*, the same monthly magazine whose editor, Buck Dipter, I had written an unanswered request to for the names of pro wrestling schools. Now, his magazine had been tipped off that something big was going to happen tonight, and I was that something big.

A walkie-talkie by my side squawked: "Go for it, Wildman."

"Ten-four," I replied, and started chopping at the ring boards with my machete. The narrow space beneath the ring made full arm movement impossible, but after several swipes the board finally split and I was able to get a clear shot at the canvas. The first shot ripped the canvas apart and spotlights shocked my eyes, which had grown accustomed to the darkness beneath the ring. Blinking rapidly, I cleared a portion of canvas away and climbed into the ring. There was Rampart, his opponent Jesse James Tolliver, and ten thousand hostile faces locked outside. All as it should be.

To the extreme horror of the crowd and delight of the magazine photographers, Tolliver and I started methodically going to work on The Prince. At one point I had Rampart in the corner and we were both stifling laughter as a photographer snapped a picture of me giving him a series of crotch-shots.

Rampart had joked previously that, far from being "the most dangerous match in professional wrestling" as advertised, cage matches were probably the safest. "The cage protects you from the friggin' marks," Rampart had said.

Now, as thousands of voices screamed angrily for my death, I realized what he'd been talking about. "Boys, we just might have a riot on our hands!" Rampart announced gleefully, making a smile look like a grimace as I choked him. No doubt he was anticipating the boost to ticket sales this would have for August's WrestleWar, an SWA wrestling extravaganza scheduled to be held at an outdoor stadium near Nashville. Looking at the pure rage on some of the faces milling dangerously close to the ring, I began to wonder whether I would live to see it.

"I'd better start coming back," he whispered, as I threw a half-hearted punch that grazed his bloody forehead.

"What marks want, marks get." With that, he

launched out of the corner with a double clothesline that flattened both Tolliver and me. Instantly the arena was filled with wild cries of approval. Rampart slammed us against all four walls of the cage. Then he just stood there in the center of the ring and waved goodbye until the house lights finally came on and people realized that the show was over.

The audience filed out with the dazed movements of disenfranchised lemmings, leaving their hero standing alone inside the cage over his two temporarily defeated adversaries. Rampart looked down at me. "This night's gonna make you famous, Wildman," he murmured with a smile.

"Be careful," Shawna warned me a few nights later, "too much exposure can be hazardous."

They were both right.

As my feud with Rampart tore through Southern towns, I began responding to the hostile behavior of fans in a manner more befitting of a Wildman. I expanded the variety and amounts of steroids I ingested in order to increase my aggressiveness. "Don't you think you might be gettin' a little out of control, doc?" B.J. remarked one night after watching me growl at two teenaged girls who had meekly requested an autograph.

"Screw 'em," I barked back. Whenever I happened to glance into a mirror or stare into the window of my Chevy while unlocking the door, the person I saw was indeed a wildman. Though the transformation felt right, I was disliking that person more and more. Whenever I

brushed my teeth I closed my eyes so as not to
encounter any reflection. *Muscular Mike had loved mirrors.* I recalled this with the fondness people use to
remember the annoying habits of old friends who are no
longer a part of their lives.

I spent the last Sunday of July on the road leading into
Arkansas, watching and sketching the sunset. The air
was mild and the sunset lacked its usual harshness. I
was able to keep my eyes open while drawing, and I
captured details my memory had never been able to
reclaim. Birds were gliding inches above the water, their
wings perfectly still. Then with one flap they ascended
into a blue playground on fire. The liquid surface of the
fields swarmed with vegetation. Mysterious ripples shot
up in evidence of microscopic revolutions taking place
below, armies of organisms seeking the unrestrained
promise of air above. An occasional car passed but after
only a few moments their interruptions faded into thin
air, its whisper already so alive with bird cries and the
earth's patient growth beneath the water.

The picture was one I had never drawn before. Its
shapes and colors had been felt and seen rather than
assumed. After it was done, I examined it until there
was no more light. A car's headlights swept past and I
became panicked, caught in something forbidden. I
rolled up the sketch hurriedly and put it in the trunk.
Before I left, I sent a howl out across the dark beds of
water.

When I got home I noticed a car parked against the

curb facing the opposite direction of the street's traffic flow. Its defiant presence impressed me; I waved at the front grill as I pulled into the garage. Climbing the steps to the front door, my knees throbbed in rebellion to the movement. "Get ready for arthritis at forty," Shane Stratford once warned me with a smile.

I was feeling very old as I straggled into the quiet foyer. The floor was tiled and a chandelier hung just above a row of dirty copper mail slots. On a small chair just inside the door was a thin-lipped woman wearing large glasses. She pulled up from her hunched position and stopped me with a look of naked distaste. "Wandering Wildman," she spat accusingly, "you're bad." The smallness of her face and hurt in her voice made her seem childlike.

But Wildman didn't give a damn. Just another mark. I waved her away with a motion adopted for dealing with fans. "Get lost, idiot," I snapped as I barreled past.

"You're a bad man!"

Her words were infused with enough venom to make me stop and turn. My knees locked up at the sight of a butcher knife clutched in her twitching hands. Her eyes glowed with true steady hatred. "If I killed you it wouldn't be a bad thing," she murmured in a trancelike tone. "God wouldn't punish me!" she cried, reinforcing her words with a few aggressive steps in my direction.

I knew I should be alarmed, but Wildman wouldn't show any fear. "Yes, He would!" I shouted blindly at her. "You would burn in hell for all of eternity!"

"No!" she looked around in a confused manner, as though God were seated nearby ready to argue. I lunged and grabbed her wrists. Her scream made me wince. I slammed her hands into the wall. The knife dropped, chipping a tile an inch away from my foot. "No!" she screamed, the pain in her voice biting into me, "No! You're bad!" The sorrow I felt for her angered me and I shoved her back against the wall. She sank down and pulled her knees to her chest. I snapped the knife up from the floor. Her next wail was so intense it sounded like she was trying to vomit out her own heart.

"Shut up!" I shouted at her. "Just shut up!"

"What the hell's going on out here?" A gruff, tobacco-torn voice from my left made me turn. In the doorway to an apartment stood a tall stout man, his bloodshot eyes wide as he took in the scene before him. "What are you doing to her?" he demanded, focusing on the shine of the butcher knife in my hand.

"This woman tried to attack me," I said loudly, then had to repeat it as a shout in order to be heard above her crying.

"I know you," he pointed a shaking finger at my orange mohawk. "I seen you on the television." His head nodded in a determined appraisal of the situation. "Oh, I've seen you," he added ominously.

"Goddammit, call the police!" I yelled. "I don't want her to get away."

The woman paused momentarily, then unleashed another piercing cry against some unseen horror. I closed my eyes. "Shut up!" I commanded. After her shriek subsided, I opened my eyes and saw that the man had disappeared back into his apartment.

"Why did you do this, lady?" I asked her desperately, hoping she would tell me before the police got there.

But she only continued to sob, quietly now, as though that last shriek signified a final failed defensive stand.

When the police finally arrived, a tall ponderous sergeant explained that they had to take me in for questioning. Finally, at about two in the morning, the sergeant came into the interrogation room where I had been sitting by myself and informed me that they'd tracked the woman's family down. She was a paranoid schizophrenic, and technically a ward of the state. Apparently she lived with her mother and sister (the father had died), helping out in their mail-order goods business by knitting blankets. While she worked alone in her room she watched television; her two favorite programs (both of which, according to her family, made her sob violently) being soap operas and professional wrestling. The last three Saturdays, she had snuck the car out and driven to Nashville. Then she had followed me home after the shows to find where I lived. I was usually drunk and numbed with Valium after these shows, so it didn't really surprise me that I never noticed.

"We found this in her car," he said, flashing a copy of *Pro Wrestling Monthly*. It was open to the page that featured me giving Rampart one of many crotch-shots. I could tell instantly that it was one of the shots in which Rampart and I were both stifling laughter. A big red "X" had been scrawled over my howling figure.

"What's gonna happen to her?" I asked quietly.

His eyes flicked over me in a glare as impassive as the room's four white walls. "Her mother and sister are gonna have her committed to an institution up north," he answered flatly.

I lowered my eyes to the rounded edges of the metal table. "I see," I said.

"You're free to go."

"Two percent," I mumbled.

"Do what now?" he frowned, suspicious of a veiled confession of some kind.

"Nothing." I pushed myself to my feet.

On my way out, I recognized a few cops from the shows. I held my breath, waiting for one of them to ask me for an autograph. Thankfully, none of them did. I checked the backseat of my car, then spent the drive home scanning the rearview mirror for tailing headlights.

Sunrise found B.J. and I sitting out on my deck, each of us with a beer. We drank and passed a joint back and forth in buzzing silence. "Are you feelin' okay?" he asked finally, "I mean, really . . . okay?"

"Really . . ." I took the joint from him, had a hit, and exhaled. "I don't know." My eyes stung as the sun began glancing through night's stubborn haze. "I don't know how I feel." I lied. Then I blurted: "That could've been me."

"Say what?"

"That woman. She was so . . . obsessed . . . with wrestling."

"She was nuts, man."

"So am I," I pointed out with a mirthless smile. "Remember?"

"That's just a gimmick," he said. "Okay?"

"Okay," I agreed. But even as I said the word I was running the smooth cool neck of my beer bottle along my inner forearm. The marijuana licked at my brain, teasing out fears and paranoid thoughts. That woman had been as determined as me to find some kind of meaning in pro wrestling; the only difference is she had no choice but to do it as a fan. I wanted to talk to her, to ask her if maybe she was conscious of something inside her that made her act in ways she couldn't control. If she had killed me, would that have silenced her demons?

But there was no way I would ever be able to ask her these things, to talk reasonably with her. We were enemies, separated by the very search for control that bonded us.

Later that afternoon when I informed Rampart that I was turning face, he sighed knowingly. "Wildman," he began, "these things happen. The woman was disturbed—"

"Billy, I'm turning," I said. My voice was trembling a little, and he looked up at me. "I have to," I pleaded.

He sighed again. "Shit," he said with a shrug.

That night, for reasons of my own, I saved Rampart from a brutal attack and became a face.

Two weeks later, I got a call from an executive of the World Wrestling Organization. He invited me up to the corporate offices. They would be happy to fly me there and back, first class.

"There's a flight next Sunday that leaves at 7:00 in the morning and gets here at 10:30, New York time. We can have you back by 9:00 the same evening."

"Sounds like you people have done this before," I said and smiled into the phone.

"We know you boys have a grueling work schedule."

"All part of the business."

"Depends on how you're doing business," he pointed out. "The World Wrestling Organization likes to give its wrestlers a little more time off. Our national television exposure makes it possible for us to do that."

"So do you send me a ticket or should I pick it up at the airport?"

There was laughter. "We'll send it to you. And we'll have a limo waiting for you at the airport."

The World Wrestling Organization's main rival was International Championship Wrestling. They were like the Coke and Pepsi of the pro wrestling business. Superstars jumped from one promotion to another with regularity, often pitting the two of them against one another in hopes of a bidding war. It was common knowledge in the business that the sole reason most young wrestlers like myself endured so much of a grind in the SWA was to gain necessary exposure in order to make the leap to one of these "Big Two." Rampart was opposed to this, and reserved a special hatred for the WWO. He didn't want his wrestlers talking to "those goddamn Northerners," as he referred to the WWO front office. He particularly detested the owner of the WWO, Thomas Rockart Jr., who had bought the WWO from his father and then proceeded to build it up into a national promotion. "Was a time," Rampart would say meditatively, his speech a little jumbled from the wad of tobacco lodged between his cheek and gum, "when this

business was run on honor and respect. You didn't promote in another man's territory. Then this goddamn
yankee comes along and fouls it all up. Runs wild over
others' territories, no respect for the old way."

I didn't respond with what I considered to be simple
logic: Thomas Rockart Jr. was following the way of the
1980s. The bigger you were, the more exposure you got,
the more you could spend to get top talent like "The
American Dream" Sonny Logan. It was apparent that
Rockart, who was beginning to exploit the then
unheard of cable avenues such as pay-per-view, represented the future of professional wrestling. That was
where I wanted to be.

Of course, I didn't mention this to Rampart. When I
landed at JFK on Sunday morning at 10:30, the limousine was right out front where they said it would be. We
slipped easily through the streets of New York, its buildings much taller and darker than the ones I was used
to seeing in the South. The driver's East Coast accent
sounded as exaggerated and foreign as the Southern
twangs I had been introduced to sixteen months ago. A
sense of déjà vu overtook me: stranger in a strange
land.

Thomas Rockart Jr.'s office was in a twenty-story
building whose rocket shape and glass exterior had
earned it the nickname "The Crystal Ship." Rockart's
office was on the top floor, and one could tell immediately that it was a space where important decisions
were made. An aquarium occupied an entire wall, hous-
ing miniature sharks and fish of such remarkable color
and design that they looked like swimming works of art.
The opposite wall consisted of a fireplace surrounded

by bookshelves stocked with the classics. Just behind the massive mahogany desk sat a globe that was at least four feet in circumference and beyond that a large-framed window looked out onto the city sprawled below. Rockart could easily lean back and spin the globe, then stare out the window contemplating the world revolving around his latest decision or dilemma. Spending enough time in that office could lead someone to believe that they were king of the world.

Thomas Rockart Jr. was almost as impressive as his office. With carefully styled black hair and dark eyes, he carried himself with the air of a man who controls others' lives both effortlessly and guiltlessly. His size surprised me; on television, where he served as a play-by-play announcer for matches, he had always seemed to be a smallish Ivy Leaguer. In person, he was an inch taller than me and looked to weigh about 220 pounds. He still retained his sophisticated presence, carrying his bulk well in a $1,000 Armani suit. My current out-fit of blue jeans and a red-and-black-checked flannel shirt made me feel severely underdressed, but he quickly put me at ease with a radiant smile that assured me there was no other person in the world he was more eager to see. His handshake featured moder-ately restrained power, and just before he released my hand he gave it an extra squeeze. "Mister Harding, it's a pleasure to meet you." His introduction managed to be smooth without sounding practiced. "Have a seat, please."

"Thank you, Mr. Rockart," I said, glancing quickly at an oil portrait hanging to the right of the window. That it appeared to be of Rockart himself was not surprising.

He seemed to have enough nerve and imagination to, with a straight face, consult an image of himself for advice.

"I'd like to thank you for coming up on a Sunday," he told me, "and please, call me Thomas."

"Only if you call me Michael," I replied, while at the same time wondering how long it had been since anyone other than Shawna had.

"All right, Michael," he said, nodding. "Would you like anything to drink?"

Over red wine we discussed various aspects of professional wrestling. It was then that he filled me in on the proud history of the World Wrestling Organization and his personal vision for the future of pro wrestling. The tactics Rampart dismissed as "stepping on toes" were, according to Rockart, necessary in order to place professional wrestling on a national stage. "People have accused me of losing the 'sport' of professional wrestling," he explained, "but I prefer to think of it as combining the best of both worlds of sports and entertainment."

As I listened, I became more and more convinced that Thomas Rockart Jr.'s ruthless strategy to become king of the wrestling world was fueled by an honest affection. "Professional wrestling is better than a bunch of country yokels with chewing tobacco caught in their teeth," he said. "It can be enjoyed by the majority of the American public." I was aware that I was being seduced, and this specific awareness led to another slightly foggier one. I sensed that Rockart possessed a control over himself that I didn't have. Beneath his determined earnestness and theatrical way of speaking lie a certain weight, as though he was under constant supervision from somewhere outside himself. Even a gesture as simple as a shrug was delivered with a confidence meant to impress.

Two hours passed quickly and easily. When Rockart suggested lunch, I agreed. As we were leaving the office, we heard: "Hi, Thomas!" The voice was instantly familiar. I'd imitated it many times before.

I turned, my eyes widening. Chuck "The Stud" Beastie was approaching us with a salutatory smile. Long black hair fell over wide shoulders that stretched against a tie-dye T-shirt. His elephant pants had legs loose enough to accommodate his larger-than-average thighs. When we shook hands, I was surprised to find his grip much gentler than Rockart's. "I've seen some of your matches," he said in a rough but subdued tone that bore little resemblance to his bellowing interview style. "You work pretty well," he said.

"Thanks, Mr. Beastie," I said. Both men broke into chuckles.

"Call me Chuck, kid," Beastie said smiling.

"Michael and I were just going out to grab a bite," Rockart said in a voice like velvet. "Care to join us?"

"Sure," Beastie responded immediately. My heart was pounding excitedly as the elevator indicator rang. Rockart held the door open for us.

We dined at the terrace restaurant of a nearby four-star hotel. The waiter didn't bat an eye at my orange mohawk, and his unflappable cool made me wonder if Thomas Rockart Jr. brought all his prospective employees here. Maybe the waiters had long since grown accustomed to this debonair, dark-suited man popping in for a midday meal in the company of men who looked as though they had just stepped off the pages of a comic book. After all, this *was* New York.

For lunch there was a fettuccine dish with chunks of salmon and lobster swimming in alfredo sauce. I didn't taste a bite. I was sitting at the same table with *Chuck Beastie.* Rockart kept up a steady stream of conversation until the waiter brought us coffee. At this point his voice lowered to a conspiratorial pitch that, though directed at me, managed not to exclude Chuck: "Michael, I'm going to take you into my confidence. I want you to come work for my company. There's a position we have for a wrestler like yourself, one who's young, but has been around. The potential is limitless."

"I'm interested," I said, ignoring my coffee and finishing my second glass of a smoky Merlot.

"Last week, one of our jobbers got his neck broken by Rand Stiffer," Thomas Rockart Jr. said.

"He used to wrestle up in Canada, right?"

"That's correct." Rockart nodded. "We brought him down here and gave him a heel gimmick as a psychopathic hockey player. Problem is, he's taking his gimmick a bit too seriously."

"Living it, huh?" I suggested.

"Exactly," Rockart agreed. "He's injured jobbers before, but this is the first time he's almost killed one."

"How is he?"

"As unapologetic as ever. Said the kid had it coming—"

"No," I interrupted him, "how's the kid he injured?"

"He's okay." Rockart nodded eagerly and continued, "We took care of the hospital bill. He's never gonna wrestle again, naturally. It happened at a house show so we weren't even able to get it on tape—"

"Be good ratings," Chuck uttered in a growl that sounded a little too rough.

Thomas Rockart Jr. peered at him out of the corner of his eye before once again focusing on me. "It's obvious Stiffer is a bit out of control," Rockart admitted. "But the problem is he won't mess with any of the boys who have been here for awhile—"

"You want me to be a policeman," I suggested, using the term for wrestlers that help keep other workers in line.

"Michael, you're a hell of a talent," Rockart urged, "but you are young. Very young. Wouldn't you agree, Chuck?" Chuck was busy studying the microscopic holes of varying width that made up the tablecloth's flowery design. He looked up, studied me with careful eyes, then nodded.

"Yeah," he agreed.

"I want to bring you in, Michael," Rockart spoke slowly until I looked back at him. "But I don't want you coming into a hostile environment. I've seen your matches in the SWA, and I know you're a good shooter. If you take this guy out, you can earn the respect you're gonna need to have the other wrestlers put you over."

"Take him out?" I asked.

Rockart's eyes settled on me from just above the tip of his wineglass. "Do whatever you have to do." His voice was firm.

I looked over at Chuck, who immediately began nodding slowly. "If I were ten years younger, I'd take the sonofabitch out myself," he informed me. "I've seen your matches. You can do it. That's why I recommended you."

"You recommended me?" I asked, my ears growing hot.

"Uh-huh," he said, nodding.

Rockart shifted forward in his chair; his eyes sweeping over both of us. "Shall we go back to the office and talk contract?" he suggested.

Chuck bid us farewell on the street, giving my hand a shake and saying he hoped to be seeing me soon. Rockart and I took the limousine back to his office, where I signed a two-year contract for $70,000 the first year, $90,000 the next, and a renewable option for a third year at $150,000. Also built in to the contract were bonuses for special appearances and pay-per-views. There was no clause that gave me any kind of percentage on merchandise sales bearing my name and likeness. I found out later that most of the superstars in the WWO were getting as much as 20 percent of the gross sales from their T-shirts and any other assorted memorabilia.

As I left the office that day, I noticed Thomas Rockart Jr.'s smile still hadn't changed. His expressions were so rigidly precise that he seemed to be a walking portrait; a mobile companion to the one that hung in his office. In following visits to his office, I would discover that the fireplace was gas-activated, the spines of the intimidating classics lining the wall were merely shells devoid of pages, and the fish in the tank had to be replaced every other week because they kept dying.

But all I knew that first day was that I had taken yet another step toward becoming the World Wrestling Organization Heavyweight Champion.

7

BLINKING HARD

Arms flail over the metal barriers, pro-viding a tentacular display in the gaps between red-shirted security guards. They stand with their backs to me so they can have a better view of potential trouble in the crowd. Everyone's role is so clear. The fans rep-resent the possibility of riotous behavior, and the guards are supposed to make sure fan behavior doesn't go too far.

What is my role? Catalyst? Prop? The answer comes from the ring announcer's diaphragm: "From Chicago, Illinois . . ." The pitch of his tone changing with the enun-ciation of the words. ". . . Weighing two hundred and twenty-eight pounds . . ." His voice peaking then receding like a patient wave. ". . . Here is the challenger . . ." Mounting and ready to explode: "Mister Michael Harding!"

My heart hammers against the chasm between the hero that name is supposed to represent and the enigma that I am. The crowd finds a reservoir of noise and unleashes it into the night with fierce abandonment. Their growing response makes me light-headed. I reach over the ropes of the mini-ring and try to touch some of the extended hands. They are too far away. I lean over the ropes, growing more desperate, until I am almost falling out. But the distance between the hands and the mini-ring's ropes is still too far.

The canvas beneath me jerks. I grab on to the ropes and fall back into the ring as the motor sputters. The miniature ring stalls. My theme music blares on. Hands gesture on both sides of the aisle, bidding me to come and touch them.

I stand on my elevated island, stranded.

My tenure with the WWO was due to begin in two weeks. When I went to the Mid-South Coliseum the next day, Mickey, the club-footed guard at the door, said Rampart had left word that he needed to speak with me.

"Have a good time in New York?" Rampart asked in greeting after I had knocked on the door of his dressing room.

"You heard, huh?" I asked, only mildly surprised.

"When it comes to pro wrestling, not too much goes on without my knowledge." He spat on the floor as if to accentuate his point.

"I start in two weeks," I said. "That's fair."

He leaned back and regarded me with a stare of careful scrutiny. "I put a lot into promoting you, Michael," he said.

"I'm still Wildman," I snapped sharply, "for two more weeks."

"Sure, Wildman, whatever you say."

――――――――

"Does this mean you're going to have a normal hairstyle?" was my mother's first reaction when I told her that I had just signed to the World Wrestling Organization.

"Jesus, Mom." I sighed into the phone. "This is the big time here. What if I told you I had just gotten a job with . . ." I struggled to come up with the name of a financial entity of comparative stature, but couldn't recall one. "Kodak Incorporated," I finally said. Kodak had a large plant on the highway that ran between Nashville and Memphis.

"Well, kiddo, I'd be pleased that Kodak would make you get a hairstyle that made you look human," she said. "Is your name still going to be Wildman?"

"I don't know," I said. "They may want something different."

"Just plain old Michael isn't outrageous enough, I suppose." She sighed.

"Fuck Michael," I snapped, reacting with the abruptness Wildman always drew upon when attacked.

A hostile silence followed. "Goodbye, Wildman," she said before hanging up.

Shawna was also curious about my future identity.

"The WWO is known as the land of the gimmick, you know." She chided, "Maybe you can come down to the ring with a pallet and a brush and be an artist. I can see it now, "Portrait of the Artist as a Young Professional Wrestler.'"

"Do you think that's funny?" I snapped.

"I was joking and you know it. Don't pull one of your Wildman roid rages on me," she snapped back. I relaxed.

"You always call me on them," I said.

"Someone's gotta keep you in line."

"Maybe you can be my valet. That can be my gimmick."

"Chuck and Mimi already have that one tied up, my dear."

"You can be my long distance valet."

"Persistent little fucker, aren't you?" She laughed.

"Is that bad?"

"It's fine. But you haven't even seen me for a year. For all you know I have a hairstyle like yours now."

"Why don't I come see you and find out?" I asked.

I had sprinkled in hints of a possible visit during more than a few of our phone conversations over the past year. The response was always a prolonged silence on her end, followed by a change of subject in a manner as subtle as a flying elbow off the top rope. This time, after four seconds of listening to the long distance connection purr noiselessly, I heard her say: "Your artwork's getting better."

I had recently sent her, in addition to sketches of the sunset, a sketch depicting a field of faces whose only features were wailing mouths.

"Don't try and flatter me to change the subject," I said, pleased by her critique.

"You know me better than that."

"Do I?" I asked.

"I should hope so!"

I hung up that night feeling the same way I always did after a conversation with Shawna: both confused and exhilarated.

————————

I had been a bit hesitant to tell B.J. how much I was making. It wasn't a million dollars, but it was a hell of a lot more than seventy-five dollars a night. Five days before I was due to leave for the WWO, he and I spent a night drinking on my patio. By one in the morning all aches had ceased and we were laughing about all our early matches back in southern California, how green we were back then, how we had smuggled steroids in from Tijuana. "You're gonna be able to afford the good stuff now, huh?" he said, his tone curious. I knew what he was asking so I told him.

He whistled. "Not bad, man," he said, laughing. "Not bad for a guy with an orange mohawk."

Both of us belched out laughter. "You'll be up there soon, brother," I said. "I'll put in a good word—"

"I talked to my dad the other night. The night you got back from New York," B.J. said. "He said that if I didn't make a million dollars as a pro wrestler, I could do it as something else. Said he had no problem with that. Said he had no problem with me never making a million as long as I was working hard at something I loved."

"You're going back, huh?" I asked reluctantly, not wanting to hear him admit it.

"I miss Terri, man," he said with a sigh.

"You could always have her move out here."

"She's a California girl. And I can see it now. A mixed-race couple in Memphis. Shit, we get enough dirty looks in southern California, and this town is a few hundred years behind L.A. Know what I mean?" I nodded. "'Sides," he went on, "I don't . . . I don't love this shit like you do. The only reason I've stuck it out this long is you were here."

I looked around at the crumpled beer cans scattered at our feet like reject pieces of a puzzle. "Quittin' the business, huh?" I asked, bracing myself for the answer.

It came with another sigh and a nod. "Looks that way."

"I'm gonna miss you," I said.

He nodded. "Me too," he mumbled into his bottle. Then he shook himself a little. "You just be sure and tell Ricky Witherspoon hello for me. All right, Wildman?"

"Sure thing." I nodded. B.J. got up. "You really love her, huh?" I said, not looking at him.

"Yeah," he sighed, "I really do. Took me bein' away from her this long to figure out how much she means to me. More than a million dollars, for sure."

My eyes didn't move. Neither did B.J.'s shadow, its shape draped across the ground before the dim porch light. "You ever been in love?" His voice scratched the moist air.

"Only with wrestling," I replied automatically.

His shadow shifted slightly. "See you in the morning." Then it was gone.

"'Night," I said to the concrete, its surface now absent of darkness. But there were still all the beer cans. I got up and made it my mission to capture them all. I collected them quickly, crushing each one very carefully before stuffing it into the empty box. Their sides split open and leaked stale beer; precious aluminum corpses. With all but one accounted for, I looked around for many seconds before realizing it was in my hand, still half-full. I downed it, crushed it, and put it in the box.

I stared at the box full of empty beer cans for a long time until I realized I was crying. All it was was a box of empty beer cans. I wanted it to be more. A casket of dead soldiers, a cachet of rare jewels, anything rare and holy. But it was a box of beer cans that would be recycled and bought and recycled again until one day they would simply be thrown away and buried somewhere deep in the earth or burned. I dropped the box and hurried inside, where I took a Valium and passed out.

The next morning I couldn't really recall the feelings of the past night. No matter, I didn't have time to worry about them. In four days, I had to be ready to face the WWO.

"Crusher Crews" was a living legend, known throughout the pro wrestling business as the last of the true mercenaries. Both the WWO and ICW wanted him, but he sneered at the idea of selling out and staying in any one territory for too long. He wrestled independently, going wherever the dollar was highest, and in the process acquiring a reputation for brawls with fans and fellow wrestlers as well as for his extraordinarily bloody matches. Throughout locker rooms across the world, wrestlers spoke in awed tones about the time Crews had once wrestled a bear on a card in the Pacific Northwest, beating the animal in less than three minutes. Some stories had him choking the bear into submission while others gave credit to his softball-sized fists, which they said he had used to pummel the bear's face in. All versions ended with tearing the unconscious bear's head off and parading around the ring with it impaled on a sharpened cedar branch.

The night after my talk with B.J., I pulled into the parking lot of Mid-South Coliseum and was jarred by the marquee's message of: *Tonight: Special Appearance of Crusher Crews vs. Wandering Wildman in a Steel Cage.* Alarm ripped through my body. I tracked down Rampart in his dressing room.

"I'm supposed to be wrestling Jesse James tonight," I told Rampart. "What gives?"

"Crews was coming through," Rampart said with a shrug. "He wanted to wrestle. I figured it would be a good experience for you."

"Experience?" I shouted. "For what, a prison riot? The guy never sells a move, and you want me to go into a *cage* with him?"

"You still work for me," Rampart smiled, "and I'm the booker. That clear?"

"As a fuckin' bell," I snarled. Wildman was taking

over. I stomped into the hallway where I collided with none other than Crusher Crews.

"Watch it!" he shouted, glaring down at me as though I were something distasteful he had just stepped in. He was at least 6'5" with the kind of frame that could fill an entire doorway. His shoulders and chest thrust out from his body like the head of a hammer. Stringy black hair fell back from a forehead littered with long jagged scars from razors, beer bottles, and (if one particular rumor was to be believed) a restaurant plate glass window through which he had thrust his head when he was told the restaurant was closed.

This creature appeared very capable of ripping a bear's head from its shoulders. I found myself scanning his body for scars which might belong to a bear claw. "Mister . . . Mister Crews." I extended my hand. He glanced at it with flickering disgust. "I'm Wildman." I coughed and found the rough tone I was looking for. "Wandering Wildman," I repeated.

"You're the punk that's goin' to WWO, huh?" he sneered, "Rockart's a fag. Logan's a fag. They're all fags up there. They must be lookin' for some young boys to molest."

With that, he stalked into Rampart's dressing room and slammed the door. I went into the other dressing room and sat, pressing my back against the two walls meeting just behind me.

As the time for my match approached, Jesse came by and kneeled down beside me as I laced my boots. "Hey, Wildman," he said quietly, "be careful out there."

"Yeah," I snarled, trying to get into character, "I can handle Crews."

"I shouldn't be tellin' ya this . . ." He sighed, speaking with a quiet urgency. "But this has happened before. There was this young dude once . . . Pud Gatorbear . . . Indian gimmick. Rampart gave him a real nice push. Six months later, Gatorbear announced he was goin' to Japan. Rampart got a little pissed."

"Rampart sounds like he's got some attachment issues," I commented.

"Uh . . . yeah," Jesse replied blankly. "So, he brings in Crews and sends the kid against him in a dog collar match. He tells Crews that Gatorbear's gonna go over. That pissed Crews off."

"I'll bet."

"So Crews broke both Gatorbear's arms, then laid down in the middle of the ring and pulled the kid on top of 'im for a three-count," Johnny said.

"Fuck this." I launched up with my boots still untied. I grabbed the torn straitjacket that I wore to the ring and threw it on. The mirror on the wall featured a jagged crack in it, and I positioned my face safely away from it so I could have a clear uninterrupted reflection of my snarl. "I'm the Wandering Wildman," I reassured myself.

When I barged into Rampart's dressing room, he was in the process of shaving his forearms. "What the hell?" he yelled. "You never come in here without knocking!"

"What the hell's the idea, Billy?" I shouted back. "You wanna see me crippled?"

He set the razor down as his lips wandered into a cocky grin. "What are you talking about?" he asked.

"Crews," I intoned. "You brought him in here to try and take me out, didn't you, asshole?"

"Just a second, you little prick." Rampart stood. "I made you what you are. That Wildman gimmick was *my* idea!"

"It's mine now!" I shot back.

"Like hell it is," he sneered. "You're already actin' like a WWO clown. If you're such a wildman, get in the fuckin' ring with Crews and stop whinin'."

"The guy wrestled a *bear*, for chrissakes!" I yelled, ashamed of my reference to a tale that was most likely untrue. "He's gonna shoot on me and try to tear me apart!"

"Then I suggest you shoot back," Rampart drawled. He picked up a towel and began wiping the shaving cream off his forearm. "Hard," he added.

My entire world broke into a maddening buzz. "Fuck you!" I howled, shoving him to the ground. The action felt good, igniting the same improbable wonder I had when I approached the ring before each match. I picked up the stool and slammed it against the mirror. Pieces of the room's reflection erupted and fell to the floor, revealing a patch of unpainted wall.

"Put down that fuckin' stool, you asshole!" Rampart's voice pulled at me. I turned to face him while I licked the saliva running down my chin. In his hand was a small dark pistol. He had shown it to me once before, bragging that he sometimes pulled it on overeager marks.

From the way he was aiming the gun at me, I was certain that he was going to pull the trigger. Fear spurred me in his direction. Before he could move, I snatched the gun out of his hand, then swung it back in an arc and slammed the handle into his left temple.

He collapsed to the floor in a moaning heap. There was a scraping behind me.

I whirled around and trained the gun on Crusher Crews, who was busy righting the stool. He sat down and gave me a bemused look. "Don't try anything," I growled. "I'm not afraid of you."

"Then why are you holdin' a gun on me?" he asked simply.

It seemed a fair enough question but I only snarled: "Don't try and stop me!"

"I won't," Crews drawled. "I know you're scared enough to shoot me." I felt more eyes from the doorway and saw that several of the wrestlers had gathered there. Crews had insulted Wildman in front of all of them.

Pull the fuckin' trigger and take this asshole off the earth! Wildman screamed.

For a terrifying instant my finger tightened sharply. Then a wave of fear consumed my body like a fever, and I snapped the gun down to my side. All the guys at the door backed away hurriedly as I charged out of the dressing room. The hallway went by in a blur, and then I was outside in the parking lot. A swell of cheers cascaded into the humid night through the walls of the arena. There was a winner being announced, but I couldn't decipher the name. I pointed the gun in the air, closed my eyes, and pulled the trigger.

All that resulted was a sharp momentary click. I opened my eyes and regarded the empty barrel of the gun in amazement. After a minute or so, a door slammed behind me. I looked over, feeling a dull certainty that it would be Crews brandishing a bloody bear's head on a stick. B.J., his hair matted with sweat, rushed up with my duffel bag in hand. "I heard what happened," he panted. "They told me about it as soon as I came backstage."

"Forget it," I croaked. "I'm outta here."

"So am I, doc," he laughed. "Rampart knows we're buddies. He'd try and fuck me over to get revenge for you cracking him."

"I'm sorry," I said.

"Damn," he said, grinning. "Did you really clock him over the head with that thing?" He pointed at my hand. I looked down and was surprised to see I was still holding onto the pistol.

"Yeah," I replied, then hurled the thing into a pool of darkness just beyond the marquee's dull blaze.

"Damn," he repeated wistfully.

"I've gotta get outta here." I winced, blinking back tears.

"We better take my car," B.J. suggested. "Rampart was talking about going to the cops. And he knows what your car looks like."

"He knows your car too."

"He didn't see me leave, though. It'll take him a little while to figure out I'm gone."

Thirty seconds later we were pulling out of the parking lot in B.J.'s car. We drove in silence as he sped along the road that would lead us back to Tower 99.

"I'm quitting," I blurted out.

"Duh," he said, laughing, "but you gave Rampart something to remember, the cocky litt—"

"I'm quitting wrestling," I announced. "Period."

These words were flung out with defiance. A silence

followed, during which every bump and rattle became unsteady pulses. I glanced over at B.J.'s impassive face. I knew I wanted a response, but I wasn't sure what kind.

It came. "Whatever it is . . . ," he said, "if you quit now, you're gonna let it win."

"Let *what* win?"

"You know what." He smiled, perhaps to put me at ease, "You've got something. I don't know why you do the things you do. Touch yourself and what not. Tap things. But whatever it is, it's gone away since you've come here."

A bewildered shame invaded my chest and soon spread to my forehead. The only time B.J. had pointed out my habit to me was during that one workout, a year ago, in southern California. But he had obviously been watching me throughout our time spent together. How many others had noticed and never said anything? Had Shawna?

Probably. People rarely reveal all they know.

B.J. was staring at me now. His eyes held a relief I wanted to share. I turned to the houses and mailboxes hurtling by. I tried to imagine who they belonged to and what their families did every year at holidays or whatever, but they were going too fast and I eventually surrendered to a gentle weariness. I was tired enough to be honest.

"It's still there," I told B.J. "It's like I've got this thing inside me—inside my own body. Myself. It'll tell me to touch this or that. It'll tell me to look at things a certain way. But when I'm in the ring, when I'm someone else, it's got no power."

B.J. stopped at a light and turned to me. "That is a fucking trip," he said. Then he started laughing, but quickly stopped himself. "Sorry," he said, "but—"

"It's all right. I know it sounds silly—"

"Don't ever say that. It sounds *real*. And when something like that is really happening, it's not silly. I'm sorry for laughing."

"B.J." I swallowed. "B.J., I was so fuckin' scared tonight. I'm still scared. What the hell am I doing going to the WWO? I can't—"

"Bullshit," B.J. spat out, putting the car in motion. We drove in silence until he turned right on to our street. He stopped the car abruptly. A police car sat parked in front of the Tower 99 front entrance. "Wonder who they're looking for?" B.J. sighed, his face deadpan. We cruised slowly past the car, and from my slouched position I could see it was empty.

"Probably inside waiting to beat the shit out of me," I said grimly.

B.J. stopped the car. "If you're gonna quit, you might as well do it now, doc," he said.

"What're you talking about?"

He hit the horn. The blasts hammered the night, attacking the still darkness of the street so arrogantly that they might as well have been the preceding notes to a cavalry charge. Even the stars seemed to dim in response to the disturbance. My mouth tried to form words: "Wha're yu—"

"What's it gonna be, Mike?" he asked in a sing-song manner. "You gonna strap on a set of balls and hit the WWO, or are we gonna end it right here?"

He mashed the horn again. In a matter of seconds four cops would be storming out of there. The police car itself was tingling ominously only six feet away from us. A flash of movement to my right made my heart jump. It was an old man walking a dog.

"I've got the Wandering Wildman down here, officers!" B.J. shouted at our building. The street was suddenly alive with motion. Leaves chuckled in wind, electric wires bulged on the verge of explosion, and shapes spun in and out of Tower 99's windows.

"Damn it, let's go!" I shouted at B.J. "I'll go to WWO! I'll go, all right?"

"You promise?" B.J. demanded, shifting his voice low.

"Yes, I promise! I swear to—"

B.J. was already pulling away. I exhaled but still watched anxiously as Tower 99 and the police car were sucked deeper and deeper into the rearview mirror until B.J. turned the corner. Then the mirror blinked, and our old street was replaced by another.

"Well, it was nice to get that settled," B.J. said, smiling.

I shook my head at him. "I think *you're* the one that's nuts, brother."

"Fuck it," B.J. said, laughing. He seemed happier than he had been in weeks. "What do we have back there?" he asked.

After thinking about it for several seconds, I joined in B.J.'s laughter. The truth was I had nothing back there. Though I had purchased numerous decorative additions for my costume I wore to the ring as Wandering Wildman, I hadn't accumulated one piece

of furniture to add to the basic furnishings the apartment had come with. The only things I brought into
that apartment were wrestling magazines, bottles of
Valium, and beer. I either ate on the road or had take-
out delivered once a week. The oven and stove were as
clean as the day I moved in; I had wandered through
that apartment like a displaced ghost.

"Nothing," I answered B.J, "nothing really."

"All I got are some pictures of Terri and stuff.
Since I'm gonna be seeing her in person, they're not
that important anymore." B.J. shrugged. "So let's get
outta this state before Rampart has us lynched. And
remember," he added, "a promise is a promise."

"I know," I said, squeezing my forearm even
though I knew B.J. was watching, "I'm going. I'm
going to the WWO."

As we entered Arkansas I tried to focus on the rice
fields I knew surrounded us, but the sun had set
hours ago and taken all light with it. All I could see
whipping by outside the window was an untraceable
darkness similar to that which Motley Mick Starr had
seen in the desert with Shawna.

———————

I awoke with a start. As usual, my body's many aches
cried out immediately. I fumbled in my wrestling bag
and popped two Valium. I swallowed them without
water, and only after ten seconds was I able to gaze at
the small portable clock B.J. had taped to his dash-
board. I squinted the numbers into gradual focus:
8:07.

I got out of the car and inhaled; the crisp country air bit my lungs.

We were parked at a roadside diner. Fields of pleasant green occupied all the available land around us, turning the parking lot into an island of exotic gravel. The assorted pick-up trucks in the lot boasted Arkansas license plates. I heard B.J. moan from inside the car. "Lordy," he exclaimed, "I forgot how miserable sleeping in a car can be."

"I forgot how miserable that damn passenger seat can be," I groaned.

"Quit your bitchin' and shoot me a Valium," he said with a laugh.

We straggled into the diner, which was packed with truckers and several people clad in hunting fatigues guzzling coffee and eggs. B.J. and I each downed a Sunrise Plate Special of grits, eggs, sausage, and grease. Then, with B.J.'s anxious eyes following me, I shuffled over to the pay phone on the back wall. Just above the phone was a stuffed owl, its wings flared, looking ready to pounce.

I placed a call to WWO corporate offices and went through two secretaries and a head of promotion before finally getting to Thomas Rockart Jr. "Michael, where are you?" he asked cheerfully.

"Somewhere in Arkansas, I think," I said. "Listen, there's been a slight change. I've left the SWA earlier than I thought."

"Hey, terrific," Rockart said. "We've got a show in Kansas City tonight. Think you can make it?"

"I don't know," I said. "I don't have a car."

Rockart laughed. "What are you, on the run or something?" he asked. My stomach issued a sour rumbling as it did battle with the Sunrise Special I had just inhaled.

"Well," I mumbled, "there may be assault charges pending." After hearing my brief rundown of the story he broke into howling laughter.

"Great job, Michael!" he exclaimed. "That fucking Rampart's known for being an asshole. About time somebody laid him out. With that kind of aggressiveness, you'll do fine with Staffer. Just fine."

After a few more pleasantries, I hung up the phone. The owl's body was still there, poised eternally for attack.

————————

What had happened to everyone? To Shane Stratford, Hal, Aries, and all the rest? The only person from southern California B.J. spoke to since arriving in Tennessee was Terri. I had contact with no one in California, and to my mother only during a few calls that interrupted months of non-communication. All the people in my past other than Shawna and B.J. had fallen away, and my lack of genuine concern baffled me. I never even called the landlord of my apartment in San Bernardino. For all I knew my belongings had been donated to a Salvation Army. Was someone sleeping on my former wrestling pillow? Thousands and thousands of faces swam before me joined by a current of screams for something that wasn't even real; did it make their screams worthless? What about the two girls who once paid five dollars to have their picture taken with me? Did they still think I was worth something? Where would that picture end up? Kept in a trunk somewhere safe with other memories of an unreclaimable youth or as just another piece to discard one day during a disposal of fan magazines and other indulgences from teenage years?

These thoughts battered at my slippery hold on sleep before finally loosening it completely and pitching me into a free-fall toward consciousness. The last image I glimpsed in sleep was of the latest picture I had sent Shawna, the one which featured thousands of screaming mouths. I awoke remembering the one thing I had left behind in the apartment I would never set foot in again. My drawing supplies were tucked in the upper shelf of the closet, which was the same place I had hidden pornographic material when I was in high school.

B.J. was pulling into the parking lot of Kansas City Memorial Stadium. He pulled up to the curb at the rear tunnel, behind a semi bearing the silver-lettered logo of the World Wrestling Organization.

We remained silent as the sun flirted with an opening in the clouds, casting intermittent glares on the windshield. "Been a hell of a ride, hasn't it?" I offered.

"You're in for another one," he said. "You need me to be here tonight?" he asked.

"No," I said. "I'll be all right."

"No backing out now, doc," he warned. "You promised, remember?"

"Under extreme duress." I grinned.

"Whatever works."

"Thanks, B.J.," I said, "for everything."

We clasped hands. Our eyes gently grew closer, a

pair of approaching reflections. This imperceptible movement was stopped only when our foreheads touched. This contact was enough. His irises like green planets. Maybe mine appeared the same way to him. Other people's eyes always have a certain measure of mystery simply because of our inability to possess them.

"My first and last head-butt," he murmured. We both started laughing. It was right that the only head-butt of his life take place out of the ring, away from the sight of any mark.

"Say hey to Terri for me," I told him as I got out of the car.

"Will do," he called. "Keep in touch."

I stood there, watching B.J.'s car swim across the parking lot's empty rows. My dirt-infested Chevy was back in Tennessee, gone for good. To hell with it. I turned and looked around.

Kansas City jutted up around me. Its buildings wide blocklike Herculean creatures paralyzed in their own steel and rock. The stadium looming over me was no exception. Its pillars looked tall and strong enough to hold up the sky. After a few minutes, I felt as good a hold of my bearings as I was going to get so I started walking toward the loading tunnel.

———————

The first time I met "Hippo" Haleberg he was in the process of stuffing a Twinkie into his mouth. "Houdimf?" he asked, shaking my hand and chewing while I glanced around the backstage area. Pipes were dripping onto the floor, forming small puddles of multi-colored liquid. I wondered idly if it was gasoline or just water from the Kansas City sewer system.

Once Hippo swallowed, he introduced himself more formally. He had been a wrestler some twenty years ago, and now worked in an executive position. He had possessed a stocky bullish frame when wrestling five nights a week, but the intervening years had turned most of what had once passed as solid fat into noticeably loose fat. His jowls sagged down to the collar of the Hawaiian shirt he wore. Perhaps he felt loose-fitting attire could camouflage his bloated stomach, but it was clear at a glance that this man was a prime risk for a coronary.

"You're Michael Harding, right?" he asked, pushing his glasses back against his sweaty brow. "Good to have you on board." His voice became lower. "We'll put you in with Staffer tonight. Don't do anything heavy. Just feel him out."

"Right," I nodded, "about my gimmick—"

"Worry about it later." Hippo waved his half-eaten Twinkie like a magic wand. "We'll just intro you as Michael Harding. Okay?"

I was still nodding as a tall, good-looking man in a tan suit glided over. "Hi there," he said with an excessively cheerful air. "You must be new." His eyes roamed my body, and I realized who this was. *Rob Robertson.* The guy who Allah had referred to as the "buggerer" who tried to molest young wrestlers and ring-boys. "You a face or a heel?" he cooed.

"I can work both ways," I stammered, then flushed red as he responded with delirious laughter. "I'm married," I announced.

"Jesus, Rob." Hippo pounded him on the shoulder. "This is the one who's gonna wrestle Staffer."

"Oh!" Robertson exclaimed. "You must be a hell of a shooter."

"Yeah," I growled halfheartedly. A well-muscled man with carefully groomed black hair swooped out of a dressing room and raised an eyebrow at Rob. Both of Rob's trimmed eyebrows jumped up in response. I recognized the man as a jobber for the WWO who went by the name of Nerve Glandon. Rob turned back to me. "Nice meeting you. Good luck tonight." The last three words carried a degree of gravity. Then he bounded off and caught up with David. The two of them disappeared through a doorway.

Hippo Haleberg shook his head as he munched with absent savagery on the last of his Twinkie. "Donletimwuryu," he mumbled, then swallowed. "He's harmless," Hippo assured me, then asked: "You really married?"

"Not in a physical sense," I answered guardedly.

"Probably a good idea to let him think you are," he said with a sigh.

————————

By five o'clock that afternoon the dressing room was filled with wrestlers, several of whom I had watched on Saturday morning television just three years ago. There was "Big Jim" Pitbull, a tall black man whose thickened 255-pound body and tightly drawn face were tempered by surprisingly gentle eyes. He usually barked and growled during his interviews, but up close he carried an air of sophistication. His nose was buried in the "Money" section of *USA Today*. Right beside him was "Officer O'Malley," a man who had a chest like a bull and exuded an impenetrable countenance. O'Malley's real name was Walter Schwartz, and he had been in the business for about twenty years. After years of working the Caribbean and other rough territories, he had finally settled into the WWO before his body gave out completely and was working the Irish cop gimmick. To his right was "The Soultaker," a relative newcomer to the WWO who worked a gimmick as a zombie wandering the earth in search of souls to possess. He had introduced himself to me as Trevor, and was now in the process of applying the makeup that created his zombie pallor.

I stood in a corner, watching with dim wonder as they dressed into their various costumes and went over spots for the night. There was a pervading smell of baby oil in the room, and I saw many of them were slicking themselves down. I hesitantly returned the few cautious smiles and nods in my direction, breathing a sigh of relief when Chuck Beastie entered the dressing room and immediately came up to me and shook my hand with a raspy "How ya doin'?" This broke the ice, and a few more of the boys came over and introduced themselves. Sledge, a squat man with a perpetually red face and thin blonde hair trimmed in a crew-cut style, complimented me on decking Rampart.

"I didn't know the story traveled that fast," I marveled.

"In this business, there ain't too many secrets," he chuckled, pulling on a plain gray shirt. His gimmick was that he was an ex-con, and he and O'Malley were currently in a heated feud.

When they found out I was scheduled to wrestle Staffer, a commiserating exhalation went around the room. "Shoot hard," Ricky "The Billion Dollar Baby" Witherspoon, a shaggy blonde-haired guy with a slight limp, informed me. I nodded weakly, remembering that as the same advice I had gotten from Rampart last night.

Witherspoon (whose real name was Richard Turkin) and I talked for a while. He had only been with the company for three months, and I got the feeling he felt as alien as I did. He had entered the dressing room wearing torn jeans and a Gold's Gym tank top, but his costume was a black suit strewn with sequins that jumped to life every time he moved.

I was too nervous to mention his generosity to B.J.'s father and his subsequent influence on B.J. I would do it later, I told myself. The next night or the next . . . my hands shook a little as I rubbed and flexed my pectorals to a fixed rhythm. Wildman was gone, last seen standing alone outside an arena in Memphis with an unloaded gun in his hand.

Staffer sauntered into the dressing room at about 5:45. He exchanged a few nods with the regulars, then staked out a mirror and began examining himself. I watched him out of the corner of my eye. Shaggy dark hair spilled over his forehead, stopping just over a crooked nose that looked to have been broken several times. His forehead was a rough map of scar tissue. I followed the movement of his left hand as he wound tape around his right knuckles. He was muttering to himself. Suddenly his voice shot up. "Hey, needle dick," he snarled at the mirror, "you gonna fuckin' propose or somethin'?"

It wasn't until everyone in the locker room had shifted in my direction that I realized he was talking to me. Determinedly swallowing my pride, I walked over to him. "We're working together tonight," I said, thankful my voice wasn't shaking.

I waited for a response, acutely aware that everyone in the now silent dressing room was watching us. "Do you want to go over some spots or something?" I asked.

"Spots!" he shouted, making me jump back. "We don't need any fucking spots!" he hollered. "I'm going over! That's all you need to know." He tore off the tape and smacked his well-taped fist into the beefy palm of his left hand. "That's all you need to know," he insisted in a sing-song rhythm.

I walked back to my corner and sat down in bewilderment. Chuck had already disappeared into his private dressing quarters with Mimi. Top wrestlers like him and Sonny Logan had their own dressing rooms, but the rest of us were packed into one. I spent the next two hours busying myself with tying and untying my boots and trying to pretend I didn't notice the other guys looking at me and talking amongst themselves.

When Rob Robertson stuck his head in the door and announced "Staffer and Michael, you're up," Staffer, clad in his customary costume of a hockey jersey and long tights, snagged his goalie's mask from the floor and stalked out of the dressing room. I followed, clad in plain blue trunks I had borrowed from Ricky Witherspoon. They were a size too big for me and I had

had to use a safety pin to get them to stay up around my waist. As I walked by my fellow wrestlers, each of them became engrossed in the floor.

Robertson met us by the red curtain that separated our backstage area from the arena. "All right, boys. Ten minutes max. Staffer, you're goin' over. Make it a cheap victory—"

"No way," Staffer barked. "This kid's doin' a clean job." He glared at me as though the idea for a cheap victory had been mine.

"This kid's gonna be feudin' with you for the next coupla months as soon as he arranges a gimmick with the big guy," Robertson said, leaving me to wonder if he was talking about Thomas Rockart Jr. or God, "so you better get used to workin' with him."

"Shit, ya send me dese fuckin' greenies and expect me to *work* with them?" Staffer demanded. Robertson's only response was to sigh and gaze at me helplessly before retreating into the darker recesses of the backstage area.

"Seems like Rob likes you, greenie," Staffer sneered. "Young kid like you, what'd you do, suck dick to get here?"

"Fuck you, man," I said in a snarl corrupted by a nervous flutter. Staffer smiled widely enough to reveal a gap where his two front teeth should have been. "I've wrestled in the South for sixteen months," I continued.

"Well, well," he said, still smiling, "we'll see how much those good ole boys taught you." He warped the last of his sentence into a slurred Southern tone that, combined with his Canadian accent, made him sound like a stoned Boss Hog.

"Ladies and gentlemen," the ring announcer's voice filtered through the curtain, "Introducing . . . from Chicago, Illinois . . ."

Hippo's head poked through the curtain. "Lesgo Michael," he said while chewing something. "Jog when you go down the aisle. Remember, you're young, fulluvinurgy."

Staffer lowered his face mask and uttered: "Shoot."

Then came the ring announcer's mechanically enhanced declaration: "Michael Harding!"

As I jogged down to the ring, a confused murmur arose from the crowd. Their lack of interest made me feel invisible. By the time I hit the ring, I was running. Once inside there was no stopping my hands as they groped my entire body. Thighs, arms, chest; all were flexed and touched by my roaming hands. "You nervous, kid?" the referee asked, smiling just a little.

I shook my head. Then Staffer was announced, and he stormed down the aisle to a passionate chorus of boos and jeers and assorted cries of "Fuck Canada!" Staffer lunged into the ring and kept charging. His body slammed into mine, sending me in an unprepared heap between the second and third rope. I sprawled onto the padded area next to the ring and was pushing myself up when a sharp pain cut across my back. The blow sent my face back down against the thin ringside padding. I glanced up and saw Staffer raising his hockey stick. I scrambled forward, but he connected once again. My body curled itself into a ball. Through labored breathing, I could hear laughter from the fans at ringside. I hated them. I hated Staffer. But for myself I held a unique loathing. I felt smeared with shit; I wanted to crawl out of my own skin and leave it beneath the ring like a used piece of toilet paper.

The bell burst into methodic repetitive tolling. I shrieked as the stick collided once again with the small of my back. Several fans at ringside howled and imitated my cry. I turned over and saw Staffer standing before the crowd with his stick raised like a trophy.

I began to unfurl with the hope of scrambling back into the ring, but he quickly turned back and fired another swing at my head, which I avoided only by rolling completely under the ring. Staffer's laughter trailed behind, settling in my ears as I lay there in the darkness. I sneezed to expel the dust tickling my nose. My eyes grew moist, and I stubbornly reassured myself this too was from the dust.

The referee eventually got Staffer on his way back to the locker room. I remained under the ring, still sneezing and swatting at my eyes while digesting the cheer that the crowd gave Staffer. *Nothing's changed,* I thought, *crowds love violence.* The referee's head poked between the draping. "You all right, son?" he asked.

"Yeah," I croaked, "I think."

I emerged from underneath the ring, and the arena exploded with hoots and laughter. Briefly I thought of the jeering response my English class had given me when I had announced that I wanted to be a pro wrestler. All the achievement of my goal had brought me was 1,000 times more ridicule.

Not a whole lot to show for two years' work.

As we approached the curtain, I got up the guts to pull my eyes from the floor and regard a few faces in the audience. "You suck!" a boy about twelve shouted at me.

"I hear there's job openings at McDonald's!" a voice bellowed from my right.

"Fuck you," I whispered.

"What?" the referee whispered back.

"I'm gonna kill them."

"Fuck 'em," the referee murmured. "They're just marks."

But I wasn't referring to just the fans. I was referring to everyone who had made me feel inferior and scoffed at what they considered a worthless dream. The faces of Max Egan and the four other kids who had first introduced me to my incompleteness floated before my burning eyes. *I'll show them,* I thought, *Goddammit I will. No matter what I have to do.*

———————

That night, in a motel on the interstate in the middle of Missouri, I popped two Valium and washed them down with tap water from the bathroom sink. Then I focused on my reflection. Hundreds of miles separated me from anything I had ever been connected with. I could become anything I wanted. A psychotic, a sexual pervert, a mild-mannered investment banker, a retired porn star who had been sold into the business by a junkie mother, anything at all. The people in the room next to mine or the next hotel or the next city would never know it.

I raised the blade in my left hand. Its steel exuded neither warmth nor coolness; gripped by my fingers it looked like an extension of myself. A nervous impulse surfaced, some scared voice urging these fingers to release the blade and touch my reflection. The reflection of a whole Michael Harding. The blade now caressing this reflection's forehead.

I recalled Rand Staffer's forehead, a map of criss-crossing scars. "Scars are good," Hal Duncan had once informed a young punk rookie named Muscular Mike Maple. "They're a symbol of dues paid."

I cut across flesh. For a few seconds there was nothing except a zipper of pain, high pitched and screaming. Then the flesh was eased open by blood. My hand was already in motion. Another cut. Then another. I imagined a million mosquitoes coming to drink this blood, proof of my existence. The wounds crossed one another like intersecting streams. Their output formed a river that washed down the bridge of my nose and over my eyes. I felt an unfocused longing to touch this blood, to make it real. But nothing was real anymore. Not even the taste gliding over my top lip and invading my mouth, a soupy oxygen-filled rust.

My bloody face hovered in the mirror. Michael Harding would never do anything like this.

Touch your reflection. Touch it.

I slowly undid my belt, looping it through the air like a lasso. A metal Coca-Cola belt buckle gave it substantial weight. I had bought it years ago because it reminded me of a title belt. Now I held it aloft for a second as though it were one, and in the next moment I whipped the buckle end out into the mirror. A crack split the mirror in five separate directions. Sections of glass tilted my reflection and offered pieces of my face to different angles of the bathroom's light.

I had the dream again that night. But after I pinned the masked man I was able to pull the mask from his head and finally see what had no doubt always been there: my own face staring back at me with wide lifeless eyes.

8

A few of the security guards temporarily surrender their scrutiny of the crowd to turn and find out why I haven't passed them yet. When they see the stalled ring, surprise and amusement infiltrate their impassive faces.

I climb out of the mini-ring and begin to navigate the rest of the way on foot. My hands reach out blindly and find others. "Go for it, Michael!" a voice manages to leap free from the chorus of thousands.

I am almost to the ring when I pause before a security guard who is blocking the view of a young girl. I snatch the red cap from the security guard's head and put it on my own. Both the guard and the girl stare at me. "I love you, Michael!" she screams.

"I love you back!" I tell her, then grab her hand and

kiss it. My chin leaves a small pool of sweat on her fingers. She screams again and brings the hand to her mouth, kissing it all over. Others are reaching out and touching my shoulders, biceps, and forearms. Their fingers explore eagerly, gliding over my skin's veneer of sweat. I look at the security guard, wink, then take off his cap and fling it out at the crowd. This elicits more whoops. I'm breaking the rules for them.

Only a few rows away from the ring area, I spot a tall thin man with a round moonlike face. He has a shock of hair so blond it is almost white. In his hands is a large coffee jar.

As I get closer he looks up and howls. I can't look away. Bits of tobacco, dark and rich like growing moss, infect his teeth. As I pass, he spits tobacco juice into the coffee jar but makes no move to throw it at me. He probably emptied it out when he tossed it all over Stud Hoss Mauler. I let my hand wander past his face and knock his glasses off. He yelps but by then I am already past him and circling the ring.

With any luck, his glasses will be crushed by someone's foot.

Tug Tyler's voice echoes inside me: "Be a champion for those people? Who needs it?"

———

"Bit off season, aren't you?" the portly clerk joked in response to my request for a hockey stick, goalie mask, and jersey.

"It's never off season for hockey, eh?" I said in a Canadian accent. I was on the outskirts of Des Moines, where the WWO was scheduled for that night. I had left the motel early that morning, having taped a one hundred dollar bill to the mirror. All they had as a record of my stay was a receipt with an unintelligible scribble for a signature.

I reached the Des Moines Municipal Auditorium at around four in the afternoon. Ricky Witherspoon and Jimmy "The Python" Jugular were already in the dressing room sipping beers. Jugular always carried a seven-foot python to the ring with him. The python's name was Choker, and Jugular would lay Choker across his opponents whenever he was victorious. When I walked in, Jugular and Witherspoon were lazily discussing how many "Chokers" there had actually been.

"They usually only last about a month," Jugular said with a shrug and began downing a beer. "Had one that lasted almost three. The fucker seemed to like gettin' stuffed in a bag and carted off to different cities in the back of a plane."

"How long has this one lasted?" I asked, causing both of them to glance up at me with surprise.

"Umm . . . about three weeks, I guess." Jugular threw a grin at a burlap sack in the corner. "Hear that, fucker?" he called tauntingly. "You only got about a week left."

"What's with the hockey stick?" Witherspoon asked me.

"I'm trying out a new gimmick tonight." I smiled.

"You turn Canadian overnight?" Witherspoon asked. I had applied a thick accent to the word "out."

"For this match I did," I told them. By then both were gaping uncomfortably at my forehead. It couldn't have been a pretty sight—swollen skin ballooned out over dried red slits. I turned and headed outside. I found Hippo Haleberg fiddling with the controls for the sound system with one hand while trying to balance a slice of grease-soaked pizza in the other. After I proposed the gimmick I wanted to adopt, he didn't seem too enthusiastic.

"A chameleon?" he asked, nibbling cautiously on his pizza. A moment later he cursed sharply and began fanning his tongue.

"Yep," I said and nodded, "I'm going to take on my opponent's personality, their speaking patterns—"

"Their gimmick," he concluded.

"Their gimmick," I confirmed, "and I'm gonna make it mine."

"I don't know . . ." He frowned.

"Let me try it for tonight at least, eh?" I smiled. He managed to swallow a careful bite of pizza.

"What do we introduce you as?" he asked, taking a bigger bite

"The Chameleon. From parts unknown. Weight unknown," I said. "The Chameleon."

"Chameleon, huh?" he mused, then tilted his head back as though noticing me for the first time. "Jesus, what the hell happened to you last night? Looks like your brain exploded."

"Part of the gimmick," I rumbled proudly. "Paying dues."

When I returned to the dressing room, I saw that Staffer had arrived. As I walked in, all conversation ceased momentarily before being resumed in an awkward rush. I went over to stand by Witherspoon and

Jugular. Staffer approached me with a guarded smirk. "What's up with the mask and stick, eh?" he asked.

"You'll see," I replied shortly.

"How's the back?" he asked.

I turned to face him. Either my glare or my freshly scarred forehead must have taken him aback because for a moment his mouth groped unsuccessfully for words. "Hell, kid," he finally allowed with a chuckle, "last night was just a little initiation."

"I'm not your fuckin' kid," I snapped back, "and from what I understand, you're an asshole all the time."

These words silenced the rest of the room. Staffer frowned, suddenly very aware of an audience. "So," he asked in a whiny mocking voice, "you wanna go over some spots?"

"Spots!" I yelled. "Yeah, I got a spot. I knock your ass out of this fucking sport, needle dick!" My Canadian accent on the "out" was thicker than Staffer's.

He frowned as everyone in the room fell into an excited shuffle. He turned and stalked back to his space. I changed into my jersey and waited for match time.

When I was announced, I backed out to the ring in case Staffer tried to Pearl-Harbor me. Sure enough, as I was halfway to the ring, I saw through the slits in my hockey mask that he was peeking out the curtain. I raised my stick and his masked face disappeared. It was like seeing my own head being enveloped by a red cloaked mirror.

Again people were unsure whether to boo or applaud for me, but this time I didn't care. I was a chameleon, able to stand motionless in the ring while the crowd buzzed in confusion. No need to touch or feel anything.

Staffer once again charged down the aisle as he was introduced, but then stopped and climbed carefully through the ropes. My legs twitched as I remained rooted in the center of the ring with my stick poised for battle. I could taste my own hot breath trapped in the mask.

Staffer approached me. The crowd's noise trickled through my ears as though it were coming from someone else's dream. Staffer reached out, pulled my mask forward, and let it snap back against my flesh. I didn't cry out. I did the same thing to him, and by the time he raised his stick, I was already swinging mine. The flat end hooked him in the rib cage. He grunted and bent over. I brought my stick down again, and this time he howled as the hard wood collided with the knuckles of his right hand. His stick fell, and I tossed mine away as well. I tore the mask off his head and hurled it away, then slammed my masked face into his nose. Through the crowd's flood of cheers came the sharp crack of a broken nose. I knew that a psychotic hockey player would live for sounds like this and true to form I felt my heart kicking ecstatically. So easy to act like this. As a chameleon, able to become anything I see. Nothing could touch me.

I whipped off my mask and tossed it away. Staffer was down on one knee, and I threw a forearm up under his chin. His head snapped back and the arena lights bore straight into his glazed unblinking eyes.

No mercy, put him out of the game—these words

blazed through my mind—*out of the game.* I shoved his wobbly form into the corner and unleashed three more short uppercuts against his jaw. I was ready to do this forever. After two or three more blows, Staffer's head went slack and sagged against his shoulder. Leaving him slumped against the turnbuckle, I backed up ten paces. The referee (the same one from the previous night) retreated to the side and made no move to stop me.

I bolted toward Staffer and jumped into a drop-kick, driving my two feet into the side of his left knee. The bone gave way with surprising ease, but the sound was sudden and a little frightening. A giant balloon bursting. This explosion flew into every corner of the arena, transforming the moderate crowd rumble into a unanimously excited *oooohhh.* If the sound of Staffer's knee breaking wasn't enough to please the fans, then no doubt his cries of agony were. As he lay on the canvas wailing, I stood on the second turnbuckle and glared out at the crowd. They roared their approval at The Chameleon, who had given someone a permanent injury in his very first match. I stared at their faces, feeling the familiar hatred from the night when Muscular Mike first bled in the ring at a rock-and-roll club in the San Fernando Valley. Yet now there was also a gap, an unreclaimable distance from the very people I once so desperately sought approval from. I looked with scorn upon this sea of marks—faces pathetically eager for something, anything, that would help draw them out of the everyday monotonous battle of their own lives.

The bell fired off a hollow call for order as the referee

waved frantically for a stretcher from the back. I
hopped out of the ring and strolled back to the curtain.

Backstage, several of the wrestlers congregated
around me. The general atmosphere was congratulatory;
most whispered to me that Staffer's comeuppance
had been a long time coming. Then the red curtain
parted hastily and a pair of anxious paramedics
wheeled Staffer back on a stretcher. The agony in his
moans excited me, drew me closer. In the next instant
I was overturning the stretcher and snarling at
Staffer's flailing form on the pavement: "I knocked
you out of the game, you needle-dicked fuck!" The
paramedics stood in frozen horror as Ricky
Witherspoon and The Soultaker each grabbed one of
my arms. A pair of hands clamped around my chest.
I glanced back and saw Rob Robertson's feverish
eyes. He was pulling me backward, pressing his body
against mine. I allowed myself to be guided away as
the paramedics scrambled to get Staffer back onto the
stretcher. Then I finally shook loose and shoved Rob
to the floor.

"I am The Chameleon!" I shouted. "Whatever you
give me out there is what you'll get in return!" I took a
deep breath and exhaled the line that would become my
trademark in all interviews thereafter: "When you face
The Chameleon, you face what you fear within yourself."

With this declaration, I turned and vaulted into the
hallway. Sonny Logan was coming out of his dressing
room. "How ya doin', Dream?" I said to him with the
same gruffly affectionate voice he had asked Michael
Harding that identical question six years ago.

His eyes were wary, but he offered a smile and took my extended hand. "Pretty good, brother. How about you?"

"Pretty good," I echoed, then strolled back to the dressing room as my future identities milled behind me, whispering uncertainly about both my gimmick and my sanity.

"I like the gimmick, Michael," Thomas Rockart Jr. told me two weeks later in his office atop the Crystal Ship. Outside the window, a gray day was pelting New York with rain. The drops buffeted the window silently, the glass was soundproof. "It's going over," he determined, leafing through some proof sheets of publicity stills that had been taken that morning in a studio downstairs.

The photographer had introduced himself as "Ivan, with an I," while breaking into giggles for no discernable reason. He was a man with huge shoulders and an immaculately trimmed five o'clock shadow. Though his hair was slicked back, it still managed to escape into unruly cowlicks.

Ivan became immediately distressed over what he termed my lack of identity. He had been forced to raid the "has-been closet," which contained costumes from now defunct gimmicks. "This was Super Ninja's," Ivan cooed, delicately admiring a black ninja suit dotted with chalk white Japanese symbols, "before he became Typhoon Witley. Now he wears a hideous plumber's outfit." Ivan permitted himself a brief shudder before casting a scrutinizing me. "This is your size," he concluded. Then he doused the outfit in black spray paint, effectively eliminating all traces of white.

True to his word, it fit perfectly, clinging to me like a thin film of sweat. He then stationed me against an all-black wall. "What kind of pose should I strike?" I asked him.

"You're The Chameleon, buddy," he grunted, suddenly all business as he fiddled with his camera. "I just shoot pics here."

I ended up crossing my arms over my heart and gazing at the lens with unrevealing eyes and tightly pressed lips. "Your eyes look a little whacked." Ivan frowned. "Can't you lighten 'em up a little? Make you look a little less nuts." But every time I tried to allow a bit of feeling in my eyes, they burned from the heat thrown off by the lights. "Jesus, you look like an alien," Ivan would protest, spurring me to once again barricade my eyes with an unfocused intensity.

"Just take the picture," I snapped. "I don't give a damn how crazy I look."

"Fucking wrestlers," Ivan mumbled, and began snapping away.

"These'll work." Thomas Rockart Jr. was nodding at the sheets. "You look a little insane, though. Aren't chameleons supposed to be . . ."

His voice trailed off as his eyes searched mine expectantly. I let the silence join the soundless rain falling outside. Then I coughed and suggested, "Chameleons mimic their environment. They aren't supposed to be anything. Except maybe a mirror. And aren't most marks a little nuts?" I added, trying to smile. He frowned.

"That's one of the myths the World Wrestling Organization is trying to dispel. Professional wrestling is family entertainment. After all," Rockart intoned, "families will always spend more on a night of entertainment than a group of drunken yahoos will. Kids sixteen and under are the ones who purchase the most T-shirts and souvenirs." He scrutinized the photos for another few seconds before nodding and announcing, "But these'll work. I can have Ivan touch up the eyes in development. Make 'em look more . . ." He regarded me. ". . . human." He was laughing as though he just discovered the punch line to a joke that had previously eluded him. Since his laughter seemed to be a cue, I joined him.

He set the pictures down. "This wasn't the only reason I asked you here today, Michael," he remarked with a fluent shift into a more promising tone, as though we were about to become co-conspirators in a grand scheme. "Doctors have ruled Staffer as unfit to wrestle for at least six months," he continued with his smile intact. "He's collecting on a policy from Lloyds of London."

Lloyds of London was an insurance company that issued policies that covered the physical attributes that celebrities deemed necessary for their continued success. These included movie stars' eyes, pianists' hands, models' lips, and also professional wrestlers' backs and knees. "He'll stay out for the full twelve months the policy is paying him, and his contract's up in nine." Without taking his eyes from mine, Rockart removed a yellow envelope from a drawer and slid it across the desk. "You saved this company the hundred thousand dollars it would've cost me to buy out his contract," he stated. "We take care of employees who help the company."

I resolutely reached across the desk, took the envelope, and pocketed it. Then we stood and shook hands. My grip matched the firmness of Rockart's.

As I drifted through the outer hallway, I thought about the first time I had heard the term *juice money* when B.J. and I had cut ourselves for an extra fifty bucks. What could this be considered? I hadn't just pretended to put someone out; I had really done it. *Blood money,* I mouthed to my reflection in a slanted mirror stationed just before the elevators. A young man stared back at me, a young man with a bonus in his pocket (ten thousand dollars in hundreds, I would discover back at my hotel room). A young man who had no need to touch his own reflection. So be it.

I did what I had to do, and I will continue to do so.

I felt the envelope tucked securely inside my jacket pocket, an excited buzz climbing into my temples. I was ready to ascend this very unique corporate ladder, where at the top waited not only the WWO World Heavyweight Championship but millions of dollars.

The timing was perfect; I was due to start a series of matches with Ricky "The Billion Dollar Baby" Witherspoon the night after next.

9

RICH MAN NOW

At ringside they are all on their feet. The only security here is provided by the waist-high metal barriers and two security guards seated at either end of the ring. Even the fans wearing T-shirts that bear the champion's name and logo reach out to try and touch me.

Four middle-aged men, their thinning hair matted back by sweat, are the only ones who jerk their hands away as I walk past. "You suck, Harding!" one of them shouts and gives me the finger. A dark stain lurks underneath the armpit of his halfway-unbuttoned white dress shirt. Two others, both in plain white T-shirts, begin to chant the champ's name. I just smile and move on. Next up is an elderly couple. They look embarrassed and I have a momentary suspicion that those guys are all brothers and these two are their parents.

"Good luck, son," the man, who appears shorter than his wife, advises me gravely.

"He needs more than luck!" shouts one of the T-shirt boys.

I pass by a group of three women in low-cut dresses who caress my arms and chest. One presses an object into my hand. Sharp ridges bite my palm. It's a hotel room key.

The items that people at ringside give wrestlers seem to be indigenous to their particular city. L.A. and New York fans usually pass vials of coke. Midwestern cities produce the most hotel room keys and phone numbers balled up inside panties. One night in Dallas someone handed me a small pill bottle that was filled with teeth. Backstage, we saw that some of the teeth were still coated with dried blood. We debated what it meant.

"Tooth fetish," someone offered.

"Edgar Allan Poe reader," Tug Tyler suggested.

"Psycho." I shook my head.

"Wrestling fan," Wild Joe Irwin said, and that settled the matter.

I threw the bottle away. I throw everything away that is handed to me at ringside. Most pro wrestlers do. Only an idiot would snort drugs given by some anonymous mark who could very well want you dead.

Drifting past a group of younger guys who high-five me, I let the room key slip from my hand.

By this time I've lost track of how many times my theme music has finished and restarted. But I recognize the notes that signal the climax. Time to head into the ring.

I climb the stairs and grip the top ring rope. It feels like a rubber snake in my hands. I lean down and step

*between the ropes. My foot catches on the second rope
and I almost slip flat on my face. I manage to recover a
semblance of balance, falling into the ring with a stum-
ble while my music peaks.*

Did other wrestlers, I wondered, have their own reasons
for choosing the gimmicks they used? I had already
noticed that all the WWO wrestlers called each other by
their gimmick names, just like in the SWA. Were gimmicks coined as arbitrarily as some porno stars make
up their stage names (their middle name first and the
name of the street they grew up on), or was a piece of
the wrestler's "legit" personality sewn into these masks
they threw at the audience? By piecing together the
identities of others in the WWO, I could emulate them
even more thoroughly while at the same time distract
myself from any thoughts about me. Since the only one
way I felt truly comfortable looking at something or
someone that closely was as a subject to be rendered in
black and white, I bought an array of sketching pencils
and an easel at a Manhattan art supply store the day
before I was set to fly to Denver for my first match with
Ricky Witherspoon.

Because my disposal of Staffer gave me immediate
respect from the other wrestlers, when I asked
Witherspoon if he would consider posing for a sketch he
looked at me strangely for only a brief moment before
shrugging and saying "sure."

This was on the afternoon before our match at
McNichol's Arena. I set up an easel down at the pool

area of the Denver Hilton as he settled into a lounge chair.

"Where'd you grow up?" I asked, choosing a pencil from the sketch kit.

"Midwest," he answered distractedly, closing his eyes against the sunlight.

"Chicago?" I prompted.

"Nah, Wisconsin," he drawled. "Can I just lay here like this?" He propped his head up and squinted at me. "You don't want me to pose or anything, right?"

"Just kick back. Close your eyes, whatever."

"All right," he said, leaning back and closing his eyes once more. I was already laying in the outline of his body. "Apple Creek, Wisconsin," he said with a sigh.

"Small town?"

"So small the census once forgot to put us on the state map," he said. "Us citizens of the town weren't even surprised. Just amused. All hundred and thirty-four of us."

"What was it like growing up there?"

"Well, we went to a high school about twenty miles away. Spent a lot of time cruising around, drinking beers, and listening to the Bear at ninety-five point nine." He chuckled and said, "Can't believe I still remember the frequency."

"Did you watch pro wrestling?"

He laughed. "I watched *Knots Landing* and *Dallas*. Seein' the way those people lived . . . it put me in awe. I mean I know they were actors and all, but still . . . the biggest event in our whole *county* was usually the Saturday afternoon high school football game. I was Kenosha High's running back," he added.

"You play ball in college?" I asked.

"Never went to college," he said, "wasn't good enough for a scholarship and we sure as hell couldn't afford it. My old man was a farmer and the market was shit. Still is."

"So you went into wrestling," I said.

"No." His eyelids tightened against a light breeze but remained closed. "I became an insurance salesman. The only reason I got into wrestling was because I was trying to sell some promoter a policy. His name was Harvey, and he had a group of wrestlers he traveled around with all over the Midwest. He saw how big I was and said he'd buy the policies if I agreed to wrestle for him whenever he came into town."

I traced the cherubic contour of his cheeks; their color was already deepening in the harsh afternoon light. While I searched for a pencil of proper thickness to record this, he continued, "So I took a few wrestling lessons from Harvey and started working whenever he got into town. Next thing I know, he's offerin' me forty bucks a night if I tour with his group. I go, 'Why not?' Nobody in the county had any money to buy insurance anyway. So I left with the tour. I remember the first time I went into Milwaukee. I was fucking amazed." He laughed. "I thought, this is just like *Dallas*! Shit . . . can you imagine getting all excited over a dirty little city like Mil-fuckin'-waukee?

"After a year of touring the Midwest, Harvey opened a promotion in Florida and made me the champion. I was wrestling with a football player gimmick back then. About a year later I went to another promotion out west. By that point I was makin' what at the time I considered pretty good money. Maybe a hundred a night, and I was happy as a pig in shit.

"But then Thomas contacted me, and two days later I flew into New York first class with a huge ol' limousine waiting to pick me up."

I grinned, recalling my identical introduction to the WWO and Thomas Rockart Jr. Although his eyes remained closed, Ricky matched my amused expression. "Yeah, I know," he acknowledged, "the WWO does that with everyone. But it was a big deal to me. First time I had ever been in a limousine. I pictured it like it was the opening of a television show. I felt like J.R. fuckin' Ewing. Then I went into the corporate offices and Thomas offered me a job and you bet your ass I jumped at it. When he asked if I had any idea for what my gimmick could be, I told him I had a great one.

"The original idea was to have a tycoon who had built himself up from nothing. But Thomas thought it would work better as a heel gimmick. So I made up Ricky Witherspoon, an oil baron from a rich family who believed he could buy anything . . . or any *one* in life. Thomas loved it. Those first few months, he gave me rolls of hundreds to pass out even when I was outside the ring. It would get me in the right frame of mind, he said. I was in heaven. Three years removed from rationin' toilet paper, and now I'm passing out hundreds wherever I go."

I started to ask about whether or not he remembered B.J.'s father, the limousine driver in L.A. he had tipped a hundred dollars, but his voice washed over my first hesitant words. "Money can make people do crazy things," Ricky Witherspoon said with a rising edge, the same one he used during on-camera interviews. "And why is that? Because money can change people's lives. Forever."

Trying to guide him away from his gimmick, I asked about his parents and their farm back in Kenosha. "They're still there," he said and confirmed with a curt nod, "tilling the soil, was how my father would put it. He said the land would always take care of us. Meanwhile, I was wearing jeans a size too small because we couldn't afford to buy new clothes. We . . ." He shook his head again, as though he were refusing to speak on a witness stand. But then the words came out haltingly. "There were times we couldn't afford soap . . . or shampoo. Christ . . ." He sighed with a resignation that made me expect him to break out into shudders underneath the July sun. "That's why I wanted Ricky Witherspoon to be an oil baron. The land had been fucking me over all my life. It owed me. It's like, yeah, Dad, the land takes care of some people. People that take oil from it. Not growing wheat and fucking corn.

"He's a good person, though," he added. "Both my parents are. In their way." He smiled blithely. "I bought them a new tractor last year," he said with a triumph that suggested he had won something. And perhaps he had. Rather than cut himself off from his parents and destroy his whole history in order to gain freedom from it, he was willing to merely recreate himself in the present and take a victory by default. The portrait was close to completion.

Should I mention his influence on B.J.?

A kid with a tuft of dirty blonde hair sprouting from his head approached Witherspoon warily. The child was wearing a Sonny Logan T-shirt and blue jeans. He moved with the awkward balance of an eleven or twelve year old whose growth has outdistanced his coordination. A dark-haired mother hung back by another cluster of chairs, her eyes careful and observant.

"Mr. Witherspoon," the kid ventured. Ricky looked over at him.

"Yeah?" he said.

His casual tone seemed to set the boy back at least ten seconds. After a few stammers, he finally bleated out: "Can I have your autograph, please?"

Witherspoon accepted the pen and Hilton notepad the boy thrust at him. "You think you'll ever beat Sonny Logan?" the kid asked. Fans' confidence levels always seemed to rise sharply once you agreed to scribble your gimmick name on a scrap of paper.

"We'll see." Witherspoon shrugged. "I may just buy the title off him."

"He wouldn't sell it to you!" the kid yelped. Witherspoon peered at him, and the kid shrugged. "At least . . . I don't think he would," he amended.

"What do you wanta be when you grow up?" Witherspoon asked.

"A professional wrestler." This proclamation came with no hesitation. "And rich. Like you."

Ricky Witherspoon scrutinized the boy with new interest. "Professional wrestlers do some crazy things, you know," he said in a tone imbued with a vague challenge.

"I can do crazy things." The boy's voice rose defensively, peaking with a slight crack.

"How about . . ." Witherspoons' eyes blinked like a

high-speed camera as he scanned the pool area. ". . . jumping in the pool with your clothes on?"

The kid looked shocked. Then he turned back to his mother and called: "Mom, can I jump in the pool?"

"Well . . . sure," she called back. "Go up to the room and change."

"I have to do it with my clothes on."

"No, I'm sorry, Bill," she said, shaking her head. "I can't allow that."

Billy turned back to Ricky Witherspoon, who had removed a hundred dollar bill from the rolled-up Hilton robe lying next to his chair. "You wanna be rich like me, Billy?" he challenged. "This hundred dollar bill is yours if you jump in the pool. Right now."

Billy's eyes widened as he stared at the bill in Ricky's hand. He shot a quick glance at his mother, then took off running toward the pool's edge. "Billy!" his mother shouted.

There was a loud clap as Billy hit the water with his legs and arms tucked in a cannonball position. He disappeared beneath a liquid mushroom cloud. His mother charged over to the pool. Billy paddled to the side and climbed out sheepishly while his mother cast a peevish glare over at a smiling Ricky Witherspoon. Billy dodged his mother's grasp and ran up to Witherspoon, who handed Billy his reward and asked quietly, "Do you still think I can't buy Sonny Logan's belt, Billy?"

"I . . ." Billy frowned, his face reflecting a battle between his loyalty to Logan and loyalty to himself. "I think you could." Witherspoon's new disciple nodded eagerly, flinging water from his damp hair.

"Billy!" his mother's shrill tone made me cringe. *Like an owner calling her pet.*

Billy slunk toward her, flinching as she gripped his arm. With a final venomous stare at Ricky, she turned and pulled Billy away. The two disappeared through a pair of doors layered with tinted glass. Ricky lifted up the pad with his signature scrawled just beneath the Hilton insignia. Billy had forgotten it. "He'll remember this day for the rest of his life," The Billion Dollar Baby remarked airily, tossing the forgotten prize to the ground and closing his eyes.

I set my pencil down. The portrait was finished.

Back in my hotel room later that afternoon, I placed a call to California. Terri answered. She was officially B.J.'s wife now; they had gotten married a week after he returned from Tennessee.

She told me about their weekend honeymoon at a bed-and-breakfast inn in Santa Monica. "That ocean air is so *thick*," she said, laughing. "I could taste it every morning."

"A desert gal, huh?"

"Always and forever," she chimed. "So when are we gonna see you on TV?"

"Probably in a couple weeks," I said. "How's the recently retired psycho dentist doing?"

"He's great. He misses you," she added. "He's at work right now, but if you want I can have him call—"

"No, that's all right," I said quickly. "I have to be at the arena pretty soon. But could you give him a message?"

"Of course."

"Tell him that Ricky Witherspoon remembers his father as a gentleman." I dispatched these words in a rush, hoping brevity would mitigate their untruth. "And also, Ricky got a real kick out of his effect on B.J."

"That is so cool," she gushed. Terri knew well the story of B.J.'s father and Ricky Witherspoon. "He'll be psyched to hear that."

I swallowed, guiltily thankful that Terri had bought the lie.

After hanging up I walked over to the thin-backed chair by the corner and sat. The wallpaper screamed out a diagonal pattern of snarled lines. Their static breakups matched my thoughts as I tried to figure out why I had just lied to my best friend's wife. After a long time I still had only one conclusion: hotel wallpaper was very, very ugly.

My series of matches with Witherspoon called for me to go over him via pinfall in nearly all of them. We worked out a finish where the referee took a bump (thus being "knocked out") and Witherspoon got his steel briefcase and tried to hit me over the head with it. But I ducked and kicked him in the stomach, forcing him to drop the briefcase that I then picked up and used to crack him over the head. Then I tossed the briefcase out of the ring and covered an unconscious Witherspoon just in time for the referee to recover and make the three-count.

Since Witherspoon was a heel who usually taunted the fans with a wad of money, I too came out with a fistful of cash. But instead of taunting the fans, I tossed the money out to them. That first night in Denver I hurled a few fifty dollar bills loosely in the direction of the first couple of rows, picturing a good-natured grab for the cash. As soon as the money left my hands, the first three rows broke down the barriers and trampled one of the poor security guards in an effort to get at the bills. While the other guards restored order, the trampled one was fished from the crowd and taken to the hospital. He suffered three cracked ribs and a puncture wound in his right thigh apparently caused by a stiletto heel.

Ricky was furious. "Shit, Cam!" he yelled backstage afterward, referring to me by what was to become my nickname among the boys. "You gotta throw those bills *far!*" he urged. "Otherwise, you'll have those fuckers rushing the ring!"

After that night I threw only one or two bills out at once, and I made sure to ball them up and hurl them as far as I could. I usually aimed for someone big, knowing that little kids might be mauled if they attempted to snag a bill meant for them. Logan always hurled his T-shirts at little kids and there was no trouble. But, as I had learned, T-shirts were one thing, money was quite another.

Even though The Chameleon was still a mystery to most pro wrestling fans, the money I dispensed at the start of each match quickly bought their cheers. I dressed in a carbon copy of Witherspoon's black sequined suit and dyed my hair a sandy brown to match his color. "You're going to be facing the one person you can't buy, Witherspoon!" I trumpeted in pre-match interviews, which were run on Saturday morning television. "That person is yourself!"

Three weeks before I made my hometown debut at the Rosemont Horizon, I called my mom to invite her to the show. She told me that she already had other plans. She had met someone, she explained. About six months ago he had come into the restaurant where she was waitressing part-time and asked for change for the parking meter. Then he had come back a half hour later and asked her out. The night of my hometown return was also the night of his lodge's annual "Starlight Dance and Dinner."

"I wish you could've told me sooner," she told me over the phone. I was calling her from an airplane, partly because flights were the only relatively calm period in my average day and partly because I liked the idea of being able to spend seven dollars a minute on a phone call and not sweat it. "Isn't three weeks enough notice?" I asked her.

"Well," she acknowledged, "it's just that this meeting is very important to Irling. And it's important that I be there."

"But this is something . . . ," I hesitated, "that will never come again. My first time wrestling in my home-tow—"

"So do it!" she snapped. I held the phone away from my ear, stunned. When I brought it back, her voice was softer, "—for almost four months, and then suddenly you call and expect me to drop everything to come see you wrestle."

"It's only been three months," I protested, though I

really wasn't sure. Travel had forced time into a perpetual string of hotel rooms, airports, gyms, and arenas. Days no longer passed, they vanished, swallowed up by the kinesis of my newfound life. "I'm sorry I didn't call," I murmured.

"Don't be sorry . . ." Her voice wandered into silence. "What's your name now, kiddo?" she asked.

"Chameleon."

"Chameleon," she said, sighing. "Don't be sorry. You're doing what you have to do with your life, obviously. But can you understand . . . I have to do the same."

"I understand," I said. "I'm still sorry."

"I'm not," she said, and laughed, "I love you."

"How's Harry and Shirley? And Jim?" I asked, wanting her to remain on the line, to keep talking.

"They're . . . they're fine," she responded, sounding surprised, "and Jim's at Harvard Business School. He's interning at some kind of savings and loan."

"That's good." I nodded at the phone. "That's good."

She invited me for lunch or dinner the day after the match. But we were going to be flying out the next morning at six for Houston. I told her I'd try to come back when I got a few days off.

"I'll watch for you on TV," she said, before clicking off.

When we landed in Cleveland I had tried to locate Bryan or Marty. I tracked Bryan down at his apartment at Southern Illinois University. He was enrolled in summer school and told me he was planning to study abroad for a year. "Maybe Italy or Spain," he said, "I hear there's a lot of women over there who like American guys. What's up with you, man?"

When I ran down an abridged version of the past four months, he was amazed. "The WWO!" he exclaimed bewilderedly. "That's too much. I can't believe you—"

"I'm gonna be wrestling at the Horizon!" I told him. "You gotta be there, man!"

"When?" he asked. I gave him the date. "Shit," he groaned. "You would pick the night of my last afternoon final."

"No way."

"Yeah," he sighed, "but if I can shoot through the final quickly maybe I can get up there in time."

"How's Marty?" I asked.

"I dunno." Bryan sighed. "He's down here, but he's not going to summer school. Just hangin' out, I guess. I haven't seen him in days. He's partyin' a lot. He's, uh . . ." He paused. "He's Marty," he said finally. Bryan and I agreed that if he could make it that day, he'd meet me in the lobby of the Radisson Hotel next door to the arena. As teenagers we had spent many hours at the tables there loitering in hopes of seeing our favorite wrestlers stalk by.

A few weeks later I was landing at O'Hare airport. My heart skipped excitedly at the thought of seeing an old friend. But when I got to the Radisson only one table was occupied. Two elderly couples sat engrossed in some kind of card game. Bryan was nowhere in sight. I approached the front desk.

"Hi," the redheaded desk clerk greeted me. Her face was sprinkled with a dizzying amount of freckles.

"Hi," I said. "Reservations for World Wrestling Organiza—"

Her expression grew officious. "Your name, please?" she asked.

"Harding," I said and glanced aimlessly around the lobby. "Harding," I repeated. Her fingers danced rapidly over the keys, and in a few seconds the smile returned to her face.

"Oh, here we are!" she said. "I didn't recognize you at first. You must be new."

"Yep." I nodded as a cry of joy went up from one of the ladies at the table. I turned and saw her waving a hand of cards triumphantly.

Once in my room I took a Valium and called Bryan. "I just had the most intense final," he moaned. "Sorry, man. But I'm too burnt to make the drive."

We talked for a few minutes and hung up with a promise to keep in touch. I sat on the edge of the bed, slowly realizing that when he moved out of the dorm, I would have no way of reaching him. I had forgotten the number of his parents' house. I could feel the Valium entering my system, soothing an incipient depression. A different phone number slipped out from a fold in my memory and I found myself dialing it. A woman answered—Charlotte's mother. I had only met her once, that night I took Charlotte to the prom. "Is Charlotte home?" I asked.

"Charles?"

"Yes," I confirmed nervously.

"She should've picked you up by now," she said, "but you know how she drives. Nervous Nellie."

"Yes, Nervous Nellie." I laughed.

"Of course, I don't have to tell you your wife is also one of the most careful drivers—"

I hung up the phone and stood. The Valium was

blotting my sensitivities, turning potential joy or depression into feelings that I could recognize but not experience. Fine with me. It was time to engage in what was becoming a pre-match ritual. I called Ricky Witherspoon's room. "Hello?"

"Spoon, it's Chameleon."

"Cam . . . gimme ten minutes. You know where the bar is?"

"Hell, yes," I chuckled dreamily, the Valium pummeling the outside world into a dim blur. "I practically grew up in this hotel."

That night, in the arena I first discovered the dream I was on my way to achieving, I worked another match in front of thousands of faceless marks. Several times during the match, the building rumbled as a plane flew by at a low altitude either on its way to or from O'Hare Airport. As a member of the audience, I had always incorporated the rumble into a general excitement that grew from the cathartic feeling of watching simulated struggle. But now the noise was merely that of an airplane flying overhead on its way to some destination. The next morning I would be on one as well, going to another city to do the same thing all over again.

"It wasn't what I thought it would be."

This was how I described the night to Shawna a week later. I was talking to her on the phone in the living room of my fashionable New York apartment. Outside the window, a throng of tiny bright dots lay packed together like interconnected vessels marooned in an expansive vein of darkness. "It wasn't what I thought it would be," I repeated, looking away from the window.

"Nothing ever is." Her laugh was tender and a little sad.

Gradually the semblance of a routine began to emerge in my schedule with the WWO. We would usually wrestle anywhere from twelve to thirty nights in a row, then receive something like four days off. Beastie told me that he had wrestled three hundred and ten days last year. Oftentimes, the only three things we saw in a city were the airport, the arena, and the hotel. If we had enough time, we went to the gym and suffered through a workout with limbs and muscles trashed from a relentless schedule of colliding with a mat. The workouts didn't matter that much; steroids made our physiques possible. Our bodies were controlled by a variety of substances; downers made it possible for us to sleep after the adrenaline rush from a match, uppers got us up in the morning so we could make a 6:00 A.M. flight, and painkillers helped us ignore nagging injuries such as torn muscles, bruised ribs, and sprained ankles. We were kept well supplied with pharmaceuticals by the physician who traveled with the WWO. His name was Dr. Randall Tingle, but we always called him Santa, partly because he looked like old Saint Nick, but mostly because his main duty was dispensing steroids and painkillers. The good doctor was most assuredly necessary, because although our pay paled in comparison to that of professional baseball or football players, we had no off-season to recover from injuries. Rather than see this as an injustice, many wrestlers took a bizarre pride in the harsh life we endured. It served as another stripe of exclusivity that separated us from the marks. "Just get me under those lights, brother," Sonny Logan said backstage one night. "It makes all this shit worthwhile."

I nodded vigorously as he drew a small bullet-shaped canister to his nose and fired a few hits of cocaine into each nostril. When he offered the vial to me, I took it immediately. We hadn't talked much, and I had the feeling this was a test of some sort.

I tilted the bullet and snorted deeply. Cocaine flew up into my nose, savagely tunneling into my mucous membranes. I winced and coughed a little as Logan began laughing. "Take it easy, brother," he advised. "Let it glide in by itself."

I did much better with the other nostril. I handed the vial back and he clapped me on the shoulder. I tried to remember him doing the same thing to a kid in Chicago years ago but at that moment was too wired to be able to call up the memory. I just kept looking at "The American Dream" and nodding, my face frozen in a numbed smile.

ANYTOWN, U.S.A.

The locker room saturated with the scent of baby oil. I sat in the corner, my body a vibrating battlefield as a Percodan buzz clashed with a hit of Dexedrine I had just taken because I only got two hours sleep the night before due to partying and some fucked up flight reservations. In the center of the room, "Dastardly" Darren Domino was holding court, talking about the woman he

H-bombed last night. An H-bombing involved slipping a Halcion in an unsuspecting rat's drink. Then after Domino had sex with her, he shit on her and deposited her naked feces-smeared body in the hallway. He bragged that he'd done that to at least a hundred women throughout the United States. I didn't know why he did this, and probably neither did he. There was no time for self-reflection. Not with our schedules and our personal appearances and photo sessions. Sixteenth straight day on the fucking road and I was supposed to give a shit about some drunk girl? All I needed to know was that I was going to be allowed to go out into the arena that night. Hit the lights and the music and then during the match I'd be counting the number of marks with my T-shirt on. That's all they existed as now—bodies wearing my T-shirt. That meant I was still saleable, and that meant I would have a job tomorrow. Unlike Sledge who, as soon as his feud with Officer O'Malley was over, had been dismissed by fans and hence let go by Thomas Rockart Jr.

The fickleness of fans toward wrestlers led to many "gimmick-lifts," in which a wrestler simply traded in one gimmick for another. There were other reasons for gimmick-lifts. Mickey Jeter had always been known as "The Lone Warrior" and was getting a good push until three months ago when he jokingly press-slammed a drunken Thomas Rockart Jr. at a riotous party after a successful pay-per-view. ("He insisted," Mickey would protest afterward.) Mickey's claim had been backed up

by several witnesses, who remembered Rockart pro-
claiming: "I can take it!" The Warrior followed his boss'
orders, sending Rockart to the ground as gently as possible. Nonetheless, Rockart suffered three bruised ribs
as a result. Three weeks later, Mickey had been
informed that the Warrior gimmick was being retired.
He now worked a drag queen gimmick as "Vivian
Vitale." Whereas the Lone Warrior had howled his way
through interviews while beating his chest, Vivian
Vitale lisped while flaunting an exaggerated limp wrist.
Before every match Mickey caked his face with
makeup, painted his nails fuck-me red and doused his
body with glitter. "What the hell," he would say and
shrug, smearing mascara on his eyelashes, "I used to
paint my face when I was the Lone Warrior, too. Just
the other side of a fuckin' coin." I would nod as if I
knew what he was saying. And I thought I did. Twenty-
six straight days on the road and nothing seems real.
Always another destination looming, adding a slippery
impermanence to every location. Even emotions
seemed too fleeting to trust. My disgust at Domino's H-
bombing was nothing more than a remote ache that
would soon be replaced by the excited heat of going to
the ring and then the exhausted ride back to some
hotel and then the listless laughter at that hotel's bar
before a confused tumble into sleep.

I had no desire to touch my own body anymore. Why
bother? I wasn't even real. I was Ricky Witherspoon.
But in rare sober moments I realized this freedom from
my compulsion was only temporary. If I stopped touring, stopped wrestling, it would all reemerge.

So I clung to my Chameleon character, remaining a

skewed reflection who experienced days like notes in a chaotic opera I had written but now failed to understand.

As my feud with Ricky Witherspoon was played out in arenas across the country, I managed to buy a Mercedes convertible and lease an expensive penthouse in Manhattan's fashionable high-rent district. "It's where the well-off reside," Witherspoon, who lived four buildings down from me, informed me proudly.

When we worked the Capitol Arena in Washington, D.C. Witherspoon made reservations for a group of us at a particular downtown restaurant frequented by the president. But during our match I bit off a small piece of my tongue while getting hurled from the ring, and had Santa shoot my mouth up with a local anesthetic. When I told Ricky I wouldn't be joining the rest of them for dinner, he expressed disbelief. "How could you not wanna go to this place?" he demanded indignantly.

"I won't be able to taste anything!" I protested.

"So what?" he cried, "We'll be eating with the same silverware the *president of the United States* eats with!"

So I went along and ended up getting drunk on a bottle of eighty dollar champagne. When I was with The Billion Dollar Baby, money was never an object.

Many months passed with Shawna and I playing phone tag. Every time her machine came on I listened to it all the way through, then hung up on the sound of the beep. Near the end of my feud with Ricky Witherspoon, she finally caught me at home on one of my rare off-days.

"You've been avoiding me," she promptly accused. "No phone calls—"

"I called a couple of times, but I always got your machine so I hung up."

"Why didn't you leave a message?"

"I hate the sound of my own voice." This was curious but completely true, and the silence on the other end of the line indicated she was just as stunned by the confession as I was.

"No artwork, either," she said, more quietly.

A sketch pad lay on one of the small black end tables bordering the couch. Except for the sketch of Ricky Witherspoon lounging by a Denver Hilton swimming pool, its pages were blank.

I shifted the phone from one ear to the other before speaking. "Not too many fields out here. And you can't see the sunset."

"Why not?"

"Buildings get in the way."

"What kind of building do you live in?"

"Place in the upper forties," I said. In response to the silence I added, "Got a doorman and everything."

"Okay, okay, I'm impressed, already," she said and laughed. "What's your apartment like?"

I glanced around, shifting uncomfortably on a thin-backed chair twisted into some kind of fashionably esoteric design. This was the first time I had been forced to fathom my apartment as a home and not just a crash pad. I surveyed the living room that joined the kitchen via a wood-paneled bar. Pieces of metallic, sharp-angled furniture crouched throughout the room like animals laying in wait. "It's . . . modern," I stammered finally, using the only word I could remember from the description the broker had recited. "It has all new furniture. I ordered the stuff out of a catalogue. Came in pre-arranged room designs."

"Prearranged?" she pronounced the word with distaste.

"I didn't have time to go through a store and pick out stuff," I protested. The chair, as though in retaliation for this insult, held its strange curvature stubbornly as I tried to scrunch into a more comfortable position. "Cost me a fortune," I added, both in justification and to pacify the chair. It didn't work.

"I'll bet," she drawled. "Do you like it?"

"It's all right." I stood up and cracked my back. "I wouldn't mind a rocking chair, though."

"So why don't you buy one?" she asked, laughing. "You have enough money, right?" she teased. "You can buy a top-of-the-line rocking chair."

Her chiding tone made me angry enough to visit a Salvation Army the next day and pick up an old rocking chair with wide thick rollers and immense cushions for thirty dollars. I set it up before my window and began rocking. I rocked and thought about the apartment, its cramped rooms and tremendous views and extraordinarily high rent. Downstairs in the parking garage sat a Mercedes convertible that I barely ever drove. It reminded me of a gun Ricky Witherspoon had once shown me. The thing was a collector's item that had never been fired. "Never gonna be, either," Ricky had maintained, patting the barrel protectively. If fired, he explained to me, the weapon would lose most of its value. I had never understood the purpose of owning a gun like that. I didn't know that I ever would; our series of matches was winding down.

The next day I traded in my Mercedes for a used Honda. Two weeks later, Witherspoon and I had our final match in Madison Square Garden. That following weekend I moved into a spacious flat in Brooklyn and decorated it with an array of mismatched, second-hand furniture. My new place had a softer feeling than the penthouse; this was a place I could actually see myself wanting to come back to.

I was helped in the move by Ricky Witherspoon, Jake Jugular, and the person who was set to be The Chameleon's next opponent, The Soultaker.

10

WRESTLING DEATH

Dark stains dot the canvas; blood and sweat from the matches that have filled the afternoon and early evening. A cup flies into the ring, fanning out a stream of beer, which for a moment becomes a rainbow under the artificial lights. The beer splashes onto the canvas, and the cup finally comes to rest by the ring's opposite edge. The referee kicks it out of the ring with a neat sweep of his leg while security guards descend upon the general area from which the cup was thrown.

The air is rich and taut, smelling vaguely of sweat. The day has been hot, and a lot of people still have their shirts off even though the sun has gone down and the air is now cool. I take off my leather jacket and fold it up carefully. The special guest ring-boy comes up to the *edge of the ring. He won a write-in contest for the privilege. About one hundred and twenty thousand people sent in essays explaining in a hundred words or less what being ring-boy would mean to them. I don't know what this kid's winning answer was.*

He is lanky with slight birdlike features. His short black hair is combed straight and moussed so that it will not fall over a gold earring in his left ear.

He looks down, bashfully I think, as he takes my jacket. Then he snaps his head back up and glares with eyes burning a metallic blue. "You're gonna lose, man," he says with a practiced steadiness. I take a step back, surprised and a little frightened by the conviction of his voice. As though he knows something I don't.

He turns and walks quickly back to the timekeeper's table. I'm watching him carefully, wondering if the real reason he wanted to be ring-boy was to psyche out the wrestlers he didn't like. Does he actually think it will make a difference?

If he has that kind of faith regarding his role in the grand scheme, I envy him.

———————

If someone were asked to describe death incarnate, chances are the description would touch on at least one of Trevor "The Soultaker" Gladstone's unsettling physical attributes. Just a few inches shy of seven feet, his elongated body was wrapped in skin so pale it looked bloodless. His movements contained a methodical quality that suggested an unconscious battle against human reflex. When in the ring, he always wore a white mask, but the emptiness of his eyes was startling even when viewed through the mask's narrow slits. His fearsome presence and demonic gimmick made him wildly popular with wrestling fans, even though he was technically a heel.

When our series of matches began in early March of 1989, Trevor invited me out to his home in upstate Connecticut. His wife, Meredith, was a lively woman whose jet black hair was alive with unruly curls. Her athletic body was dominated by a set of remarkable breasts, which Trevor had told me she had done about eight months ago, shortly after their third daughter, Helena, had been born.

I sketched him in his backyard, surrounded by foliage awakening from winter. Fledgling greenery had already climbed halfway up a chain-link fence, which enclosed the yard's perimeter. Trevor sat by a small fountain, clad in an overcoat similar to the black one he wore to the ring. He was missing the expressionless mask, as well as the top hat. "Jim, Janis, and Jimi," he was saying in response to my query as to what had prompted him to be a wrestler. His voice split the air with the audible consistency of a tire crunching hot gravel.

"You wanted to be a rock star?" I asked.

"Nah, I just wanted to be someone who would be cheered by others. I guess," he said and shrugged. "I guess I also respected the way those three lived and died."

"You mean young?"

"Not just that. It's like they lived life so intensely

that they almost *couldn't* make old age. Know what I mean?"

My throat caught. Sure, I knew all about people dying young. I quickly shifted to the topic of his gimmick.

"Like a cross between Michael Myers and Freddy Krueger," he explained, as his thin red hair was stirred by a short gush of spring breeze. "When I saw that movie *Halloween*, I couldn't sleep for two weeks. Something about that fucking guy just freaked me out."

"I've never seen it," I said.

"Oh, you gotta!" he enthused. "I've got it on tape. That and *Nightmare on Elm Street*—"

"What about *Friday the 13th*?"

"Nah," he shook his head with authority, "it's just a cheap knockoff. *Nightmare on Elm Street* is okay because Freddy's so witty. So I use a few aspects of him for interviews. But *Halloween*, now that was the original. Michael Myers is the real deal. I love the way he *walks* after his victims; he doesn't have to run, because it's inevitable that he'll catch them."

"Like Death itself," I murmured, frowning at the picture taking shape on my sketch pad. The Soultaker's tall sinewy figure was well-formed, but without the mask to guide me, I couldn't capture the usual expressionlessness of his facial features.

"You got it." He exhaled. "It comes for you at its own pace. You see the sun rise and set every day and one day it's gonna be the last time you ever see it and you don't even know. Seems like a shitty deal, doesn't it?"

I shrugged, a bit startled at the unease erupting in his gray pupils. Whenever he was in the ring, the only thing in those eyes was an unflinching gaze as trapped and soulless as a shark's.

A breeze swept through again, bringing the trees to life. He took a deep breath and shifted his body lower, as though going into a fighter's defensive crouch. "I wonder—" he began. Then over the rustling branches came a series of high-pitched exclamations from inside the house. "My girls are home from school," he said, standing quickly. "Come in and meet 'em."

Trevor's two oldest daughters were named Dawn and Elektra. Dawn was five years old and possessed the same thoughtful eyes as her father, as though she were storing the world away in the back of her mind for further consideration at a later time. Elektra was nine and given to fits of shrieking laughter, as though she had an ability to reach into air and pluck a joke that no one else was able to grasp. Through dinner, Trevor smiled at Elektra proudly whenever she underwent one of these episodes.

"What's so funny?" Dawn asked her sister.

"Nothing, dummy," she responded. "Everything." She smiled, then giggled again.

"What exactly, dear?" Meredith asked her.

"Let her laugh." Trevor smiled. "It's good for her."

Throughout the meal I snuck looks at Trevor, and saw his face shining with contentment. The children were extremely well-mannered, both saying "please" and "thank you" while passing various items around the table. I had the feeling of being part of a well-oiled machine.

After dinner Trevor suggested we go "to a little place down the way." It turned out to be a strip joint that catered to Connecticut's upper crust citizenry, and stocked dancers that were accordingly devastating. The doorman, the wheelchair-bound bartender, and many of the dancers all greeted Trevor with comfortable enthusiasm, calling him both "Trev" and "The Soultaker."

Trevor spent the next couple hours surrounded by strippers. While a stream of women danced for him, he chugged beer after beer. The tips of his fingers were soon sparkling with glitter that he had rubbed off the strippers' waxed thighs. By the time we left, his eyes were completely glazed.

Fifteen miles of winding road stretched between the bar and Trevor's house. Dark trees manned both sides of the road. The speed limit was 40 mph. Trevor had obeyed it on the way there, but on the return trip he jacked it up to 70. We skidded dangerously close to losing control on several occasions. "Live a little, my lost soul!" he growled after I implored him to slow down. "Tomorrow we die!"

"It's 1:00 A.M.!" I screamed along with the tires of our car as we tore around a tight corner, "It *is* tomorrow!"

We made it home intact. My new opponent emerged from the car with a slow and fatigued momentum; the several moments of potential death on the way back seemed to have drained the fevered energy he had briefly possessed. After stumbling inside, he showed me where the guest room was. "We'll finish that painting," he said and sighed. "Gonna finish that painting tomorrow."

"Right," I said. "Sweet dreams."

"Tomorrow." The word fell from his lips along with a

thin trail of drool. He turned away and staggered off down the hallway, leaving me in the perfectly still pool of light that filtered down from the ceiling fixture.

That night in bed I finished his portrait, remaining awake until four in the morning as the pen in my hand closed in on the haunted stimulation that I had seen grow from his eyes and gradually consume his entire face. Becoming The Soultaker, I concluded, enabled Trevor Gladstone to confront and perhaps feel a measure of power over his own mortality.

I put the pen and sketch pad down and tried to fall asleep. But every time I took a breath, the memory of almost overdosing in Memphis swept through me. Only when I saw the first rays of dawn seeping through the curtains was I able to trust unconsciousness.

In the coming months I took on the same deliberate movement and gravelly voice that were a part of The Soultaker's character. But with The Soultaker's physical mannerisms came Trevor's peculiar love/hate relationship with the idea of death. One night while lacing up our boots backstage I asked Trevor what he thought happened when we died, and he answered firmly, "This is it. When we die, we cease to exist."

"What about our souls?" I wondered.

His hands froze in the middle of a knot while he looked at me like I was on the moon. "Souls?" he snorted. "What do you think, because some book says we have souls, that automatically makes it true?"

It seemed like an odd statement from a man who

sent his two kids to Sunday school. When I pointed this out to him he shrugged. "I want them to make up their own minds," he said. "Besides, I don't want them to feel like I do," he added.

"How's that?" I asked.

"Doomed," he answered, looking back down at his laces and pulling them tight.

My father's skin is sticky with pungent sweat. Sores swollen with pus covered his chest. They exploded one by one, flinging infection onto my skin. My flesh crackled and bubbled before dissolving completely and my father's disease now burrowed through my muscles and split apart my bones in search of my heart, in search of my soul. It laid waste to my body from within, and I released my father's body as life slipped away—

I awoke screaming. The hotel room was dark. "Just a dream," I whispered, wiping the sweat from my upper lip. "My soul cannot be taken," I recited, "for I am the taker of souls." Then I reached over to the half-pint of vodka I was now keeping by the side of all my temporary beds. I had a sip and repeated what had become my common prayer.

Five sips later, I was finally deadened enough to believe it and slipped away into sleep.

For a while I frequented libraries whenever we had downtime in a city. Although I could never check any books out because I would be gone from that city the next day, I managed to get a lot of reading done during scattered episodes at various library tables. I pored through books on religion, searching through theories about the origin of life and what happens after death for something to dispel the unease that now clutched me during every sober moment. Nothing worked. So I did the next best thing, I began making sure I had as few sober moments as possible. It soon got to the point that during our matches, Trevor and I would sometimes be so drunk we'd be giggling with impish glee beneath our death masks. I had been doing steroids on and off for years, and with my increased drinking I feared my kidneys or liver were giving out. After three months of this I went to Dr. Tingle, complaining about pains in my side. Santa gave me blood tests and assured me that everything was fine; my organs were still functioning as they should.

"This is all in your mind," he announced, pulling out several different rows of the portable medicine cabinet that he was always wheeling around. "Ah-ha! Here," he said. His fingers closed around a small red bottle jumbled among other containers in the bottom row. "Take one of these a day," he recited, "preferably after meals. Tell me if you feel better in a month."

After leaving the office, I looked at the small plastic canister. Its label read *Prozac*. I tossed the present into a wastebasket and went off to get drunk with Soultaker at the nearest strip joint.

———————

Most nights on the road I was too drunk and blitzed on pot or painkillers to even dial numbers, much less talk coherently. But on off days, holed up in my apartment,

I was able to remain sober enough to call Shawna. Our conversations were, at that time, the only things that felt stable in my life. One night, over two thousand miles of wire, I asked her: "What do you think happens to us when we die?"

One of her customary silences followed. I looked across my sparsely furnished living room into the kitchen. One of the pictures she had sent me was stuck to the fridge with a small rubber magnet spelling out *I Love You* as one uninterrupted slogan with the words distinguishable as separate entities only by their differing colors. The picture featured her sitting on a wooden fence next to a pond. Her eyes were on the water, questioning its depth. She had told me a friend took the picture after a day of hiking. I hadn't asked whether the friend was a man or woman.

Her voice gently parted my thoughts. "I once asked my brother about death," she was saying. "I was probably about eight years old. We had been rafting down the river all day and were gonna go out to dinner with our parents. And it was one of the first times in my life I had felt good. I felt so good that I became afraid that it would end. Not just that day, but all of it. My whole life. That day was one of the first times, after all the foster homes and bullshit, that I actually cared about whether or not I was alive." She paused. "So I asked him that same question you just asked me."

"What did he say?" I asked.

"He looked down at me, and even though he must've been only twelve at the time, to me it sounded like the voice of a wise old man. He told me 'Simple, Shawn. You become a star.' It was still afternoon so there weren't any stars out yet, but I looked up and imagined myself in the sky looking down over everything and it seemed all right. Everything seemed all right." She took a long breath that reminded me of the ones I would take after waking up from nightmares about my father.

"You ever imagine you see him up in the sky at night?" I asked her.

"I don't need to imagine," she replied. "How about you?" she asked. "What do you think happens?"

"I don't know," I answered with a sigh, "but I like the idea of becoming a star."

Strippers and professional wrestlers go well together. "It's the common bond of creating an illusion," a stripper in Detroit once told me. "You studs are, like, pretending to really fight. And we pretend to really dig the dorks we're dancing for. All it usually takes is a look or a small kiss in their direction. You'd be surprised how easily these dweebs, who're supposed to be all educated and shit, fall for it." She had popped her chewing gum and I had nodded, more wearily amused than surprised, as her silicone-enhanced breast poked against my steroid-enhanced arm.

Later that summer, a pack of us went out on the town after a show in San Diego. San Diego was known as a "three wake-up call" town; it contained an abundance of hot rats and rich marks who just loved showing pro wrestlers a good time. Getting to bed at four in the morning made it hard to get out of bed and catch a nine o'clock flight.

That particular night, after hitting the rounds of clubs and drinking on the tabs of a few La Jolla doctors, we finished up at Les Girls, a popular strip joint downtown. Trevor talked two strippers into coming back to his hotel room. They went at it for several hours before passing out. Trevor awakened to a scream.

His eyes flew open and he saw his wife in the doorway. She had a room key in one hand and a bottle of champagne in the other. Trevor later related the incident to me in a trembling voice, "The first few moments, I thought it was some kinda dream, and then it hit me. It was the morning of our tenth wedding anniversary. She had caught the red-eye to be with me. At first I didn't know why she looked so surprised, but then I saw the two strippers leaping out of the bed. Both of 'em nude as newborns, of course.

"I tell ya, Cam, I didn't know whether to shit or go blind. There was a buncha screaming, and the next thing I know here's Meredith just kicking the shit out of these two naked beauties." At this point in the story his chest swelled with pride. "She was really doing a number on 'em, man. It was all they could do to grab their clothes and get the hell out of that room with their lives. But then Meredith turned her attention to *me*. Shit . . ."

He shook his head. We were in the bar of a Miami hotel, sipping from large bowl-shaped glasses that contained a frosty purplish alcoholic concoction. Sprouting from the slush were tiny plastic showgirls. "She shattered the bottle of champagne and sat there shaking the broken neck at me," Trevor recalled, nervously thrusting one of the showgirls in and out of the drink. "I remember tasting that dried-up pussy juice around my lips and thinking, 'Well, shit. Isn't this some way to finally go. After all the morbid thoughts about dying, I'm gonna go with dried-up pussy juice in my mouth.' I knew she was damn sure angry enough to do it. My life flashed before my eyes and everything. Well, not my whole life, just all the time I'd been wrestling and screwin' around on the road and all that."

He sighed and took a long swallow of his drink, not bothering to lick the purple foam that remained on his top lip. "But then she broke down crying," he murmured. "She confessed that she had had her share of *indiscretions*—her word—while I was on the road over the past couple years."

"Damn."

"Two days later we went to this marriage counselor. He said our lives were being disrupted by all my traveling. We had grown apart, all that kinda shit. But I'll tell you this, Cam, I do still love her. And she says she still loves me and I believe her. And my daughters . . . I'd . . ." His voice fell off momentarily before surfacing in a tone desperate enough to make his next words sound like a prayer. "I would die before I'd want them to be hurt."

"I meant what I said that first night at your house," I told him. "You've got a great family."

"I agree." His face relaxed and he wiped the froth from his lip. "It's funny. All this time I was so worried about death and all that shit. Now I feel like . . . death is gonna come, that's all there is to it. But that doesn't mean I can't enjoy life while I have it.

"There was once a great swordsman. He won many

wars for his country before retiring. Though he claimed to dislike war, he kept his sword in his den. Became very successful in business and had a son. When he was dying, he asked that his grandson be given the sword. The rest of the family was upset; they wanted to know why, if he claimed to hate war so much, he gave the sword to such a young boy. His father had done the same.

"What I am giving the boy is a tool," the old man said. "The same tool my father gave me. War occurs, and a young man needs tools with which to sometimes fight. But I have cherished this sword for so many years because every day when I look at it, I am reminded of the men it felled. I am respectful of their lives, and this makes me even more appreciative of mine. This sword reminds me every day of how fragile life is. This is a lesson we must learn for ourselves. The world is not always a pretty place; battles must be fought. But hopefully, and he turned to his grandson, you will learn the lesson I have: Live your life as a human being, not a slab of metal."

Trevor paused. "Not as a slab of metal," he contemplated, raising his glass. "I really like that. Here's to being human."

"Here's to it." I touched my glass to his and tilted it back, careful not to poke an eye out with one of the tiny women bobbing in the cocktail.

"Well, part of my being human means getting off the road and back to what's important: my family." Trevor finished his drink. "So congratulations, Cam. You're gonna put The Soultaker out of professional wrestling."

So it came to pass that at the annual Fall Maul,

Soultaker and Chameleon engaged in a "coffin match." To win, one of us had to dump the other in a coffin, which was stationed on a platform near the rear rows of the main floor. We battled throughout the arena, slamming into chairs and hurling fireballs at each other. This match was the wildest one we'd ever worked with each other; we both performed maneuvers we never wanted to risk while drunk. After being tossed out of the ring, I looked up and was legitimately shocked to see Trevor's 6'10" frame leaping over the top rope. I managed to catch him successfully, and we went down in a carefully jumbled heap.

"I had never done a move like that before," he explained to me later, "and I knew it would be my last chance to ever try it."

In the closing moments of what *Pro Wrestling Monthly* would term "an epic battle," The Soultaker was placing me in the casket when I shifted my weight and flipped him inside with me. We pulled the cover shut, giggling like a couple of kids as the coffin lowered.

Once safely below the platform, a couple technicians opened the coffin. Trevor hopped out and was immediately congratulated by Hippo Haleberg, who patted Trevor's sweaty back with a hand caked with Twinkie crumbs and said, "Hell of a match, boys." Trevor nodded, then turned to me.

"Match of a fuckin' lifetime, brother," he panted.

After we shared a quick embrace, I laid back down in the coffin. A simultaneous gasp escaped eighteen thousand mouths above and I knew that all the lights in the arena had just been extinguished. Above me, I could hear liquid spilling over the coffin's steel-coated cover. Then came the sound of flames crackling to life. Production values. I smiled, my satisfaction ascending with the coffin. Though the coffin's space was stifling, I felt ready to fly, a million miles removed from that night in Tennessee when I had hacked through the bottom of the ring with a machete.

The padding next to my head was equipped with a small speaker. Once the coffin made it safely to the top, a voice squawked in my ear: "All right, Cam. You're all clear. Take it home."

I threw open the flaming cover of the coffin and climbed out. The broadcasters were Thomas Rockart Jr. and Robby Redondo, a former pro wrestler. The two worked very well together; they had a natural animosity for one another that extended over to the broadcaster's booth and enabled them to effectively play off one another, with Rockart assuming the babyface role and Redondo the heel. Although they both knew Rockart signed Redondo's checks, they also both knew Thomas Rockart Jr. would never break up a winning team over something as trifling as his own personal feelings.

For this event, their comments were being broadcast not only for the pay-per-view audience, but for the arena as well. As I stood in darkness, the arena's only light coming from the flames swarming the coffin, their voices boomed:

"Who is that?" Rockart shouted, "Is that The Soultaker . . . or—"

"It's The Chameleon, I think!"

"No, it can't be! It just can't—"

"It is!"

"No, it's not!" Rockart cried. "You've got too much of that fake hair falling over your eyes, Robby!" (Robby, prematurely bald from steroid use, was never without his lengthy red and blue toupee).

At this point the house lights ignited and shone down on The Chameleon standing triumphantly above the flaming casket. I slowly removed The Soultaker's trademark mask from my face. "It's The Chameleon!" Rockart was shouting, "I can't believe it! The Chameleon has vanquished The Soultaker!"

With the mask off, my hair was free. Dyed back to its natural color, it stood out in a violent display of static electricity which had taken a hairdresser hours to create. "Wait a minute!" gasped Rockart, who tended to turn melodramatic whenever behind an announcer's table.

"You know who that looks like—" Robby began. Then I pulled off my Soultaker attire, revealing a Chuck "The Stud" Beastie T-shirt. This touched off a unanimous buzz from the crowd. I hurled the black overcoat into the coffin and slammed the blazing lid. The fire's light disappeared beneath the platform as the coffin lowered out of sight. I grabbed a microphone conveniently draped across the edge of the platform's railing.

"Aallllll riiight," I growled in the Chuck Beastie imitation perfected long ago on my high school's high jump mats.

"The Chameleon is going after Chuck Beastie next!" Rockart howled excitedly over a storm of cheers.

I turned and hopped down the platform in the same agile fashion The Stud always bounded about.

Like father, like son. The words ricocheted around my skull, and I found myself mouthing them without conscious thought. I mouthed them two more times before I realized their source: My own feeling of nonexistence that, unlike The Soultaker, remained unvanquished.

11

CHASING SHAWNA, FINDING MOM, AND A FATHER'S ULTIMATE JOB

"Better work the corners," the referee, now at my side, tells me. His name is Billy Harren, and he has been with the World Wrestling Organization for twenty-five years. Set to retire next year. He originally got into the business because he wanted to be a wrestler, but his 5'6" ectomorphic frame made that an impossibility. He worked his way up from ring-boy to referee. A few years back there was an angle in which he started favoring the heels in every match. The story line culminated in his being "fired" as a referee and becoming a manager. After two years managing, he opted to go back to refereeing. "As a ref, you're more a part of the match," he explained. So his manager character disappeared, and after a six week vacation in Hawaii with his wife, Billy came back and was quietly reinstated as a referee. By that time, most fans had forgotten he was once a "horribly biased" referee.

Many critics consider it ludicrous to have a referee for a match that is "fixed," but the third man in the ring is crucial. Not only does he enhance the theatrical element, but he watches the crowd. Billy Harren often speaks of the night eleven years ago when he was reffing a match between "Howling" Hunter Thomas and "Waco" Willie Falk and a crazed fan streaked into the ring with a knife. The fan (who later was found to be an animal rights activist) went after Hunter, who was notorious for bragging about wiping out entire species of animals. The wrestlers were in a clutch and didn't see the attacker, but Billy did. He tackled and disarmed the animal lover, but in the process suffered a cut on his shoulder that required twenty-two stitches to close. "Battle wound," Billy will term the scar while displaying it with considerable pride. "In a weird way, that was one of the coolest experiences of my life. Goin' to the hospital an' gettin' all sewed up, an' every moment I was feelin' like a wrestler. Like one of the boys, y'know?" That night has become a part of wrestling folklore and cemented his reputation as the best ref in the business.

"Do the corners, Michael," he is urging me now, teeth gritted so it doesn't look like he's speaking. "This is SlamFest, for chrissakes!"

I head over to the first corner and step onto the turnbuckle. *The crowd gets louder when I press my arms above my head, as though there is an invisible volume switch I am pushing against. Their screams crack with enthusiasm and hostility, but the passion in them seems forced. They do not really care.*

This thought makes my knees lock on the turnbuckle. I stand frozen, outside of myself and able to watch all the collections of vocal energy sailing past my body. A few die at my feet. None are able to penetrate the invisible shield of despair that holds my body in a dim black cloud. Seeing myself, I see no hero. Just a scared kid who is unworthy of the dream that has nursed him through life. A premonition of death seeps through the cloud and just as quickly retreats, leaving my body limp and restless.

To myself, hiding in plain sight before millions of people, I look like the only person in the world.

One of the things that made Chuck Beastie so popular with men was the constant presence of his beautiful valet, Mimi. With her playing the faithful and loving companion, he remained true to his gimmick by unleashing a storm of verbal abuse on her during every match or interview. Wherever Beastie wrestled, it was not uncommon to find a few representatives of the National Organization for Women outside the arena carrying picket signs that bore slogans such as: *Studs Don't Yell at Women* and *Mimi—Why Do You Stay?* The picketers lent a nice touch of authenticity, and I often suspected Thomas Rockart Jr. of setting them up as shills. But when I asked him about this, he denied it. "They're out there on their own accord," he said, sounding as mystified as I was. "Great publicity, but I'm kind of tempted to let them know it's really a gimmick." In truth, Mimi and Chuck had been married for six years. I would soon find out just how much of a gimmick their in-ring relationship really was.

But first I needed to become Chuck, and to do that I would need a Mimi. I told Rockart about Shawna. "If she'll work for a straight two hundred dollars plus transport and lodgings a night, she's in," he said. When I relayed this info to Shawna, her silence over the phone made me wonder if she was stunned, offended, or perhaps both.

"Shawna?" I ventured.

"When do I start?" she asked.

Chuck and I were set to have our first match at the San Diego Sports Arena, and I met Shawna that morning at San Diego International Airport. I arrived for her flight two hours early and spent the time pacing the gate and telling myself this was no big deal. Shawna was coming out here for a job, pure and simple. It had been more than two years since we had seen each other in person—what the hell did I expect to happen?

I careened back and forth between posts, discarding various scenarios of our being reunited. I remained mercifully unmolested by fans. Fans rarely bothered me; my status as a chameleon made it difficult for them to recognize me when I was stripped of the complementing presence of an opponent.

Shawna was one of the first people off the plane and

was hard to miss in a pair of jeans that gripped her thighs like cellophane wrap. Above her narrow waist dangled the bottom of a pink Gold's Gym boat-neck top. A narrow sea of flesh parted the two articles of clothing, and a belly button ring glinted like a sparkling island. Her skin had taken on a deeper tan over the past two years; this increased glow shadowed the fresh red highlights in her hair. I was squinting as I stepped before her. "Wow," she said, her eyes taking me in. "You grew." She reached out and touched my shoulder. This first real contact vanquished all the fantasies I had been entertaining for the past couple of hours, leaving me empty of everything but the passing moments and Shawna's very real presence.

I blurted out an improvised line using Chuck Beastie's growl: "Been eating three square meals a day."

"I'll bet, Mister Stud." She pulled me in for a hug. Her neck smelled like lilacs. As we headed toward baggage claim, our sides bumped together in a gently irresolute tempo. Her presence altered the airport's makeup, transforming what before had seemed merely a corral for purposeless travelers into a buzz of motion that suggested everyone there was either arriving from or preparing to depart on a search for possibilities only they could see.

I wanted to spend some time with Shawna that afternoon, but she insisted she had to prepare for this first match. "I need to meet with Rockart," she said as we drove toward the hotel in our rented Ford Taurus. "And I should meet Mimi, too. Besides, you haven't sketched Chuck yet, have you Chameleon?" she added.

"Not yet," I admitted, although Chuck had told me

he was looking forward to it. "I've always wanted to see myself as others do," he had told me.

So that afternoon I headed off to the San Diego Zoo with the same man who, as a child, I had fantasized about accompanying to father-son softball games. The zoo was his idea; when I asked him why, he shrugged and spent the next few seconds exhaling an unintelligible mumble. "I like animals," he announced finally. "Meem and I have two dogs, a cat, and a parakeet at home."

Our first stop was the chicken cage. Chuck watched the parade of feathers and precise pecking, his lips sewn in still concentration. His hand was slapping his thigh with the same whiplike snap imbued in his ring moves, but at that moment the limb's energy made it seem cut off from the rest of him.

"You uh . . . like chickens?" I asked idiotically. His brown eyes remained fixed on the chickens but his hand abruptly stopped. It sagged, a melancholy weight, to the side of his right thigh.

"Do you know," he suggested, his voice grappling with what sounded like an unfamiliar wonder, "that if one chicken is different than a group of other chickens, those chickens will peck the different one to death in twenty-five seconds or less?"

"Where'd you hear that?" I asked.

"Discovery Channel," he answered.

After we left and were wandering by the peacock cage, I noticed a group of children ogling us from over by the lion pit.

"The peacocks . . . ," Chuck was saying, his voice now a soothing hiss that made me picture a snowy television screen. "I love it when they let their feathers come out. They're beautiful."

"I think we've been spotted," I mentioned, nudging him and pointing out the gaggle of kids. Chuck's face assumed a look of alarm, as though he'd been caught doing something forbidden.

"Shit," he said quickly, "let's move."

We hurried down to the southern area of the zoo. Chuck stopped before the zebra exhibit, then motioned toward a bench across the dirt trail. It was tucked under a blanket of shade provided by surrounding pines. "How about there for the sketch?" he suggested.

"All right," I agreed.

He positioned himself on the bench with one leg tucked to his chest. "How's this look?" he said.

"Great," I said.

"Do you want me to sneer or anything?"

"No," I laughed. "Just relax." A careful wind teased his long frizzy hair. My pen traced this movement and the sketch was underway.

"Have you always . . . talked like this?" I asked.

"I had a real high-pitched voice when I was younger. It stuck around until I was about fifteen." His smile receded further into the folds of his mouth. "The guys used to tease me about it all the time. Called me Chuck Whiner. That's when I started rasping like this . . . so I wouldn't sound like a fucking girl all the time."

"Did you always want to be a pro wrestler?"

"I never had much other choice," he said. "My old man was in the biz, as you probably know."

I did. His name had been Randall Montgomery, and he had been the first person to hold the WWWO (as the

WWO had been called back then) Heavyweight Singles
and Tag-Team Championships simultaneously. "He
had me training by the time I was twelve," Chuck
informed me. "Other kids were out playing softball, I
was in the basement taking bumps in ninety degree
heat. Used to call it 'the pit.'" He shook his head. "I never
had any choice but to be a pro wrestler," he stated
flatly.

"You mean you wanted to be something else?" I
asked, a little stunned. The desire to lose myself in professional wrestling had been so all-consuming that it
was hard to imagine anyone begrudging so wonderful a
birthright.

"I don't know." Chuck shrugged again. "I always
looked at it like a plumber pulling his kid into the family business."

"I guess . . . ," he began, peering past me with eyes
that were overcome momentarily by a terror so intense
that I felt certain he'd spotted a sniper aiming for my
head. "I just don't know," he sighed, looking to the
ground. But my fear remained, held taut by an extreme
feeling of déjà vu. I glanced behind me, but the only
thing I saw was a couple shuffling past many yards
away. Even from this distance, it was easy to see the
painful beet-red glow throbbing on their faces, arms,
and legs. They continued along with determined steps,
gesturing gamely at the animals.

"How did you meet Mimi?" I asked, turning back.
Chuck's face immediately filled with fierce pride.

"I met her walking out of a cloud," he announced. "It
was a show back ten years ago, when I was starting in
Texas. There were these three jokers . . . real assholes

. . . Eric, Billy, and Jeff. Old-time veterans who used to give hell to all the newcomers. Naturally, they were hard partyers, too. Eric used to have this LSD liquid. Pure stuff. One time they dipped a candy bar in it and offered it to this Samoan kid. Poor bastard ate the whole fucking bar. He was tripped out for about a week, then claimed afterward that Satan had come and possessed his soul."

"Sounds like Trevor's old gimmick."

"But this was a shoot," Chuck said severely. "The kid wound up in a mental hospital."

I thought of the woman who had stalked me in Memphis. How many people had landed in mental hospitals because of pro wrestling? "What happened to the guys who gave him the stuff?"

"Nothing. They thought the whole thing was hilarious," Chuck said. "So I shot on Eric in our next match and beat the shit out of him. Later that night they slipped some Halcion into my drink backstage. I woke up at dawn. They had hog-tied me and set me out by the side of the road. I was one of the most hated heels in Texas about that time. All it would've taken was for some local boys to find me and I woulda had the shit beaten out of me.

"I hear this car pull up. Then there're these cowboy boots walking in my direction. I managed to turn around a little. The wind's kicking up dust everywhere, and I couldn't see a damn thing. I was getting ready to plead for my life with some idiot redneck. But then through the dust stepped the most beautiful woman I had ever seen."

His voice became softer and softer as he described

how she had used a bowie knife to free him from the ropes and then taken him back to the farm she ran. Her father had recently died, and her mother had slipped away only three weeks later. "I told her that was the most romantic thing I had ever heard, and she laughed. But it was a nice laugh," he insisted. "And then she fixed me one helluva terrific breakfast. Fresh hotcakes and eggs that weren't too runny or too stiff. The coffee was rich and strong. And as she did this she talked, and I just sat there. Not hearing a word she was saying 'cause I was too busy falling in love with her."

He was convinced that they were soul mates. "She used to always describe our meeting as kismet. She knows words like that," he said and smiled. "I looked it up in the dictionary. It means fate. Beautiful, huh?" A delicate chuckle escaped from his lips.

"How about kids?" I asked.

His mouth drew back into a tight thoughtful line. "We're on the road a lot, so . . ." He let the sentence dangle helplessly before sealing the dismissal with a shrug. "We'll see."

Out of a strange reluctance to continue meeting his eyes I turned my attention to the portrait in my hands and was stunned to see that I had ceased drawing. His form was complete, but details had eluded me. The only characteristic that could possibly identify the shape as Chuck Beastie was the long black hair fanning out like wires seized by current. "We'd better get moving," I heard him say, and when I looked back he was already on his feet. I jumped up and hurried after him, still half-studying the incomplete sketch. "Did you get me down?" he asked, peeking over my shoulder.

"Sort of," I mumbled, "I guess I got distracted by that story—"

"Hey, I like it." He slowed his pace for a few seconds, rubbing his elbow carelessly as he grew closer to my shoulder. By the time I slowed down, he had already resumed his previous stride. We passed the sunburnt couple, who were laughing and calling "yoo hoo" and "hey there" to a pair of hippopotamuses basking in the sun among a freshly constructed jungle.

"Mind if I . . . keep it?" Beastie's request was backed up by an assertive look.

"Well . . . ," I stammered. "Sure." I tore off the piece of paper and handed it to him. He rolled it up and very carefully placed it inside his jacket.

"Do you regret it?" I asked as we continued back the way we had come.

"Regret what?" his words flew back with a tense expectancy.

"Becoming a professional wrestler," I suggested.

"I love pro wrestling. I'm grateful as hell to my old man for giving me the chance to compete in it." In spite of the rapid mumble in which he thrust these words forth, he managed to give each one a careful pronunciation. "The only thing is gimmicks like Vivian Vitale," he added, his voice claiming a measured intensity, "they make the sport seem . . ." He paused, seeming to consider and disregard several definitions before settling on the appropriate one. "Goofy," he concluded. "And my father always used to hate goofy stuff in this business."

"A little strange," I replied, when Shawna asked me how the session had gone. We were backstage, preparing to go out for the match that night.

"What do you mean, 'a little strange'?" she asked, adjusting her low-cut sequined dress that ended mid-thigh.

"A woman walking the streets of Hollywood in that thing would either be arrested or discovered," I teased her, trying to change the subject for a reason I couldn't quite apprehend.

"Ha-ha," she retorted. "Why was it a little strange?"

I shrugged.

"Let me see the portrait," she demanded.

"Chuck wanted to keep it," I told her.

"Hmmm . . ." She gave a pondering frown.

"How was Mimi?" I asked.

"She told me it would be a relief to have another collection of estrogen around all this runaway testosterone," she said.

"What about the wannabe woman, Vivian Vitale?" I laughed.

Shawna shot me a cool stare. "That's a *gimmick*," she said in a voice that contained enough shaded hostility to make me both confused and nervous.

"Actually," I pointed out hurriedly, groping at a bit of information Santa had once given me, "steroids are metabolized by the body as estrogen. So there are really *several* collections of estrogen around here."

"So I've noticed." Her face reclaimed a smile as she jabbed my chest with a disapproving finger. But her touch was hesitant, as though she were touching a vase she was afraid might crack.

"Alll riight," I rasped, ignoring what Chuck had told me about the origins of the voice I was mimicking.

The match went well that night. Afterward, Mimi and Shawna both changed into dresses more suitable for the terrace restaurant where the four of us were planning to have a post-match meal. Chuck and I both wore elephant pants and tank tops. There was some resistance to our attire at first, with a shaky-eyed greeter informing us that "coats and ties were required." Chuck bribed him with a twenty and we wound up seated at a table near the kitchen. The reservations people had overbooked the restaurant, and new diners were being herded in with flustered speed only to be placed at folding tables covered with red tablecloths. These makeshift dining spots dotted the aisles, making it hard for the waiters to move around and adding to the chaos.

Mimi immediately ordered two Hawaiian chocolates, a sweet mixture of Kahlua and sours, for herself. Chuck and I discussed the first couple spots of the match while Mimi tossed back both drinks. "I had a fan reach out and try to grope me as I came down the aisle tonight," she hurled the words into the empty glass of her second drink, then turned accusingly to Chuck. "Where the hell were you, *Stud*?" she sneered.

"Honey," Chuck laughed nervously, "I was on my way to the ring. I had to be playing to the crowd." His hands settled palms up at shoulder level, as though he were weighing two stones.

"Some stud," Mimi muttered. With a shared look, Shawna and I mutely asked each other if we should excuse ourselves. Then a waiter appeared, and instead of giving us menus, he informed us that they were putting in another table. Regretfully, they would have to move us. Immediately two large smiling busboys stepped up, lifted the table at either end, and hustled it eight feet to the right. After we readjusted our chairs, the waiter said he would bring menus. Mimi demanded another drink, and Chuck ordered a beer.

"My pleasure, sir!" the waiter cried, then swooped away.

"His pleasure . . . for moving us?" Chuck asked, looking at me. I shrugged. We strained to make conversation. At one point Shawna asked how Chuck and Mimi had met. Chuck quickly replied that he had already told me; Mimi snorted with a level amount of disgust.

"Do we have to talk about *wrestling* right now?" she asked her drink. Shawna apologized carefully, and I got Chuck off in a discussion of the pets they owned.

Two more times, once just after we ordered and once in the midst of the meal itself, our table was moved again by the same two burly workers. The waiter expressed his sincerest regrets, referring deferentially to us as "ladies and gentlemen" at every opportunity and assuring us after each move that it had been his pleasure.

"Ha!" Mimi slurred, after the third time he'd moved us. She slammed her fork down onto her plate. The waiter and Chuck's eyes both became equally nervous. "This *gentleman*," she indicated Chuck with a blind thrust of her thumb, "wants to know why it's your goddamn *pleasure* to move us and inconvenience our meal?"

"Meem . . . ," Chuck murmured, "come on, he's just doin' his job."

"She does have a point," Shawna piped in. I turned to her, eyebrows raised. She shrugged at me. Our waiter's face twitched as though he were trying to repel a fly attempting to land on his nose.

"We consider it our pleasure to serve ladies and gentlemen such as yourselves—"

"Ha!" Mimi shrieked, downing the last of her drink and slapping the glass down disdainfully. "This isn't a *gentle*man next to me. He's a *no* man! Oh, be a man!" she cried to Chuck. "If you can't be a stud, at least be a man! Christ, why can't you ever be a man?"

"That's enough . . . ," Chuck muttered in the low grated tone he used in interviews.

"I suppose it's too much to expect for you to be a man in a restaurant if you can't even be a man in the bedroom—"

"I said—Enough!" Chuck bellowed. It would have been audible even in an arena packed with thousands of screaming fans. In this much smaller area of restaurant, it knifed through the busy chatter of diners with the force of a meteor crashing through space, leaving only anticipatory silence in its wake.

I looked back cautiously at the sea of eyes staring at us. The waiter coughed, but stood rooted to his spot like a necessary prop. Mimi shoved her chair away, clambered to her feet, and strode out of the restaurant with impressive agility for someone who had been slurring as severely as she had. "I'm sorry," Chuck said, his eyes sweeping over the waiter before settling on Shawna and me. The waiter nodded dumbly and retreated between the potted ferns cloaking the kitchen entrance-way. "You guys finish dinner. Please." Chuck cast an embarrassed glance around the attentive restaurant as he stood. "Just sign the check to my room." Then his wide back was threading awkwardly down the narrow aisles crowded with waiters and busboys.

Our own waiter emerged from the ferns. "Will there be anything else, sir?" he asked me.

"Another drink, I guess," I replied.

"Right away, sir." He snapped his anxious eyes over to Shawna. "And madame?"

"Nothing, thanks," she said and shook her head. He departed with a relieved air.

"I kind of like it in here," I said.

"I'm not surprised." Shawna chuckled. "Nobody would dare call you by your name. You're just another characterless 'sir' to them. Must feel safe, huh?"

I regarded her with bewilderment. "Shit," she said, "I'm sorry." Her hand found mine under the table. "It's just seeing you dressed in that get-up he wears. Even at *dinner*. It seems . . ."

"Let's draw the line at living whatever gimmick Chuck and Mimi are," I suggested.

"You mean you're ready to actually create a rela-tionship . . . of your very own?" she suggested.

"Yeah." I kissed her hand. She drew it back with a grin.

"Good friends, Romeo." She specified our status as she wrapped her fingers lightly around her water glass.

"Is there someone else?" I asked.

"Nope," she answered quietly, "but you're still a pro-fessional wrestler, remember?"

I turned my eyes up to the ceiling, seeking comfort in the impartial striped pattern I expected to find there. Instead, a skylight suffering the absence of sun threw my reflection back. "How could I ever forget?" I asked myself.

The next day neither Chuck nor Mimi mentioned the incident. Shawna and I didn't press the issue, and soon the four of us had managed to establish a respectful camaraderie. Shawna quickly became popular with the rest of the boys, which was no surprise. She was able to hold her own in raunchy conversation, attitude, and drinking games. But she drew the line at any kind of heavier drugs. "I've been down that road before," she said in explanation, refusing to either elaborate about her previous consumption or lecture anyone about their current use.

Two weeks after she joined the company, we hit San Francisco for a show at the Bay Arena. Afterward, Shawna and I went out alone for a night of cocktailing. We followed a string of windowless bars along Market Street, and in honor of our night out decided to play one cut from *The Doors Greatest Hits* at each of them. I would drink three shots of tequila and she would drink two before the song ended, and then we would seek out another bar with a juke box.

It was early morning by the time we finished the album and made it back to the tenth floor of the San Francisco Hilton. I was staggering spiritedly down the hallway, nursing an idle desire to somehow wind up alone in a room with Shawna when I turned and found she was no longer beside me. I spun around and saw her kneeling at the other end of the hallway next to what appeared to be a dead body.

I hurried to her side. Shawna was holding the naked body of a young girl. "Bastard," Shawna mumbled, "that fucking bastard. Drug her up, shit on her, then toss her out like a goddamn room service tray." I wondered blankly at this, then focused on two large turds clinging to the girl's back. My vision was so blurred that at first glance they had appeared to be nothing more than grotesquely oversized moles.

Shawna tore off a piece of her shirt and swept the shit off the girl's skin. Then she knocked on the door. Soon she was pounding on it. I was busy wrapping my jacket around the girl's naked body and slapping her lightly, trying to make her come to. Finally, the door opened, and I turned just in time to see Shawna fire a punch at the face of a bespectacled middle-aged man wearing a Hilton bathrobe. She pulled it in time, and her fist stopped about two inches from his slack jaw. Drunk as she was, this kind of control was truly impressive.

Shawna and I stared at the dumbfounded man. "Harry?" a female voice came scratching from the darkness behind him.

"Aaaahhh . . . ," the man exhaled. The girl surfaced from her Halcion-induced coma and let out a mournful wail. The man's eyes went from us to the naked victim cloaked in my coat. Shocked outrage took over his face, triggering in me a shame similar to what I had felt in Tennessee when a different man standing in a different doorway had witnessed the Wandering Wildman threatening a crazed stalker with a knife.

The door slammed in our faces. The girl was crying by now, and I took her up in my arms before Shawna and I bolted off down the hall. Once we turned the corner Shawna wordlessly took the girl from me and disappeared into her room. I retreated into mine and, unable to sleep, sat staring out the window at silver blades of moonlight until a knock came at the door.

It was Shawna. She walked inside and sat on the edge of the bed. "I gave her some clothes," she said. "She went downstairs to call her friends for a ride."

I nodded. She looked up at me. "Can I sleep here?" she asked. I was not prepared for this. Inky guilt spilled from my heart, catching in my throat and making me cough. What could Shawna have gotten out of the past ten minutes that made her suddenly want to have sex with me?

My coughing fit must have revealed this anxiety, because she let out a bemused chuckle. "Take it easy, Cam," she said mildly. "All I want is to sleep in the same bed with a guy I know isn't a total asshole."

"Sure," I said, relief and disappointment reducing my voice to a whisper. But even though sex wasn't an issue, my guilt lingered. We spent that night side by side, shoulders touching.

In Cleveland the next day, Chuck and I were backstage discussing some spots for that night's match when we heard a series of yelps erupt from the bathroom. This was followed by a toilet flushing repeatedly, and finally silence. Several seconds later Shawna strolled out with an impassive smile. By the time

"Dastardly" Darren Domino made his way out, a bunch of us were waiting for him. He had obviously washed his face, but the humiliated look on his face was as unmistakable as any layer of shit.

I started the chant. "Swir-lee! Swir-lee!" Soon the rest of the guys had joined in. Domino's only response was to put on a brave smirk and half-strut, half-shuffle off to a corner.

"That was great," I told Shawna later that night, after the match.

"Seems like everyone enjoyed it," she said.

"Yeah," I said. "I guess he had it coming," I added.

"I wonder . . ." Her face locked into a hard expression that matched the tone of her next words. ". . . why the hell no one else ever did it, then."

She got up and walked off. I didn't follow; I had no worthy response to offer. We didn't speak again until the next afternoon in Dallas. I was backstage wrapping my wrists and fingers, using the same excessive amount of tape Beastie always used every night, when Shawna came up to me. "I'm sorry about the way I acted toward you yesterday," she said. "You didn't deserve that."

In the past twenty-four hours I had thought a lot about how I would respond to her apology, which I knew she would make eventually. Now that it was here, I said something I had not once considered. "Actually," I answered, "I suppose I did."

She smiled, and we drifted into a hug. It tightened, but as soon as her breasts touched my chest she jerked back. She gave me a furtive smile, then turned and loped off. I stared down at the piece of tape dangling from my wrist, then felt a hand caress my back. I turned quickly to see Rob Robertson. "Better be careful," he whispered, "the little woman might find out." He cut his eyes at Shawna's retreating figure, then strolled away. After several confused seconds, I figured it out: he still thought I was *married.* He must have seen something in the way Shawna and I were interacting that suggested an intimacy closer than friendship.

I pressed the remainder of tape down across my wrist, taking a few moments to consider the tiny explosions going off below. They were unruly and strong; they scared me. I stood and went off in search of Beastie to plan the finish of that night's match.

The WWO gave its employees Christmas Day off. I worked a match with Beastie in Minneapolis on Christmas Eve, and we were scheduled to work again the day after Christmas at the St. Louis Civic Center. I arranged for a stopover in Chicago to see my mom. Over the phone, I apologized to her about not being able to bring a gift. She cut off my excuse about the blur of travel making it difficult to even think with, "Just you coming will be gift enough.

"Even if it's only for a few hours," she went on, referring to the just under five hours I would have for my visit.

When I mentioned this to Shawna, she asked if she could come along. "Sure," I replied, stunned. "I mean, I'd like that."

We were standing outside the Minneapolis airport,

waiting for our rental car to pull up, when I finally asked her why she wanted to come.

"I want to see where you come from," she replied, her cheeks lighting up like small cherries against the sub-zero temperature.

The next day, Christmas, I called my mom just before we were leaving and learned that Harry and Shirley were "dying" to see me. I knew something was up. Finally, my mom spilled the story. Jim had been apprehended in a sting operation regarding the collapse of a savings and loan. Apparently, he had been involved in the disappearance of several hundred thousand dollars worth of bonds. There had been so many that he figured the government wouldn't miss a few. However, the bonds he had chosen to steal had been marked by the Treasury Department. The percentage of these marked bonds in relation to the total amount that had been issued was comparable to the percentage of bicentennial quarters Jim had managed to disfigure as a child before giving up. But now, his ambition carried a penalty more severe than a simple surrender to the odds; he had been sentenced to ten years in a federal penitentiary.

"Harry and Shirley are still in shock," my mother said, then warned me not to mention Jim.

We all met at Barnaby's, a darkly lit pizza place in a Chicago suburb. The booths were the kind that, when I was a kid, had always made me feel like I was sitting in the cockpit of a race car. But my bringing Shawna and my mom bringing Irling made us a party of six, too many for a booth.

I had always pictured Irling as a gruff, large man,

similar to the way my father was supposed to have looked. To my surprise Irling was tall and thin with a face of neatly arranged features. His demeanor was unassuming and tinged with gentleness. All of his movements, even those as simple as pulling out a chair for my mom, were conducted with the swiftness of a deer bounding down a hillside. When Mom introduced us, he immediately recited what he did for a living (administrative assistant for a microchip company) and listed his hobbies (golf, pinball, and tinkering) with the shaky eagerness of a game show contestant.

Harry and Shirley had both become a bit chunkier, and Harry's hair was now a field of gray. But they seemed in determined good spirits, with both of them expressing how proud they were of my current position as, in Harry's words, a "sports superstar." His advice to me now was to simply "get married" with no mention of "and have children."

He told me this while Shawna was in the ladies' room. "Now that's a woman to settle down with," Harry said. I glanced uneasily at the ladies' room, as though Shawna might be able to somehow hear through the door.

"She seems nice," my mother added with a distant approval, touching my frizzed out, dyed-black hair with a puzzled finger.

"She seems very . . . forward," Irling commented.

"Bet your ass she is," I agreed.

Ten minutes later, Shawna had returned to the table and Irling had excused himself to the washroom. "What do you think?" my mom asked me as soon as the men's room door had swung shut behind him.

"He seems all right," I replied, realizing too late that I was mimicking her generic evaluation of Shawna.

Before I could add anything, my mother announced: "We're moving."

"No!" Shirley exclaimed.

"When?" I asked.

"I don't know." Mom said. "Irling's getting transferred to a new plant opening in Nebraska. I think it'd be good for me. To get away from the city—"

"Are you going to marry him?" Shirley asked, her mouth opening and closing like a fervent guppy.

"I'm not sure yet," Mom said casually and continued munching her pizza. I stared at her in the candlelight and noticed she had accumulated some gray hairs herself. The sight of them triggered a thought I had never before allowed myself: Bonnie Harding was a person with her own collection of fears and confusions. For so many years she had been strong and raised me, never once complaining or feeling sorry for herself about losing a man she had loved. She suddenly seemed like someone who might like booths as much as I did. Even though it scared me a little, I began to flirt with this newfound concept, wondering if she might also have trouble distinguishing dawn from dusk.

"Congratulations, Mrs. Harding," Shawna said, smiling.

"Thank you, Shawna." My mom's voice unfolded into a genuine appreciation.

"Yeah, Mom," I said. "That's good. I'm . . . glad."

"Thank you," Mom repeated with a girlish smile. I wanted to grab a flower from the table's vase and tuck it behind her ear.

"Well," Harry said, his voice as skeptical as a foregone conclusion.

"I'm glad to see you're doing so well for yourself, Michael," Shirley announced loudly.

"Why?" I wondered aloud. "You never supported the idea of me going into wrestling. If it had been your decision, I would've gone into the same field as Jim—"

Mom choked as Harry's face settled into a rigid vexation. "Jim is . . . ," Shirley paused, then turned anxiously to Harry as though waiting for him to tell the rest of a joke she had fouled up.

"Jim is gone," he related this information to Shawna in a stern flat tone, no doubt assuming she was the only one at the table who didn't know what had happened.

"Jesus!" she exclaimed. "He's in prison, not dead. He's still your son!" ("It got to me," she would tell me later. "I don't like parents that write off their kids.")

Irling suddenly reappeared, landing in his seat like an excited bird. "You know those sinks in the bathroom?" he asked, "My company's working on a chip that will give them an eye. Soon you won't have to turn a faucet at all. Just stick your hand under and—ta-da!—water comes out. Tell me that won't cut down on germs."

He spun a proud smile around the table, seemingly oblivious to the silence usually reserved for blind dates that are failing miserably. My mom reached over and squeezed his hands. "That's great, sweetie," she said.

Harry and Shirley left hastily before the check arrived, offering only a few murmured farewells to mark their departure. As soon as they were gone, the table's mood unwound. Soon my mom was telling a story about the time I had named a turkey we bought at the store "Daffy" (having convinced myself it was a duck) and then broke down crying when my mom tried to cook it.

"I remember that," I said and grinned. "You wound up taking it back to the store, where you told me they would bring it back to life there because it was a 'special duck.'"

"Actually," she smiled, "I kind of pulled a fast one on you. I just circled the block and came back with the same turkey. We had it for supper that night and you never noticed a thing."

I laughed along with everyone, a little chagrined that this possibility had never occurred to me. I wondered how many other things in life I had missed.

Outside the restaurant, Irling and I shook hands. When I hugged my mom I noticed she was wearing perfume. "Mom, what kind of perfume is that?" I asked her.

"Concord," she answered. "The same kind I've always worn, kiddo." She leaned in closer and whispered into my ear, "I really do like her."

"And I like him," I whispered back.

"Hey, Mom," I said, as we pulled back a little, "I'm sorry, you know, about missing Christmas that one year. And about . . ." But what exactly I was sorry about escaped me. It didn't matter. She reached through flying snowflakes and touched my cheek with a warm hand.

"Dawn." She smiled.

The next morning, before leaving for St. Louis, I called information and tried to track down Bryan and Marty. Marty's old number was disconnected, and Bryan's parents promised to give him a message the next time he called from Spain, where he was now living with a young woman he had met in a youth hostel there. This inability to reach two of my oldest friends only underscored a growing realization that I had nobody close enough to talk to about my growing feelings for Shawna. I had begun sketching a life-size drawing of her on a six-foot-long scroll of leaf paper I had tacked to a wall in my Brooklyn apartment. I didn't know whether that could be classified as deranged or not, and there was no one around to ask. B.J. and I hadn't spoken much since I had joined the WWO. During a four-day vacation in the slushy weeks of February, I finally got in touch with him one night. Ever since lying to Terri about Ricky Witherspoon remembering B.J.'s father, I had been reluctant to talk to B.J. Maybe he would be able to tell that I had lied. Maybe he already knew. What really scared me was that he would ask me why I had lied, because I knew how hard I would have to probe myself to come up with an honest answer.

But when I got him on the phone he made no mention of Witherspoon. He was working at a warehouse and going to night school. Terri was studying nursing as well. "We're gonna need two incomes real soon," he told me. "Families are expensive."

"What do you mean, 'families'?"

"What do you think I mean, bro? We got ourselves a little Bobby Joe Junior!"

"What?" I cried. "When?"

"Damn, Mike," he laughed. "We've been married for a year and a half." With a start I realized this was true. Kansas City still felt too close and too real for that kind of time to have passed, but there it was.

"How come you didn't tell me sooner?" I asked.

"Terri wanted to surprise you. When you came to visit," he added pointedly.

"Sorry, B.J.—"

"It's cool. The travel schedule must be hectic as hell, but try and get out here soon."

"I will," I promised, knowing I probably wouldn't. These little lies, exaggerated promises . . . each one peeled another strand off the rope of our friendship. What had once seemed unbreakable was now stretched by miles and time to the point where I couldn't mention something that would make me vulnerable. Telling any of my fellow wrestlers about Shawna would only have been inviting ridicule. Her absolute refusal to get involved with pro wrestlers was well known by one and all. Even Chuck Beastie was off-limits as a potential confidant. Although we got along well, his intense demeanor frightened me too much to be able to confide in him.

Our feud was ending soon anyway. SlamFest, the WWO's yearly pay-per-view extravaganza, was set to take place the first week of April. Chuck Beastie and I were about to engage in a series of cage matches that would see him emerge victorious. He would then challenge "The American Dream" Sonny Logan at SlamFest, while The Chameleon would most likely be retired. This made me exceedingly nervous; I had no idea what other gimmick could replace it.

A day after I learned B.J. was a father, I was spending the final evening of my four-day vacation working on my giant sketch of Shawna when I heard the knock.

I stared at the door with curiosity and a dash of fear. Nobody had ever come knocking before. The sound came again, a bit more violent this time. I crossed over and opened it, revealing Shawna. "Surprised?" She grinned.

"Yeah," I lied. Shawna's arriving at my door totally unannounced seemed right. At this point in our relationship, if she had sprouted wings I doubt I would've done much more than wonder what took her so long.

We hugged and, before I even had a chance to remember it was there, she caught sight of her portrait. "My God," she exhaled, "I don't know whether to be completely flattered or fucking terrified."

"It's just something I do to pass the time," I mumbled.

"Sure," she intoned, drawing the word out with an exaggerated gentleness that made me blush until I saw she was laughing. "So," she piped, "what's good around here?"

I was held speechless, searching for an answer. On my days off I rarely went outside, preferring instead the cool gray walls of my apartment where I could listen to jazz and sketch life passing by outside the window. My living room window provided me with a pleasant view of the tree-lined street outside. The houses stood with a quiet dignity. Many of them looked as settled as the families that inhabited them; these houses were possessors of secrets, collections of memories, and catalysts of dreams. They were the kinds of buildings, I realized while sketching one day, my grandfather had taken pride in building.

I had never ventured far past the small corner grocery store that stood at the end of my block, its rusted sign boasting *Best Prices*. I often looked at that sign as a silent signal, bidding me not to wander out of its sight. Alone, I had been able to pass it and continue on for a minute or so, only to feel my resolve dissipate after about twenty paces. Then I would turn back and trudge underneath the sign and into the store to purchase boxed pastas and macaroni and cheese, the only two meals I ever cooked when off the road.

"I don't know," I heard myself confessing to Shawna.

We took the subway into Manhattan and strolled along a small crowded street lined with bars. We passed a blues bar with harmonies riding waves of cigarette smoke out the open door. A saxophone broke into life, swelling within a horn's rhythm. I grabbed Shawna's hand. "Come with me," I said.

I guided her into the bar. Two dark-suited men with fedoras were blowing while people watched and clapped from just a few feet away. I swung around and began dancing with Shawna, who matched my strides. When they saw us, the musicians kicked it into a jazzier mode. After a five minute session they wrapped it up and we finished with a flourish that had me dipping Shawna down to within inches of the hardwood floor. We applauded with sweaty hands, and both men tipped their hats to us.

Then we were back on the street. "Pretty good moves in there," Shawna was laughing. "When was the last time you danced like that?" she asked.

"I don't know," I said, "probably high school prom."

"Long time," she whistled, and bumped my hand. But I didn't take it. I was too busy remembering the last woman, Charlotte, I had danced with like that. The last woman who had insisted I give up professional wrestling for her.

We stopped at a corner and debated whether or not to buy a couple of hot dogs from the vendor leaning against the streetlight. He immediately noticed our interest and pounced. "I don't sell hot dogs!" he barked. "If you want a hot dog, go up to Seventh Street where all them amateurs are. These," he informed us, his cheeks pushed up by his smile, "these are genuine Fourth and Broadway chili cheese dogs with the works."

"Sold me," Shawna said, pulling out her wallet. She cut off my mild offer to pay with, "You buy the drinks, I'll buy the food." I watched as she opened the wallet. There was a photograph resting in the top fold of transparent picture holders. It was of a sinewy young man with long blonde hair and skin whose tone almost matched Shawna's. He was wearing wrestling trunks, and it was obviously a publicity shot of some kind. I quickly looked away, and was sulkily absorbed in the dynamics of the street as she turned to me with a chili cheese dog.

We parted later that night at the door to my building. With the trace of her perfume still on my shoulder from when we had hugged, I lay in bed with indigestion. Because I didn't consider myself the jealous type, I told myself it was just the result of the chili cheese dog. Across the room, her sketch hovered in the shadows strewn against the wall.

The cages in WWO were similar to the ones in the SWA. They consisted of four walls made up of the same chain-link fence that surrounds school playgrounds. But WWO cages possessed a unique feature: a trap-door in the roof allowed wrestlers to actually clamber on top of the cage and brawl there in order to give the marks an extra thrill in hopes that one of them would go flying off and plunge thirty feet onto the arena floor.

Naturally, Beastie and I worked out a spot toward the end of the match where we brawled on the top of the cage. The finish of the match had Beastie kicking me back through the opening. After I fell back onto the mat he would scale over to the turnbuckle, unload with a flying elbow, and pin me.

The afternoon before our first match, Beastie responded to my greeting with a grunt. When I suggested we go over a few spots, he merely grunted again and started out toward the ring. I scanned the back-stage area. No Mimi.

The cage had been lowered from pulleys so that it fit neatly over the ring. After about twenty minutes of working on spots, he suddenly snarled at me: "You can't be drunk or fucked up on pills when we do this match, kid." It was the first full sentence he had uttered all afternoon.

"I don't do it to get drunk," I responded carefully. "I do it to kill pain. My knee's still fucked up from—"

"What the hell do you know about pain?" he retorted. "I've been in this business eleven fucking years, wrestling at least three hundred nights out of every goddamn one of them. So don't tell me about pain."

He stormed out of the cage and stalked down the aisle toward the backstage curtain, leaving me alone in the ring. I stared at the fence, through all those tiny separate holes, out into the empty arena.

Backstage, Chuck sat alone in a corner speaking to no one. Mimi finally arrived at ten minutes before show time. As soon as she peeked into the community dressing area, Chuck shot to his feet and hustled her into a private room. I made sure to pass by the closed door a couple of times. Instead of the expected shouts, I picked up snatches of what sounded like an earnest conversation.

Fifteen minutes later Chuck emerged smiling. He immediately apologized to me for behaving as he had. I assured him it was fine, and underwent a complete renewal of faith in him. "Alll riiight!" we bellowed in unison, before going out and having one of our best matches. Out in the ring, he hollered at his beautiful valet with gusto and flexed for the crowd as though this display of machismo and people's reaction to it were his very reasons for being. Naturally, I did the same.

————————

A week later we had a one-day layover in St. Louis. I was lying on the bed of my hotel room, studying the hideous curtains when a knock came at the door.

Shawna came in and presented me with a long thin gift wrapped package. "Open it," she urged, as though whatever was inside might explode if not revealed quickly enough. I did as she asked and found a set of fifty colored pencils.

"Whoa," I said. "These are . . ." Unable to determine a proper adjective, I let the ascension of my eyebrows supply one.

Shawna watched my reaction carefully, then said: "I want you to draw me. In color."

"Umm," I said, nodding, "okay."

She draped herself over a chair.

"Now?" I asked.

"Sure," she explained, "we've got the whole evening."

This comment sent me into a state of mental and physical fumbling that lasted until I finally had a sheet of blank paper stretched tautly on the easel before me. Then came the same mix of dread and anticipation that had consumed Muscular Mike Maple back in a southern California YMCA so many years ago. Now, finally, I was having that feeling in a situation that had nothing to do with wrestling.

As I worked I asked Shawna questions. Her responses were neither evasive nor confessional. When I carefully asked why she had no boyfriend, she provided an airy shrug and answered, "My life is complex enough without adding in *men.*" She instilled the final word with an assemblage of hope and confusion usually reserved for words like *infinity.*

I drew on, my hand becoming more and more animated as it discovered the richness of color. I shaded Shawna's dark flesh with a combination of brown, yellow, and gray, then added slashes of red and green to simulate the shine a certain wave of light mined from her flesh. Where this light came from was a mystery to me; it may have even been brought on by my own mind, but there was no doubt my eyes and hands saw it as real.

At one point I asked her, "Why are you in this world, Shawna?"

"To learn, I hope."

"What could you learn from pro wrestling?" I joked.

"Oh. You meant *this* world. I thought you meant this *world.*"

"What could this world teach you?" I asked seriously.

"I'm going to just be quiet and watch you draw," she said and smiled in gentle rebuff. "Let me know when you're done."

I finally stopped at about eight o'clock. My new excitement over color had resulted in an abundance of details. Imagined shadows and tones swirled together to form a visual overload. But there was no doubt I had captured Shawna. The portrait's eyes twinkled. Face impossibly alive, looking soft enough to caress.

When Shawna looked at the result, I assumed her silence meant she hated it. I was ready to say the hell with it and tear the thing to shreds when she asked me if she could keep it. I nodded mutely. She seemed to sense how drained I was, and left quickly with the sketch, squeezing my hand in farewell.

As soon as she left, I leapt to my feet and began to pace my room. My brain was still humming. I wanted to talk to someone, anyone, about something or anything. I left my room and took the elevator down to the hotel's lounge.

The first thing I saw was Chuck Beastie marooned

at a table in the corner. Above him, a halogen light shone down, its glare clouded by a piece of metal that had been sculpted into an ambiguous shape. The rest of the light shone down on Beastie's body, which was slouched with the confusion of a lost child. I stepped up to the table. "Mind if I join you?" I asked. He waved haphazardly at the chair across from him. I sat and flagged down a brunette waitress, who took our order for two martinis and disappeared.

"I lied to you," Beastie drawled quietly.

"About what?" I asked, staring across at his wrinkled brow. Listless piano music floated from the other side of the lounge, where a mustached man was playing out his final set of the night. Beastie's eyes met mine sullenly.

"I didn't meet 'er on a road," he slurred. "I didn't see 'er walkin' out of a cloud." His chin sagged down and rested against his chest. "I met her in wrestling. She won a contest to be my valet for the night. Way back when I was in Texas."

He didn't seem to expect a response, and I didn't trust myself to provide one. The waitress brought our drinks and Beastie drained half of his in one swallow. I did the same.

"She's leaving me," he croaked dissonantly. "We went on separate vacations. Thought some time apart might do us good. But all it did was show her how much she enjoyed being away from me."

"I can't give her what she wants," he said. "When we first got together, it was like . . . it was the first time in my life I could see myself together with someone. I never wanted to be apart from her. And because I met her as a valet, it was perfect. Of course, once we had kids she would retire from the road to raise 'em. For eleven years we tried . . . tried to make it work." His words gave me a dull chill and I inhaled the rest of my vodka to fight it. "It was supposed to be like a dream," he repeated. Sweat was running down his forehead. His voice was receding from the low rasp that he had forced himself to develop over the years. The tone now had a pathetic hollowness, as though it were a limb or organ he no longer had any use for.

"I hate that goddamn picture you drew of me." The words flew from his mouth like darts "It makes me look . . ." He withdrew back into a melancholy silence before pushing out the final word: "Goofy."

"Hey, it's . . . it's all right, Chuck," I said. "I'll take it back."

"Ask me that question again, kid," he mumbled.

"What question?" I whispered tightly.

"Do I . . . regret it?" he said.

I opened my mouth only to find I couldn't speak.

"I love pro wrestling." Chuck's voice suddenly sounded young and scared. "I'm grateful as hell to my father for giving me the chance to compete in it."

He sighed with a final gasp of force. "But yeah. I regret it," he said and drank more of his martini. "It was supposed to be a dream. Now I gotta get a fucking life."

He drained his glass, and this bit of liquid seemed to push him over the edge. As he slumped toward the table, I quickly reached over and righted him. "A fuckin' life," he mumbled. I stood and stepped over to him.

"Come on, Chuck. Time to go," I said. I managed to get him out of the chair and hoist him over my shoulder. I carried him like this past the disapproving stares of a middle-aged couple nursing drinks at a table, past the ceaseless drone of the piano, and finally escaped out the door under the pitying gaze of our waitress.

I dug Chuck's room key out of the pocket of his elephant-legged pants and finally managed to haul him the rest of the way to his room. After I carried him inside and laid him down on the bed, he seemed to gain a slight foothold on consciousness. "I'm all right." He blinked at me and nodded. "How'd I get up here already? I pass out?"

"Yeah," I answered, "I carried you."

"No shit." He laughed. "Haven't passed out in years. Felt damn good."

"Hey," he called as I turned to go, "I lied to you."

"You told me," I said. "It's all right. I hope you and Mimi can work it out," I added helplessly.

"Huh?" He shot me a puzzled frown, then nodded. "Oh, yeah. That too. But also about that day we first met. It was a setup."

"Say what?" I snapped the light on and approached the bed. He wiped his brow and rolled over so that his back was to me.

"Rockart wanted you to put Staffer out of wrestling. He wanted you on the team. It was my job to help coax you on board. Rockart knew I was your favorite wrestler from that questionnaire you gave Shane Stratford."

The elaborateness of the plan stunned me, and I even felt a sting of pride at the trouble to which Rockart had gone. This slight boost in self-esteem was dashed by Beastie's next comment: "He figured that if you got hurt, no big loss. But he knew you were young and hungry enough to get it done." He turned back to face me. "His original plan was to drop you after your first year. I talked him in to keeping you on."

Beastie seemed to be groping for a specific response. For an instant I was tempted to go to the bed and throw my arms around him. This notion passed quickly and I took a step back. *Thanks,* I mouthed the word to him. He leaned back on the pillow.

"Like a dream," he murmured. "Was gonna be like a dream."

His eyes closed. I stood very still for several seconds, afraid to move. Then I turned and crept out, extinguishing the light before closing the door on his silent breathing.

———————

The next night Rockart flew into Atlanta, where we had an event at the Omni. Mimi no-showed that night, and Beastie and I worked the cage match without her or Shawna at ringside. The match was rocky, and at one point Chuck accidentally stiffed me in the jaw. After the match Chuck had a private meeting with Rockart. I stuck around backstage, sprawled out on a table in a Valium-induced daze that gave the familiar desirable result of dulling the pain enough to make me an observer within my own body. I turned my head and watched a scruffy rat dart from a gaping hole in the wall. The animal paused before a mirror, staring up at it while its long pink tail whipped to and fro like an uneven pendulum. I was too buzzed to be frightened; even if I had been, I couldn't have screamed. My tongue was glued to the roof of my mouth. Then the door to the dressing room slammed, sending the creature back into the opening from which it had emerged and leaving me to wonder whether or not it had even been real.

I struggled to sit up. Shawna stood before the table. "I'm leaving tomorrow morning," she announced. "Rockart just gave me my walking papers."

"Shit," I slurred. "Mimi's not coming back?"

"Apparently not," she said.

"Shit," I repeated. "That sucks."

She looked at me and snorted, then without a word turned and left the dressing room. "Shawna!" I shouted. "Wait!"

I stumbled off the table and into the hallway just in time to see Shawna leaving with her gear. "Wait!" I yelled again, and this exertion made me dizzy enough to have to lean against the wall. The world was in the throes of a rapid spin. When my surroundings finally straightened out, the first thing I saw was Beastie at the other end of the hallway, gazing sadly at me. I pressed my head back against the wall, suddenly very sober and miserable.

Back at the hotel I went straight to Shawna's room. There was no answer at her door. After checking the lounge, the pool, and the fitness center, I finally spotted her sitting by the fireplace as I hurried through the front lobby. "How long have you been here?" I asked her.

"The whole time," she said. "I was going to call out to you, but you looked so determined to find me yourself that I decided to just let you run." I collapsed onto the couch.

"What was that back there?" I asked. She furnished an answer by focusing a stoic gaze on the knuckles of her right hand. "You tell me you're leaving tomorrow morning and then you just walk out?" I demanded.

"What do you expect?" she snapped, cracking her knuckles. "A lay for the road? Something to reward you for all your trouble?"

"Hey, what the hell?" I charged, "I didn't deserve that!"

"How would you even know anything about what *you* deserve?" she shouted. "Either you're pretending to be someone else or so zonked out on drugs or alcohol you can barely think!"

"Well, in the last two years I've had three broken bones, at least a dozen concussions, and more sprained wrists, ankles, and dislocated shoulders than I can count. So if I have to take a few pills for the pain, excuse the hell outta me!"

"You'd take those pills anyway," she said in a voice that was more saddened than accusing.

"Maybe I would," I allowed. "I like the way they make me feel."

"You mean *not* feel!" she cried. "Why are you so afraid of yourself?"

"I'm not afraid of myself!" I shouted.

"Michael Harding!" she shouted back. "Why is he so bad? Why don't you want to be him? That's who I was falling in love with! Not Chuck Beastie or Chameleon or whoever the hell else you pretend to be!"

Those words made everything leading up to them instantly worthwhile. I reached out to touch her but her eyes stopped me. There was something familiar about the look they possessed, and I quickly recognized it as fear. It was the same fear that had been lurking underneath the noncommittal answers she provided while I had been sketching her.

I reached out and drew her to me. We kissed and I parted her lips with my tongue. When I felt her respond, I closed my eyes. The world fell away and I was almost tempted to put a hammerlock on her to ensure she'd stay there forever. As though she were reading my mind, I felt her immediately pull away. I opened my eyes and she was on her feet. "I haven't fought with anyone like this for a long time," she said.

"Who was the last poor bastard?" I grinned weakly.

She just shook her head and grabbed her bags. Then she rushed over the shiny marble floor and fled through the doors into the waiting night.

———————

The next day the WWO was in Cleveland. I took a cab to the arena straight from the airport and simmered backstage all afternoon. "You hurtin', kid?" Chuck asked when he found me.

"I'm sorry," he stammered. His eyes were bloodshot and cloudy.

I nodded.

"About all that shit I said the other night . . . ," he began.

"It's okay."

"I *like* the picture you drew," he blurted, then paused. When nothing happened, he seemed relieved and continued: "That's how I'd wanna . . . picture myself. Hell . . ." He gave his voice plenty of rasp. "I'm thinkin' about taking some time off."

"To get a life?" I asked.

"To get something." He seemed to be struggling against his own words. "It's a mixed-up game, huh, Michael?"

It was one of the first times anyone other than Shawna had called me by my name, and I felt my face flushing uncomfortably. "I suppose," I mumbled.

"I mean . . . ," he began with an arcane hope.

"You're still my favorite wrestler, Chuck," I met his eyes. "And always will be. Even if you're not a wrestler anymore."

He smiled and nodded, biting his lip. "Thanks, man." He reached out hesitantly, then rested his hand on my shoulder, "I've worked with a lot of people. And what you just said is mutual."

I should've been overjoyed. Chuck Beastie had given me his approval. But the moment lacked the magical sheen it possessed in my dreams. I wanted to jump up and cry with joy, to throw my arms around Beastie and thank him. To hold him. But I did none of these things and was still nodding and biting my lip when he suddenly got to his feet and wandered off.

We had done the spot dozens of times. On top of the cage. Marks screaming, all falling away below as we wrestled in a dimension that belonged solely to us. The match had been a beautiful one, as effortless as a dance while appearing as chaotic as an army of souls rioting in hell. Chuck and I were like two actors locked in a scene so good that the barriers of reality and fantasy had long since fallen away, leaving a world that felt so right you never wanted to leave. "What a fuckin' match," Beastie whispered as he jabbed me, his fist brushing against my neck.

"Fantastic," I agreed and accepted his knee coming up gently into my mid-section.

"I love you, brother," he whispered as he swung me around.

"Love you too, Stud," I whispered back as I reversed him. Dozens of times. He would let go of my arm and then charge toward the edge of the cage before stopping himself and teetering there for just a second and then turning and flattening me with a clothesline.

But this time he kept going and for an instant he seemed suspended in air and the moment was senseless as a dream and I was waiting for him to turn around and charge me but he was already falling. I scrambled over to the edge of the cage and saw that he had landed on a table. His body was fixed and peaceful, still glistening under the lights. His positioning was perfect, like the set pose an action figure would assume while waiting patiently for a child's hands to grant it the gift of movement. But then his motionlessness became too complete for him to be anything more than a perfectly obedient son to the end, blood leaking out of his ears like a regurgitated secret.

12

SHOOTING WITH MYSELF

Perched on the turnbuckle, my eyes become microscopes. I focus and draw out individual faces, seeing them as cells of an amorphous organism. Every one a pulsing collection of eyes and nose and mouth and ears but no combination exactly like another. A vague amazement passes through me as I consider how many combined sensations have helped shape these people's lives. A world of sight, taste, sound, and touch has been filtered by eighty thousand individual arrays of senses, melted down by thought and strained into action that has brought them together as a combined force.

Why are they here? Why am I here?

I pause now on the fourth and final turnbuckle. A woman with hair dyed blue is at the end of a row, holding up a sign with both hands. The sign is a white poster board with red letters pasted on: Michael: U Are Already a Champ! *A girl about six, possibly her daughter, is in the next seat. I picture this woman sitting up last night, working to finish this sign. Carting it to the stadium and spending all afternoon guarding it against being crushed. Then picking the right few moments to hold it up. All for the hope of what? Connection? Support? I search her face for familiarity, but she is unknown.*

Her lip begins to quiver, then slowly melts away. The rest of her face follows. Her skull, white and unimpeded by flesh or muscle, swivels atop a body still melting. Now she is nothing more than bones given the gift of movement. I look away quickly, but all around me skin is dissolving. Rivers of burnt flesh run down the aisles. All that remains are cheering skeletons. Then like stars dying before twilight, their cheers vanish. The skeletons are collapsing into piles of dust. One by one.

My own flesh is gone. Terrified, I look around to see how many skeletons are still left in the audience. About half. When they all fall to dust, it will be my turn.

I bellow against this fate but cannot hear my own voice.

The champion's music bursts my silent bubble. The audience's reaction is an intense tidal wave of sound that fills the air so thoroughly I have trouble breathing. But it is all right. I will not die. The audience has been made real once again by the promise of the champion's entrance.

I stand in the ring, ready to battle the man who has just brought me back from the dead.

Chuck Beastie's death was ruled "accidental," even though it was determined he had struck the table headfirst. Chuck had been in the business for eleven years and knew how to absorb a fall and how not to. To his fellow wrestlers, it was obvious he had chosen not to.

Two days after the "accident" Rockart called me in to New York. Predictably, a limousine was waiting for me at the airport. When I got inside, I was a little surprised to see Thomas Rockart Jr. sitting in the backseat. "Hello, Michael," he greeted me smoothly. After a few minutes of standard small talk, it became apparent the limousine wasn't going to move. "How are you, Michael?" he finally asked me, his tone reflecting that we had now moved past the introductory chitchat. I listened to the rain assaulting the roof and watched it run down the windows. It looked like transparent blood.

"I'm all right," I lied.

"Good to hear," Rockart said, nodding. "I've watched you the past couple of years. You're the kind of person we would like to have around. How you handle this is very important."

His words landed like tiny jabs against my mind. "I understand," I said and nodded blindly.

"I've booked you for three title matches with Logan," he said. "We'll see how they go over. Then we'll see about giving you a push for a series of matches with him."

"When?" I asked, trying to feel excited.

"Starting tonight in Boston," Rockart said. "Then for the

next two nights in St. Louis and Baltimore, respectively."

"Chuck's funeral is two days from now," I pointed out.

"True, but we need you wrestling in Baltimore that night," he said mildly.

"You know how much Chuck meant to me, Thomas," I said, a nail of rage pounding through my voice. "You knew from the very beginning," I shot.

"He finally told you about Stratford, huh?" he said, with the easy chuckle of a parent who had just discovered his kids indulging in predictable mischief. I wanted to kill him. "I'll be honest, Michael. I didn't know how long you were going to last. He had as much faith in you as you seem to have had in him. And now is the chance for you to confirm that faith. We are in the business of sports entertainment. Now the key word there is *business;* no one gives a damn anymore if pro wrestling is real or isn't. The vast majority of the American public takes it for granted that it's not. It's our job to provide them with the best product available. I can't afford to play favorites—"

"I'm not asking you to," I snapped. "All I want is for you to let me—"

"Wallow in Beastie's death, Michael?" he asked. I seethed, but remained silent. "I know what you're going through." Rockart squeezed out the words. "Believe me, in my own way I know." He coughed and regained the confident timbre that was his trademark in the announcer's booth. "Chuck Beastie will be given a proper tribute by the World Wrestling Organization."

"Another fallen product, huh, Thomas?" I sneered, a little amazed at my own willingness to offend the one man who held the key to my childhood dream.

"Look here, Michael," Rockart said. "'The American Dream' Sonny Logan sells ten million dollars worth of T-shirts, visors, mugs, vitamins, and other assorted merchandise a year. But before he joined our company he was Steve Strong, a bulky tan body builder from Venice with thinning blond hair. I made him what he is. He may have done a hell of a job with the role provided to him. But *I'm* the one that gave him his gimmick. He is the trademarked property of the World Wrestling Organization. And so are you." I could see this sonofabitch envisioning himself as the head of a Hollywood studio, all his stars flexing and screaming and ranting within the confines of his uncalloused palm.

"I'm looking for loyal people to guide this company into the nineties," he said to me, his tone shifting into an earnest pitch. "If you can—"

"I'll do it," I said. "Just give me the address of the funeral home where I can send flowers."

"Done." Rockart confirmed with a nod. I opened the door to get out without waiting for him to end the meeting. I stepped out of the car, slammed the door, and paced carefully across the slick pavement back into the airport to catch a flight for Boston.

———————

Before my first title shot against The American Dream, I shaved the front of my head and bleached the remaining strands of hair in order to match both his hair color and his premature baldness (due mostly to roids, he had once admitted. "Hell with it, brother," he smirked, raising and flexing one of his arms. "I think these cannons are worth losing a few hairs.")

In addition to adapting a facial look similar to Logan's, I came out to his theme music wearing one of his tank tops that boasted his trademark phrase *American Dreamin'*. I tore it off with the same exaggerated show of strength he always displayed, then throughout the match tried to ingratiate myself with the crowd using his spastic appealing gestures.

But after a few matches it was painfully clear that it wasn't working. All my moves in the ring were forced; I sure as hell didn't feel like a hero. The crowds were lethargic during our matches, as though they shared in my confusion. With no persona to guide me through my moves in the ring, I was lost, trapped by the dread an alcoholic finds the day he drinks and drinks and nothing happens.

———

Meanwhile, all hell was breaking loose in the world of professional wrestling. ICW (International Championship Wrestling), the WWO's main rival, had been purchased a few weeks ago by a mogul named Brad Burner; Burner had made billions of dollars by launching cable channels that featured cartoons, world news, and sports. The history of the feud between Rockart and Burner reportedly dated back to their days as kids growing up in the same Connecticut suburb. One afternoon Thomas had supposedly refused to let Brad have a swing of the baseball bat, or some believed it started when the two future tycoons were pre-teens and Brad hadn't let Thomas have a ride on his new motor scooter. Whatever the first occurrence, it quickly grew into a heated rivalry. In high school, they had run against each other for student body president, with Rockart winning narrowly. The two had lost touch when Burner went on to college and Rockart had started in the pro wrestling business. By the time Thomas Rockart Jr. was buying the WWO from his father, Brad Burner had begun introducing cable channels. He had casually called Rockart and asked for some WWO footage for a sports channel, thinking their shared past could serve as sufficient payment. Rockart, however, had demanded top dollar. This infuriated Burner and succeeded in rekindling their war. Now, three years later, Burner had achieved enough financial success to spend ten million dollars to take over ICW and attempt to exact revenge by raiding the WWO of its talent. To accomplish this, Burner was offering large contracts to several WWO superstars.

This was all explained to me in Buffalo on the afternoon before my fifth match with Sonny Logan. I arrived at the hotel to find Ricky Witherspoon in his room packing a bag. Apparently, he had arrived at the hotel an hour ago, and as he was unpacking had received a phone call from ICW. He had accepted an offer over the phone and was leaving for Atlanta right away. After filling me in on the battlefield that served as the backdrop for Rockart and Burner's current war, Witherspoon revealed the terms of his new contract.

"One point two million dollars for two years," Witherspoon recited, sounding a little dazed as we zipped down to the lobby in the mirrored elevator.

"That's what they offered me," he continued. "I have to be in Atlanta by eight o'clock to sign the contract."

"Wow," I remarked, fighting an inexplicable twinge of sorrow for Ricky. "Rockart doesn't know?"

"Nope," he said. "I feel a little bad, but what the hell. Business is business. And Ricky Witherspoon goes where the money is."

Before I could make a comment about living the gimmick, the elevator halted and the doors opened to the lobby.

"Darren Domino is on his way, too," Witherspoon informed me as we drifted through the lobby. "And supposedly Burner's gettin' ready to make Sonny Logan an offer he won't be able to refuse."

"Sonny?" I questioned sharply. "He won't go. No way."

"We'll see," Ricky said. "I can put in a good word for you over there. They may make you an offer anyway, but, you know . . ." He let his voice fade and be swallowed up in the din of pedestrian traffic shuttling through the lobby.

"I don't know," I said, reaching up to massage my temples. "I don't really know what my plans are right now," I specified.

"Yeah," he said quickly, "I can understand. How're you doing . . . ?"

"I don't know," I repeated.

We emerged from the doors and were immediately hit by the crisp raw air so prevalent in late afternoons during the tail end of winter. A limousine was already at the curb. It was a longer one than Rockart had and this elongated style gave it the air of a confident predator.

The bellman, outfitted in a blue suit and top hat, hustled up to us. "Sirs? Did you call for a limo?" he asked.

"I did." Ricky Witherspoon smiled, then turned to me. "Christ, I think I may just buy myself one of these. I'm gonna be able to afford it now, that's for damn sure."

We shook hands. "See ya in Atlanta," he said and grinned at me as he got in the limo. I watched the beast glide away, smiling as the breeze stroked tears to life in my eyes. I suddenly pictured Richard Turkin as a little kid, identical to the one he had paid a hundred dollars to jump into a pool. As much as Witherspoon liked to think of himself as a tycoon, he would probably always be that little kid, forever jumping in and out of pools for the highest bidder in search of more money. I waited until the massive limo became lost among the river of taillights hustling toward the airport in the sharp dusk chill, then turned and walked back into the hotel.

That night at the arena was my worst match with Logan yet. The crowd was hostile toward the very idea of someone mimicking Logan. Many shouts of "Stupid!" and "Boring!" rang out. Obviously, The Chameleon gimmick was wearing thin.

After the show, Thomas Rockart Jr. met with me backstage to discuss what he termed a "necessary shift in direction." Also present at the meeting were Hippo Haleberg and Rob Robertson. As Rockart justified the growing need to alter my Chameleon gimmick, I was almost ashamed at how respectful I was of his poise. Hanging over this man's head was Burner's blatant intent to bring down the company he had spent his life building, and yet his manner remained coolly focused on business at hand. During the past week he himself had been present backstage at all house shows, like a general reinforcing his actual existence among his troops. He had taken Ricky Witherspoon's pre-show defection in stride, and already knew about Darren Domino leaving and claimed to be unconcerned. He also had to deal with the paradoxical opportunities that Chuck Beastie's death offered. Although Rockart had already assembled a tribute to "The Stud" that would air on all of the WWO's television shows, there was a wordless desire to further capitalize on (while at the same time not appearing to exploit) Beastie's death to hype the upcoming SlamFest.

But if any of this was causing Rockart stress, he kept it well hidden as he spent a half an hour patiently expounding the many indications that signaled my current gimmick had run its course. "Nobody really feels *connected* enough with The Chameleon to love or hate him," he concluded.

"Happens to the best of 'em," Hippo boomed reassuringly as he plunged his hand into a bag of potato chips.

"Remember 'Breakout Jones'?" Robertson tittered, then turned to me. "This was when rap was hot for . . . oh say, fifteen minutes. We had this guy who used to rap in the ring. Well, of course when rap went out, the gimmick was kaput. So what happened? We threw a skull necklace around his neck and pushed him as a voodoo master from Africa. He's wrestling as 'Black Magic' now, as over with the marks as a sheet over a Ku Klux Klanner."

"We stick by our workers," Hippo confirmed, and shook a potato chip at me in the same manner a judge would wield a hammer. "Gimmicks come and go, but if you stay loyal, we'll always have a spot for you in the company."

"I'm thinking . . ." I coughed, then winced as my ribs throbbed with the effort. "I'm thinking I may need a week or so off."

A cool distrust leaked into Rockart's eyes. Robertson issued a tired sigh. "How much did Burner offer you?" Hippo demanded.

"Nothing," I answered. "Nothing yet. And that isn't even what this is about. I've gotta go . . ." Their six eyes regarded me carefully with a stillness that was marred only by Hippo's methodical chewing. "I've gotta go find a gimmick that I can . . . live with." I stopped briefly, and was ready to continue when Rockart cut me off with a sharp cough.

"Where are you going to find it?" he asked. I patted my chest gingerly.

"In here," I said.

"Oh, for Christ's sake." Robertson groaned. "If you're going to ICW, at least have the courtesy—"

"Quiet, Rob," Rockart commanded. Robertson immediately became silent. "Okay." Rockart nodded slowly. "Do what you have to do. But I want you back *in character* in no more than two weeks. We'll be doing a live TV simulcast from Chicago. Call me in a week. We'll need to get your costume designed and set up a storyline to bring you back in."

"How do we know he won't just sign with ICW?" Robertson protested.

"He won't." Rockart shook his head smoothly, and our eyes locked in a shared knowledge of yet another confession I had made in the application to Shane Stratford's wrestling school—that my ultimate reason for becoming a pro wrestler was to become the World Wrestling Organization Heavyweight Champion. It was the WWO I had seen in my dreams as a child, and Thomas Rockart Jr., with characteristic certitude, was sure that I still wanted to be that child.

Staring into his eyes, I began to fear that he knew me better than I knew myself.

I drove west for four days, stopping at chaotic intervals to eat at local diners and sleep in anonymous rest stops. I called B.J. from Nevada on a Friday afternoon and spoke to Terri. She told me that B.J. was working an afternoon shift at the distribution warehouse where he had recently been promoted to loading supervisor. When she learned I was just roaming around in Nevada, she ordered me to come for dinner that night. Six hours later I was turning down B Street in a subdivision of Lancaster. The layout of B Street was identical to the layouts of the other twenty lettered streets that surrounded it, dual rows of houses identical in both structure and color. Tract homes, the kind my grandfather had viewed as an insult to those who lived in them.

"You sonofabitch!" B.J. whooped, throwing open the front door of his house and wrapping me in an embrace. His body, no longer inflated by steroids, was now smaller but tighter. Oddly, his face seemed to have grown. There was a completeness to it, as though life had been filling in imperceptible gaps.

A shriek from inside the house broke our hug. "Joey!" he turned and hollered gleefully, "what kind of nonsense are you into now?" He turned back to me and smiled with proud annoyance. "Joey," he said in way of explanation.

Joey was his two-year-old son. Although still chubby, his coordination was already impressive. The one feature on the child that clearly belonged to B.J. were his ears. Like B.J.'s, they were lean and plastered tightly against his scalp. Throughout a dinner of spaghetti and garlic bread, Terri rubbed Joey's ears frequently, as though they provided her with proof of motherhood. The child giggled delightedly whenever his mother touched him. B.J. occasionally patted the boy's head, and Joey stared at his father with wide awestruck eyes.

The assemblage of houses known as Lancaster was about fifty miles north of Covina, home of the junior high school building where they had first met, and therefore some distance away from the town where they had originally dreamed of settling down. But, as B.J. explained to me while we drank beer out on the porch after dinner, property prices were cheaper out here.

"With a family and all, well . . . ," he said, shrugging. I nodded eagerly. "It's good to see you again," he said.

"You too," I agreed, wanting to say something more but unable to articulate what it was. I had no more phrases to fall back on. So I just sipped my beer and stared out at the neatly trimmed bushes crouching in the darkness.

"He's not mine, you know," B.J. said suddenly. I just looked at him. "I . . . we couldn't have any." He sighed. "I guess it was the steroids . . . the doctor said maybe, maybe not."

"I'm sorry," I managed at last, pushing the words hopefully into the silent night.

"Yeah," he said, "we did it with artificial insemination. Went to one of those banks. I remember I used to joke about goin' and getting paid fifty bucks to whack off."

"You did that?"

"Yeah. Twice," he said. "Back when I just turned eighteen. Before I started takin' all that shit." He grinned with a tired humor. "I always like to think that maybe I got my own sperm, you know?"

"He . . ." I stopped. "He's a great kid," I said.

"Yeah." He nodded stubbornly. "I don't know why I told you that just now." He shook his head. "Just wanted to tell someone, I guess—"

"Ricky Witherspoon didn't remember your father," I blurted. "I mean . . . he wouldn't have. I never even asked him. He might've but I just didn't know . . ."

Just ahead of me the bushes were swaying, moving back and forth like lost fish under a blurry ocean. "I lied to you and I'm sorry, B.J." I turned to look at him. He was nodding, his eyes curious. "I don't even know why." I went on, "I just wanted it to be true. I wanted it to be true and the only way to make sure it would be was to not question it and just tell you what I knew you'd want to believe."

I stopped and took a breath. The vague aroma of flowers wound into my nose, making me think of daffodils even though they had no scent that I knew of. All I remembered about them was popping off their yellow heads as a kid. So many afternoons on the way home from school had been spent decimating bright armies that seemed to lay over every block and grow back overnight.

"It wasn't that important, Mike. Really," B.J. said slowly. "But I'm glad you told me." He paused before asking: "You feel better?"

"Yeah," I replied. "You?"

He nodded and we both looked away from each other. A horn sounded in the distance, jabbing at the awkward silence B.J. and I were sharing. That confession had left me more naked than I had been in a long time.

"Michael, we've got a surprise for you!" Terri's voice rang merrily from the doorway behind us. She trooped out onto the porch carrying a box, the Sears slogan clinging faintly to the cardboard. She set it on the porch, and the first thing I saw resting on the top was my grandfather's catcher's mitt.

"Oh my God," I said, dropping to my knees beside the box.

B.J. laughed. "Hell, yes, I forgot to tell you," he said, "Terri went and picked up your stuff from your old apartment while we were down wrestling in Memphis." The glove seemed to have accumulated a few more cracks, and as I slipped it on my fingers, it was dryer and tighter than I remembered. But then I inhaled and caught the smell of leather and pictured my grandfather clearly for the first time in . . . *what, how long had it been?* . . . *six months, a year, two years?* In all that time I had seen only snatches of him in dull and unfocused memories. Now I held a clear image of him as the accompanying gravelly voice drifted through my mind.

I placed the glove next to the box and lifted out some old art books. "Oh, shit," I said, laughing, "these must be years overdue." I opened the cover and saw the stamp: March 9, 1987.

"Amnesty day," B.J. said. We all kept laughing and remembering as I sorted through the other items from my old apartment in San Bernardino. There was the alarm clock that I had brought from Chicago, a quilt I had purchased at a local Pic 'n' Save, as well as several pro wrestling magazines. Holding the alarm clock made me remember a lot of mornings in that small San Bernardino apartment, the clock's steady beep signaling the start of another day at Shane Stratford's Wrestling Academy.

One of the final objects was a small tattered book called *Underground Steroid Guidebook*. As soon as I brought this out of the box, I dropped it back inside. My eyes met with B.J.'s but neither of us spoke. I hurriedly yanked out the object I had been saving for last, the pillow I had wrestled with since I was fourteen. I gave it a light jab and watched it drop to the floor.

As Beastie's body fell from the cage.

"Memories." I blinked. "They're something."

Later that night in the bathroom I took the last Valium in my pill case. I had forgotten to get a refill from Santa before I left Buffalo. A low murmur of nervousness passed through my body as I tried to recall how long it had been since I had gone an entire two days without taking a painkiller of some sort. There was no way for me to get more without going back to Santa, since I had no legal prescription. As I opened the door, I looked back at the mirror and maintained eye contact with my reflection for a few seconds before turning and stepping out into the light of the hallway.

Before leaving the next morning I gave the pillow to Joey, who immediately wrapped it in a bear hug. "A natural born pro wrestler," I proclaimed.

"God help us." B.J. laughed.

Outside by my car, B.J. ran his finger along the hood. "Been doin' a little traveling, huh?" He nodded at the dust clinging to his fingertip.

I shrugged and looked at the house. Terri waved. She was on the front steps in a bathrobe. Her damp hair clung to her cheeks like a golden picture frame. She sat watching Joey, who was hurling the pillow to the ground then picking it up and doing it again.

"Sure you don't wanna stick around a little while longer?" B.J. suggested with a murmur of concern.

"I can't," I said. He looked unconvinced. "I appreciate the offer, man. I appreciate everything. But I've got a few more things to do."

"Before what?"

"Before . . ." I looked up at the sun, a hot and angry blade in the sky. "Before I start traveling again."

"Do your thing then. You know where to find me if you need to." He hesitated. "What do you think, doc?" he asked quietly, gesturing vaguely at the house behind him. Terri was still on the front steps. Joey picked up the pillow and threw it in the air. He shouted happily when it landed, then ran to pick it up.

"I'm jealous," I said.

"Bullshit." He grinned. "I'm jealous of *you.*"

"Bullshit." And we laughed.

I drove away, watching my rearview mirror. The houses were still identical in appearance but now I found myself imagining the individual worlds they contained. Separate realities where human emotions and memories could endure. My grandfather's glove sat beside me as proof. I hoped my old wrestling pillow would be happy there.

The old Shane Stratford's Wrestling Academy sign still hung above the door; given its original filthiness, it was impossible to tell if the years had added any dirt. As soon as I walked through the doors, I recognized the same old smell of sweat that I associated with desire, as though the stifling confines of the gym only served to stoke its inhabitants' dreams of wrestling in arenas that seated tens of thousands.

Many of the same posters still adorned the walls. In the ring were about a dozen students in differing stages of bulk. I spotted two bloated juicers right away. All of them were watching Aries, who appeared a little stockier and a lot slower than he used to be. He was announcing in a loud tone: "When you go over the top rope, it's easy to look like you're controlling it. The key is making sure you look like you have *no control over it.*" He ran the ropes, and just watching his body's instinctive tentativeness with every step made me wince a little. I had seen enough people wrestling with injuries to determine at a glance that he was obviously on a pill of some kind that was fooling his mind but not his body. In addition to the usual knee and elbow pads, both of his thighs and hands were heavily swathed in tape. An itch sprang to life on my right forearm, and I scratched it furiously as Aries launched himself over the ropes with a fierce abandon. He landed with sloppy but undeniable force on the mat outside—a human car wreck. The students watched silently for about fifteen seconds as Aries struggled to his feet.

"Damn," one of them whistled, "that looked good."

"'Cause I had no control," Aries specified immediately. "What you just saw was a guy who legit could've broken his neck. And that's what the crowd wants to see."

"Looks like it hurt," came another much deeper voice from the mass of bodies in the ring. Aries laughed and reached over for a small pill bottle that was resting on a metal folding chair. "That's what our little friends, Soma, are for," he said, and chuckled grimly. I remembered how Stratford had used to offer us nail polish to kill the pain in practice; it appeared the stakes had gone up.

At this point a hand fell upon my shoulder. "Hey, kid," a voice from what seemed like several lifetimes ago triggered a shrill alarm inside of me. It was not the reassuring bluster of Shane Stratford, but instead came with an unmistakably Canadian accent that belonged to Rand Staffer.

His lips were twisted into the same gap-toothed smile I had mimicked so long ago. "Long time," he said with a smirk. I wanted to extend my hand and see if my fingers would go through him or not.

"What are you—" I stammered.

"Shane Stratford went a little batty about a year ago. They said he was starting to have hallucinations and all. Part old age, part nail polish abuse." He chuckled wryly. "So, I get a call from Hippo, who asked me to take over as WWO West Coast Rep. Part of the deal included running the school. I said, 'Why not?' My wife always wanted to live near the ocean." He snorted. "I didn't count on being stuck here in the desert, but what the hell, eh? Life isn't always perfect."

I had never comprehended the fact that he might have been married. "Tough break about Beastie," he continued. "How are you?" His voice was disarmingly curious.

"Okay," I said, casting a quick glance back at the class. Many of them were looking over at us, and I tried to read the expressions on their faces. Was Staffer setting me up for an ambush? Would he order these young hungry wrestlers to try and put me out of commission? I was too nervous to be amused at the potential irony.

"Let's talk in my office for a few minutes," Staffer suggested. For a second I thought he meant to step into the ring. But he had already turned and was walking to the door that led to Stratford's old office. His left leg showed the sheer hint of a limp.

Once inside, he closed the door behind us. A ceiling fan had been added, lending a circulatory freshness that had dispelled the room's former odor of nail polish. Aside from the fan, the layout of the small office was unchanged.

"Do you hate me?" I asked.

"I did," he acknowledged slowly. "For at least a year,

I had fantasies about showing up at the arena and charging the ring with a baseball bat. About a year after . . ." An edgy sarcasm took control of his voice briefly. ". . . *the incident*, I got drunk and hopped on a plane. I knew the WWO was there, and I knew what hotel the boys always stayed at. Waited in a car in the parking lot of the Hyatt with a pint of Scotch and a crowbar. You finally got back around midnight, and I watched you stagger in with Trevor and two women. I just watched you and I wanted to get out and hurt you so bad."

I tried to place the exact night but couldn't. My feud with The Soultaker had been an exhausting chain of pills, women, and too much alcohol. If Staffer had attacked me that night, not only would I have been an easy target, but I probably wouldn't have even remembered it.

"But I didn't move." Staffer was now speaking in a voice blunted with softness. He seemed to be groping with a confession. "I just kept sipping from the pint and waiting for the old Staffer . . . the old Rand Staffer *fire* to hit me. The bloodlust, the need to hurt someone. Then damned if I didn't start crying like a fuckin' baby. It hit me what a true sonofabitch that Staffer had been, and how miserable his life had been. My kids had been terrified of me, my wife had been ready to leave me. But over that past year things had gotten so much better. Even though I wasn't wrestling, I was . . . *happier* than I had ever been when I had that stupid gimmick I couldn't turn on and off."

"I can relate to that," I commented, "or at least the part about not being able to turn it off."

"I guess that's what I figured. And it hit me that

what you had done was . . . nothing personal," he said. "So, I just finished the pint, slept it off, and flew home in the morning."

The breeze from the ceiling fan was making the top strands of his hair drift like small ripples over a dark pond. "That's why I don't hate you," he said. "In a way, you ending my career helped me keep what, although I didn't realize it at the time, was most important to me: my family."

I nodded. "Not that there aren't times when I still don't fantasize about kicking your ass," he said and smiled, "just a little."

"What's your real name?" I asked.

"Rand Staffer," he replied with a shrug. "My parents were always a little annoyed that I kept it throughout my career."

We both stood. I extended my hand. "Good to meet you, Rand," I said. His hand was warm.

"What's yours?" he asked.

"Rand Staffer?" I replied with a shrug. He chuckled.

We walked outside, where I spent a few minutes talking to the students in the class. I scratched both my burning forearms and provided monosyllabic answers to their questions about how I had risen so fast in the WWO.

"Hey, Chameleon," Rand Staffer said as he came out of the office and unrolled a poster. It featured one of the shots "Ivan with an I" had taken of me in the downstairs studio of the Crystal Ship. I was standing against a black wall while clad in a black outfit. The picture had been touched up in such a way that my body blended completely with the wall, thus leaving a pair of ridiculously wide searching eyes as sole proof that an animal of some kind was occupying the space. *Those eyes do look insane,* I admitted to myself, remembering Ivan's admonition.

Staffer handed me a bottle of Wite-Out. "Better use this to autograph it," he said with a grin.

I dipped the small brush in Wite-Out and scrawled "Chameleon" across the poster's pitch black background. Then I dipped it in again and added "M.H."

"All right, M.H." Staffer nodded. As he taped it up to the wall alongside the many posters I had seen while in the ring as a student, I talked with Aries. He seemed surprised when I told him I had just seen B.J.

"Haven't talked to him for a while." Aries's shoulders jerked up in a random shrug. "Been kinda busy." In a weary, petulant voice he filled me in on the new responsibilities he had acquired in the past few years. He had married the daughter of one of his parents' lifelong friends and was now running all three of his father's car dealerships, with a fourth one scheduled to open next spring.

"Sounds like you're rolling, Aries," I offered.

"Am I?" he glanced above my head, throwing the question at the sagging ropes of the ring behind me. "I can't really wrestle anymore. It's all I can do to teach." He sighed. "Well, hell. Why aren't you still wrestling?"

"Ahh . . . ," I said. "The thing with Beastie . . . it kinda got me."

"Beastie . . ." He nodded, then mumbled, "Lucky bastard."

"What are you talking about?" I demanded.

"He died doing what he loved," Aries declared defensively.

"You have no right to call him lucky," I said. "You didn't know anything about him. About *him*."

"Maybe not," he relented. He reached down and massaged his knees. "But I know plenty about me," he said. I left his comment unanswered, lingering in the unventilated air. *It's fucking dry in here,* I thought, scratching the prickling sensation that by how had grown up to my upper arms.

"See ya around." Aries sighed, turning back to the ring.

"Yeah," I said, "see ya."

I had originally planned to leave southern California immediately after visiting the school, but signing that autograph had awakened a memory in me. It kept growing in a manner as similarly ominous as the itch that now consumed both my entire arms. So I drove to the Denny's where I had first made an inarticulate attempt to scrawl a gimmick name as an autograph. I took a booth by the window where I would have a good view of the doorway and ordered a "Moons Over My Hammy." My stomach wasn't feeling too good, so I only ate one or two bites. I drank several glasses of water and kept scratching my arms and chest, waiting for something.

I stayed there until sunset, and by then I knew I was in trouble. My arms were on fire, and my organs felt like they were slowly imploding. With an involuntarily trembling hand, I slowly removed a pen from my pocket and scrawled the name "Michael Harding" onto a napkin. I wrote it again, watching the curves and dips of the letters, trying to grasp the sum total of their connection.

An overpowering urge to vomit made me drop the napkin. It floated on to the table. I added some bills to it. Staggered to the bathroom and puked all over a stall. I caught the reflection of my sweaty face in the mirror. *You stupid sonofabitch. You're hooked.* My arms were an ugly, irritated red from nonstop scratching. Buried just under the red I glimpsed the small scar from that mosquito. Still a tiny white snowflake. Mine for life.

My vision reeling, I made my way out of the restaurant.

Well, I could check in to a hospital or deal with this thing on my own. Hospital, hell. The WWO fired people for going to rehab. Bad publicity. Although it was night, I knew that I could drive back to the wrestling academy and more than likely score something, some Soma at least. I hadn't done Soma in years, having been spoiled by Santa's easy access to more popular painkillers.

That's what I'll do, I reassured myself. *I'll go get some Soma. Shoulda gotten some this afternoon.*

I pulled out of the Denny's parking lot and began driving with sickened resolve back in the direction of the wrestling academy. But I heard Aries's bewildered, unhappy tone ricocheting within my ear over and over, and every time I stopped, *there he was* . . . landing in a fantastically impossible bump on the hood of the car. *My God,* I thought, *I'm going crazy.* However, whenever the car began moving again, the image would disappear and his voice would recede. So, to ensure myself constant motion, I forgot about going back to the wrestling academy and instead followed the green arrow of a stoplight onto an entrance of the freeway. It would pass below my old apartment before stretching on into the darkness of the desert.

In August even the nights were hot out there. The hotel room was strange; it was vibrating like a frayed drum. Finally, I realized this assault was coming from my own heart. Chest shuddering each time the life-giving organ pumped blood through a system in rebellion.

My brain dragged along a rocky terrain of consciousness, throwing up sparks of heat, which made even the simplest thoughts painful. I didn't know how long I had been there. It could have been hours or days. When I checked in I had given the skeptical-eyed clerk my credit card and told her to charge for as many days as I stayed. Perhaps even then, I unconsciously expected to die here. So be it. The Do Not Disturb sign hanging on the door would buy my corpse enough time to begin rotting. Stomach rolling, my hands kept swiping uselessly at invisible bugs that were feeding on my burning skin. The shades were pulled but I knew that somewhere in the surrounding void there was a liquor store. Got to buy a pint of vodka and maybe some Primatene tablets. *Pseudo-ephedrine, what the fuck desperate times call for—*

My stomach gagged, and I pictured the worms crawling in and out of it. I couldn't go anywhere, I was too sick. My body throbbed, every parched beat of agony colliding against ragged nerve ends like an open hand into a thin sheet of glass. I knew each injury like an old friend; where and how all of them had happened. My knee blown out in St. Louis. My hand fractured in Buffalo when a chair slammed against it. My back reduced to a riotous assemblage of crooked dried-out bones grinding against one another like rocks in an arid forest. My spine with no fluid left; it had leaked out through tiny holes that had sprouted as a result of the innumerable times I slammed myself down against canvas and concrete. The flesh on my forehead seized revenge for all the times I had cut it apart with razors, reopening and oozing puss and blood. I gazed up at the ceiling into a vacuous hell of miming reflections; their battles had no connection with one another. They crisscrossed with unrelenting ferocity in a collection of visions so twisted it was impossible to term them dreams or nightmares.

And Beastie's body fell and the coffin was lowered and money was thrown and people were trampled and I tore the gun from a man's hand and pulled the trigger and frothed at the mouth and flexed and then the blade sunk into virgin flesh.

Maggots swarmed my forehead. Their small green bodies falling into my eyes, but I wiped them away, entranced now by the visions on the ceiling. I watched myself slam Bryan and Marty on one of the mats at school and sit back down to watch television on Saturday mornings and Max Egan was chanting "Bastard" and I was running and crying and pounding my own fist into my forehead, wanting to bleed as my mother stood in a doorway shaking her head and saying, "Your father's dead." I held his ghoulish frame in my arms, the bones so pronounced against the taut stretch of flesh/canvas that I am afraid one of them will penetrate his skin and pierce mine.

I recoiled, squirming on the bed, afraid to touch him, afraid to be him. Reeling out of the hospital room in horror. Never, I said to my reflection, never will I be like him. He is not a man. He is not my father. I reached out and touched the muscular vision on the screen, this Dream that will hold its pose forever and never ever die.

The vision dissolved, seizing the child's finger and pulling it off in a sea of sparks and the child melted into its own shadow, vanishing. Gone.

––––––––––

The awakening took place in stages, with my mind laying claim to limbs and muscles one at a time. When I was finally able to stand, the first thing I noticed was sun peeking between the curtains. An air-conditioned breeze stirred the shades to movement, granting their scraps of brightness a fluid quality similar to that found on shifting waves of a sun-drenched lake. I threw open the curtains and was blinded by a rising sun.

Turning on the television, I saw from a morning show that four days had passed since check-in. I turned off the TV and went to take a shower. I winced as water hit my naked body, every drop a tiny blade on exposed sensitive skin. But I remained under the water for a long time, amazed at how much I could feel.

13

UNMASKED

The champion is a master at making the crowd wait. Their cheers build. A fan leaps into the aisle and starts running toward the curtain but is tackled by security guards. The wide red line remains unbroken.

The lyrics of the champ's song begin. He will not emerge until the first chorus. All as scripted as a character's entrance in the scene of a play.

"When it all feels wrong and you're goin' down . . .

"You gotta stand tough, gotta hear the sound . . ."

Billy Harren steps up beside me. "Jesus, get ready for a roar," he says.

"How long have you two known each other, Billy?"

"Since he started in the WWO," he says and laughs a

little. "You know he was a heel at first?" he asks.

I look at him. The lyrics landing against my ears but not penetrating.

"Dig down deep inside your soul . . .

"Gonna pay the price, gotta lock and load . . ."

"No way," I say.

"Sure," he nods. "He came out as 'Dastardly Duke,' or some such thing. Crowd hated him. But then our most popular face jumped ship. So Rockart flipped Duke, and he became a big all-American hero. Won the belt a year later."

"I didn't know that."

"Take the reins, kick into overdrive . . .

"That's what we're here for, to be alive . . ."

"No reason you should. It was only two matches," he chuckles. "Damn . . . eight years ago . . . eight or nine—"

"That's a long time," I comment. "You gonna call this one straight, Billy?" I ask.

"For the first time in my life," he says and smiles.

The chorus kicks in:

"I am a true American . . ."

The crowd swells, a giant raging hand strong enough to reach into the night and pull down the stars. Billy and I look to the curtain, where the champion has just emerged.

Twelve hours later, I was at a pay phone in a rest area just outside of Phoenix. Clouds provided the sky a quiet gray shield while peppering the ground with rain.

Shawna answered on the third ring. "Hey, Shawna," I said, "the mountain just came to Mohammad."

———————

Her house was located in an upscale neighborhood. Just outside her door stood an Indian sculpture of an eagle adorned in a red and blue headdress. The bird's expression and crouch suggested imminent flight. Next to this work of art stood Shawna, wearing a smile similar to the eagle's. "So," she called as I got out of the car, "you still a pro wrestler?"

I waited until I stood in front of her before I spoke. "I'm on my way to Chicago," I told her. "I'm supposed to be there . . . in a couple of days I think." My hold on time had become precarious; minutes felt as temporary as the drops of rain melting upon contact with Shawna's cheeks. "Just passing through."

She nodded. "Fair enough." She stepped aside. "Come on in."

"I love you," I said. She continued to regard me with an impenetrable gaze. Then without a word she turned and walked inside. I followed. The living room had a stream running through its center. It began in a fountain and drifted along a sloping floor, its flow guarded by rocks on either side. It ended up in a small reservoir near the kitchen, where it was washed outside. All the furnishings were made of wood, and several more headdresses adorned the wooden walls. In the corner was an umbrella holder in the form of a penguin.

"Beer? Vodka?" she asked.

"Do you have any water?" I asked. She gave me a

doubtful stare. "It's been kind of a rough few days," I explained. "I don't think I could handle anything stronger right now."

I drained the glass she handed me in one long swallow.

"Thirsty, huh?" she smiled.

"Very," I answered. She went back into the kitchen and came out holding a copper pitcher. She refilled my glass. I wet my lips before setting it down on a beaded coaster. "Shawna, I don't know what's happening," I said. "I have no idea. I want you . . . I need to wrestle . . ." I inhaled sharply, "I don't want to lose you."

Her mouth opened and I saw the familiar look cross her face that signaled a sarcastic remark was coming. But then she swallowed and nodded, her expression vanishing like a page on fire. "Wait here," she said. "I'll be back."

She walked back into a hallway and disappeared through a room.

I paced the living room, my heart beating tremulously. It was as though this were a main event of some sort, and we were searching for the proper finish with no rehearsal. While I berated myself for thinking about wrestling at a time like this, she reappeared with a photograph in her hand. She held it out to me at arm's length. I examined it. It featured a trim young man standing in a wrestling ring, whom I recognized instantly as the same one I had seen in Shawna's wallet. "I see . . ." I nodded.

"I don't think you do," she said and sighed. "He wrestled in Memphis under the name of 'The Brawler.'

But his real name was Sean." She paused. "He drove west one night and never came back."

"You must have loved him very much," I said quietly.

Her short burst of chuckles grew into a fit of laughter that then graduated into a storm of guffaws. I walked over to her and tried to put my arms around her.

"I'm sorry," I said. "It must have been hard for you to lose him—"

"Damn it, Michael!" she cried, "I *was* him!"

My ears erupted into a disbelieving hum. I wrestled with her admission, imagined myself in the ring with those words-slamming them, hip-tossing them, but I couldn't pin them. "You were *him*?" I asked slowly.

"Yes," she declared, "I was him." My eyes expanded as I took in this person before me, my vision inserting masculine features on the face and body I had always regarded as the ultimate in feminine desirability.

"Shawna," I pronounced the word carefully, its sound suddenly seeming alien to me. "Jesus Christ. *Shawna!*" I began laughing. "It's too perfect!" I howled.

She gave me a dark look. "Told you I could surprise you," she said edgily. "By the way, I was one hell of a shooter. Believe it or not, I still am."

"Oh no . . . Shawna. I'm not gonna . . ." I wasn't sure of what I was going to do. "Mind if I sit down?"

She nodded slowly. I sank into the bamboo couch. "I've never told anyone about this before," she said, "so this discussion is going to be as new for me as I'm assuming it will be for you."

"Oh, no," I cracked, "I've fallen in love with tons of transvestites in my life."

"Transvestites are men who *dress up* like women," she said sharply, giving me the same dark look as when I had made the comment about Vivian Vitale.

"Sorry," I exhaled. "I meant transsexuals."

"I prefer to be called a woman."

"Right."

"Maybe you'd better go," she said.

"No." I looked up, surprised at how quickly the word leapt from my mouth. "I mean . . . I'd like to stay."

"All right," she said, nodding slowly. She suddenly seemed so vulnerable, more than I had ever thought her capable of being.

"Why did you do it?" I asked. My eyes were darting carefully, keeping her face in a pleasant state of unfocused flux.

"I don't know, I was bored one Friday night." Her wit rose faintly before she succumbed to a sigh. "I always thought of myself as a woman," she said. "Always."

"Huh," I responded hesitantly.

"Native Americans felt that men who believed they were women possessed supernatural powers," she said.

"Are you . . . Native American?" I asked.

"I don't know," she said. "There was never any information about my parents available to me. But judging from my skin color, I'd say there's some kind of Indian blood in me."

"Did you ever tell your adoptive parents?" I asked.

"They wouldn't even talk to me about sex," she said. "I learned all about that from my brother. There's no way I could have told them about this."

"How about your brother?" I asked.

"In a way," she said cautiously, as though trying out

a new voice. "I don't know that he really knew. My freshman year of high school the coach recruited me for football because I was big. But I had trouble when it came to tackling people. I didn't like the idea of hurting anyone. So I would just try and tackle people by pulling them to the ground. The coach would say things like, 'Every time Miller misses a tackle, that means we run an extra lap at the end of practice.' The kids started calling me sissy and faggot. But I still couldn't hate them enough to hurt them. I *wanted* to. But I just couldn't."

As she talked I watched her hands move in graceful circles. In spite of my mental protests, my mind formed a picture of her as a little boy. *Good God, this must be so wrong. What the hell am I still doing here?*

I closed my eyes but didn't move from the couch. "Are you all right?" I heard her ask. "Do you want me to go on?"

"Yes, I'm fine," I said. "Go on. Please."

"It was the same way when they teased me about being adopted. I would try and fight one of them, and the kids would be screaming at us to kill each other. It all seemed so stupid to me. I couldn't hit the other person, and my brother would have to help me out."

"Sounds like wrestling," I commented, eyes still closed tightly.

"Yeah," she agreed. "I think that may be why I became a wrestler. To get revenge. It's like . . . this way I can feel superior in a way to the marks . . . to the crowd. I'm not sure.

"So one time after a fight, my brother took me aside and told me basically that all these other kids could go to hell. But I shouldn't be ashamed of who I was. At that point I was aware that I was . . . different. But I don't know whether he was referring to that or to the fact that I was adopted." There was a silent gap. "That was about four years before he jumped off that bridge and died."

I blinked. "So how'd you become a pro wrestler?"

"Like I said, I was always big." Shawna shrugged, squeezing one of her forearms. "And one day in the gym someone spotted me working out. He was a pro wrestler, and he offered to train me. I was pretty sure pro wrestlers didn't really hurt each other. Not on purpose at least." She grinned, the first time she had done so while telling me her real history. "So he trained me and I went to Memphis."

"Did you ever . . . have sex with anyone all those years?" I let my eyes close again.

"You mean did I fuck other guys?" she asked, her humorous tone suggesting that her smile was there. "No. I never wanted to make love to another guy as a guy. I wanted to be a woman. All this terrified me, of course, so I tried even harder to be a rough pro wrestler. I drank every day, then used pills after matches. Then I started using them during matches. One night I blacked out in the ring and woke up in a hospital room. The doctor who had pumped my stomach told me that if I kept it up, I would be dead soon. That's when I realized that was precisely what I wanted: to die. I was fucking miserable. As a man." She paused. "About two weeks later I was driving out of Memphis to a show in Arkansas. As soon as I crossed over into Arkansas and saw those rice fields, the ones I told you to sketch . . . that was when I made up my mind. So I just kept driving west.

"But a few years later, after I had gotten the operation, I found I still wanted to be a pro wrestler. Something about it . . . the cheers, the theater . . . I was hooked. So I went to Billy Rogers's Power Camp and started a new career with a new name, a new body . . . everything."

I opened my eyes. Shawna was still sitting there, legs crossed, staring at me with those wide green eyes. "But the funny thing," she said with a throaty tenderness, "is that although I've been a woman for five years . . . the first time I truly felt like a woman was when I saw the picture you drew of me. It was like some kind of a . . . validation. I saw myself as a woman through another's eyes for the first time."

"You must have guys hit on you all the time."

"It happens," she acknowledged, "but I've never responded to one." She paused before uttering, "Until now."

I bit my lips. "You mean until that night in the hotel lobby—"

"Who kissed who, Romeo?" she asked with a guarded smile.

"Guilty." I smiled. The moment felt similar to many we had shared in the past, except that all those previous thin hints of defensiveness and discomfort were almost gone. "I'm glad I helped you complete your change," I said.

"There's also a Native American tradition for the change you're undergoing. A vision quest," she said. "It means a search for one's self," she added.

"That's a nice name," I remarked idiotically.

She laughed. "You're not done with it yet, obviously," she hesitated. "I just wanted you to know the truth about my history. You shouldn't give up your search on account of a false hope." She swallowed, seeming to weigh her next words. "As much as I would have liked you to," she added.

My mind spun like a planet thrown off its natural orbit. I stood hurriedly and took a few careful steps.

"I'm glad you told me," I said.

"I'll bet," she remarked with the old defensive smile.

"No, I mean really," I insisted. "It shows trust." She looked up at me with a kindled attentiveness. "Trust," I repeated, as though it were some kind of password.

The dust dancing through the air became invisible as all hint of afternoon light vanished from the window. "I'd better go," I said.

"Wait," she said softly, "before you do, there's something I'd like to give you." I nodded and remained where I was, weaving in place as she once again strode down the hallway. *What could possibly be next?*

This time she returned with a piece of poster board. Stretched across its surface was a drawing of the rice fields lining the road that wound down from Tennessee into Arkansas. But it was no longer just black and white; streaks of color mixing reds and yellows with blues and grays had been shaded in. A lean slice of silver represented water lining the fields.

"It's beautiful," I admitted.

"Dusk or dawn," she stated, holding the poster out to me. I took it.

"Damned if I know," I said.

We paused at the door. I wasn't sure at all what to do. She held up her hand in a motionless wave. I did the same. We held those positions for a ridiculously long time before she issued a chuckle and let her hand drop. "All right," she said. "Whatever happens or doesn't happen, I'm glad I told you."

I nodded, a statue granted only slight movement. My hand remained suspended. "Good luck, Michael Harding," she said softly. "Have a good journey."

She was still standing on her porch, framed in my rearview mirror as I drove away.

14

MR. MICHAEL HARDING

The champion parts the curtain. He strides out facing backward, his back a huge inverted triangle of flesh. His mammoth arms are raised toward the sky, like an orchestra conductor's. After a few yards he swings around and continues down the aisle, his blond hair snapping behind him.

He reaches the mini-ring in the aisle and gazes incredulously at this obstacle. The crowd cheers him on as he tips it over and storms ahead.

Jesus, he's big.

By the time he makes it to the ring, the air is filled with eighty thousand voices chanting his name. I glance over at the four guys who were chanting earlier. Their mouths now move silently, just four more parts swept up into the sum of the crowd's worship.

A crushed aluminum can misses my head by a few inches. I whirl around, but it is impossible to tell where it came from. Hostile eyes stare back at me. The champion's presence has transformed me from a young man with a dream to a destroyer of idols. I look for the woman with the blue hair, but can't locate her. Maybe she got out. Just as well. I've seen crowds like this rip unpopular signs to shreds and threaten those who made them.

I stare across the ring at the referee holding the ropes open for the champ. The champ slips through and parades around the ring, eliciting cheers from all. He makes it look so easy. Could I really take this guy's place? A vague guilt knots my stomach. If I beat him, I will upset the natural order of things.

If I were out there in the audience, I would be booing me.

As though some invisible hand had protected the buildings from either renovation or decay, the quiet Chicago street I grew up on looked exactly the same. The street's gutters even seemed cluttered with the same moderate amount of trash. A fresh smoky smell from a rooftop barbecue traveled through the air.

My door was opened by a short squat man with a tuft of black hair poking up from a swollen cherry of a face.

What happened to Irling?

"Hi," I said, "I'm Bonnie's son."

"Who?"

"The woman who lives here," I said, mentally double-checking the address that had always been stored in the recesses of my mind as *home*.

"Bonnie!" he exclaimed. "She sold the place to us about three months ago."

"Oh," I said. He was studying me. "Do you know . . . where she went?" I asked.

"Nebraska, I think," he said, "but she left something for you. Said you were on the road all the time." His eyes clicked into sharper focus and he snapped his fingers excitedly. "You're oneathose pro wrestlers, right?" he exclaimed.

Was I? I still hadn't called Thomas Rockart Jr. "Yeah," I managed, "I'm kind of on vacation right now."

"You mean you're not wrestlin' at the Horizon tonight?" he asked.

So it was Friday. Two weeks to the day after I had set out from Buffalo on the search for a new gimmick. "No," I said, "I mean yeah." From the way he was peering at me I could've been growing horns right on his front porch. "Yes," I finally concluded, "I'll be there."

"What's your name?" he inquired. "I'll look for ya."

"Not sure yet," I mumbled, "We're trying out a new . . ." My voice trailed off before I could get out the word *gimmick*. "Did you say my mom left something for me?" I asked.

"Oh. Yeah, wait. I'll get it." He turned, then glanced over his shoulder. "I'd invite you in, but me and the wife were just gettin' ready to take a bath. Conserve water, ya know?" he added with a wink.

Soon he was back with two envelopes. I wished him a happy bath, and he winked again and guaranteed that it would be. After he closed the door, I turned and sat on the stoop. One of the envelopes was stamped and addressed to me, while the other simply had "Michael" decorating the envelope in looping writing I immediately recognized as my mother's. The note inside was on stationery dotted with planets:

Dear Michael,

As you probably discovered by now, we've moved. We're going to be living just outside Lincoln, Nebraska. I'll call you with a phone number as soon as we have one. I've also sent a letter to your apartment in Brooklyn, but since you never seem to be there, I thought you might try and call or come by before you actually received it. I really enjoyed your last visit—it seemed to be the calmest and warmest time we've had together in quite some time. Shawna is a wonderful person, and I wish you all the best with her. Irling says hi as well.

Love, Mom

The other letter read:

Dear Mike,
Seems funny to be addressing this letter to you. I'm not even sure if you go by Mike or Michael. Anyway, I wanted to write to you and say that if you're blaming yourself for Chuck, don't. These things do happen. Been doing some reading lately, in addition to running my gym. Came upon a great

saying: "Death tweaks us by the ear and says, 'LIVE—I am coming.'"

Back a while ago, that idea would have depressed the hell out of me. But now I see it as a challenge and an invitation. Hope you feel the same. Take care, buddy. Meredith, Dawn, and Elektra all say "hi." Helena says "da."

Still a human (not a slab of metal),

Trevor

I stood and slowly descended the steps. On the way to my car, there was once again the scent of burning charcoal. I looked over and glimpsed a small army of ashes being whisked through the air. I thought of my grandfather, and although I knew they were from the barbecue, I reached up and let them touch my hand.

I had visited my father's grave only once before in my life. After wandering among the gravestones for almost a half an hour, I was ready to give up. The place was too damn quiet, I told myself angrily. But then at the end of a plot I spotted the name *Steven Harding.* Once I stopped walking I was able to pick up the trilling of birds coming from somewhere.

I read and reread the inscription: *Alive in Our Hearts and Memories Always.*

I crouched down and ran my palm along the marble, smearing the residue of ashes across this message. For the first time in my life, it was true. He had been real, a person with dreams and aspirations, some of which he had met and conquered but some of which must have remained undisclosed or perhaps undiscovered. Had he ever considered the possibility of dying so young?

I wanted to proclaim something, go on a rant of some kind. But with the tips of my fingers shadowed by ashes that had been blowing in the Chicago winds, I thought of my grandfather's advice: "Keepin' your mouth shut is the best way to keep your options open." So that's what I did.

When I was ready, I whispered, "I miss you, Dad. I love you." As I stood, a flock of birds rose from the oak trees that bordered the row of plots and flew into the sticky air. I walked off, still confused but no longer hating the silence that had reclaimed the cemetery.

———————

When I got to the Rosemont Horizon, a few fans were already gathered by the tunnel that led to the backstage area. I strode past and half-listened to their bewildered whispers as they tried to place me as a wrestler they recognized.

The first person I saw backstage was Sonny Logan. He was touching his nose delicately with one hand and clutching a newspaper with the other. "What's up, brother?" he greeted me. "Where have you been? Tom is goin' crazy. He's sure you signed with Burner." He gave me a slim conspiratorial smile.

"Nah," I replied, as we exchanged a soft handshake. "I went and got lost for a while."

"Did you see this yet?" He shook the newspaper at me.

"What is it?"

"Shit," was all he said as he handed me the copy of *The Tribune.* I glanced above the fold that had been creased by his grip. It was an editorial by a local sports journalist. The heading read: *No Hero's Death for a Local "Beastie."* A burning erupted on my forehead and got hotter as I read more:

When hometown boy Charles Clifton, known in the bawdy world of professional wrestling as Chuck "The Stud" Beastie, fell to his death last week during a professional wrestling match in Boston, it was indeed a tragedy.

It was not, however, a sports-related tragedy.

Professional wrestling is, and always will be, an odd curiosity in the parade of never-ending fads that contribute to that vague semblance of "Americanana." The World Wrestling Organization would like you to believe Clifton died the death of a sportsman. He did not. He died in a freak accident during a rehearsed move, the same way a stuntman might perish in a botched stunt. For the WWO to somehow assert that this death was the result of combat is ludicrous. Noble? Perhaps. But Charles Clifton's death will do nothing to alter the general public's attitude regarding pro wrestling.

It can then be seen as a shame. Pro wrestling is cheap, often exploitative (Clifton's death being no exception) entertainment, but represents no kind of athletic contest. To compare Beastie's death to those of men who have died on a football field or a racetrack is absurd. It is an ironic tragedy that young men are willing to take such risks in the name of a wanna-be sport.

> But there is a truer tragedy: that of Chuck Beastie,
> a character who died in vain as a wanna-be athlete, not
> even bearing his real name.

I tore the paper in half and stormed up the stairs. Thomas Rockart Jr. was hunched over the public-address system, going over the music and lighting cues with the engineer. As soon as he saw me, his lips tightened. "Where the hell have you been?" he demanded. "Why haven't you called?"

"I'm sorry, Thomas," I replied. "I had to work some things out. And I've got an idea," I announced before he had a chance to respond.

He tilted his head curtly. "Give me a live interview tonight," I said.

"What are you going to say?" he demanded.

"I want to try something," I urged. "Trust me."

His features pulled back in thought. After a minute they assumed their usual structured confidence. "You'll get two minutes just before intermission," he told me. "And it damn well better be good."

"It will be," I promised, turning around.

"Wait!" he shouted. "We've gotta get you a costume! We've got to—"

"No costumes," I said. "I'll be in the audience. Just introduce me and I'll come up to the platform."

Excitement awakened in Thomas Rockart Jr.'s eyes, as though an infallible inner sense had just been positively stoked. "Okay." He nodded. "What do we introduce you as?"

"Michael Harding," I replied. I descended the same narrow passageway where Sonny Logan had first shook

my hand, then strode out through the tunnel. After
buying a ticket, I milled about in the anonymous sea of
marks. Two young boys were performing wrestling
moves on one another, and people shot them bemused
glances as they filed inside. Soon it was show time, but
the boys were still wrestling, lost in their own world. I
hung around, waiting to see who would win. Soon I
realized the show had been going on for twenty minutes
already and hurried inside just as one of the kids
wrapped the other in a Boston Crab.

My seat was in the middle of one of the corner sections. When the announcer called my name, I was
ready. I ambled down the rows of seats and climbed
over the barricade. Security guards escorted me to the
podium, and once there I took hold of the microphone
and gave a speech that would be replayed many times
on WWO telecasts over the following weeks:

"The fans of the World Wrestling Organization have
been watching me wrestle for years but almost none of
them know who I am. Up to this point I have been The
Chameleon. Two weeks ago, I was in a cage match with
a man named Charles Clifton, known to millions of fans
around the world as Chuck 'The Stud' Beastie. He was
an amazing athlete and, more important, a great
human being. He was not a character; he was a man
with many different facets to his personality. He was
also a true hero not only to millions of fans but to me.
He taught me many things, and his death taught me
the most important thing: that it is time to shed my
skin. My name is Michael Harding. Period. I came into
this sport for one reason: to become the World Wrestling
Organization Heavyweight Champion. And that's what

I'm gonna do. As myself! This is no script. This is no character. This is one man going after a dream. And I will not rest until that belt is mine!"

"Immediate" and "unbelievable" were the two adjectives Thomas Rockart Jr. later used to describe the crowd's reaction that night. He sent me out to work with Officer O'Malley, who was one of the WWO's most popular wrestlers. It was an assumption that since I had all but challenged Sonny Logan, the fans would treat me as a heel. But as the name "Michael Harding" boomed out of the Horizon's scratchy public-address system, the crowd launched into cheers. Then as the match progressed, it became more and more apparent that I was the fan favorite.

During live events, the referee always wore a small flesh-colored earpiece that enabled him to receive any changes from backstage. While we were in a rest-spot (O'Malley had a headlock clamped around me in the middle of the ring), the referee leaned in close. While he pretended to test my arm for consciousness, he whispered frantically, "The big guy just came through . . . said to change the finish." The finish had called for me to gain a cheap victory over O'Malley by pinning him with my feet on the ropes for support. "Big guy said O'Malley should do a clean job," the referee whispered.

"All right." Officer O'Malley nodded, then said to me sotto voce, "How do you wanna beat me, Mike?"

Several blank seconds followed; for more than a year

my moves in the ring had been limited to the ones used by whomever I was working with. Then I recalled my last glimpse of the two boys outside. "Boston Crab," I whispered.

"Ah, a traditionalist," O'Malley laughed approvingly. And that was the way it happened. Five minutes later I wrapped him in a Boston Crab, and his face strained in mock struggle until he finally indicated that he was beaten.

The referee rang the bell, and as he raised my arm in victory the chant began: "Har-ding! Har-ding!" In the midst of it all a plane soared overhead. I listened and hoped that wherever those two kids were, the building was trembling for them too.

"Amazing," Thomas Rockart Jr. claimed, adding a third adjective to what he was calling "the Harding phenomenon." He was seated in his office, surrounded by letters and cards. In the last two weeks I had been working as Michael Harding, nearly 40,000 responses had poured in supporting my quest for the WWO title. T-shirts had been printed with *Michael Harding* on the front and *Period* on the back. They were selling out at every house show. Upon seeing the sales figures for the week, he had immediately doubled the order for T-shirts, Michael Harding cups, baseball caps, and key chains. The highest compliment a wrestler can be paid by a promoter is to be called a commodity. Sonny Logan was a commodity. "Bad Boy" Benny Flare, the Champion of WWO's rival ICW, was a commodity. Now I was a commodity, and Thomas Rockart Jr. wanted to make my name a trademark owned by the World Wrestling Organization.

"Absolutely not," I told him, when he brought it up casually. "My name is my name," I said, getting a kick out of the momentary uncertainty in his eyes. It was the first time I could remember seeing that, or at least noticing it.

We finally agreed that the WWO would introduce me as "Mister Michael Harding." That would be the trademarked name, and the WWO's exclusive license on that name would expire upon my departure from the company.

"Which will never happen anyway," Thomas Rockart Jr. stated with an assured smile. "Not when you hear this latest offer."

Because of some "tax maneuvers," Rockart explained, he wanted to renegotiate my contract to cover only the next two months leading up to SlamFest. I would receive a substantial raise, earning $40,000 each month. The updated contract also contained a clause that stated if I left the WWO, I couldn't work for another wrestling organization until a full year had expired. With this safeguard in place, Rockart felt secure that I wouldn't hop from the WWO to ICW after the two months ended. What Hippo later told me was that Rockart wanted to throw this money at me for two months while making sure that the "Harding phenomenon had legs."

"Any moron can be popular for a few months," Thomas Rockart Jr. was fond of joking. "It takes a real moron to connect with pro wrestling audiences for longer."

That week the card for SlamFest, the WWO's annual "Night of Titans," was announced. In the main event, "The American Dream" Sonny Logan would defend the World Wrestling Organization Heavyweight Championship against "Mister Michael Harding." Thomas Rockart Jr. informed me that our match would end with a Logan victory by default. I would juice and bleed so profusely that the referee would be forced to stop the match. This could then set up a feud that would carry Logan and I through a summer of main events.

As the weeks counted down to SlamFest, the WWO hype machine launched into overdrive. I was engaged in a series of "face versus face" matches with Scotty "The Body" Fitzman, who had been working an all-American fitness gimmick the past five years. Our matches were purely scientific, meaning neither of us resorted to cheating. I always pinned him cleanly, and we shook hands at the end of every match. The purpose was to establish me as a legitimate contender for the WWO belt. Also, by having me take on a fellow face, Rockart was preparing the fans to witness me take on Sonny Logan, the ultimate face, at SlamFest.

In addition to these matches, I was making a string of public appearances. My days were spent at children's hospitals, orphanages, and other places rife with photo-ops. But these events also provided me with a chance to connect with people on a one-to-one basis. The orphanages always hit me hardest; after an afternoon of talking with parentless kids, I would often sob alone in my car on the way to the arena. All my senses felt like those of a newborn, nerves raw and eager to experience emotions for their own sake. Because my heightened feelings also included the aches and pains that are part of a pro wrestler's everyday life, it was a small miracle that I hadn't yet hit Santa up for a single painkiller.

Since ceasing all steroid use, my physique had lost the added thickness granted by water retention. Each night I felt smaller and smaller in comparison to Scotty Fitzman, who religiously injected himself with 1,000 milligrams of testosterone cypionate once a week instead of taking the Fitzman One-A-Day Vitamins he endorsed.

But in spite of all this, as well as the knowledge that I wasn't going to win the belt, I felt on top of the world. The days passed like steps down the aisle, filled with that infinite possibility I always compared to the opening kickoff of a football game. I was that football, climbing higher and higher before a crowd of eager faces.

"This world has been through countless revolutions and periods fueled by emotion and violence. Professional wrestling taps into both of those needs in a safe manner that at the same time is thoroughly entertaining. There is violence, but it's contained, and the fact that these gladiators often reflect facets of the audience's own personalities enables people to undergo a catharsis while watching them engage in battle."

"A bit of a highly inflated opinion, wouldn't you say?" speculated the host, Harry Winters. "A lot of people would say it's just a couple of fat slobs pretending to hit each over the head with chairs." He chuckled and gave the camera a sly glance, sharing this joke with millions of his late-night viewers.

"Obviously they're not watching very closely." I alternated my focus between Winters and the camera. "Anyone who watches pro wrestling can see these are athletes, not 'fat slobs.' But there has been a certain stigma attached to pro wrestling due to its over-the-top approach. As a result, many people are closet fans. But the WWO's worldwide popularity makes it impossible to deny that pro wrestling touches a very primal nerve in people. The whole situation is almost overwhelming, a brutal ballet with larger-than-life characters—"

"But you're not claiming to be larger-than-life, are you, Michael?" he pounced. "I mean after all, your name is Michael Harding, period. You're supposed to be the young lion."

"Sure . . . ," I fumbled for a panicky second, watching the red dot just above the camera swell, a large eye tunneling into my thoughts. I touched my arm, flexing it, and found an answer of sorts: "When I get in that ring I become something else. It's like a connection to a past point, a kid jumping around on mats with a dream, and something greater, a man who is on his way to making his dream a reality—"

"But let's get real," Harold Winters chortled. "The endings are all predetermined. The moves are choreographed. Given those two factors, how can you really feel like you have any control or independence? How can you expect people to cheer for you?"

"When you see a movie or watch television, those

things are all predetermined. Hell, Harold," I said and smiled, "before we started the show, you and I planned out what we were going to talk about in this interview. Now you didn't mention that you were going to question pro wrestling's authenticity. So you just went off the script for our interview.

"And since you went off the script," I continued loudly as Winters' mouth parted, "I'll do the same. I'll draw an analogy between pro wrestling and your show. Given that your show is planned out beforehand, you know that there's one thing none of your guests will ever mention. The fact that you've been married and divorced seven times and are currently on your eighth wife. Everyone knows that's your Achilles heel, the thing you're very sensitive about. That," I added, "and your three face-lifts."

Harold Winters' expression compressed itself into a stern frown. "We'll be right—" he began.

"See there?" I announced. "You dug at me, so now I'm digging at you. This kind of stuff happens in professional wrestling as well. With all the variables and personalities involved, you can never be sure what's scripted and what's not."

Harold turned abruptly to the camera and almost shouted: "We're right back." The red light shut off.

"Ninety seconds!" the cameraman called out. Harry waved off the makeup people that swooped over to us.

"Those were some low blows," he said, sounding more genuinely stunned than angry.

"Don't fuck with my sport, sweetheart," I said and winked at him.

———

This episode was rerun the next night on CNN and wound up making the national papers. Two days later, *USA Today* had a phone-in poll on who had emerged as "the victor in our debate on the merits of pro wrestling versus late-night talk shows." Seventy-nine percent of the 13,000 readers who phoned in said that I had won. Backstage at the Pittsburgh Civic Center that night, Hippo Haleberg informed me that, with the event still a week away, advance pay-per-view orders for SlamFest had hit the million mark, an all-time high.

When I got back to my hotel room after the show, I found a manila envelope had been slipped neatly under the door. Inside was a standard employment contract for International Championship Wrestling. Under section E, which was labeled "Payment," the sentence read: "I will be paid the sum of for 365 days of employment under International Championship Wrestling." Over the line were the handwritten words: "Name your price." A cover letter signed with best regards by Brad Burner invited me to call him "day or night" if I had any questions.

I shook my head and laughed. Thomas Rockart Jr. had been right. There was only one title I had spent my life fantasizing about winning. That was the one possessed by Sonny Logan.

The next morning I was awakened by a phone call from Thomas Rockart Jr. He informed me in an urgent voice that in six days I was going to become the World Wrestling Organization Heavyweight Champion.

I grabbed on to the sides of the bed as if to brace myself. The football was about to start falling.

15

TRUE AMERICAN

Off comes the champ's blue and red T-shirt, ripped from his bronzed chest in a show of mock strength. He hams it up, face stretching in exertion when everyone knows the shirt's material is so thin a five-year-old could pull it off. He cocks his arm, preparing to give the crowd something to fight over, then pauses.

He whirls back around and fires the shirt at me. I catch it on instinct, as surprised as the crowd. The champ and I didn't plan that one. The T-shirt clings to my hand. People at ringside throw up their arms in expectation. I'm holding a sweat-soaked treasure.

I let it unfurl. American Dreamin' is stitched in red letters across the shirt's glossy blue. I look out at the crowd. More hands fly up and the same people who were hollering insults at me seconds ago now beg me to toss them what's in my hand. Even the champ himself is watching me curiously.

My eyes scan the ringside area for who I know I will see . . . the guest ring-boy, standing on the floor next to the ring's far corner and staring intently at the champion. I walk over and stand in front of the kid. He scowls, and I toss the T-shirt into his hands. "See there, kid?" I tell him, "I'm not such a bad guy, am I?"

Before he can refute this, I turn and face the champ, who is waiting in the middle of the ring.

He winks at me. I don't wink back.

––––––––––

The dream I had spent my life living for now lay within the palm of my hand, its coming as inevitable as the end of the world predicted in the dusk/dawn painting. Instead of being thrilled, I was scared as hell.

Thomas Rockart Jr. informed me on the phone that morning what had happened: last night an exact duplicate of the contract that I received had been delivered to Sonny Logan in the same surreptitious manner. Apparently, Logan had been waiting for something like this (I remembered the smile he had given me at the Horizon when he mentioned Rockart's suspicion that I had signed with Burner). He had called ICW headquarters in Atlanta, and even though it was midnight, Burner had called Logan back at the hotel. Logan had named his price, and the next morning left for Atlanta to sign a one-year contract for four million dollars.

Naturally, Thomas Rockart Jr. was enraged. Because he had considered Sonny Logan to be one of the few wrestlers whose loyalty was unshakable, there wasn't even a clause in Logan's contract that stipulated he couldn't work for another company after leaving the WWO. His contract expired a week after SlamFest, and Rockart had intended to use that time to hash out a new agreement with his champion.

"That sonofabitch," Rockart ranted over the phone after telling me the story. "I *made* him and he goes and does *this* to me! Fuck it! We'll see how well that jerk Burner does with The American Dream! *I'm* the only one who can market that balding rhinoceros!"

"I wish Sonny Logan nothing but continued success," Thomas Rockart Jr. said the next day at a press conference in the lobby of the Crystal Ship. There were about two dozen reporters in attendance. Logan and I sat on either side of the podium where Rockart, dressed in a white suit instead of his usual black, was standing. I assumed the white was supposed to make him look more benevolent. "After all, this is a business that is rapidly growing. And with that comes higher stakes. I must say I dropped the ball here." As Thomas Rockart Jr.'s lips stretched into a smile of tolerant resignation, I pictured him practicing rigorously in front of a mirror all morning long. "I even must tip a grudging hat to Burner for so aggressively recruiting such talent," he continued. "Sonny Logan knows wrestling very well because he has been around a very, very long time."

This subtle rib at Logan caused a stirring among the lines of reporters.

"I have a wife and two kids, with another little boy on the way," Logan announced, "so I've got to look to where the future of this sport lies. By signing with ICW, that's what I've done." He cast a challenging smirk at Rockart's impassive face.

"What about SlamFest?" a reporter hollered.

"Sonny Logan's final match for the WWO will indeed take place at SlamFest," Thomas Rockart Jr. declared. He turned to me. "Michael Harding will challenge him for the World Wrestling Organization Heavyweight Championship."

"So given Logan's departure, it can pretty much be a foregone conclusion he'll be dropping the belt," a reporter shouted, eliciting a roomful of laughter that made me want to scream.

"This match will, like all WWO matches," Thomas Rockart Jr. pointed out steadily, "be a prime example of sports entertainment at its best—"

"I've worn this belt proudly for five years," Logan cut him off. "I definitely plan to leave as a champion—"

"And I definitely plan to make sure you don't," I asserted, like any good challenger would. Logan looked around Thomas Rockart Jr. and smiled quirkily.

"We'll see Sunday," he said.

"We sure will," I responded.

"One can never know for sure." Thomas Rockart Jr.'s smile remained fixed, a beacon of teeth to match his suit. "All I can say is I have never before been so looking forward to a match between two WWO super-stars. I see this as a battle between old and new. No offense, Dream." He laughed. Logan just shook his head and continued to offer up his own smile for the photographers. "The WWO is a place where anything can happen," concluded Rockart. "That's what makes our brand of sports entertainment so much fun."

"What do you mean you're *not certain* you want to do a job?" Thomas Rockart Jr. screamed a half hour later, after the three of us had gathered in his office. The only other living things in the room were the fish swimming languidly through the tank's green water.

"Don't scream at me, Thomas," Logan responded coolly. "You can scream at any other wrestler you've got working for you, but not at me."

"There's a tradition, Sonny," Thomas blustered. "When a wrestler leaves a federation, he does a job in his final match. If he's a champion, he *always* drops the belt. I know Michael is young—"

"It's got nothing to do with Michael," Logan said. "I'm serious, Michael." He turned to me. "If I was ready to drop the belt, I would have no problem doing a job for you. But the fact of the matter is I just don't want to drop it."

It was odd to see him explain this so rationally; if his tank top and stretch pants were a three-piece suit, he could just as easily have been dissecting a corporate takeover. Then it hit me that this could be considered precisely that; Brad Burner was taking over the license to "The American Dream." An uneasy pang stitched its way across my side.

"*You* don't *want* to?" Rockart was demanding. "When the hell did you start booking this federation?"

"I'll be happy to wrestle Michael to a draw," Logan maintained. "That way, nobody loses face."

"Bullshit!" Thomas Rockart Jr. cried. "That means you leave the WWO undefeated as champion. That means our heavyweight title is weakened. Sonny." Rockart's voice dropped to a husky whisper. If Logan was discussing a corporate takeover, Rockart seemed more like he was pleading with a departing lover. "You, more than anyone, know that this business is built on *perception*. People see a belt as having value only because of the person wearing it. And people see the person wearing it as having value only because of a company's push of that individual. If that person's real habits were made public, then the public might not accept him as quite a hero."

"What are you insinuating here, Tom?" Sonny Logan demanded. "That if I don't drop the belt, you'll issue a press release stating that I drink, do coke, take steroids, fool around on the road, et cetera?"

"It's a funny business." Rockart gave a ridiculously affected shrug. "Things leak out."

Logan laughed. "We both know there's no way you'll ever let that 'leak out,' Tommy. Because if it does, it may weaken me, but it also destroys the character that's been the cornerstone of your company for five years. And I know you, you'd sell your own kids to the devil before you'd do anything that'd damage the company."

Thomas Rockart Jr. stared at the champion of his company with a cool hatred. Sonny Logan stood and nodded at me. "Sorry, Michael," he explained. "Again, it's nothing personal." I gave a numb nod, and Logan turned and left.

After the door clicked shut, Thomas Rockart Jr. began a furious beating of his fingers upon the oak of the desk. "Damn it, damn it, damn it," he chanted in tune with the steady beat of his drumming. I watched, fascinated, as he quickly turned to the portrait looming just behind him. "We'll figure something out," he told himself. "We'll figure something out."

I headed quietly out of the office, leaving Thomas Rockart Jr. still staring into the stern eyes of his self-portrait.

Out in the lobby I found Sonny Logan waiting for the elevator. We nodded at one another. The silence was heavy enough to make the *ding* of the elevator sound like a gunshot. Once we were inside, he said, "You know what we call him, right? Herr Rockart?"

"He does have an ego," I allowed. "I mean hell, how many people do you see with portraits of themselves hanging in their office?"

Logan looked at me blankly, then shook his head. "That's not him," he said. "That's his *father*. Thomas Rockart Sr."

"No shit," I said. Suddenly I realized that the *something* I had sensed in Rockart the first time I met him, the same something I was lacking, was a father's presence. Maybe, when he had accused me of wanting to dwell on Beastie's death, he *had* understood. *In his own way.*

"I met his old man once," Logan was nodding. "My first year here was the year Thomas took over operations. He was an even bigger hard-on than his kid."

The elevator reached the ground floor and its doors slid open. Sonny Logan and I both made simultaneous gestures indicating the other should go first. "I insist," Logan said, in a tone that awakened in me some stubborn need to stand my ground. "After you, Dream," I challenged, trying to keep my voice diplomatic.

Logan's hand flashed out and stopped the doors

from closing. He stepped out of the elevator, and I began to follow. He stopped and turned, his massive frame taking up almost the entire elevator doorway. I stumbled and bounced lightly off his chest. He smiled down at me from his seven inch height advantage. "See you on Sunday, Michael," he said evenly.

Then he was walking away. I watched him until the elevator doors began to close once more. Then I barged through them, stumbling across the lobby and into a humid New York City spring.

In any given week, the combined roster of WWO wrestlers received more than 5,000 fan letters requesting a reply of some kind, be it autographed pictures, personal meetings, or simply a written acknowledgment. During the weeks leading up to SlamFest, that weekly total had quadrupled. This meant a greatly increased workload for "the three priestesses," the trio of women who made up the response department on the fifth floor of the Crystal Ship. Two of the three might have been more properly referred to as witches. Both suffered from severe middle-age; they were unhappily married, and their tired brittle faces matched their personalities. They seemed determined that every word or thought they shared be a cynical one.

Via Kavanaugh, however, really did seem to be something of a priestess. She was a large-boned woman with facial features that were more comforting than beautiful. When she spoke, it was with a voice so cheerful that you were inclined to believe anything she told you. She was much gossiped about throughout the Crystal Ship offices, for although she had been working for the WWO for many years, she would talk to the boys about past and upcoming matches in such earnest tones (offering luck for the future and commiserating on losses) that many of us wondered if she wasn't a little mad. It was as though the innocence from the thousands of letters she opened every week had seeped through her skin. She would often give us letters if she thought, as she put it, "we would especially like them."

Via was the one who made me aware of Robert Brown, a ten-year-old boy dying of cancer in a New Jersey hospital room. She had slipped me a letter about two weeks before SlamFest.

Robert wrote that he admired my courage, and even though he had been in hospital for the past couple of months, he was sure that he would get better in the same way I was sure I would win the WWO Championship. I read his letter eight times the night after Via gave it to me. Even the shaping of the letters was clean and polite. The postmark was from Fairfield, New Jersey, about a two hour drive from Giants Stadium, where SlamFest was taking place. I got in touch with the local hospital and made arrangements to visit there on the day before SlamFest. Three days before leaving for New Jersey, I poked my head into the response department. It was lunchtime, and Via was the only one there. She was at her desk with a view of a narrow alley, responding to letters while eating a chicken salad sandwich.

I told her that I was going to visit Robert. "See

there?" she cried, with a justified air. "I knew you'd like that letter."

"Thanks for giving it to me, Via," I said, then reached out and clasped her hand.

"Good luck on Sunday," she urged. Her routine wish of luck was, for once, undeniably valid; the finish of my match with Logan had yet to be determined.

This changed on Saturday morning, when I met Thomas Rockart Jr. in the rear booth of a coffee shop. He had called me in my hotel room at the Sheraton that morning, saying that he had to meet with me urgently "somewhere out of the way." I copied down his directions and agreed to be in the rear booth at the specified coffee shop at 10:30 A.M. The shop was abuzz with activity when I walked in ten minutes early. Rockart had instructed that the meeting was to be top secret, so I had tried to dress incognito, in a football jacket and a sports cap pulled down low over my forehead. I was stopped for an autograph three times on my way back to the rear booth, where I found Thomas Rockart Jr. sitting with an impatient expectation.

"I've got a plan," he told me as soon as I slid in. This self-assured man bore no relation to the scared little boy I had seen staring up at his father's picture. "We let the big lummox think he's getting his draw. No problem. But at around the twenty minute mark, you're going to get him into a Boston Crab. He'll crawl to the ropes and break it. He'll love that. The egotistical sonofabitch loves to get out of other people's finishing maneuvers."

"So what about after that?" I asked.

"There won't be any *after that*." Rockart's smile was

sinister. Then he coasted into silence as a waitress whisked by and deposited two cups of coffee on the table along with a pair of stained menus. Before she could speak, Thomas Rockart Jr. nodded at her with a smile that was pleasant and dismissive; she took the hint and disappeared.

"As soon as you wrap Logan in that Boston Crab," Rockart continued, his face reclaiming its former malevolence, "the ref is gonna pretend to ask him if he submits, then ring that bell so fucking fast Logan won't have a chance to get within three feet of the ropes."

"Isn't that a little . . . dishonest?" I ventured.

"Michael, this is *pro wrestling*," he reminded me. "It's not like we're planning to fix the World Series."

"True, but there's a way it should be done," I protested. "There's a right way for a title change to happen—"

"This *is* the right way. I'm the fucking booker—don't forget that."

"You're as bad as the reporters," I mumbled.

"Michael." His tone was patient. "I love this goddamn business. I love it even more than you do—because you still want to shape it to fit the way *you think is right*. Well, I love it enough not to see anything in it as right or wrong. That's the audience's job. They decide who to cheer for. We just give them something to watch."

I remembered my first exposure to pro wrestling. I had wanted something to watch, and I had gotten it. Meeting The American Dream must have meant *something* to me, enough for me to chase the WWO heavyweight title all the way up to this point. Now my dream was being granted not in the ring but in a fucking New Jersey coffee shop. It was nothing like I thought it would ever be. *Nothing ever is.* The words repeated themselves over in my mind several times before I remembered they were Shawna's. Thinking of her made me even more confused and upset and I pushed her from my mind.

"I understand," I said.

"Good." Rockart nodded. "Three people know about this. Billy Harren is the ref; he's been employed by the company for twenty years and is looking forward to his pension. So there's no problem there. The other two are sitting at this table." His clasped fingers swung back and forth between us like a pendulum. "So there will be no problems. And no leaks," he commanded.

I nodded at the tips of his fingers. He smiled, unclasped his hands, and rose from the table. I sat alone, shifting the salt and pepper shakers as though they were checkers. I realized vaguely that I had forgotten how to play the damn game, but was too unsurprised by this to laugh at it.

The specific name for the cancer that was slowly destroying Robert Brown's body was neuroblastoma. It had first afflicted him when he was only fifteen months old. Chemotherapy and radiation had cured it, but in rare cases neuroblastoma returns after absences as long as nine years. Robert, now ten years old, was a rare case. Two months ago the cancer had attacked again. Robert had waited two weeks, vomiting quietly at night and forcing himself to act well, in hopes that he would be able to fight off the disease himself without going back to the hospital. By the time he confessed to his mom that he might be sick again, the cancer had spread from his abdomen to his spine. He would be in the hospital at least another month while undergoing further chemotherapy.

Robert Brown's hospital room was lit by sunlight which framed his thin skeletal face in an unrelenting brightness. An official SlamFest cap covered a scalp made bare from countless radiation treatments.

"Hi, Robert," I said shyly. The room's silence was amplified by the beeping of a few monitors at the side of his bed. A television on the wall was playing a pro wrestling show with the sound turned all the way down.

"Omygod. I didn't know if you were really coming." His voice, squeaky but layered, surprised me. For some reason I had thought he would only be able to whisper.

I stepped up to his bed. The room smelled like chalk dust. When he shook my hand, I wanted to grab him and run down the hall and outside and just keep running. His palm was damp.

"You're my favorite wrestler, Michael Harding," he announced.

"Thanks. Thanks, Robert."

"How'd you get to be one?"

How indeed. "I took the train. Out west."

"Wow!" he exclaimed. "You went out west?"

"Sure." I nodded. "You've never been out there, huh?"

"No. What was it like?"

I started talking about Shane Stratford's Wrestling

Academy, the heat, and the desert. Just before I reached the line I had practiced so many times, the one about the tumbleweeds and me being the only things that grew out there, he broke in: "Are you gonna win the title tomorrow?"

I took a deep breath and told him the truth. "I don't know."

"It's your dream, right?" he insisted. His eyes were trusting, staring at a hero. I nodded helplessly, captive to everything I had always wanted. "That's why I think you're gonna win," Robert maintained hesitantly. "My dream is to get better. Sometimes I visualize my body, all my cells like wrestlers, body-slamming and drop-kicking the disease out of my system. Neuroblastoma. That's what I've got. So I've got a name for my body: the Neuroblaster. It's Neuroblaster versus Neuroblastoma—" His words were cut off by an abrupt frown; his bottom lip was twitching nervously. "Hey, what's wrong?" he asked.

I wiped the tears away and said nothing. The doctor had mentioned that Robert Brown would be lucky if he saw sixteen. "Sometimes I just get . . . emotional," I whispered. "You know?" I asked.

"I sometimes cry, too," he admitted reluctantly. "The doctors say it's like a release. But wow, I . . . I never pictured you crying."

"When something hurts bad enough, I cry."

"You ever get . . . down?" he asked, "'Cause some-times, I don't know. I wonder if I can beat this. It just . . . hurts. I try to picture the treatments like matches . . . like radiation as my manager. But then I'll feel so tired after-ward, I'll throw up. Sometimes I don't think I'm . . ." He was whispering now, confessing a sin, ". . . strong enough."

I reached out and took his narrow hand. "Robert, the morning I left Chicago to be a pro wrestler I threw up too. I threw up because I was scared. I've always been scared. But it's okay. It must be. Because it's part of life. To see a guy like you fighting the way you are . . . let me tell you something. You're my hero, Robert Brown."

"You're mine too."

"Okay. Then let's do that. Let's be each other's heroes." His hand squeezed mine and I squeezed back carefully, his fingers like brittle straw. "Let's both keep fighting. No matter what. And don't be afraid to cry, or to feel down sometimes . . ." I pulled his small body to mine. "Don't be afraid to be afraid."

His fingers dug into my back with a tightness that was familiar and unnerving. His father, I knew, had died of colon cancer when he was five.

———————

"We need to talk," I told Sonny Logan that night at a banquet to celebrate tomorrow's SlamFest. I was sickly aware that I couldn't go through with Thomas Rockart Jr.'s plan. "Tonight." I went on quietly, scanning the crowd to make sure Thomas Rockart Jr. nor any of his spies such as Hippo Haleberg or Rob Robertson were watching us.

"All right." Logan nodded, speaking out of the side of his mouth. "Room 1023 in ten minutes."

Room 1023 was the presidential suite; furnishings

such as marble table-tops and golden sink handles all paralyzed in a state of luxury by sterilized air. We sat on two reclining chairs swathed in leather. "Thomas is going to fuck you tomorrow," I informed him. He started laughing. It occurred to me that he may have been doing coke all night long. "Maybe I should talk to you about this later," I said, beginning to stand.

"No, wait!" he announced. Then he peered at me a little suspiciously. "What are you talking about?" he asked.

After I ran down the entire plan, he once again began to laugh. "Damn, that's a relief," he smiled. "I thought I was gonna have to tell *you*."

"What?"

"Harren told me all about it this afternoon."

"Harren told you . . .?" I frowned. "Why?"

"He's going to Burner as well." Logan winked. "Burner's got a contract for him that'll make the pension he's getting from the WWO look like the peanuts that it is."

A silence engulfed the room. Outside the magnificently framed windows came a shallow trickling of laughter and splashes from the pool below. "There's a question I've been wanting to ask you. This seems like the right time for it." Logan fingered the palm of his right hand. "How come you never drew me?"

Still stunned that he already knew about the setup, I responded to his question with a distracted shrug.

"You drew everyone else you feuded with," Logan continued, "but you never asked me."

His earnest tone marked a huge contrast to the feral teddy bear persona he hurled at television cameras and audiences in arenas throughout the world. A curiosity burgeoned inside; why hadn't I wanted to draw him? "You know, I first met you years ago," I revealed, "backstage at the Rosemont Horizon."

"Outside?"

"No, on the staircase. One of the ones going from the dressing rooms to the cargo area."

"No shit?" he smiled politely, attempting to show a fond remembrance for a moment he obviously didn't recall, a moment that had opened up a new direction in the course of my life. I wondered idly if every human being lived in their own individual dimension, all joined only by a bare thread of what we were taught to label as reality.

"So, you were Sonny Logan. The American Dream," I went on gingerly, wanting the words to be right, "and I . . . wanted to be like you. But at the same time, it seemed impossible. It was a comfortable goal, I guess. I thought that if I became WWO Champion, everything would be . . . right."

He chuckled. "Shit, you sure were a mark." His head bobbed up and down.

"I think I still am," I said. "And that's why I didn't sketch you. I was afraid that I would lose something." I found myself reaching out to touch his face. He shifted back instinctively, and I quickly dropped my hand.

"Huh," he grunted.

Then his hand patted my shoulder. "You know what I wanted to be when I was growing up? A rock-and-roll star." He seemed to be speaking with the same care I had just used. "Sometimes I look out at these people who wear my T-shirts and cheer for me and I wonder how the hell I got here. Barely any of these people know my real name is Edward Hemmings and that I sucked a pacifier until I was six and still don't know how to swim and . . ." He shook his head and took a breath. ". . . was always picked on in junior high for being at least six inches taller than everyone else. When I went back to my reunion, all these people were there. It was during my second year as champion. They were all clapping me on the back in this condescending way, joking about old times that hadn't even happened, and I just kept thinking *you don't know me, you don't know me.* But when I become Sonny Logan . . . I go under those lights and sometimes . . . there are moments . . . when I really feel like I'm living a dream." He sighed. "You know how weird it is to be called 'Dream' all night and then come home and stare in a mirror?"

"The only mirrors I like are the ones that come with smoke."

He grunted. "Tell me about it. I sometimes wonder if there's someone out there who was born to do this gimmick, and through some fucked up twist of fate I'm taking his place. You remember when you came out and threw your gimmick away? That was so goddamn great to see. I respect you, brother."

"But not enough to do a job for me," I countered with a smile.

"Shit," Logan determined. "My whole gimmick . . . the American Dream . . . has been mapped out from the get-go. I'm pretty tired of it, frankly. So this one time, I wanna feel like I've had some say in who I am; I wanna go out on champion or not as champion on my own terms."

So the American Dream's desires were only a desperate reflection of my own. The thought both reassured and scared me even more. "So, do we blow off the match tomorrow or what?" I asked.

"Tomorrow." He said the word like the name of a poem he had just read and failed to grasp. "Tomorrow we do our job and give the crowd a show. All up to the point where you're supposed to get me in a Boston Crab. Then we shoot."

There was nothing more to say. I got up and left the suite, unsure of everything except my need for sleep.

I spent a long time in bed staring without thought at visions that tried to pull me into unconsciousness through an offering of illusions.

There was no need to touch my own body. Soon I would be forced to find out just how real Michael Harding was.

I closed my eyes.

16

IN THE RING WITH THE DREAM

I approach "The American Dream" Sonny Logan without hesitation. There is no *why* anymore. There just is. Our chests touch. Sweat from our skins mingles and locks us together. He looks down at me.

"You ready, Michael?" His voice like a tractor's rumble, turning over dirt.

His gaze locks me in. Eyes so blue and limitless. But they do have limits, I know this. This dream can bleed, this dream can feel pain, this dream may not be real. I won't leave this ring until I find out for sure. My nervousness lifts, carried away by outside noise, which suddenly ceases to matter.

"I'll see you in twenty minutes, Dream."

"Let us know when to start shootin', Billy," Logan tells our ref.

"Ol' Tommy boy's gonna shit his pants," Billy drawls.

Sonny Logan staggers me with a shove. I shove him back.

Although for the next twenty minutes our moves are choreographed, the expectant tension results in some very real damage. At one point I leap off the turnbuckle, and since my left ankle has been bothering me, I put more emphasis on my right. My right knee buckles as soon as my feet hit the canvas, and a hot poker of flame tears through my knee. It is soon reduced by an influx of adrenaline to only a vibrant throb. A few minutes later, after leveling Logan with a suplex, I hear him grunt and turn to see him clutching at his ribs. Later I will learn that he has cracked two of them.

As the bout wears on, our surroundings dissolve. The only thing I see, hear, and feel is The American Dream, his sweat mingling with mine as we throw affected blows and grapple with an abandoned precision that would have made Shane Stratford proud.

I am dripping with exhaustion, picking myself up from the canvas after a missed elbow-drop when suddenly Billy Harren reenters my existence. "Twenty minutes, boys," he whispers excitedly.

The spot Thomas Rockart Jr. wanted to pull the ruse with was a simple one; Logan was to slam me, then attempt his famous leg-drop and miss. At that point I was supposed to get him in a Boston Crab, and this was to be where Billy would immediately ring the bell. I instinctively allow Logan to slam me, then roll out of the way as he drops the leg. When I get to my feet and turn,

I find him already on his feet. "Now," he pants, "we shoot."

The audience senses something amiss as we circle one another slowly. From a small pocket of my hearing, I can make out Thomas Rockart Jr.'s frantic shouting. Logan and I launch into a tight lock-up. His force knocks me off balance briefly before I am able to slip around and wrap a headlock around him. He shoves me off, and as I turn, his huge arm slams against my chest. My back hits the mat awkwardly; vertebrae jolt with sudden terror. Logan leaps on top of me. We grapple with a series of amateur moves . . . half nelson, grapevine, wraparound . . . I am surprised at how quickly they come back to me, and even more surprised at how their fluidity makes them feel less real than the solidly placed fake ones that preceded them.

Logan manages to get me in a half nelson cradle. He rolls me over and plants my shoulders on the mat, and I hear two slaps of the mat before a burst of adrenaline fuels my kick-out. Using our sweat for lubrication, I slither out and slip both arms around Logan's massive trunk. He howls in pain as I apply pressure to his already broken ribs. I struggle to close my hands around his back. "Do you give up, Dream?" Billy Harren demands.

"No!" The word lands forcefully on my ear alongside a spray of saliva and sweat. His arms wriggle inside of mine. My hands are thrust apart. He staggers back to the corner, holding his ribs, and I move in and unleash two hard forearm shots to his temple. His head snaps back, and I stare into the two dazed milky balls of gray that regard me helplessly. A victorious chill makes my neck tingle. *I'm going to beat him.* This realization comes free of any terror or loathing. I snap him out of the corner, drop an elbow onto his chest, and hook his leg. He squirms a shoulder up at the count of two and a half.

"C'mon, you fucker!" Thomas Rockart Jr. is screaming. I glance over and see him standing at ringside, hammering the edge of the ring with his palm. "Count faster!" he cries.

I don't want to risk rolling Logan over for a Boston Crab, so I give him another elbow-drop and pull him over another foot and then climb the corner turnbuckle with sweat glazing my eyes and blurring my sight. I am too exhausted to raise my hand in a symbolic gesture of victory and to do so would seem unnecessary and even a bit silly as I stand on the top turnbuckle and regard my prey below. Down on the mat, Logan lays twitching like an unconscious dog in the clutches of a nightmare. I launch off the turnbuckle. Aim for his chest and ribs. Knock every last bit of fucking wind out of the champion.

For a moment I am suspended in air. Flash bulbs split my vision like lightning. I blink. Logan is gone. Nothing for me to do but absorb the blow of landing on the bare canvas with no body there to break my fall. My right knee explodes. Roll over on the canvas just in time to see Logan's massive leg drop down on my face. Blackness. Then I hear the slap of a hand against the canvas and I kick out hurriedly. A uniform gasp is given by 80,000 throats in response to my escaping Sonny Logan's *trademarked finisher.* Thomas Rockart Jr.'s joyful cries drift into my left ear;

the owner of the company is adrift on an excitement comparable to that of any random mark among the millions watching.

Logan stands above me, his own face mute with wonder. I begin to crawl away when he grabs my right leg and twists his left knee around the thigh. I know what he is doing but am too tired and stunned from the leg-drop to stop it. After cinching my legs into a figure four, he falls back onto the canvas. Instantly, the inside of my right knee splits apart as though sliced with a drunken surgeon's blade.

I grit my teeth. Logan twists his legs further, sending new waves of pain that tear through tendons and travel up my spine, lighting up every pain signal there is. I scream, hoping somebody hears me.

"Give it up?" Billy's face is inches from mine. The words come as a statement.

"No!" I shout. "No, I don't!"

Logan presses down harder. Suddenly the pain leaks from my knee like final drops from a worn sponge. It swarms the rest of my body and seeks out hidden spots with a familiarity that indicates it is no longer a stranger. I am the pain. "No, I won't quit!" I say clearly.

"C'mon, kid!" Logan implores, his voice strangely pleading, "Give it up!"

"No!"

"I'm gonna break your leg if this keeps up!"

"Then break it!" I snarl. I look at his face that reflects a battle between his concern for my welfare and his desire to keep the belt and defeat me fairly. His eyes meet mine and in that moment we are joined in a raw connection deeper than when we first met, deeper than any choreographed moment before this. His frightened eyes reveal that even dreams complete an inevitable cycle, finding death in victory as well as defeat. Lose respect for this death and you lose respect for life. Relieved tears kiss the sweat on my tongue. I feel I belong in this ring right here, right now; every moment I refuse to submit is its own accomplished dream. "No way!" I scream louder, "Never—"

Then the bell is pounding. Logan immediately releases the hold and crawls over to me. He drapes an arm over my chest and hugs me. "You are one crazy sonofabitch, brother," he mumbles in my ear. I smile, bathed in a euphoric haze as the spotlights above draw both my body and the surrounding night into their incandescent womb.

When I come to, my body is lying flat on an unmoving stretcher. Thomas Rockart Jr.'s voice echoes through the backstage area. I sit up and see him in a hallway, gesticulating wildly at Sonny Logan and Billy Harren. "How in the hell could you ring the bell?" he is screaming at Billy. "He never submitted!"

"For Christ's sakes, Thomas. The kid's leg was ready to snap," Billy spits. "'Sides, you wanted to pull a false finish with the Dream. So don't give me this 'moral routine' shit."

"You're fired!" Thomas Rockart Jr. roars. "Fired, fired, fired! And you," he turns to Logan, "you get out of my face, you big balding gorilla—"

Logan cracks Thomas Rockart Jr. square on the jaw, sending his former boss to the ground with what looks like a pretty painful bump. The legit ones usually are. Logan regards the unconscious Rockart and cracks his knuckles. "I've always wanted to do that." He smiles.

A trio of paramedics hustle into the tunnel. They rush past Rockart's prone form and surround the stretcher. "I'm all right, guys," I tell them. But as soon as I put my foot on the floor, my knee ignites with angry pain. I cry out and tumble back onto the stretcher.

"We'd better take you to the hospital, Michael." The tallest paramedic, who seems to be in charge, nods his slender head with enthusiasm. "You've got a bad one there."

"All right," I admit sheepishly.

"Great match, by the way," the paramedic says and smiles.

Sonny Logan ambles over to me. "I'm headin' out, Michael." He extends his hand and says, "You gave me one hell of a run in there."

"You didn't beat me, Dream," I say, holding on to his hand.

"You're right," he acknowledges.

We both give an extra squeeze, then laugh and release one another. "Maybe we'll see each other again one of these days."

I merely shrug, thinking of my grandfather and his piece of seasoned advice. My former idol is almost halfway through the tunnel when I call out: "Hey, Edward."

He turns carefully. "Thanks for the fight," I say.

"If you think I'm gonna say 'any time,' you're nuts," he remarks.

I'm still laughing as the World's Gym insignia on his leather jacket disappears into the night lapping at the end of the tunnel.

17

MICHAEL AT LAST

One knee surgery and two weeks later I am in the living room of the house my mom and Irling have bought in Nebraska. The three of us are all assembled on the couch, watching a press conference on WWO superstars, a new weekly show appearing on a twenty-four-hour sports cable channel that's in competition with Brad Burner's twenty-four-hour sports cable channel. In the conference, Thomas Rockart Jr. claims that "The American Dream" sucker punched him, then publicly challenges Sonny Logah to a face-to-face match. Footage of the SlamFest match is then run, and while the television belts out my screams of defiance, my mom squeezes my hand and regards the wraps on my leg with a noticeable amount of pride. Thomas Rockart Jr. reappears onscreen and mentions Billy

Harren's defection to ICW, thus insinuating that Logan and Burner were in cahoots with Harren to throw the match in Logan's favor. Thomas Rockart Jr., unique genius that he is, is turning his failed plan into a boost for his company.

He still has no knowledge that I tried to inform Logan of the plot, so I am his current golden boy. As mock flash bulbs click before him, Thomas Rockart Jr. calls Michael Harding "one of the greatest professional wrestlers I have ever had the pleasure of working with." He then declares that I am undergoing physical therapy with a specialist in the Rocky Mountains (this elicits a laugh from my mom, a look of puzzlement from Irling, and a knowing shrug from me) and will be declared the number one contender to the heavyweight championship upon my return to the World Wrestling Organization. Thomas Rockart Jr. has, in fact, promised me a long title reign upon my return, which the doctors are speculating could be anywhere from six to twelve months away.

"Are you going back, Michael?" Mom asks later that night as the two of us rock slowly on the porch swing. Their house is at the end of a gravel road dotted with two other houses spaced a mile apart from each other. Apple trees swarm their front lawn. Silvery leaves shift like bright fleeting smiles in the moonlit breeze.

"If I do," I say slowly, "I won't be going back to what it was. That make any sense?"

She nods with satisfaction. "It feels so good to finally be able to call you Michael and get a response," she says. I shrug and keep rocking. "So, how's Shawna?" she asks.

I raise my eyebrows in response to a sudden eruption of crickets. "They do that every night," Mom explains, laughing. "Some kind of timer. They'll die down in a few seconds." Within ten seconds, silence's only spoiler is the gentle breeze whispering through the apple trees.

"I haven't talked to Shawna for a couple months," I confess.

"Why not?"

"I just . . . ," I stammer, then finally come up with, "She's a complex person."

"I liked her," Mom insists.

"I like her too," I say quietly. For a second I am almost tempted to reveal Shawna's former identity, but I quickly dismiss this as the kind of secret that, like my grandfather's $7,000 for "care of the glove," would be better kept to myself. For a while, anyway.

The two days I stay with my mom and Irling pass swiftly. The only tense moment comes the first night at dinner. After informing me with considerable pride that his sink dispensers were enjoying successful trial runs in the cities of Sacramento, Milwaukee, and Lincoln, Irling peered at my knee with intense interest. "Mind if I ask you something?" he asked, "How do you get an injury that bad if pro wrestling is all fake?"

"It's not fake!"

My head snapped to the source of these words: my mother. "It's known as a work," she informed Irling.

"Go, Mom." I laughed.

After leaving Nebraska, I continue west. It is only when I am sixty or so miles outside of Denver that I realize what was missing about the visit. *Broken Dock*, the portrait of a planet's final moments, was nowhere to be seen.

I pull into the parking lot of a general store bathed in red from the sun dangling just above the horizon. The walk to the phone booth takes a while. Even though I no longer need crutches, the doctor warned me to walk with care. "Little steps," he said.

Once I pick up the receiver, I realize I did not pull in to call my mom.

Shawna answers on the third ring. "Hello."

I reply, "It's me, Michael."

"Well, hello." Her voice is soft. "Congratulations. You wrestled quite a match."

"Yeah, I . . ." I pause. "I was thinking about stopping by, telling you about it. Think it's a story you might get a kick out of."

"Really? You still a pro wrestler?" she asks.

"No," I answer, touching my fingers to the surrounding glass. Outside the red sky wraps Earth in a hushed splendor. I tap the clear barrier in time with seconds that move the sun, a collection of energy patiently approaching this planet. Millions of years from now an unseen cycle will find completion, and the same force that has brought life for so long will bring death. Outside red turns to black, but I am not afraid. I feel a part of this transition of light somewhere deep inside, ready to challenge the potential of dreams and make life a wonderfully ungraspable portrait. "I'm just me," I say at last.